The Education of Joshua Chastain: A Gay Mormon Memoir

A novel by Nicolas Shumway

Table of Contents

Prologue

"Do you have a urologist?" asked Dr. James "Jimmy" Blanchard, my personal physician and a lovely gay man from Louisiana who at that particular moment was performing a digital rectal exam. Finger, rectum—you get the idea. It's one of the indignities inflicted on men over a certain age during their annual physical.

"Why would I want a urologist?"

"Because I don't like the feel of your prostate. If you're free, I'll try to get you an appointment with Dr. Singh this afternoon."

"Dr. Singh? Sounds brown. Is he good-looking? I don't want just any old doctor poking around down there."

"Joshua," Dr. Jimmy said with uncharacteristic sternness, "This is not a joke. You need to take this seriously."

That afternoon, I met Dr. Singh, who was indeed brown, forty-something, and handsome. After palpating my prostate for what seemed an eternity, he scheduled a biopsy for the following morning. The biopsy confirmed that I had prostate cancer of a fairly aggressive type. Dr. Singh immediately ordered a bone scan and an MRI which revealed that the cancer had

1

metastasized, producing small tumors at several sites throughout my body. The cancer was deemed inoperable, although other forms of treatment, albeit with unpleasant side effects, could arrest or at least slow the progress of the disease. Incidentally, anyone who believes in intelligent design should consider the prostate; there's nothing intelligent about the way it's put together.

A high percentage of men with my diagnosis die within five years. Time management being one of my strong points, I coolly noted that five years would give me plenty of time to tie things up at the university where I teach music history and oversee an orderly transition out of my position as organist and choir director at All Saints Episcopal parish where I have been employed for nearly twenty-five years. I also realized that, if there is any truth in the Nicene Creed, I might soon see Benjamin, my husband of thirty years, who died of pancreatic cancer only months before my diagnosis. I miss him terribly. In fact, my first thought after learning of my illness was how to break the news to Benjamin.

Treatments began immediately, a combination of chemo, hormones, and radiation therapy that left me nauseous, achy, and weak. I was also frightened and lonely. Aware of my darkening mood, Dr. Jimmy, who sang tenor in my church choir, suggested that I consult a social worker. Despite my initial reluctance, I eventually agreed to talk to an Episcopal chaplain who specialized in helping people with end-of-life issues.

The chaplain turned out to be someone I knew, or at least had known some twenty years previous: The Reverend Anthony Murphy. Father Andy was a former Roman Catholic priest who "jumped over the wall"— i.e., became an Anglican priest. He later sealed his defection by marrying a former RC nun. As part of his transition to the Anglican priesthood, he spent a year internship in my parish. Short, with big ears and a bullfrog voice, he made no attempt to modify his working-class, Boston-Irish accent. An engaging preacher and great storyteller, he served successfully as a diocesan priest and enjoyed a modestly lucrative second career writing crime fiction under a pseudonym. After nursing his wife through a long illness that left him a widower, he felt called to leave parish ministry and accept a medical chaplaincy which is how I reconnected with him.

Although age had whitened his hair, thickened his midriff, and given him a certain gravitas, the big voice and big ears unmistakably identified the man who entered my hospital room as Father Andy. Taking his chaplaincy very seriously, Father Andy was present for each of my treatments and sometimes provided transportation to and from the hospital when I was unable to drive myself. We soon became fast friends and frequent dinner companions, perhaps in part because, as recent widowers, we both understood the loneliness that results from losing a life partner.

As our friendship grew, we became increasingly intrigued by each other's life stories. I was fascinated by his descriptions of growing up Roman Catholic in an Irish neighborhood in South Boston. His experiences as a big-city ethnic kid who attended Catholic schools from kindergarten through seminary could hardly have differed more from my early life in Rosales, a rural Arizona community settled by Mormon pioneers. A kind of Mormon *shtetl*. Add to this our different sexual orientations—he a straight kid who never questioned his sexuality and hoped to play professional baseball, and I a gay kid who realized he was queer at a young age and wanted to become a classical musician. We did, however, discover common ground in that we had both been happily married, and we shared a profound interest in religion. In an early conversation, he remarked, "You know, I've never really known a Mormon, much less a gay Mormon."

"Ex-Mormon, if you please. I was excommunicated from the Mormon church years ago and am now an officially confirmed Episcopalian. I currently have no formal connection to the LDS Church."

"So, you left Mormonism and never looked back? I find that hard to believe. I left the Roman Catholic Church years ago, but some of it still gets up with me every morning and goes to bed with me every night."

"Gay folks don't walk away from the Mormon church. They get kicked out. Excommunicated."

"Excommunicated?!? Just for being gay?"

"Well actually, they'll let you remain as long as you're celibate."

"Celibate, eh? Probably works as well for them as it does for the RCs. So, did you just walk away, or are you still a residual Mormon?"

This question surprised me because I remember my early years with a contradictory combination of gratitude and anger, nostalgia and resentment. I had not managed to just walk away. Mormonism was still in my cell structure, a part of my religious DNA. After a long pause, I answered, "No. I suppose some of it is still in me. But I've tried to leave it behind."

"Leaving things behind isn't easy. Our early experiences hold on to us no matter how hard we try to escape them. Somewhere in me, there is still a South Boston Irish kid who thought that God wanted him to be a Roman Catholic priest."

As our conversations progressed, I ended up telling him snippets of my life—how I grew up in a small Mormon town in Arizona, coped with being a gifted misfit, discovered that I was gay, ran away from home to escape aversion therapy supervised by a Mormon psychologist, got excommunicated from the Mormon church, and eventually embarked on a rewarding career

5

as a university professor and church musician. Particularly shocking to him were stories of three near-rape incidents, an affair with a Roman Catholic priest, lots of anonymous sex, and a short stint as a prostitute. After a particularly detailed conversation, he said, "These are great stories. You should write them up."

Eventually, with Father Andy's urging, I started writing a novelized story of my early life. Fortunately, the cancer treatments proved effective, and after several months, I was deemed to be in remission—a precarious category since it means that, although temporarily dormant, the cancer could return at any time. This respite from the illness, however, gave me time to write.

The result is this manuscript. Reconstructing my early life, especially those pivotal teenage years, turned out to be a challenging and possibly futile task since nearly fifty years separate the current me from the young Joshua Chastain portrayed in these pages. Although I trust my recollection of events, my reconstruction of thoughts and conversations inevitably relies on plausibility more than fact. Hence, the term "novelized." Lest this sound too apologetic, I hasten to add that even "real memory" is often a form of fiction, a way for the human mind to impose narrative order on disparate events and people. Fortunately, I was not writing entirely from memory. Despite moving around a lot, I've managed to keep a good number of my datebooks going back to 1968.

While the information they contain is minimal, they have helped me keep the narrative on track.

Father Andy read early drafts of the manuscript and proved adept at asking good questions. He also suggested additions, particularly to explain Mormonism to people like him who know some of the stereotypes of the LDS Church and its doctrines but none of the details. "To most of us," he said, "Mormonism is weird. You can't rely on what people already know or think they know if you want them to understand your story." Consequently, much of the information included in this memoir about Mormon doctrine and church history is here at his behest. Father Andy was the catalyst, but the story is mine.

--*Joshua Chastain*

PART I

Chapter One:
A Weird Kid and His Family

Since I refuse to think of myself as *just* a homosexual, I tried several starting points for this story, but sex kept intruding. My sexuality does not define me, but it has been essential in determining who I am. A heterosexual Joshua Chastain would have become a quite different person. So, I start with sex.

I first became aware of male beauty in the spring of 1958 shortly after turning five years old. His name was Manuel Guerrero, and he was helping my mother set up scenery for a Rosales community theater production she was directing. Dressed in Levi's and a tight white t-shirt, he was probably sixteen or seventeen when I first noticed him. I remember the soft curves of his adolescent muscles, the short black hair on his forearms, his narrow waist expanding upward to his broadening shoulders, and the smooth timbre of his recently changed voice. I later told Mother that he was very beautiful. She quickly informed me that men were handsome, and girls were beautiful. Subtext: I should never mention male beauty.

My second sexual experience as a five-year-old could have been much less benign. In September of 1958,

Mother took some of her students to the county fair with me tagging along. At some point, probably because I was being a pest, she entrusted me to a young man, possibly a college student home for the weekend, whose name and face I honestly cannot remember. I remember being carried on his shoulders. I remember women making over me because of my mop of blond curly hair. And I remember him taking me to a toilet stall in a public restroom where he lowered both our pants and shoved his large erection between my legs. I remember him saying something about having to get that good stuff into me. But I then heard my mother honk and call for me. I ran out of the restroom with my pants half buttoned, which caused Mother's students considerable merriment.

Who was he? I don't know. Did he intend to rape me? Possibly. While I remember elements of the event with startling clarity (his abundant pubic hair and his big hard penis), I never ascribed much importance to the event, possibly because he didn't hurt me. But, as with the beauty of Manuel Guerrero, this was an experience I could discuss with no one.

I was of course aware of girls, my first playmates being a family of five girls who lived down the block with their harried mother, some twenty cats, and their Jack-Mormon alcoholic father. (Jack Mormon: a Mormon who doesn't attend church or abide by all the rules, most often the prohibitions against alcohol and tobacco.) These girls and I sometimes "played nasty" which meant little more than dropping our pants and comparing equipment. Even at that early age, I found boys' equipment more interesting than theirs. Throughout childhood, I developed intense crushes on other boys and was keenly aware of the good-looking men in town.

I am the youngest of five children. My four older siblings were born in quick succession, Jeff in 1941, Terri in 1943, Clarissa in 1944, and Keith, the sibling closest to me in age, in 1946. I was a surprise baby, born on April 2, 1953, seven years after Keith and, as my father noted, a day too late for an April Fool's joke. I have only vague memories of my siblings—Jeff who tried to teach me manly things like how to catch a ball and sit with my legs spread, and Keith who often felt duty-bound to twist my arm behind my back, force me to the floor, and demand that I say "uncle." In response to my tearful protests, he would taunt me with, "What's the matter? Can't you take it? Are you too big a sissy to take it?" Keith left for BYU just as I entered the sixth grade. I did not miss him or his bullying. Following the pattern of most Mormons, my sibs married young and soon had families of their own. Except for holiday visits, I saw little of them after they left for college.

Chapter Two:
Music, Hygiene, and Enemas

Keith, of course, was not the first or last person to call me a sissy. Name-calling and bullying were daily occurrences on the school playground. I ceased complaining about such things since my father always responded with something like "You either have to fight back or learn to take it." He bought boxing gloves and tried to teach me to fight. I was a hopeless student, partly because I had little athletic ability, but mostly because I had no desire to hit or be hit by other boys. While my father never criticized my failures as a boxer, I sensed his frustration and disappointment, particularly since my two older brothers had been successful high school athletes.

Powerfully built and very much a man's man, my father was an auto mechanic and the proud owner of his own business—a service station, garage, and tire shop—that he had built from scratch. As a young child, I saw little of him, simply because he was gone much of the time. Looking back now, I realize that during most of my childhood he was working twelve-hour days to support my four siblings either in college or on church missions. I have early memories of sitting on his lap, but I also remember being told when I was three or four years old that sitting on a man's lap was not appropriate for a boy.

12

Physical contact between men in the Rosales of my childhood seldom amounted to more than a handshake or a pat on the shoulder. For this reason, I particularly cherish the memory of the few times my father touched me gently and lovingly. These occurred when I was ill. Run almost entirely by volunteers, the LDS Church ordains adult males in good standing to the Mormon priesthood. Being a member of this lay priesthood empowered my father to bless his family just as ministers in other churches might bless a parishioner. Consequently, when I was ill, my father would kneel at my bedside, anoint me with consecrated oil, lay hands on my head, and pronounce God's blessing upon me. His touch was warm and gentle, made doubly so by the strength and roughness of his hands.

Being bullied as a sissy did not keep me from discovering a love of classical music. My first-grade teacher, a kind woman named Mrs. Brewer, had her students take a short nap after lunch, during which she played a recorded selection of classical music. One afternoon after classes (as Mrs. Brewer told my mother) I sneaked into the auditorium and picked out on the school piano both the melody and the bass line of the selection heard during that afternoon's nap. Much impressed, Mrs. Brewer urged my mother to arrange piano lessons for me. My parents hardly knew what to do with a musical child, but they acted quickly on Mrs. Brewer's suggestion and bought me a much-used Lyon & Healy upright piano for my seventh birthday, placing it on the service porch where I could practice for hours on end without disturbing anyone.

Fortunately, Rosales had a superb piano teacher, a childless widow lady named Josephine Jespersen. Known to her students simply as Mrs. J, she held a master's degree from the Cincinnati Conservatory of Music. During the school year, she spent several days per week teaching at Arizona State College in Flagstaff. But she kept Rosales as her home base, largely to be near her extended family, all of them descendants of Danish immigrants who converted to Mormonism in the 1870s. Students came from all over northern Arizona to study with her.

Entering Mrs. Jespersen's living room was like entering a shrine, far from the bullies and name-calling. Except for a small sitting area around a coffee table, the room was dedicated entirely to music. Two midsize Baldwin grand pianos dominated the room, surrounded by bookshelves laden with music scores, books about music, and tiny busts of famous composers. Music quickly became much more than a hobby for me; rather, it was a refuge and a means of self-affirmation in which Mrs. Jespersen became my spiritual guide.

Town gossips held that her husband had died in a car wreck while returning from a tryst with his mistress in Kingman. She kept a framed photo of a fine-looking man in a band uniform on her mantel. I once asked if he was her husband. "Yes," she said. "He was very handsome, wasn't he? Perhaps too handsome for his own good."

Although Mother supported my musical interests, her first love was the theater, having performed in numerous school and community plays in her younger years. Singlehandedly, she founded and maintained the Rosales Drama Society. Complementing her work in community theater, Mother taught speech and drama courses at high school—courses I resolutely refused to take. A striking, carefully groomed woman, she did almost everything as though playing to an audience. She didn't just read to me; she played the role of a mother reading to her child as though an audience were watching.

Her vivid accounts of the founding of the Mormon church, Joseph Smith's martyrdom, and the bravery of the Mormon pioneers made her a particularly effective Sunday-school teacher. Someone once remarked that hearing her tell a story was better than seeing the movie. As I grew older, I found her theatrics embarrassing. Hence, my private nickname for her: Loretta as in Loretta Young.

Although Mother assiduously defended Mormon notions on the proper role of women, she just as assiduously avoided the traditional duties of a Mormon housewife by having a full-time job and involving herself in every school, church, and town function possible. As a result, my clothes were so filthy that my third-grade teacher gave me a grade of "unsatisfactory" in hygiene. Deeply embarrassed, I learned to wash and iron my own clothes, transforming myself from one of the dirtiest kids in school to one of the most fastidious. Of course, this gave the bullies another reason to call me a sissy, but at least I was a clean, well-dressed sissy, and possibly the only kid in school wearing pressed Levi's.

While our home never lacked for food, it mostly consisted of prepared cereals, canned goods, and sandwich makings—items requiring minimal preparation As with keeping my clothes clean, I early became adept at preparing simple meals for myself which often consisted of little more than TV dinners or fish sticks. Fortunately, kind people who knew that my mother didn't cook often invited us to share meals with them on Thanksgiving and Christmas.

What attention Mother did not give to housekeeping, she lavished on my bodily functions. Among my earliest memories are daily interrogations about my bowel movements. A day without a bowel movement meant an enema in which she would strip me to my nothings and lay me on my side on the cold bathroom floor so she could insert a hard rubber nozzle up my ass and fill me with water, making me hold it as long as possible before shitting it out. If no hard stuff came out, a second enema immediately followed. Very quickly I learned to lie to her about my bowel movements and everything else concerning my body.

Chapter Three: Rosales

My hometown of Rosales consisted of some 3000 souls, roughly two-thirds Anglo Mormons and one-third Mexican American Catholics. Commanded by Brigham Young, leader of the great Mormon trek westward, Mormon scouts bought land west of the Rosales River, across from a small Mexican settlement whose name they kept. Arriving in the early 1870s, the Mormon settlers laid out a town following a north-south, east-west grid with wide streets and large lots, just as they did in countless other Mormon settlements in Utah, Arizona, and Idaho. They constructed two reservoirs on the Rosales River, built an irrigation system, grew crops, raised farm animals, and built both a grade school and a high school. The more enterprising acquired large tracts of land that provided considerable income for a few wealthy cattle ranchers.

Rosales Mormons never forgot that their town was built by God's command. I remember well a sermon given by one of the General Authorities, as members of the upper church hierarchy are called. He began by reciting the words of a stirring hymn written specifically for young Mormons:

> Shall the youth of Zion falter
> In defending truth and right?
> While the enemy assaileth,
> Shall we shrink or shun the fight? NO!

True to the faith that our parents have cherished,
True to the truth for which martyrs have perished,
To God's command, Soul, heart, and hand,
Faithful and true we will ever stand.

"Brothers and sisters," he continued. "Look around you. Look at your homes; look at this beautiful meeting house; look at the reservoirs and the irrigation system that allow you to grow food and prosper; look at the public schools that, as you all know, were originally Mormon academies. Brothers and Sisters—and particularly you young people—never forget that you stand on the shoulders of giants. Consider the Prophet Joseph who was murdered for his courageous role in restoring God's only true church and bringing God's holy priesthood back to earth. Consider those courageous Mormon pioneers, your forebears in many cases, who fled persecution and endured untold hardship to cross the Great Plains and build towns and cities like Rosales. Be loyal to your heritage. You are a royal priesthood, heirs of the covenant, the new Israel. Never betray that legacy, and never forget your debt to those brave and faithful Saints who came before you."

Of course, he did not mention the Mexican population, nearly a third of the town. Nor did he acknowledge that Rosales, which means rose bushes in Spanish, drew its name from the local Roman Catholic parish named for St. Rose of Lima.

Chapter Four: Craig and Patty

Throughout grade school and high school, I had few friends, partly because I preferred practicing the piano to socializing with kids my age. I did, however, have one good male friend and one friend girl—not a girlfriend but a girl who became a near daily companion. My male friend, perhaps my only real childhood friend, was Craig Bowen, a chubby kid with a keen mind and a sharp tongue. Craig's mother died when he was a toddler, leaving him to be raised by his father, a Jack Mormon and tireless womanizer who never remarried. As a commercial realtor specializing in agricultural properties, Mr. Bowen had clients all over the state. But he kept his home base in Rosales to share childrearing responsibilities with Craig's maternal grandparents, devout Mormons who raised Craig in the faith. Consequently, Craig grew up in two households, the staunchly Mormon home of his grandparents and the Jack-Mormon home of his father.

Perhaps as a way of justifying his own philandering, Craig's father was also an unending source of malicious gossip that he generously shared with his son who in turn shared it with me. Through Craig, I learned of Mrs. Jespersen's unfaithful husband. Also through Craig, I found out that my maternal grandfather, Roger Giles, had sired one of Laura Bumstead's three sons, each of whom had different fathers. Mr. Bumstead allegedly consented to his wife's adulteries because he was shooting blanks. Whether true or not, such knowledge about the private lives of Rosales adults undermined the respect that Craig and I were supposed to have for our elders.

My friend girl (not girlfriend) was Patty Burleson, my second cousin by adoption. Patty was possibly the most mistreated kid in town since, no matter how hard she tried, she could never meet her adoptive mother's high and often cruel expectations. Nowadays, she would probably be diagnosed with a learning disability. Since her mother and my father were first cousins, Patty and I became playmates at an early age. Beginning in the fourth grade, under the tutelage of a one-time member of the BYU ballroom dance team, Patty and I became dance partners and were often featured in floorshows at church and community functions, she dressed like Ginger Rogers, and I attired in a boy-sized tuxedo. As our friendship developed, I started assisting with her homework, correcting (writing) her English papers, and helping her cheat on exams.

Although not a great student, Patty had one major asset: she was drop-dead gorgeous. With thick wavy brown hair, large dark eyes, and a megawatt smile, she emerged from puberty with a movie-star figure and a clear complexion never marred by a single pimple. My father once remarked to her mother how pretty Patty was becoming to which Mrs. Burleson snipped, "Well, we hope that that isn't her only good quality." Aware and perhaps a little jealous of Patty's beauty, Mrs. Burleson kept her daughter on a short leash. But for some reason (because I might be queer?) she considered me safe company for her daughter and was delighted with our success as dance partners.

Chapter Five:
Sex and Chewing Gum

In April of 1965, I turned twelve years old and, like all Mormon boys at that age, I was ordained a Deacon in the Aaronic Priesthood. As such, I had an annual interview with the local bishop to determine if I was living a righteous life. My first bishop's interview occurred just after my twelfth birthday, months before I had sprouted a single pubic hair.

"Josh, you're now twelve years old, you've been ordained a Deacon in the Aaronic priesthood, and you must start assuming the responsibilities of a man. Now, one of those responsibilities is to keep yourself morally clean and live the law of chastity. Are you morally clean?"

"I suppose so. What does morally clean mean?"

"Have you ever touched a girl inappropriately?"

"Like what?"

"Have you ever tried to touch a girl's breasts or maybe feel between her legs?"

"No."

"Have you touched yourself inappropriately?"

"Like what?"

"Do you masturbate?"

"I'm not sure what that is."

Starting to find his own questions embarrassing, the bishop mumbled something like, "Well, you're probably too young to know about such things. But very soon you will experience changes in your body that will tempt you to commit immoral acts."

Turning twelve also meant joining a church-sponsored Boy Scout troop. Pursuant to earning a hiking merit badge, sometime in the January after my twelfth birthday, I was on a hike with three other boys, including my friend Craig who had already entered puberty. Our conversations often broached sexual topics on which we no doubt compounded considerable ignorance. Out of the blue, Craig informed us that he could come. When asked for a demonstration, he dropped his pants, jacked off, and did indeed squirt out a respectable puddle of adolescent cum.

My initiation into the pleasures of masturbation occurred several months later, shortly after my thirteenth birthday. Pubic hair had started sprouting in my lower abdomen, which initially alarmed me, and I noticed my genitals getting larger. But so far, I had not been tempted to "abuse" myself. One summer afternoon, however, while passing through the dressing room of the municipal swimming pool, I noticed a boy recently graduated from high school who was totally naked and taking a shower. Transfixed by his young man's body, profuse pubic hair, and fully adult genitalia, I stared a bit too long at which point he asked in a threatening voice, "What are you staring at?" I meekly replied "Nothing" to which he responded, "If you ever look at me like that again, I'll beat the shit out of you."

I rushed home and locked myself in my bedroom. With the image of that beautiful young man in mind, I dropped my pants and started to massage my immediately responsive and by this time nearly adult penis. The pleasure intensified until I felt like I was about to explode. This paroxysm of pleasure ended in a copious ejaculation that left me stunned, delighted, frightened, and ashamed. I knew that I had both transgressed a church teaching and discovered something quite wonderful that my body could do. I fell to my knees and begged God for forgiveness. But before the day was out, I tried it again with similar results. From that point forward, daily masturbation became almost an obligation, possibly a subconscious way of claiming ownership of my body.

That said, I was not a solitary masturbator. Circle jerks became regular occurrences after Boy Scout meetings, school functions, or just about any time that pubescent boys could meet in a safe place. I can describe in detail the genitals of most of my male classmates—how their dicks came in several lengths and girths, some more attractive than others; how some dicks curved down, up, or to one side; and how some boys had balls that held tightly to the bottom of their crotches while others had balls dangling between their legs. Our circle jerks often involved jacking each other off. Occasionally we had contests to see who could come first or shoot the farthest. Initiating a jerk-off session was never difficult:

"Hey Josh, what was the last time you did it?"

"Maybe a couple of days ago. How about you?"

By this time, we each had a hand on the other's crotch. Within minutes we would find an old barn or a clump of trees where the deed could take place unobserved.

Were these homosexual experiences? Probably yes, but none of us would have ever used that term. My jerk-off buddies included most of the boys in my class and several in the classes above and below me. With few exceptions, these boys eventually married and produced offspring. They probably remember our circle jerks as a passing adolescent aberration. Or maybe they continued finding occasional male sex partners like many married men do.

The topic of sex was hard to avoid because the Mormon Church could not leave the subject alone. Once in a Sunday-School class, a particularly imaginative teacher held up a stick of gum. "You see this stick of gum?" he asked. "It's brand-new and still in the wrapper. Who would like it?"

Several students raised their hands.

"Now," he said, "let's make things more interesting." He then unwrapped the stick of gum, wadded it into a ball, and passed it around the class, telling each student to take turns playing with it. Then, after everyone had handled, twisted, and crushed it, the teacher asked who wanted to chew it. In response to the protests of "That's so gross," he solemnly informed us that the same was true of the human body, that no one would want to touch someone whose body had been handled by other people. "So, keep yourselves morally clean. Then, when the time comes, you will be acceptable to marry the right kind of person."

Reinforcing the scare tactics of the church was the fear of getting pregnant. Condoms, the only viable birth control method at the time, were available, but only under the counter at the local Mormon-owned pharmacy and not to teenagers. Of course, things occasionally got out of hand. One of my childhood playmates got pregnant in her senior year. Abortion and marriage being out of the question, she bore the child. During her pregnancy, she was not allowed to attend school. Mrs. Waltz, the home-economics teacher, took her class assignments to her so she could earn her high school degree, but she was barred from attending her own graduation. There were also rumors of girls traveling two-hundred miles to a Mexican border town for illegal abortions.

My father never mentioned sex to me. For Mother, however, telling me about sex allowed for a dramatic performance of the overwrought heroine variety. We had just driven home. After parking the car, she let out a histrionic sigh and declared, "There's something very important that I need to tell you." Then, with appropriate pauses and exhalations, she declaimed on the God-given gift to create life, to be a co-creator with God by bearing children—or "filling the measure of our creation" to use a phrase drawn from one of Joseph Smith's revelations.

Mormons believe that every person before birth was a spirit in a preexistence. According to LDS doctrine, spiritual children need to acquire a physical body by being born into this probationary world. If they live worthy lives, they are resurrected to exaltation in the highest degree of glory. The final goal of this "eternal progression" is to become a god just like God the Father. Or as the Mormon adage has it, "Man is as God once was; God is as Man may become." Consequently, Mormons often have large families to provide bodies for as many spirit children as possible. Failing to have children betrays one's obligation to God as well as to those spirit children anxious to begin their cosmic journey toward Godhood. This of course posed a big problem for a gay boy like me since I felt no inclination to make babies.

Hearing Mother talk about sex, even in these abstract terms, made me uncomfortable. Unduly interested in my adolescent body, she often referred to my broadening shoulders and deepening voice. Frequently, she would barge into the bathroom or my bedroom without knocking. Hoping for what? To see me naked? To catch me masturbating? She would then apologize, saying she didn't know I was there, which we both knew was a lie.

By my freshman year, she had become seriously addicted to prescription drugs, downers and uppers. She justified her drug use by dramatic appeals to women's special needs which she explained to me in discomfiting detail. I was an expert on menopause by the age of ten. Obsessed with apocalyptic prophecy, she preached that the End Times were near, possibly because she could not imagine the world going on without her. Her drug use and increasing religiosity seemed to feed on each other.

Puberty was also a time of strange dreams. I remember three dreams with great clarity. In the first, I was an old man, looking something like Benjamin Franklin, but I was wearing a dress and had huge female breasts. He (I) was playing the piano. I feared that my destiny was to become that grotesque, androgynous figure. In the second dream, my mother told me that I would never need to marry, that she would always take care of me. I woke up choking and fighting for breath. The third dream was the weirdest of all. I dreamt that someone was in bed with me. That person turned out to be my mother, but she was dead, and her body was partially decayed.

When I first heard of Freud's oedipal theories about how sons want to kill their fathers and sleep with their mothers, I burst out laughing. Nothing in my experience could have been farther from the truth. Although grateful for much of what she gave me—books, proficiency in proper English, and piano lessons—I avoided being alone with her. I do not for a minute think that I am gay because of her weirdness. I wonder, however, if my relationship with my mother helped me accept myself as a gay man. To put it bluntly, having a wife didn't seem worth the trouble.

Chapter Six: Billy Schaeffer

After Keith left for university, I started helping my dad at his garage after school and on weekends, mostly pumping gas but also doing, under my father's tutelage, some tire and mechanical work. One Saturday morning in October of 1966, just after we opened, Bud Crothers, a local rancher, slipped through the front door. Addressing my father and ignoring me, he asked, "Jim, did you hear about Billy Schaeffer?"

"No. What about him?"

"He died early this morning in a car wreck. Crashed head-on into one of them overpass columns on the new interstate. According to the sheriff, he must've been doin' a hundred."

"What in hell's name was he doing up there? That's over twenty miles from here. I thought he was clerking nights at the Rosales Inn to save up for his mission."

"He was. He had passed all his interviews and was waiting for his mission call any day. But this morning, just as my wife and me were finishing breakfast, the sheriff showed up with some questions. You know, she works at the motel restaurant, and last night it was her turn to close. Just as she was leaving, a really drunk young cowboy came into the motel lobby and asked for a room. Looked like a rodeo bum, she said. Billy checked him in, but the cowboy was so shit-faced drunk that he couldn't find his room. So, Billy asked my wife to watch the desk while he helped the guy to his room. A few minutes later, she heard someone yelling. She ran out into the parking lot just in time to see Billy get in his car and drive off. His face was all bloody, so she called the sheriff. The cowboy, or whoever the hell he was, accused Billy of trying to fiddle with him. You know...play with his private parts. That's why he beat him up. In fact, the sheriff thinks Billy might have crashed on purpose because of what that cowboy said about him."

Then after a long pause, he added, "But you know, just between you, me, and the gatepost, I've long had doubts about Billy. He always was sort of a girly boy. It wouldn't surprise me if he was a little queer. And if some damn queer tried messing with me, I'd beat him up too. Can you imagine a kid like that on a mission? Living full time with another missionary and them maybe even sleeping together in the same bed? Better that it happened now instead of then."

Without agreeing with him, my father answered, "Well, whatever happened, it's a damned shame about Billy. I can't hardly imagine what his parents are going through, Billy being their only child and all."

That night, Sister Irma Taylor, the ward choir director, called me at home to invite me to a special rehearsal the following evening to prepare music for Billy's funeral. My voice still hadn't changed, so I could sing alto and fake a decent tenor if it didn't go too low.

Unlike most of the choir members, I could also read music.

The following evening, a few singers and I gathered in the choir loft of the Rosales Mormon chapel to rehearse. I sat next to Sister Leona Barnes, a large-framed, kindly woman who always wore flowery dresses. She liked sitting next to me so I could teach her the notes. Sister Taylor still hadn't arrived, which surprised us since she was never late. About ten minutes after the hour, she rushed in all flushed and nervous. "I just got a call from the bishop," she said. "The Schaeffers don't want a funeral. There will be a burial service of some sort, but just for the family."

"Really?" asked Burt Jacobs. "Why I've never heard of such a thing. Everyone in Rosales has a funeral. Why not Billy?"

Bertha Perkins, the meanest woman in town according to my father, sniffed, "I bet that the Schaeffers are too ashamed to have a public funeral now that everyone knows the truth about Billy."

"What truth?" exclaimed Sister Taylor. "All we know is that a nice young man is dead. We have absolutely no right to assume anything else."

"We're not assuming," insisted Bertha. "We know what that cowboy said about him, and we know why he beat Billy up. I'd hope that any son of mine would do the same under similar circumstances. Besides, you all remember how Gladys Schaeffer babied that boy, how she used to dress him up in little white shorts and a bow tie and how all the other kids made fun of him. And he was such a crybaby when he was little! He'd cry at the drop of a hat. And he never played sports. Which is a good thing since the other boys probably wouldn't want someone like that gawking at them in the shower rooms."

"Why Bertha Perkins!" retorted my friend Leona. "How can you say such mean things when that poor boy's body isn't hardly cold yet? And just imagine what Gladys and Will are going through! If having your boy die isn't enough, they also have to deal with all these rumors that nobody knows are true. Don't forget that that cowboy was so drunk that he couldn't even find his motel room. Now why should we believe someone like that? And how would you feel if Billy was a boy of yours?"

"No boy of mine would ever do anything like that. I raised them to be men. In fact, if any of my boys turned out like that, I'd just as soon they were dead."

"Okay folks," interrupted Sister Taylor. "There's not going to be any singing tonight, so let's go home before someone says something they'll regret. But I agree with Leona. It's not right to spread rumors. Even if they're true." Bertha Perkins scowled in disagreement, but at least she kept her mouth shut.

As we were leaving the building, Sister Barnes pulled me close to her and whispered in my ear, "If I had Bertha Perkins for a mother, I might want to be dead." Then with a hint of a smile and a light slap on my head, she added, "And Mr. Joshua Chastain, if you ever tell anyone what I just said you'll be just as good as dead. And keep your mouth shut about Billy. There's enough ugly stuff going around about him without spreading more of it."

Despite her warning, everyone in Rosales "knew" that Billy had tried something sexual with a rodeo rider who had reacted by beating him up. They speculated that Billy had killed himself because he couldn't live with people knowing that he was queer, much less face the likelihood that the Mormon Church would withdraw his mission call and possibly excommunicate him.

I said as little as possible about Billy because I didn't want anyone to suspect me of being queer. I first ran across the word *homosexual* in a dictionary game when I was in the fifth grade. The word terrified me because I intuited that it was something I was and had to hide. Shortly after his death, I dreamt about Billy. There was no narrative to the dream, just a series of images. In one image he was the handsome, well-dressed, smiley guy everyone knew. In another, he had been beat up and had blood all over his face. In a third, I discovered Billy's wrecked car, but the dead guy in the car was not Billy. It was me. I woke up in a sweat, terrified that Billy's death could also be mine.

Chapter Seven: AMPS

Adolescence for most of my male classmates meant discovering girls and arguing about which girls had the biggest tits and the most beautiful asses. At first, I thought they were merely parroting what they heard in movies, but I soon realized that they were feeling something that I was not. The sexual development of my female classmates made no impression on me, but the bodily changes in my male classmates left me transfixed, especially those of the Mexican boys who tended to be older than the Anglo students, having been held back in first grade to learn English.

Watching them in the gym showers, I loved the way hair was sprouting on their arms and legs and snaking down from their navels to form a hairy thicket around their genitals. I was fascinated by their muscles, their hair-rimmed nipples, and their broadening chests and shoulders. Of course, such feelings had to remain secret. Thus began my acquaintance with one of the loneliest places on earth: the homosexual closet.

Same-sex attraction, of course, had no place in the cultural rituals of our community, and certainly not in the LDS master narrative of filling the measure of our creation. Love stories, movies, popular songs, and social rituals were all about men with women. Both the church and the school sponsored dances to get boys and girls together in wholesome circumstances. At junior and senior proms, everyone was expected to have a date, and the church never stopped preaching on the importance of saving sex for marriage. Mormonism may be the only Christian body for which getting married and having children are commandments. "Multiply and replenish the earth" is as binding on young Mormons as it was on Adam and Eve. Paradoxically, the Church explicitly warns Mormon boys and girls against premarital sex while at the same time creating narratives and social situations to keep sex center stage—which leads many Mormons to marry young.

Making out became common among my classmates. Occasionally kids went too far—too far being anything that involved hands below the neck or above the knees. On several occasions I tried making out with girls just to see what the fuss was all about. I even attempted a bit of below-the-neck groping. Without exception, these sessions were clumsy, uncomfortable, and unpleasant. Thankfully, the Mormon girls I experimented with never wanted to go too far. Nor did I. A chastity-obsessed religious community is a great place for a young homosexual to remain closeted.

While I enjoyed the all-male company and circle jerks with members of my Boy Scout troop, my first scoutmaster was a horrid individual named Andrew Manchester Perkins, son of Bertha Perkins, the meanest woman in town. A short, thickly muscled troll of a man, he had wormed his way through family connections into positions of responsibility in both church and school. He taught high school social studies and general PE, spoke in an artificially deep voice, and loved manly back slapping and hearty laughter, making him impossible to ignore. Craig Bowen and I invented a private nickname for him based on his initials, AMPS, which our adolescent minds configured as All-Merican-Pile-of-Shit.

AMPS took a special dislike to me. I remember a three-day Boy Scout camping trip as three days of hell. Everything I did inspired AMPS to make comments like, "Josh, you do that just like a girl. Maybe you should start wearing a dress. Are you a girl? Or just a queer boy? Maybe we should start calling you Q-B for short." Barely twelve years old, I felt powerless to respond. I was most grateful when Craig Bowen whispered in my ear, "Why is that stupid bastard being so mean to you?"

While Craig's sympathy warmed my soul, it did not stop other boys from taking up AMPS's harassment. The Q-B moniker was never widely used, but neither did it disappear. Occasionally, some bully would ask, "Hey, Q-B, when you gonna buy that dress?"

Craig hated scouting and AMPS as much as I did. Using the Boy Scout law (a scout is courteous, kind, obedient, etc.) as a point of departure, we cultivated a special language that we called Boy Scout Speak—BS Speak for short, like Orwell's Newspeak. If a teacher told me to sit down, I might reply "Since a Boy Scout is obedient, I can't wait to obey." If a teacher asked Craig to hold open a door, he might answer, "Since a Boy Scout is courteous, nothing would give me more pleasure." BS-Speak thus became our obsequious private code for addressing adults, few of whom realized that we were mocking them.

Just as I was finishing eighth grade, AMPS and I had another memorable encounter. I was waiting for Mother to finish an after-school rehearsal. With nothing else to do, I wandered into the teachers' lounge, which I suppose was off-limits to students. I suddenly heard AMPS growl, "What do you think you're doing in here?" Probably stunned, I looked at him without responding. He then rushed toward me, kicked me across the room, and smashed me into the far wall just as he closed and locked the door behind him. He grabbed me, pinned me to the floor face down with his full body on top of me and his left hand over my mouth. "You worthless little faggot. You're about to get what you deserve." Pressing his erection against my thirteen-year-old butt, he started grabbing for my belt buckle with his right hand.

Frightened but not paralyzed, I twisted my head around and bit his thumb as hard as I could. He let out a curse and loosened his grip. I squirmed out from under him and tried to stand up. He grabbed my left leg and pulled me back to the floor with a thud and placed one of his troll hands over my mouth. Just then the janitor knocked on the door and said in a loud voice, "What's going on in there? Is everything alright?" AMPS whispered in my ear, "Okay, Q-B. You got away this time, but if you ever say a word about this, you can kiss your ass goodbye because no one is going to believe a little faggot like you." He released me, opened the door, and informed the janitor that we were just indulging in harmless horseplay. I walked away as fast as I could, but not without hearing AMPS tell the janitor, "You know how boys his age like to test their strength" which I suppose the dimwitted janitor believed.

After her rehearsal, Mother could see that I was upset, but I pretended that everything was okay, so she let it drop. But everything was not okay. AMPS's calling me a worthless little faggot who was about to get what he deserved stayed in my mind, partly because the "little faggot" part was true. And as a gay boy, I wondered what I deserved. It took me a long time to forget the awful sensation of his thuggish body on top of me, the pressure of his erection against my ass, and his attempts to unbuckle my pants. In the meantime, it pleased me to see a bandage on his thumb. I wondered what his mother, the beastly Bertha, would think if she knew that her son enjoyed sexually assaulting adolescent boys.

I informed my parents that I would not attend scout meetings as long as AMPS was the scoutmaster. When asked why, I replied, "Because Andrew Manchester

Perkins is a bully and a bastard, and I don't want to be around someone that stupid because stupidity is contagious." My mother was appalled that I would use a word like *bastard*. My father scolded me for speaking disrespectfully of an adult, but I suspect he was secretly amused at the notion of stupidity being contagious since he once referred to AMPS as an NRB, for "not right bright." Because scouting and church were linked, my father hoped to resolve my difficulties with AMPS. But that very week, AMPS resigned as scoutmaster, perhaps fearing that I might say something about the attack. Whatever the reason, it was a relief to not see his ugly ass at future Scout meetings. I got revenge of sorts by occasionally placing nails under his tires or throwing rocks at his house late at night.

Chapter Eight:
Fawn Brodie and the Nibley Challenge

Shortly after my fourteenth birthday, something clicked in my brain, and I started to become me, or at least the me that I recognize now: a contrarian smart-ass who almost always resents authority. Mostly out of conviction but partly to annoy conservative adults, I became a self-styled liberal and intellectual—both viewed suspiciously by conservative Mormons. News sources in our home consisted entirely of the conservative *The Arizona Republic* and *Time Magazine.* Another source of information for me was Larry Posner, a traveling wholesaler who sold tires and auto supplies to my father. Noting my political interests, he often slipped me copies of *The Nation* and *The New Republic,* both magazines way left of anything available in Rosales.

Armed with these limited resources, I supported civil rights and racial integration, although not a single black person lived near Rosales. I may have been the first person in Rosales to object to the Vietnam war. In a social studies class, we read an excerpt from Barry Goldwater's *Conscience of a Conservative.* My summary that almost got me kicked out of class: "I can see the conservative part, but where's the conscience?"—undoubtedly a line that I had filched from one of Posner's magazines. Parley Hanks, a wealthy rancher, became so concerned about how Communists were indoctrinating me that he gave me a subscription to *Human Events,* a paranoid rightwing rag that is still going strong. It had no effect. Rather, I began arguing for wealth redistribution, suggesting that we start by dividing up the huge Hanks ranch to give land to poor Mexicans.

Shortly before my fifteenth birthday, Lucy Ramírez, a non-Mormon volunteer in the Rosales public library with whom I had developed something of a friendship, recommended Fawn Brodie's *No Man Knows My History* to me. Lucy had often suggested books, encouraging me to read serious literature—the Brontës, Dickens, Hemingway, Cather, and Steinbeck, to name a few. But this time her motives were not entirely innocent.

Brodie's heavily documented book was the first academically recognized biography of Joseph Smith, the Mormon prophet, previous biographies being either by apologists or debunkers. Despite being the niece of a president of the church, Brodie basically concludes that Joseph Smith was a fraud, although she allows that he might have been a self-deluded, charismatic, and highly imaginative fraud who for complex psychological reasons believed in himself and convinced other people to believe in him—people like my great-great grandparents who figured among Mormonism's earliest converts.

Knowing that Mother would disapprove mightily of Brodie's book, I hid it in my sock drawer. Of course, she found it. Although Mother did little to keep a clean house, much less wash and fold socks, she periodically searched my room, perhaps hoping to find a *Playboy*. (Fat chance of that.) Predictably, discovering Brodie's book inspired a tremendous Loretta moment. She confronted me on a Saturday morning just as I was leaving for my dad's garage. With all the drama she could muster, she cried out to the last row of her imaginary theater, "Why are you reading that apostate filth? Why betray everything we've tried to teach you? Think of your heritage! Think of yourself as a bearer of God's priesthood! Why lay your family to an open shame?" And on and on.

I usually remained silent during her Loretta episodes since responding just prolonged them and sometimes led to a hard slap on the face. But this time I was really pissed. "And why are you going through *my* stuff in *my* bedroom?" I demanded.

"What do you mean?" she asked disingenuously. "I was just placing clean socks in your drawer."

"And just when did you start washing and folding my socks? Like maybe never? I wash and iron all my clothes because otherwise I'd be the filthiest kid in Rosales."

"That's not true!" (It was true.) "How can you say such mean things to me?!?! I'm your mother!"

"Yes, but you don't have the right to sneak into my room and snoop through my stuff."

"I am only trying to protect you." Then with a dramatic inhalation and eyes looking heavenward, she cried out, "Joshua, we live in perilous times. The last days! The time is very short! If you only knew how short! We must constantly guard against evil and apostasy. And that's what Fawn Brodie is: an evil woman and an apostate."

"Whatever she is, you don't have a right to snoop through my stuff." Sensing an impending flood of tears, I left the house as soon as I could, slamming the door behind me. I hated seeing her cry, partly because her tears made me feel guilty, but mostly because once the waterworks started, a hard slap might follow.

The next day, a Sunday, my bishop, Bishop Flake, asked me to meet him in his office after Sunday School. On entering, I saw that Brother Bateman was with him—not a good thing. Bateman worked for the church education department and taught in the LDS Seminary program—seminary for Mormons being courses for high school students on church teachings, church history, and the LDS scriptures. He got along famously with my mother since they could converse for hours about arcane points of Mormon doctrine, Jesus's second coming, and the imminent end of our wicked world.

A rigid and dogmatic man with a tired wife and eight kids, Bateman was both feared and disliked by most students, including me. In one of his first classes, he remarked that his job was to help us "master" the curriculum for that year, thus allowing Craig and me to call him Master Bateman as in masturbate-man. Bishop Flake began. "Josh, we've been informed that you are reading Fawn Brodie's so-called biography of Joseph Smith."

So that's what Mother had done. Not wanting my father to know of her snooping, she had gone directly to the bishop. Bishop Flake continued, "Do you know that the Church authorities have forbidden that book?"

With a patronizing smile, Brother Bateman interrupted. "Actually," he said, "the LDS Church does not forbid books. We leave that to the Catholics. But we should listen to our leaders and heed their counsel. Josh, do you know that Fawn Brodie was excommunicated for heresy?"

"No. I didn't know that she was excommunicated for heresy" I replied, parroting his question in a sing-song voice.

"There's no need to get sarcastic," Master Bateman replied. "God gives us our free agency to choose what we read, but he also expects us to follow the counsel of our living prophets—those very living prophets who excommunicated Fawn Brodie for apostasy. Now, you may think that you are such a bright boy that you can read apostate literature and not be affected by it. But you can't. You can't play with pigs and not get dirty."

How was I supposed to respond to that? That Fawn Brodie didn't strike me as a pig? That her book contained hundreds of footnotes, references, and citations? Noting my silence, Bishop Flake continued. "Josh, since you read Fawn Brodie, Brother Bateman would like to loan you a copy of Hugh Nibley's rebuttal to Fawn Brodie called *No Ma'am, That's Not History.* You will see that Nibley really puts Brodie in her place. After you read it, we can discuss the matter further."

No way was I going to discuss the matter further, least of all with the creepy Master Bateman. Nibley's rebuttal, however, did interest me. For decades, Hugh Nibley was the LDS church's chief apologist on virtually everything. His sarcastic rebuttal of Brodie's book was highly entertaining. Paradoxically, I sort of wanted both Brodie and Nibley to be right. Dethroning Joseph Smith would free me from some of the shame Mormonism gave me as a gay man. But I was not at that point in my life prepared to see Joseph Smith as a con artist.

Nibley ends his refutation by declaring that the Joseph Smith described by Brodie could not have done what the real Joseph Smith did, chief proof being the *Book of Mormon,* a book allegedly written in

Reformed Egyptian (whatever that was) and recorded on gold plates that Joseph Smith located through the divine guidance of the Angel Moroni. Joseph Smith claimed to have translated the plates with the help of seer stones, which he called the Urim and Thummim—some sort of holy eyeglasses. After completing the book (translation?), he returned the plates and the seer stones to the Angel Moroni, thus leaving no material evidence to corroborate his version of things. Nibley's argument in a nutshell: read the *Book of Mormon* and you'll conclude that Joseph Smith's story, no matter how fantastical, is still the best explanation for such a remarkable book.

So, shortly after turning fifteen, I accepted Nibley's challenge and began reading the *Book of Mormon.* It was not love at first sight. The faux King-Jamesian prose of the book was an immediate turn-off, especially since every other sentence seemed to start with "And it came to pass" if not "Behold" or "Verily" or "Verily, verily." With cause, Mark Twain called the book chloroform in print. But what really gave me pause was the episode of the so-called small plates of Nephi.

Needing financial support, Joseph Smith convinced a prosperous farmer named Martin Harris that he was indeed translating a sacred history of ancient America from gold plates. Harris's wife questioned Smith's story, so Joseph allowed Martin to show his wife the first 116 pages of the manuscript, supposedly a section of the Book of Lehi, which was originally intended to be the first book in the *Book of Mormon*. These pages mysteriously disappeared, which left Joseph Smith with a major problem. If he reproduced the first 116 pages through another act of translation, someone might bring forth the original, show that the two versions didn't coincide, and thereby denounce Smith as a fraud.

What to do? Joseph solved the problem by announcing that the Angel Moroni had given him a second set of plates called the small plates of Nephi that miraculously just happened to retell the same story as the missing pages. Consequently, the first book in the Book of Mormon is 1 Nephi, and there is no Book of Lehi. The *Book of Mormon* goes to great lengths to explain that the small plates had been prepared for a special purpose that only God understood—i.e., in anticipation of the disappearance of the 116 pages of manuscript. This was just too neat for me, so I discontinued my reading project, but with mounting doubts about one of Mormonism's key foundational stories.

My experience with Bishop Flake and Master Bateman also brought me face to face with another disturbing aspect of Mormonism: its top-down authoritarianism by which church leaders expect unquestioning obedience. Basic tenets of LDS doctrine hold that obedience is the first law of heaven and that one must avoid "evil speaking of the Lord's anointed"—i.e., disagreeing with church authorities.

Even if I weren't gay, I probably would have had trouble with church dogma and leadership. Maybe that's what a liberal is: someone who resents being told what to do and believe.

Chapter Nine: Mother Harold

What really confirmed my fate as a rebel was befriending Mr. Harold Prescott. Shortly after my fourteenth birthday, my parents decided that I needed braces. Since the closest orthodontist was in Phoenix, this occasioned the need for trips to Arizona's capital city every two weeks for orthodontic work. My parents teamed up with other Rosales families whose kids needed braces so that each set of parents took turns driving us to the orthodontist. Going to Phoenix usually meant spending a night in a hotel, which for me and my fellow braces wearers was great fun.

These trips also allowed me to indulge my growing interest in the organ by visiting music shops and checking out different brands of electronic instruments—Allen, Baldwin, Conn, Hammond, Lowery, and Wurlitzer. I collected brochures and stop lists, and probably drove some of the sales personnel crazy. But people were kind, and visits to organ and piano stores became a regular feature of my trips to Phoenix. Of course, the inexperienced Joshua Chastain of that time did not know that real organ aficionados considered electronic organs to be appliances. Several years would pass before I could participate in the snobbery of seeing only pipe organs as the real thing.

On one memorable trip to Phoenix, my fellow braces wearers and our chaperones announced that they were going to a baseball game. I begged off, saying that I would rather visit music stores. Accustomed to and amused by my eccentricities, they went to the game and left me alone for the afternoon. At the Baldwin Piano and Organ store, I met Harold Prescott, a college student majoring in organ at Arizona State University.

Cute in a skinny, nervous, and slightly effeminate way, he was helping his parents' church purchase an electronic organ. He played several of the Baldwin organs for me, commenting knowledgably on each instrument. Then, out of the blue, he asked, "Would you like to hear the new Casavant pipe organ at the church where I work? It's got eighty ranks and it's simply fabulous. I just know that you'll love it." (Elongated vowel in "know" as in "knooooooow").

Charmed by his attention and sensing that he might be the gay friend I was longing to meet, I accepted the invitation, casting to the wind my parents' warnings about getting into cars with strangers. After a short drive in a beat-up Volkswagen bug, he took me up to the choir loft at the back of a large empty church crowned by a stunning display of organ pipes.

"Sit next to me on the organ bench so you can check out the stops."

Of course, I wanted to check out the stops since the Hammond B-3 electric organ at my LDS church in Rosales didn't have stops. But I also wanted to check out sitting next to him. He raced through Mulet's "Thou Art the Rock" and a couple of other noisy and to my ear magnificent pieces.

"Now," he said, "you play something for me."

"I don't know any organ pieces."

"Then play a piano piece, something by Bach maybe."

I played one of Bach's two-part inventions. Although complimentary, he said, no doubt with faint praise, "You've got good *piano* technique but clearly you've never studied the organ."

"So, maybe you'd like to teach me."

"Tell you what. I'll lend you an organ method book and then the next time we get together, I'll give you a lesson." From a filing cabinet behind the organ case, he fished out a much-used copy of Flor Peeters' *Little Organ Book*. Handing it to me, he said, "This is the first organ book I ever used. If you learn what's here, you'll be well on your way to developing a solid technique." As I took the book, he gave one of my shoulders an affectionate squeeze. Immediately aware of his touch, I felt a surge of excitement course through my body. No doubt sensing my eagerness, he asked, "Would you like to see the church apartment where I live?" I didn't need a second invitation.

I had just turned fifteen when Harold, a college undergraduate probably in his late teens, embraced me, kissed me, and gently began undressing me while I did the same for him. It was like opening a Christmas present. His body was a slightly older version of mine with a bit of body hair and genitals that seemed way too large for our skinny bodies. But my spirit soared as his naked body embraced mine. And when he sought my mouth for a prolonged kiss, I knew exactly what to do—so unlike my clumsy attempts at physical interaction with girls.

We lay down on his bed, and there, in a staff apartment of a Presbyterian church, I enjoyed my first full sexual encounter with another man. I found the experience pleasurable beyond description and entirely natural, almost as though I had been programmed for it. Afterwards, we lay naked together without speaking, gently caressing each other's body. Before taking me to my hotel, he gave me his telephone number and asked me to contact him for an organ lesson the next time I was in Phoenix—adding with a knowing smirk, "for an organ lesson of a different kind."

Since my traveling companions had not returned from the ball game, I was able to sit quietly in the hotel room to think about what had just happened. On one level, I knew that according to the LDS Church I had committed a grievous sin. Yet, on another, I felt neither guilt nor shame. Rather, I was overcome with a profound sense of gratitude for having met someone like me. I then sank to my knees and thanked God for allowing me to meet such a wonderful new friend.

This was in 1968, a time when gay activism was beginning to gather strength in large American cities but most certainly not in Rosales, Arizona. Terms like "coming out" and "gay pride" would not enter my vocabulary until several years later. Family, the LDS church, the law, psychology, rural Arizona, society in general—all would tell me that homosexuality was a sin, a crime, an illness, or (when they tried to be compassionate) a tragedy. Gay sex for the LDS Church was and remains grounds for excommunication. I wish that such entrenched "authoritative" homophobia did not affect my struggle for self-recognition and self-acceptance. Still, it has always helped to remember that my reaction to my first real homosexual experience was a profound sense of gratitude for meeting someone like me with whom I could celebrate friendship through sexual intimacy.

Since my mother fantasized that God had chosen me to become Tabernacle Organist, my parents began allowing me to travel to Phoenix by bus, stay overnight with a great aunt, and then have time for both an orthodontist appointment and an organ lesson. Over the next year, Harold gave me a solid foundation in organ technique. Following each lesson, we made love in his apartment where Harold taught me both the mechanics and varieties of gay sex. He considered himself "a proud bottom" which meant that I developed considerable proficiency as his top.

Harold also introduced me to the pleasures of camp. He confirmed the stereotype of a nelly queen—a term I would learn later—along with *butch, diesel dyke*, and *dropping hairpins* (i.e., hinting that one might be gay). He referred to himself as Mother Harold, minced when he walked, spoke with a slight lisp, and made no attempt to keep his wrists straight. He habitually used feminine pronouns for men. When an attractive man wearing a tank top and shorts walked by, he would say something like, "Would you look at that shameless hussy showing off her muscles and hairy legs! And in public! Oh, be still my beating heart! Be still!!" He would then pretend to fan himself lest he suffer "an attack of the vapors."

He often began answers to my questions with "Sweetie, listen to your Mother Harold." People in his world were fabulous or awful, utterly divine or unspeakably horrid, demigods or douchebags. He saved his best descriptions for other organists. E. Power Biggs was a total soporific; Anthony Newman played okay for straight trash; Richard Elsasser had the subtlety of a rhino in rut; and Virgil Fox— "I will not hear you say a word against Miss Virgil! She is the holy mother of us all. Genuflect and cross yourself if you dare utter her name!" While I found camp amusing (and still do), in my literal-minded speech, males continued to receive masculine pronouns.

Music, sex, and camp were not Harold's only areas of expertise. When I complained about not having enough time to practice, he responded, "Joshua dear, lucky for you, your Mother Harold is a world-class maven of time management." We then worked out a daily schedule that allowed me two hours practice on the piano before going to school in the morning and almost two on the organ by combining my lunch hour with a study period. He also advised me to buy a datebook and budget my time in writing. Datebooks thus became a lifetime habit. I've kept most of them, and they've proven invaluable in helping me write this manuscript.

While Harold's help allowed me to use time more efficiently, my new schedule left little time for socializing. Music was quickly becoming my best friend and my primary means of self-affirmation. Perhaps like many young homosexuals, I considered racking up accomplishments to be an excellent strategy for surviving in the homosexual closet. By being both a good student and an accomplished musician, perhaps I hoped people might overlook my being queer.

Since Harold and I had sex in his church-owned apartment after every lesson, I eventually asked if the church had a problem with his being gay. "Not really," he replied. "God knows that I'm gay. *She* should know since *she* made me this way. Most people in the choir and congregation just look the other way. Besides, I'm a damned good organist, and this church has the best music program in town, so people respect me and leave me alone."

"What does your priest think?"

"*Pastor*, sweetie, *pastor*. Presbyterians don't have priests. Only Catholics and Episcopalians have priests. What does my pastor think? He's okay with it. Several parishioners are gay, and he knows about them. In fact, there's a gay guy on the session." Seeing me frown in miscomprehension, he added, "The session is the committee that oversees the parish. Josh dear, Presbyterians simply *love* committees. You get three Presbyterians together, and they'll organize five committees within a week. Anyway, this guy attends church with his partner, and they give many dollars to the parish."

"But don't Presbyterians believe that homosexuality is a sin?"

"Some do, but we smart girls don't take those people seriously. Why should I let other people tell me who I am? You and I have become great friends with, ahem, physical benefits we both enjoy. Where's the sin? What harm are we doing? Is there any reason to think that we are hurting ourselves or anyone else? No, no, and no. Besides, sweetie, if you're going to be an organist, you better make peace with the church because organs are in churches."

"Does your *pastor* know about you?"

"Yeah. We've talked about it. He basically said that a gay life is a gift like any other life and that I should use what he calls my life-force to do good. He loves our music program, by the way."

"That was it?"

"Well, actually he gave me another piece of advice that he called the eleventh commandment."

"Which is?"

"*Thou shalt not fuck the flock.* And Joshua sweetie, Mother Harold obeys that commandment to the letter. I will never become involved sexually or romantically with anyone in the parish, even if he looks like Adonis incarnate."

"How about your parents? Do they know you're gay?"

"Ah, my poor parents. They belong to this ghastly Bible church that hates homosexuals. They caught me fooling around with a neighbor kid and made me attend a Christian counseling group."

"Did it work?"

"Yeah, but not like my parents wanted. Sweetie, that group was filled with gay boys dying to have sex with other gay boys. I even got it on with Mr. Christian Counselor himself. When I got this job and the apartment that came with it, I moved out of my parents' home forever. It was the best thing I ever did. You can't stay healthy living with people who hate what you are."

58

Then, pursing his lips, he gave me some strange but prescient advice: "Joshua dear, listen to your Mother Harold. Never take shit for being gay, especially from dickwad shrinks and douche-bag religious fanatics. They are the worst. The *very* worst. Remember that you know more about yourself than they do. Don't ever let them tell you who you are."

We exchanged a few letters after he went back east for graduate school, but we eventually lost contact. We were never in love, but I remember him fondly and am grateful for the solid introduction he gave me to organ technique. I am also thankful that my introduction to being gay occurred with such a kind, experienced, and entertaining slightly older guy.

Chapter Ten:
Meeting Father Tovar

I finished my sophomore year on a high. I had exchanged my braces for a winning smile, and my attraction to men had led me to an intense year-long friendship with a kind man who was also an excellent organ teacher. Most surprising, however, was discovering the singing voice bequeathed to me by puberty—a resonant baritone that according to Mrs. Jespersen had "definite solo potential".

Now approaching six feet tall, I started doing chin-ups on my father's tire racks and pushups wherever I could. Probably no one else noticed the slight muscular bulges in my arms and chest, but I noticed them and deemed them remarkable. My self-confidence was further bolstered by placing in the 99th percentile on the junior level national achievement test taken at the end of my sophomore year. I still enjoyed circle jerks with some of my classmates, but I kept quiet about knowing how to do more than beat off. A gay boy in 1969 Rosales was still in treacherous waters.

But not so treacherous that I didn't find time for Father Tovar. My father discounted gas prices and car services for the Rosales Catholic priests, so over the years I became acquainted with several of them. Until Father Tovar, all had been imports from back east with virtually no proficiency in Spanish. Always curious about religion, an obsession almost as great as my interest in music, I engaged them in conversations about Catholicism. They acquiesced to long discussions with me probably because they were lonesome and grateful for someone to talk to. For Catholic priests, Rosales must have been a kind of Siberia. Rumors held that several were heavy drinkers.

Father Tovar arrived in Rosales just after Harold went back east, probably in late May or early June of 1969. The first Rosales Catholic priest who spoke Spanish, he was young, slender, and tall, with skin the color of milk chocolate. He had a head of thick black hair, large almond-shaped brown eyes, a broad smile with even white teeth, and beautiful large hands that reminded me of Michelangelo's David. We took an immediate liking to each other. My father's garage was only a half block from the Catholic rectory, so Father Tovar would often drop in for a short conversation. He explained that he would not be in Rosales for long since he was covering for a priest who had to leave because of a medical emergency. Not at all innocently, I asked if he could teach me Latin. This was not just an excuse. I really wanted to learn Latin. But I also wanted to spend more time with this lovely man, especially if he wasn't going to be in Rosales for very long.

He loaned me an old textbook, told me to study the first chapter, and agreed to meet me in his office the following Saturday morning for a Latin session. We sat next to each other at a worktable in his study and began identifying parts of speech and discussing how declensions functioned. An electric charge surged through me as I realized that his knee was touching mine. I held my knee in place and noticed that he did not move his. I gave a slight push. He pushed back. I pushed harder.

We both began pushing harder until it was almost a question of who would knock the other person out of his chair. He then placed his left arm on the back of my chair and gently let it slide up over my shoulders. I slipped my right arm behind his back and pulled him towards me. We remained in this awkward position for a few more minutes, still discussing Latin declensions as though nothing were happening on the sidelines. Eventually, he turned towards me and slowly bent forward for a kiss. After making out a bit, he suddenly pulled away and said, "We have to stop."

"Why?" I asked.

"We just do."

We both stood up. As I picked up my book and notebook, I noticed that he had not moved away from me and that there was a conspicuous bulge in his pants. I pulled him towards me. We began kissing again. I felt his erection pressing against mine—the start of a quick but exciting sexual encounter. After we both climaxed, he asked me to sit with him on the small sofa in his study, my head resting on his chest with his arms around me. His eyes were damp with tears.

"What's the matter? Why are you crying?" I asked.

"I thought it was over. I thought I could control it."

"Control what?" I asked disingenuously.

In a soft voice, he replied, "I am a priest in the Church of God. I am sworn to celibacy. I cannot do things like this. Besides, you're a minor and we might get caught."

"Not if I come to your house at night," I said, totally ignoring everything else he had said.

He remained silent for what seemed an age. Then, with great deliberation he said, "Come tonight around nine o'clock. Knock on the back door. The house lights will be off, but I'll be waiting for you."

It was early summer. With no classes to attend, I worked days at my father's garage. At night I was free to do almost anything, so sneaking to the Catholic parsonage was not a problem. I arrived as planned and knocked lightly on the backdoor. No lights were on. Father Tovar opened the door and pulled me inside. We immediately embraced, crazed in our desire to touch and hold each other. In total darkness, he guided me to his bedroom. We undressed each other. Like the first time with Mother Harold, I found myself in the magical presence of a totally naked man with a lean, taut body that was almost hairless except for his armpits and crotch.

Sex with Father Tovar followed a different rhythm from my encounters with Harold. He taught me the difference between having sex and making love. (Both retain an honored place in my value system.) He took sex seriously, moving slowly and ceremoniously, making sure that every moment counted. He assigned great metaphorical importance to the intense intimacy of intercourse and insisted that we perform both active and passive roles lest one of us feel more manly than the other. Despite my initial reluctance, I soon learned to relish the feeling of him inside of me and me inside of him, possibly because he showed great concern for my comfort and pleasure, and taught me to be similarly sensitive to him.

Over the summer, I became intimately acquainted with his beautiful brown body, the smell and taste of his skin, and the feel of his thick black hair. For almost three months, we managed to meet at least two or three times a week, always well after dark. Knowing that our encounters were both dangerous and transgressive no doubt enriched our sexual pleasure.

Chapter Eleven:
Father Tovar's Story

After our second sexual meeting, we lay naked, arms around each other and legs intertwined. Slowly, he began to talk. I adored the timbre of his smooth baritone voice and his slight Spanish accent. "I am taught that I shouldn't do these things. I have taken a vow to not do these things. Yet here I am with an underage Mormon boy, ten years my junior, doing things that could get me defrocked and maybe sent to prison. What does it all mean?"

This was a bit much for a sixteen-year-old Mormon Rosales boy, so I just waited quietly hoping he would say more.

"I come from a large family with three older brothers and four older sisters. Ever since I was a little boy, I wanted to be a priest, and my parents wanted to give one of their sons to God. Since I was a good student, a Jesuit school in Phoenix gave me a live-in scholarship when I was thirteen years old, all expenses paid. Since then, the Catholic Church has been my entire life and my only home. After high school, I went straight to seminary. I was only eighteen. My father died a couple of years ago. I had just turned twenty-five and was recently ordained. My family was very proud to see me celebrate at his funeral mass."

He stopped talking, so I asked, "Why did you want to become a priest?"

"Because I felt that God had called me to priesthood. I also received lots of encouragement from my high school and seminary teachers."

He removed his arm from under my head and turned on his side to face me. "I think that I am a good priest," he said. "I put in long hours, I attend to my parishioners, and I work hard on my sermons in both Spanish and English. I want our liturgies to be worthy of God so that my parishioners feel consoled by the grace available to them in the Church's sacraments. As a priest of the church, I am an instrument of that grace. I take it very seriously."

As a Mormon lad, I had no idea of what he was talking about. Liturgy? Grace? Sacraments? These are not LDS terms. Searching for something to say, all I could come up with was, "But you are a good priest, aren't you? The high school kids like you, and you're the first priest in Rosales who can speak Spanish."

"I try to be a good and faithful priest." Then with a rueful grin, "But making love with an underage Mormon boy isn't part of the plan."

"Could you do something else? Something besides being a priest?"

"Being a priest is my entire identity. I also know that I can do more good from within the church than anywhere else. When I give people communion and administer the sacraments, I bring God to them, and they feel God's love. When I say mass, I'm participating in a ritual that is nearly two thousand years old, and I see myself in communion with all those Christians who came before me. And when I give my parishioners absolution, they know that their sins are forgiven."

"You can forgive sins?"

"I can't, but God can, acting through me."

Seeing the confusion on my face, he quoted John's gospel, explaining how Jesus gave his apostles the authority to forgive sins, and how that authority has been passed down to all properly ordained priests. His words came from the heart, and I found them very moving.

But I was suddenly overwhelmed by the *utter weirdness* of this conversation. We had just made love. We were lying next to each other totally naked with the smell of sex still floating in the air. Yet here he was explaining his faith with great beauty and sincerity. If he had asked me that night to convert to Catholicism, I would have accepted in a heartbeat. From that point forward, we often discussed religion after making love.

Partly because at that time I didn't know any of the "hot-button" issues, we never discussed the Vatican, the pope, or the Catholic church's obnoxious teachings on sex, women, divorced people, and homosexuality.

Rather, Father Tovar saw the church as a divine instrument for helping people through the difficult process of living—by offering consolation, absolution, and real contact with God through the mass.

I once asked him what seminary had been like since I was clearly not his first sexual partner. A smile played at the corners of his mouth as he said, "Actually, the seminary was one of the gayest places I've ever been. At least half of my fellow seminarians were gay, although almost no one talked about it. As gay men, they had no plans to marry, so going into the priesthood was the perfect alternative. And to be fair, I believe that most of them were sincere in their religious vocation and that they have become good priests. Just as good as the straight guys. Maybe even better."

"Did you have sex with any of them?"

"With a couple when I first got there, but it was dangerous. The brothers who ran the seminary kept an eye on us and did everything possible to prevent close friendships. In some ways, the seminary is a very lonely place. The brothers didn't want us to have close friends."

"So, you lived that entire time without sex?"

The smile returned. "I didn't say that. Truth be told, I had a sexual arrangement with one of the brothers. It was consensual. I never felt exploited. And he didn't make a big thing of it. Whenever I felt guilty, he would say, 'Don't worry about it. Things happen.

God understands. If it really bothers you, discuss it with your confessor'."

"Do you have a confessor?"

"I see my confessor at least once a month."

"Do you tell him about me?"

"Of course. But don't worry. The seal of the confessional is such that no priest can reveal what is said there. Besides, like all smart Catholics, I choose my confessor carefully."

"Is he gay?"

"I've never asked. But nothing seems to shock him, and he always grants me absolution.

I left these conversations with my head spinning. No one could have given me a more beautiful, heartfelt, and convincing introduction to Catholicism. He explained that the Roman Catholic Church was the Church founded by Jesus, and he introduced me to the passage in Matthew's gospel where Jesus changes Simon's name to Peter, which according to Father Tovar, meant rock. Jesus then says that upon that rock he would build his church, which is why Peter is considered the first pope. He taught me about apostolic succession and how the keys of the kingdom given to Peter, including the authority to forgive sins, had been passed down through the ages to all properly ordained clergy.

Apostolic succession was easy for me to understand since Mormonism claims that the apostolic order was restored through Joseph Smith. Unfortunately, the Mormon version left out the authority to forgive sins. Recalling these conversations, I marvel that they took place after we made love as I lay naked next to Father Tovar's beautiful, brown, consecrated body. Could that possibly be the best way to discuss religion?

One Saturday afternoon in mid-August, Father Tovar came to the garage and informed me that, due to an emergency vacancy in a Spanish-speaking parish near Tucson, his bishop was assigning him to a new parish—immediately. He would have to leave the following afternoon after mass.

"Do you really have to leave?" a childish version of me asked.

"Yes. I'm bound to obey my bishop. Besides, this was only a temporary assignment, and my bishop has good reasons for placing me in a Spanish-speaking parish. I also think that God wants me there."

"Do I get to say goodbye?"

"Come by tonight, but you can't stay long."

I went to the parsonage that night. We made love quickly so he could finish packing. At that point, I almost lost it. "Father Tovar," I said with tears in my eyes, "I think I'm in love with you."

He embraced me and held me for a long time. Then, with a catch in his voice, he said, "And I love you too, but we can't love each other this way. There's no future in it for either of us. Josh, we can't hold on to each other. We both need to figure out what God wants us to do with our lives, and we can't do it together. You are only sixteen. You have a lot of living in front of you. You're beautiful, you're smart, you're talented, and you're wonderful. Please remember me. I'll always remember you. But memories are all we will have."

Instead of going straight home, I walked south of town, out to the tamarack flats just below one of the town reservoirs. The night was cool and brightly illuminated by a full moon—the kind of summer night that one finds only in the high deserts of Arizona. While Mother Harold had been a good friend, Father Tovar was the first man I ever fell in love with. Aware of his scent still on my body, I sat down on a large rock. Heartbroken at the thought of never seeing him again, I began to cry, at first just a few sniffles and then loud sobs that I didn't know I was capable of.

Everything Father Tovar had told me was true. We couldn't see each other again, and my very presence in his life could do him great harm. Adolescent breakups between straight couples were weekly occurrences at Rosales High School and a source of much commentary, side-taking, and commiseration. But my situation was different. The first real love of my life was leaving me, and I could tell no one about my sadness.

I suddenly became aware of something looking at me. About thirty feet away, sitting on a flat rock, was a gray, striped bobcat, tufted ears erect and yellowish eyes looking intently at me. Arizona bobcats are not friendly animals, and they usually avoid human contact. Why was this elegant creature staring at me? Maybe because she had never heard a human cry? As Boy Scouts we were taught to never run from a bobcat, lest we provoke a chase response. Instead, we were to make lots of noise so that the bobcat would run from us.

Yet, I sensed no hostility from this exquisite animal. Rather, I wondered if she was commiserating with my heartache because maybe in her bobcat heart, she had also known grief. As soon as I stopped crying, she rose to her feet without taking her eyes off me. She then slowly turned around and silently padded into the brush. Animal behaviorists might call me crazy, but I remain convinced that the only creature to share my sorrow that night was a beautiful wild animal not known for empathizing with humans. I got home later than usual and said goodnight to my parents. More out of duty than interest, they asked where I had been. I answered with total honesty, "I have been with a friend."

In later years, I often wondered about my affairs with Harold and Father Tovar, if that's what they were.

My involvement with Harold started when I was fifteen and lasted about a year. I met Father Tovar a couple of months after turning sixteen. Since Harold was in his late teens when we met and Father Tovar was in his mid-twenties, both men were transgressing the law by having gay sex, particularly with a minor. Father Tovar might be considered especially culpable in view of the pedophile scandals that continue to besmirch the Roman Catholic priesthood. Stories about priests who force themselves on vulnerable, unsuspecting boys truly repel me, and I am much saddened by the reports of emotional trauma such priests cause in those boys' later lives.

Yet, I do not see myself in these stories. I was delighted by Harold's and Father Tovar's sexual attentions and participated willingly. These relationships were entirely consensual. In fact, I probably had more to do with seducing Father Tovar than vice versa. Further, both Harold and Father Tovar contributed greatly to my education while also providing examples of how gay sexual desire can lead to friendship, love, and community. I remember our time together with fondness and gratitude.

Chapter Twelve:
Mme. Jacqueline Arnaud

Father Tovar was not the only remarkable person to enter my life that summer before my junior year. Every week I had a piano lesson from Mrs. Jespersen. One day in early July, she introduced me to a houseguest. "Joshua, I would like you to meet Jacqueline Arnaud. Jacqueline just retired after a distinguished career as an opera singer in Europe. She will be a visiting professor at the University of Arizona this coming fall, and in the meantime, she is spending a few days with me. You may call her Madame Arnaud."

A handsome, tall woman with neatly combed blond hair tied back in a bun, Madame Arnaud wore loose navy-blue pants, a long-sleeved white blouse, and a light blue scarf casually draped around her neck and shoulders. With simple pearl earrings, light makeup, and piercing blue eyes, she was surely one of the most elegant women I had ever seen. Extending her hand palm down, she said, "Joshua, *il me fait plaisir de faire votre connaissance*" which she quickly translated in lightly accented English as, "It gives me pleasure to meet you."

Not knowing what to do, I wrapped my hand around her fingers and mumbled something profound like, "Glad to meet you."

With a slight scowl, she leaned close to me and whispered, "When a lady offers you the back of her hand, you should kiss it and not grab her fingers. That is what gentlemen do."

"Now Jackie," Mrs. J intervened. "Don't be too hard on him. After all, he's a country kid from Arizona, just like me."

"*Bien sûr, ma chère Poupette*," Mme. Arnaud replied with a smile. "But one is never too young to learn good manners. Besides, you were never a very convincing country girl."

"Josh, Jackie was my roommate back at the Cincinnati Conservatory. We've remained friends all these years. My goodness, Jackie, how long has it been?"

"Nearly forty years, *ma chérie. C'est incroyable, n'est-ce pas?*"

"You will need to speak English to Josh, I'm afraid."

"*C'est bien*, but then you must speak French to me. Your French used to be so good. You should bring it back." Then looking at me, "Oh yes. Poupette's French was excellent, and she was by far the best pianist at the *conservatoire*. In fact, one of the pianos you see here was given to her because she won a competition.

"Jackie, you're making me blush. And you shouldn't call me Poupette in front of my students."

"But it is such a lovely name!" Then looking at me, "It just means that she is my dear friend. Besides, I don't like the name Josephine. It's too *bonapartiste*."

Seeing my confusion, Mrs. Jespersen explained, "Josephine Bonaparte was Napoleon's first wife. Half of France hates Napoleon, and the other half adores him. Jackie belongs to the first half."

"Only ignorant people adore him. Napoleon betrayed the ideals of the *République* and became a dictator. He also destroyed castles and churches all over Europe. No one should like him." Then, turning to me, she continued, "Poupette tells me that you have a good voice. Would you be so kind as to sing something for me?"

"I don't have anything prepared."

"Then sing a hymn. Surely you know some nice Mormon hymns."

So, with Mrs. J at the piano, I sang a couple of verses of one my favorite hymns, "Love Divine, All Loves Excelling" set to the Welsh hymn tune *Hyfrodol*. After I finished, Madame Arnaud said, "Joshua, you have a lovely instrument, especially for someone so young. And it will only get better with age."

After a short lull in the conversation, Mrs. Jespersen said, "Josh, Jackie will be here for a month, and I would like you to take a few voice lessons from her. It's time you received some professional vocal training."

Over the next month I had eight lessons from Madame Arnaud. I could not have had a better first voice teacher. After one of my lessons, Mrs. Jespersen invited me to join them for a glass of lemonade which allowed me to eavesdrop as they reminisced about their student years in Cincinnati, often bursting into peals of laughter about people and events they had known.

Oh, how I wished I had been at the conservatory with them! Music saturated their lives, but what I most envied was the exuberance of their friendship. Mrs. J seemed almost girlish with Mme. Arnaud, nothing like the dignified woman I knew as my piano teacher. Madame Arnaud insisted that Mrs. J was the most talented pianist at the conservatory, but then she said with some sadness, "But the call of family and duty were too strong. That is why you have such an excellent teacher of piano in this little town."

"Now Jackie, you know I was not cut out for the concert stage," Mrs. Jespersen replied.

"And why not? If you played better than everyone else?"

"Because I didn't have your stamina and ambition."

"Stamina and ambition! So maybe that is why I liked singing the role of witches like Ulrica and Azucena, and man-killers like Elektra, Carmen, and Delilah." Then with a hearty laugh she turned to me and said, "You see, Josh, I never wanted to marry, so I became famous for roles that scare men away."

Knowing nothing about the opera characters she was invoking, I didn't get the joke, but I looked forward to a time when I might.

After my last voice lesson, Madame Arnaud gave me an old French edition of songs by Henri Duparc. "Joshua, you are not ready to sing these songs yet, but when the time comes, I want you to learn them and remember me. And you must sing them in perfect French." On the inside cover she had written, "*Á mon talentueux et charmant jeune ami, Joshua Chastain*" followed by an elaborate signature and a date, also in French. She kissed me on both cheeks and whispered "*Au revoir.* God has given you a beautiful instrument. Be grateful and use it well." Mrs. Jespersen then informed me that I would not have piano lessons for the following two weeks because she wanted to help Madame Arnaud get settled in Tucson.

The next day, I ran into Craig Bowen. "I hear you met Mrs. J's girlfriend," he said with a smirk.

"Who? Madame Arnaud? Yea, I met her, and she gave me some great voice lessons. She's fabulous."

"You know she's a dyke, don't you? She's Mrs. Jespersen's girlfriend. Her husband kept a mistress in Kingman because his wife wasn't putting out. Too bad that the horny old bastard got killed in a car wreck."

"Craig, how do you know these things?"

"My dad told me, and he doesn't lie."

In truth, I thought that his father lied a great deal—anything to make people think that he wasn't the only womanizer in town. Still, it was oddly pleasant to think that "Poupette" and "Jackie" might be more than friends.

Chapter Thirteen:
Mother's Meltdown

Two weeks before beginning my junior year classes, I got a call at the service station from my father, telling me that he was taking my mother to a hospital in Winslow. "What's wrong?" I asked.

"I'll explain later. You'll need to close the station this evening and open it tomorrow morning if I don't get back in time. Don't say anything to anyone. It's nobody's business."

Dad didn't come home that night. I opened the garage the following morning as instructed. Late in the afternoon, he walked in looking drained and tired. "How's Mother?" I asked.

"Not good, but she's out of the woods. She'll need to stay in the hospital for a few more days."

"What's wrong with her?"

After a long pause and some obvious struggling for words, he said, "Sonny, women have a real tough time of it. They've got that monthly business to deal with, they go through the valley of death to give birth, and then their bodies go haywire at the change of life. Your mother has had a particularly rough time of it. Maybe you've noticed that she takes a lot of pills."

Yes, I had noticed the pills. I had also noticed how she slurred her words at night and some mornings seemed drunk. I was well acquainted with how rough women's lives are since she talked about it a great deal. I was especially well informed about Mother's very extended menopause. But her version of the story usually ended with, "Thank heaven that we now have medicines to meet women's needs."

My dad sketched the events of the previous day. He had come home for lunch, leaving me at the garage. Mother was still in bed and barely breathing. Fearing the worst, my father pulled her out of bed and tried to revive her. After a few minutes of what must have been sheer terror for my father, she finally responded, but only by saying how much she needed to sleep. My father dumped all her prescription medications in a box and drove her to the Winslow hospital. Why Winslow? Because it was far enough from Rosales for the locals not to find out. He showed the physician the medications that she was taking. His response: "Good God! I'm surprised she's alive at all."

By checking the prescription labels, my father realized that mother had been seeing several area doctors, none of whom knew about each other. She was buying medications at different pharmacies so that no single pharmacist would know what or how much medication she was taking. The medications included powerful tranquilizers and equally powerful stimulants. Mother remained in the hospital for around two weeks.

She went through withdrawal and at one point had to be shackled to her bed. My father stayed with her almost the whole time, leaving the garage entirely to me. Nonetheless, she was back in Rosales when classes started. We told everyone that she had suffered a sudden case of summer pneumonia.

Despite that experience, Mother never stopped taking pills. Her drug use coincided with her growing religiosity. Never short for words, she could speak graphically about the End Times, the special responsibilities of belonging to the only true church, the coming persecutions, the need "to endure to the end," and the importance of "filling the measure of our creation." Some Rosales Mormons found her mesmerizing and highly spiritual. I, however, increasingly wondered if I was seeing a person or a drug-enhanced performance.

If any good came from Mother's nearly fatal overdose, it allowed me to miss summer football practice which always started two weeks before classes began. Despite my failures at boxing, my father made me go out for football in my freshman and sophomore years, perhaps to keep me from becoming a sissy—which clearly didn't work. I hated every minute of it. I hated the faux-macho bullshit of having to do calisthenics while chanting "Blood. Guts. Blood. Guts." I hated the smell of sweaty bodies and mildewed uniforms. I hated running from the practice field back to the dressing room while shouting "Kill, Kill, Kill."

And I hated the coach's supposedly inspirational nonsense about "We owe it to ourselves, we owe it to each other, and we owe it to all those great football players who put Rosales on the map. So, let's get out there and fight!" Owed what? I would ask myself. What was all the fighting about, and whoever said that Rosales was on the map?

My anti-football epiphany occurred during the previous season in the fall of my sophomore year. Since I could neither throw nor catch a ball, I played offensive tackle. We were pitted against one of the Navajo Indian schools. My job on a particular play was to lunge forward and push aside the guy opposite me (knock him on his ass, as the coach put it) so that our quarterback could run through the gap in the line that I had helped create. As we sank into our stinkbug crouch, I looked at the Navajo boy opposite me. Given the padding we wore, all I could see were a beautiful pair of dark, almond-shaped eyes framed by equally beautiful long black eyelashes.

It suddenly occurred to me: "I do not want to hit this boy. I have no reason to hit this boy. This is a really stupid game." So, I didn't hit him, and our quarterback got creamed well behind the line of scrimmage. Our muscle-brained coach immediately pulled me onto the bench and yelled, "Hey Chastain (last names were obligatory in high school sports), what the hell are you doing out there? Do you want to play football or not?" And the answer was no.

Dropping off the football team did not please my father. For him sports were essential to every young man's education. To compensate, I promised to run every day and start working out with weights. I showed him that I could already do fifty pushups and twenty-five chin-ups, which greatly surprised him. I also argued that not playing football would allow me more time to help out at the garage.

Distracted by Mother's drug problems and possibly amused by my earnest bargaining, he relented but not without adding, "If you don't learn to like sports, people will think you're an oddball." Like a homosexual maybe? With the extra time, I continued doing pushups wherever and chinning myself on my father's tire racks. I also began working out in the high school weight room, guided by an old book on bodybuilding that I found in the public library.

Chapter Fourteen: AMPS Again

A week after fall term started, Mr. Boggs, who was scheduled to teach a required civics course, had a heart attack. Much to my horror, the school principal assigned AMPS to take over the course. Remembering how he had humiliated me on a Boy Scout trip when I was twelve years old, not to mention the time he tried to rape me when I was thirteen, I resolved to get kicked out of his class.

On the first day, I listened to his mangled English while he droned on about the importance of "learning" patriotism, accompanied with a few muffled sobs about his love of country. I made a list of the dumb things he said and crafted some snarky comments for the following day. Early in the next class, he gave me a lovely malapropism: *intrepretate* for *interpret*, prompting me to blurt out: "Interpretate? Is that something like perpetrate between two people? Or maybe you had inter-penetrate on your mind, like two people penetrating each other? Isn't that a little kinky for a high school class? We are, after all, impressionable minors."

Stunned and red faced with anger, he mumbled something about not intending to take any smart stuff from kids, to which I replied, "But I thought we were supposed to be smart. Is this a class about being dumb? That's something you could teach well with your mail-order degree and all." My classmates gasped and a couple of girls told me to shut up. But I was on a roll and not about to stop.

With murder in his eyes, AMPS lunged toward me, growling, "You need to go to the principal's office right now!"

"Would you like to show me the way? We can even hold hands. You really liked it last time."

My parting remark stopped him in his tracks. The color drained from his face, for he knew only too well what I was referring to. He also knew that a sixteen-year-old wise mouth like me would be harder to intimidate than the thirteen-year-old he had attacked three years earlier. But by that time, I was out the door.

Principal Barnes, the oldest son of Leona Barnes, my church-choir friend, was basically a nice guy. He was also handsome in a big-framed, muscly, old-guy way. Like most of the male teachers in Rosales High School, he had majored in PE. But he had also played professional basketball and was a first-rate coach known for fairness and giving students second and third chances. He began our conversation with the obligatory bullshit about my bad attitude problem to which I responded with a carefully rehearsed answer: "Actually, the school has a bad teacher problem. Mr. Andrew Manchester Perkins is dumb enough for twins, he can hardly speak English, and he has no business being in a classroom. I hate him more than I hate any other human being in the world."

Surprised by my passionate response, Barnes asked, "Why do you hate him so much?"

Looking straight into the principal's eyes, I said quite slowly, "Believe me. You really do not want to know."

After a long silence, he asked, "What do I not want to know?" To which I replied, "Do you remember Bobbie Tyler? Believe. Me. You. Really. Do. Not. Want. To. Know."

Mentioning Bobbie Tyler turned the trick. In the previous year, Mr. Barnes had dismissed from the faculty an old pervert who asked Bobbie Tyler, a gentle, effeminate boy two years my senior, if he had to part his hair to pee. The scandal got ugly because gentle Bobbie did not have a gentle father. Big Bob did not rest until said pervert was forced into early retirement. Clearly, Mr. Barnes did not want a repeat on a similar theme. He probed a bit, but I revealed nothing, mostly to avoid broaching the subject of homosexuality. After a long silence, Mr. Barnes said, "The civics course is a state requirement. If you don't complete it, you can't graduate."

"Then let me study it on my own and take the exams."

"We can't do that."

"You did it when Jenny Johnson got pregnant and couldn't attend school."

"But that was different."

"Was it really that different?"

Again, the hint of something sexual gave Barnes pause. He sent me to study hall and said that he would discuss the matter with "Mr. Perkins." The stalemate was resolved when AMPS agreed, probably with relief, that I could study the civics textbook in a supervised study hall, take the tests, and have another teacher grade the exams. Since AMPS was too lazy and too stupid to make up his own tests, I knew the exams would be torn out of a teacher's manual and therefore keyed exactly to the book. Fearing what I might say, AMPS went along with this arrangement although he would no doubt have preferred smashing in my head with a sledgehammer.

This last confrontation with AMPS was one of the great triumphs of my young life. I do not know if AMPS ever attacked another boy, although his raging hardon when he assaulted me clearly revealed a sexual affinity for adolescent boys. Perhaps he started consorting with men on the sly like lots of married guys do. Or maybe he settled for occasional sex with his fat wife and furtive wanking in the shower.

Chapter Fifteen:
The Remarkable Mr. Spears

What really got my junior year off to an amazing start was a new boy in our class. His name was Rod Spears, and he was drop-dead gorgeous in a thuggish, sullen kind of way. His slightly undersized shirt revealed a muscly, well-tanned body. With dirty blond hair, grayish green eyes, and a dimpled chin that was showing the first signs of a beard, he struck me as movie-star material and someone I absolutely must get to know. And that phallic name! Rod Spears.

Our first-period teacher introduced him as the son of Velma Farnsworth and Bob Spears, who were returning to Rosales after a long absence. An entertaining but ne're-do-well bunch, the Farnsworths were a large Rosales family, none of whom excelled in school or went to college. Rod's father's family, the Spears, were one of the few ranching families that still lived on their ranch, a good twenty miles outside of Rosales. My sister Terri had dated a Spears boy, whom I found very handsome, but other than that I knew nothing about his father's family.

A contractor, Rod's father had moved back to Rosales to build a house for Glenn Twynam, a hayseed of a man who had just sold his ranch and had a pile of ready cash on hand. Rod's father had reportedly moved to Rosales to escape a mob of suppliers and subcontractors he owed money to. Since Twynam could pay in cash, Rod's father could cover construction costs without needing credit—ideal for someone with his financial record.

Whatever their family histories, Farnsworth and Spears genes had combined to produce a spectacular adolescent hunk with the suggestive name of Rod Spears. Within the week, I maneuvered myself into a seat next to Rod in our first-period class, which was general biology. I turned on all the charm I could muster, but he remained unresponsive. Maybe he was shy. Maybe he was dumb. Maybe he suspected my motives. Maybe all the above. In third-period English, I again managed to sit across from him but again failed to strike up a conversation. After a few days, however, I figured out his weakness: he really was a bad student and needed all the help he could get. Clearly, he was someone Joshua Chastain could rescue.

Within a short time, I was helping him with his homework, and basically writing his English papers. Since I was doing the same for Patty, our tutoring arrangement soon became a threesome. Occasionally, Rod would sleep over at my place. Since I had inherited my sisters' bedroom with twin beds, he and I didn't share a bed, but he gave me ample opportunity to feast my eyes on his yummy body. My father disapproved of Rod's sleeping over, but he never forbade it. I once heard my father say, "I never say no to my kids unless it really matters." Evidently, Rod's sleepovers didn't matter that much.

I also spent time at Rod's house. Their home had belonged to Velma's recently deceased mother and was quite a dump, way too small for Rod, his parents, and his three siblings. Their television ran constantly, the furniture was mismatched and ratty, and there was hardly a book in sight. But what really made the Spears household unpleasant was Rod's father. A paunchy, muscly man who in his youth might have been as handsome as his son, Rod's father was verbally abusive, saying things like, "You're wasting your time on Rod. He's stupid like all his mother's people. He can't hardly pound a nail in straight." Rod's mother, a once pretty woman now faded by age and worries, tried to relate to me with questions like "Which one of them pretty girls are you after?" If she only knew.

Rod soon fixed his romantic gaze on Patty—hardly a surprise since she was the most beautiful girl in the school. As their unofficial tutor, I became their excuse for getting together and learned how to make myself scarce when they wanted to make out. Keeping their grades up, however, was a challenge. I could write their English papers, but I couldn't take exams for them. I tried to sit next to Rod in biology quizzes so he could copy from me, but despite having a gotch eye, our science teacher, Mr. Bowles, saw well enough to prevent cheating.

An opportunity to solve this problem soon presented itself. Our music teacher, Mr. Green, had a nice singing voice. Periodically he would get together with Melanie Woolsey, also a singer, to perform at church and community functions. As their accompanist of choice, I rehearsed with them at the high school. On one such occasion, a Saturday morning, Mr. Green called to inform me that he would be late, but that I should meet Melanie at the prearranged hour to run over some songs for solo soprano. I picked up his keys and promptly ran to the local hardware store and had copies made. As luck would have it, one key opened the outside door, and the other was a master key for all the classrooms.

In a matter of days, Rod, Patty, and I were sneaking into the high school late at night. Mr. Bowles used the exams and answer keys that came with the teacher's manual for our biology textbook. We made copies of both, and, just for good measure, we found his grade book, raising our grades on previous exams and lowering those of people we didn't like. Patty's and Rod's biology grades improved remarkably. With shame, I confess to also taking advantage of the purloined answer sheets.

Patty and Rod soon became a romantic item. We continued our tutoring sessions and occasional nocturnal visits to the high school, but increasingly Rod wanted time alone with Patty, making me feel like a fifth wheel. Worse, Rod started hanging out with the high school tough guys, a group that Craig and I called the duh-duhs—two duhs because they were too dumb for one duh. When Rod was with them, he seemed ashamed to know me.

Chapter Sixteen:
Truck-Stop Mike

Not to be loved is to feel unlovable. I missed my friendship with Mother Harold and the love I had shared with Father Tovar. My crush on the totally unavailable Rod only made things worse. I didn't just want friends. I wanted gay friends, friends I could be open with. I also wanted sex.

One day, someone at my father's garage let slip that "perverts" were taking over the truck-stop restrooms and picnic area on the new interstate. Rosales lay about twenty miles south of I-40, previously the legendary Route 66, where I knew there was a truck stop. At a school dance on the Saturday night after Thanksgiving, I was feeling particularly lonesome. Dances affected me this way since the pairings on the dance floor often led to make-out sessions between boys and girls that did not include me.

So, on a whim, I decided to check out the truck stop. My parents weren't expecting me home until after the dance, so I had a perfect excuse for staying out late. With money my father paid me to work at the garage, I had purchased a used 1956 Chevy pickup, so driving to the truck stop was not a problem. Since the pickup was green, I named it Bercilak after the green knight in *Sir Gawain and the Green Knight*.

The truck stop lay just west of the junction onto I-40. Needing to pee and consumed by curiosity, I entered the large public restroom, moved to a urinal, and began to do, as Cervantes delicately put it, what only I could do for myself. A tall man wearing boots and a cowboy hat moved to the urinal just to my left. He cleared his throat and stepped back a couple of inches so I could see him massaging a full-mast erection. Of course, I stared. And of course, I started to get hard.

He pulled up his pants and beckoned me toward one of the toilet stalls. Driven by God knows what mindless, primordial impulse, I entered the stall. Smelling of tobacco and aftershave, he closed the door latch, sat down on the toilet seat, unbuttoned my pants, and started to blow me. After I climaxed, he told me to wait for him outside. I slipped outdoors as though nothing had happened. Luckily, no one else was in the restroom. In less than a minute, he joined me and invited me to a soda pop in the truck stop restaurant.

He introduced himself as Mike Bryant. Attractive and well-tanned, he didn't look that old. After offering me a cigarette, which I refused, he lit one for himself. "So," he said. "That was very nice. What's your name?"

I lied and said my name was Nick.

"How old are you?"

I lied again and said I was nineteen.

"You're probably lyin' to me, but it don't really matter. You could be forty and named Richard Nixon, and I wouldn't give a shit. No one tells the truth in these places. Do you live around here?"

"I live on a ranch up north," I lied. "I just came down to get gas."

"I suppose there ain't no gas stations where you live, right?" he smirked.

Seeing that he had caught me in a stupid lie, I blushed without answering. After he paid the check, we walked out into the brightly lit pump area.

"How would you like to see my camper?" he asked.

Again, driven by a mindless compulsion, I followed him to his camper which sat in the bed of a large new Ford pickup. Although small, the camper included a tiny kitchen and a sofa. He pulled me down onto the sofa and started to kiss me. Yucky tobacco breath but a wonderful hard body. I muttered something about needing to go.

"Not so fast," he said. "You need to do something for me." When I didn't respond, he added, "Don't worry. It won't hurt, it won't take long, and I'll make it worth your while."

After more hugging and kissing, we both undressed. He opened the sofa into a small double bed. Although I didn't like the taste of his ashtray mouth, his scent of aftershave, fresh sweat, and tobacco struck me as worldly, sophisticated, and possibly dangerous. I reveled in the feel of his lean, hard body and the soft but abundant hair on his chest, abdomen, and legs. He soon made clear that he was looking for a top, which I gladly provided. After climaxing, I reached for his penis, but he pushed me away. "Can't do that. I gotta save myself for the wifey. Whenever I get home from a rodeo run, I gotta perform so she don't suspect that I been foolin' around."

So, he was a rodeo rider. That explained the tan face, the rough hands, and the lean body. But the wife? "I didn't think you were married," I said, possibly with some disapproval in my voice.

He grabbed my right shoulder and looked hard into my eyes. For a second, I thought he might hit me. He then relaxed his grip, saying with great seriousness, "Nick, or whatever your goddamned name is, don't you be judgin' me. You're too young to know how complicated life is. Most of the guys here at the truck stop are married. What I do with you is stuff I can't do with her, so it all works out."

Lapsing into BS-Speak, I said, "I'm sorry if I made you angry. That wasn't my intention." Then in my most innocent voice, I asked, "Do you like sex with your wife?"

"It's okay." Then with a sly smile he added, "I just close my eyes and think of someone like you, and she don't know the difference."

He looked at his watch. "It's time you n' me got back to wherever we're from." He gave me a quick peck on the cheek and folded the bed back into a sofa. We got dressed. Just as I opened the camper door, he said, "Wait a second. I want to give you somethin' to remember me by. Don't look at it until you get home."

He stuffed a piece of paper into my shirt pocket. I climbed out of the camper and started walking towards Bercilak. He gave a short toot on his horn as he drove by in his fancy pickup. On the back bumper was a sticker proclaiming, "Cowboys for Christ."

I drove back to Rosales as fast as my aging pickup could make it. My immediate problem was the stench of cigarette smoke on my clothes. I managed to creep into my bedroom without my parents noticing. After that, I kept a clean change of clothes in Bercilak. While undressing for bed, I felt a piece of paper in my shirt pocket and remembered that Mike had given me something to remember him by. I almost stopped breathing when I pulled out a brand-new twenty-dollar bill, probably from rodeo winnings. Twenty dollars in 1969 was a nice chunk of money for a half-hour's work. I had just been paid for sex! Which made me a what?

Aware of Mike's worldly scent on my body, I had a hard time getting to sleep. I kept wondering about Mike and the life he led. As a rodeo rider, he probably spent a lot of time on the road. I wondered if he got it on with other rodeo stars. He was handsome enough and certainly fun in bed. The thought of him having sex with other cowboys was quite a turn-on.

But what was it like for his "wifey" to be married to a man capable of having sex only by thinking of a man? Did she suspect anything? And what was that crap about "Cowboys for Christ"? Did he blubber about how much he loved Jesus and then pick up guys at truck stops? Was I that different? I attended church, read the scriptures, participated in religious discussions, and lied to my bishop about jerking off. Mike was leading a double life, but so was I.

Then, there was the money. Had I just sold my body? What a stupid question! My body was intact, and it still belonged to me. I hadn't sold it to anyone, nor had I asked for money. I had sex with Mike because I wanted to. With Harold and Father Tovar, sex came with friendship. Sex with Mike was just sex. It was exciting, it was hot, and it was great that a handsome older man found me attractive. Whatever my reservations about money and anonymous sex, I wanted to do it again.

Chapter Seventeen:
Rod Goes off the Deep End

After Thanksgiving, our music teacher, Mr. Green, put together a community choir to perform excerpts from Handel's Messiah. I had to do some serious practicing to learn the accompaniments since orchestral reductions for piano are often quite challenging. The performance was probably pretty good for a backwater like Rosales. The following Sunday, the church choir performed some dippy Christmas cantata complete with little kids dressed up as Mary, Joseph, the shepherds, and the wise men. Again, as the cantata accompanist, I spent a lot of time in rehearsals.

Just before Christmas break, Rod and Patty had a big fight. Howard White, a senior and a very handsome athlete, had started flirting with Patty. Rod became convinced that she was two-timing him—which was probably true. If Howard White ever showed interest in me, I wouldn't resist.

Rod started seeking my company again. He'd rant about what a whore Patty was and how mean his dad was. Since he never once asked anything about me, I started wondering, "What am I getting out of this relationship?" And the answer was not much. Rod used me like a library book. When he wanted me to write his English papers, help him cheat on exams, or give him an excuse to be with Patty, he pulled me off the shelf. But when he wanted to be alone with Patty or hang out with the duh-duhs, he expected me to remain on the shelf until he needed me again. I was starting to tire of him and no longer found him that attractive.

Every New Year's Eve, Rosales held a dance in the high school auditorium. Without fail, some of the Jack Mormons came to the dance a bit buzzed if not outright drunk. Just before midnight, Rod entered the auditorium, so smashed that he could hardly stand up. He was accompanied by Burt Larson and Barry Cummings, two of his duh-duh bully friends, who were only slightly less drunk than he.

Seeing how far gone they were, Mr. Barnes, the high school principal, quietly told them that they needed to leave. Rod started yelling that nobody could tell him what to do. He then lunged toward Mr. Barnes and took a swing at him. Barnes adroitly stepped aside and let Rod crash to the floor. Rod tried to get up but couldn't. Then he threw up, getting vomit all over his shirt and leaving a putrid puddle on the floor. The sheriff appeared out of nowhere and forcibly escorted Rod and his friends out of the auditorium and, I suppose, straight to the county jail to dry out.

I was heartbroken. However much I was beginning to resent our one-sided friendship, I hated seeing Rod humiliated. The high school janitor mopped up the mess. The band tried valiantly to get things moving again, but the sense of celebration was gone. Midnight came, people put on paper hats, blew toy whistles, and shouted "Happy New Year." The dance ended shortly thereafter. Rod had effectively wrecked the party.

Classes started the following Monday. Rod had been suspended. Barred from school and too embarrassed to go to church, he virtually disappeared. Sometime in mid-January, he called me at the garage and asked me to pick him up that night on the road behind the high school. As he approached Bercilak, I noticed that he was walking with a limp and that his right eye was swollen shut. As I began to drive, I asked if he'd been in a fight.

"Yeah. My dad beat me up. Nearly broke my leg with a two-by-four. I gotta leave. If I stay around that son of a bitch any longer, I'll end up killing him. It's gonna be either him or me." What followed was a painful narrative about how he felt abandoned by Patty, abused by his father, and disgraced in front of the entire town. I wanted to hug him, to tell him that I forgave him—as though he had offended me. But all I could do was listen. He saw no future for himself in Rosales. After a couple of hours of driving aimlessly around town, I dropped him off near his house. Two days later I learned that he had run away from home, possibly to join the army. I missed our friendship, however lopsided it was, and I missed basking in the presence of such a beautiful man. I also worried about him.

In early December, just before the end of fall term, Mr. Green took me and a couple of other students to Arizona State College in Flagstaff for regional auditions for all-state choir. In mid-January, shortly after Rod ran away, I received confirmation that I had been accepted and should commit myself to two days of rehearsals followed by an evening concert at the University of Arizona in Tucson. The catch: my school would have to cover my expenses. Since I was the only Rosales kid chosen for all-state choir, my high school originally refused to pay. Only after my father pointed out that the school always found money to support travel for athletic events did the school agree to support the trip.

The guest conductor was Lara Hoggard, an exceptional musician who worked especially well with young singers. Three nights of sharing a hotel room with the unlovely Mr. Green was a bit off-putting, but the musical experience was glorious. At the first rehearsal, I was so overcome by the beauty of the opening chord that I could hardly sing. Mr. Hoggard was a superb technician who paid lots of attention to phrasing, word color, syllable stresses, and vowel-matching—items totally beyond the ken of Mr. Green. But he also alluded to the spiritual dimension of music and its capacity to bring us in touch with the transcendent. Since our time was mostly spent rehearsing, there was little opportunity for social interaction. Still, I sensed that in that community I wouldn't feel weird, there would be no bullies, and no one would call me Q-B or sissy.

Chapter Eighteen: Mike's Party

Returning to Rosales after all-state choir was a letdown. Having glimpsed a beautiful world of music and a possible community of musicians, I felt more isolated than ever. I began hanging out with Craig again and regretted letting our friendship languish because of my infatuation with Rod. But even with Craig, there was so much that I couldn't share. Fearing that my whole life could collapse if people knew about my sexual activities, I sometimes felt that God had given me a great hand of cards. I was smart, I played the piano well, and I had a good voice. Moreover, I enjoyed plenty of outward signs of success—high national test scores, all-state choir, and good grades even when I didn't cheat.

But then I remembered the wild card in my hand, the one that said homosexual, the one for which Billy died, and the one that placed me on a collision course with church, family, Rosales, and classmates. I felt like a fraud and often wondered if I shouldn't just end it all by killing myself like Billy Schaeffer had done. Lonesome and horny, I started sneaking up to the truck stop at least once a week. Given my involvement in music and my willingness to tutor other students, I had good excuses for being out at night, and my parents never suspected that I was lying to them.

At night, there were always men at the truck stop looking for sex, including some with wedding rings. I marveled at how powerful the sex drive must be to impel them to take such risks. Or maybe it was more than sex. Maybe, like me, they just needed to feel desired by other men, even for a few minutes. Although most were older and often not very attractive, I invariably ended up having sex in a bathroom stall or in the wooded area behind the main building.

My mind turned off during truck-stop sex. It was like entering another world where all that mattered was feeling attractive for a short moment and getting to climax. After these encounters, guilt and shame often overwhelmed me, and I could hardly wait to get back to Rosales. On numerous occasions, I resolved to never return, but soon I would feel lonesome, horny, and needing to feel desired, and again find myself having sex with a stranger.

One night in early March, just as I was entering the parking lot, I saw Mike getting into his Cowboys for Christ pickup. "Hey Nick," he called. "You just getting here?"

"Yeah, and it looks like you're just leaving."

"Actually, I'm going to a party. I stopped here to pick up an old friend. Why don't you join us?"

"What kind of party is it?"

"Just a few rodeo friends. All men, if you get my drift. There'll also be some good food and plenty to drink. You should come."

"I can't stay long. My parents think I'm at a school dance."

"And I can't stay long either because the wifey is expecting me at home. Give it a try. I'll have you back here in a couple of hours."

Since my mind had already moved into truck-stop mode, curiosity won out over caution. Mike introduced the other man in the pickup as Jerry, who according to Mike was "the greatest jockey of all time." Shaking my hand, Jerry said, "Used to be a good jockey. Nowadays, I just teach the youngsters." Jerry had the weathered and wrinkled face of an old guy but the slim wiry body of a younger man. He also reeked of aftershave and tobacco.

After a short ride on the interstate, Mike turned onto a dirt road, crossed a cattle guard, and eventually came to a small clapboard house with a peaked tin roof and a wraparound front porch, set well away from the highway and surrounded by a clump of trees. Some twenty guys were there, several who looked like virtual clones of Mike and others built more like Jerry. From all over the country, they were on their way to a rodeo in Las Vegas and had been planning this pre-rodeo gay party for some time. Above the stench of tobacco smoke, I could smell what promised to be good Arizona chili.

Still a good Mormon boy (?), I accepted a soda pop instead of a beer. In the meantime, the crowd was getting increasingly friendly. The men asked obvious questions like What's your name? Where are you from? How do you know Mike? Are you a rodeo rider? Along with the small talk, we were getting more physical, placing our arms around each other and feeling up each other's bodies. I finally let a guy about Mike's age massage my crotch through my pants until I got hard. He suddenly slipped his hand down the front of my pants, grabbed my dick, and called out in a drunken yell, "Hey everybody, you better get in line. This kid's the real thing."

Everyone laughed. I didn't know whether to be proud or embarrassed. Soon, the owner of the house, a skinny old guy with a limp and a craggy face, called out that the food was on. The groping stopped as we stood in line for a bowl of excellent chili and cornbread. As we ate, someone said, "Fuck man, if the food's this good, the dessert is going to fabulous." Smarter than the average bear, I realized that as the youngest person at the party, I might be the cherry on the cake.

After eating, we started dancing, hugging, groping, and making out. For years, I had fantasized fondling other men's bodies with utter abandon. That night, this fantasy came true. We eventually drifted into the bedrooms where guys in various stages of undress were starting to have sex in an atmosphere of fresh male sweat only partially disguised by cologne and deodorant. I joined a group of semi-naked men, my body mingling with their bodies, my scent with their scent, my kisses with their kisses. Over the course of the evening, I climaxed two, maybe three times. I would be hard pressed to remember with whom or in what configuration.

After nearly two hours of mindless, anonymous sex, I gathered my clothes and made my way to the living room where Mike was sitting on a sofa with a sardonic smile on his face. "From what I saw, you just had yourself a helluva good time."

"Let's just say it's been interesting."

"Interestin' hell. I saw you carryin' on in there. You looked a lot more than interested. In fact, I'd say that you were fuckin' enjoyin' yourself. You ready to go?"

On the way back to the truck stop, Mike said, "You know Nick, I have a friend you should meet. He ain't an ignorant rodeo bum like the rest of us. He would enjoy the company of a smart kid like you. And he knows how to be generous."

Not understanding, I asked, "What do you mean by generous?"

"You know. He'll pay you and pay you well." Then with a sly smile, "After all, there ain't no reason for a cute, young guy like you to just be givin' it away."

It took me a second to realize that he was talking about prostituting myself. Totally unprepared for such a proposition, I was temporarily speechless. Finally, I said, "I don't think I could do that. I can't have sex with just anyone. They have to be attractive." (Which wasn't true; I had had sex with plenty of unattractive men at the truck stop.) Then I added, "Besides, I don't need the money."

"You never know about money. Besides, this guy's got money and an education. He could be a good friend to a young kid like you." He slipped me a card with a phone number on it, and said, "If you change your mind, call this number. If a woman answers, ask for Sheldon. That's my real name. Mike is my rodeo name. If she asks, just say that you are a rodeo friend."

Sex with all those men had felt great at the time. Now that it was over, however, I felt like I had overdosed on junk food—tasty at first but nauseating afterwards. Driving back to Rosales, I sensed a major funk coming on and wondered if it wasn't time to end it all before people found out who I really was. Kill myself the way Billy Schaeffer did. That way, no one would know that the bright, smart-mouthed, and talented Joshua Chastain—the curly headed kid with good grades, top scores on national exams, and membership in all-state choir—was really a fraud hiding a nasty secret.

That night I had a strange dream. I was driving back from the truck stop. Feeling ashamed and worthless, I spied an overpass pillar and resolved to ram Bercilak into it. But just as I turned toward the pillar, I glimpsed the vague figure of a man standing in front of me with his hand extended as though to warn me away. I swerved to miss him and suddenly awoke, breathing hard and soaked in sweat. The man who kept me from killing myself was Billy Schaeffer.

Why was Billy in my dream? Was he welcoming me to the world of the dead? Or was he telling me that both of us did not need to die? I recalled how Father Tovar spoke lovingly of the clouds of unseen witnesses who surround us, the communion of saints who protect and pray for us. Was Billy such a saint—a gay Mormon saint commissioned to help gay Mormon boys? I was much consoled by this possibility.

Chapter Nineteen:
Patty's Problem and the Most Godless Woman in Town

After running away from home, Rod was out of sight and out of mind, but not for long. The week after Mike's party, Patty stopped me in the hallway and asked to meet me that night near the swings at the grade school playground where no one would see us. With tears in her eyes, she told me that she had missed two periods and was late for a third one, thus convincing her that she was pregnant.

As a gay man, I knew zilch about menstrual periods and even less about pregnancy, but I soon realized that my best friend-girl was in trouble. Rod, of course, was the father. She claimed that they had had sex only a couple of times, largely to convince Rod that he was the boy she really loved. Were it not for the desperation in her voice, I might have felt trapped in a soap opera. But this was no soap opera. It was Patty's life, and she really was in trouble.

Why did she turn to me? Because I was Rod's friend? Because she thought that someone who could get copies of school keys and help her cheat her way through high school could also help end a pregnancy? Whatever the reason, I felt obligated to help. But how? For Mormons, sex outside of marriage was the big no-

no in the sky. Getting knocked up was even worse. For good reasons, Patty was frightened of how her mother and the town would react.

I knew nothing about terminating a pregnancy, but I knew someone who might: my library friend Lucy Ramírez who introduced me to Fawn Brodie's biography of Joseph Smith. Although never a member of the Mormon church, Lucy had scandalized good Rosales Mormons by getting pregnant in her senior year, marrying a Mexican named Gabriel Ramírez, and running off to Alaska. Several years later, she returned to Rosales with twin daughters, and moved in with her mother. Gabriel had been killed in a construction accident.

Back in Rosales, Lucy began managing her mother's small farm and rental properties. With platinum blond hair, generous makeup, turquoise jewelry, and clothes that showed off a shapely figure, she had a flirtatious friendliness about her that men adored and women hated. Lucy further irritated good Mormons by buying a sleazy bar on the edge of town called The Outpost. Changing its name to Lucy's Outpost, she turned it into a nice place—a cocktail lounge with a restaurant rather than a seedy bar. Of course, people still called it a bar. Whenever we drove by it, my mother would repeat the refrain from an old temperance song: "A bar to heaven, a gate to Hell; whoever named it, named it well."

Knowing that Lucy was the only person I could turn to, I ditched my last two afternoon classes and rode my bicycle to the Outpost. I didn't take Bercilak so no one would see my pickup parked outside a bar. Alone and setting up for the evening, Lucy did a double-take and smiled when I walked in. "Well, will you look at this: Joshua Chastain in this den of iniquity. Sweetie, this isn't the public library. It's a bar and it's off limits to minors." Then with a big laugh, "Besides, your mommy would kill us both if she knew you were here, and God knows that I'm too young to die."

"I've got a big problem."

"Everyone's got big problems. What kind of big problem could a pretty young thing like you have that an old dragon like me might solve?"

"A girl I know is in trouble."

Lucy smiled mischievously. "Josh, dear. Have you been sticking your little weenie where you shouldn't?"

"It's not little," I retorted. "And the baby isn't mine."

"Lordy, Lordy!" she exclaimed with a hoot. "I swear to God, that's what every man says. They've all got big dicks, and the baby's never theirs!"

I thought of saying, "I'm gay, I don't make babies, I've got a great dick, and the kid really isn't mine." But I chose to revert to BS-Speak and act courteous and respectful. "Please don't make fun of me. I'm talking to you because you're the only person in Rosales who might help us out."

"I don't do abortions, sweetie, and I don't raise orphans." When I didn't reply, she continued in a softer voice, "Okay, my sweet young friend. Sit your cute little butt down and tell me who the lucky girl is."

When I told her it was Patty Burleson, she let out a horse laugh. "No shit. Boy, you really know how to pick 'em. Both of you from super-Mormon families. This could get messy. Your parents will probably make you get married. And at your age, marriage will screw up your life. Do you want to get married?"

"I'm too young to get married."

"You're too young? Hell," she added with a guffaw. "I'm too young. I was too young thirty years ago, and I'll be too young the day I die."

"Besides, I shouldn't have to get married because it's not my kid."

"You keep saying that. But if people find out that you're trying to help Patty end a pregnancy, everyone will think you're the father. Why are you involved at all?"

"Because Patty's my best friend. And the guy who knocked her up is also a friend. Or at least he used to be."

"Is the father that Spears kid who threw up at the New Year's dance?"

"Yeah."

"I'm not surprised," she said. Then with a wink, "Actually, I thought that you were sort of sweet on him."

I must have turned bright red because this was the first time anyone besides AMPS had suggested that I might be gay. Seeing my embarrassment, Lucy placed her hand on my arm. "I'm sorry I said that. Don't you worry. You're trying to do a good thing for your friend. We can talk about other stuff some other time."

Other stuff? Like me being gay?

Suddenly very serious, she said, "Abortions aren't cheap, and they're often not safe. You'll probably have to go to Mexico for it. No doctor this side of the border will take the risk unless you pay him in the thousands."

"We could never get that kind of money."

"So, Mexico's your only option. Tell you what I'll do. I have a friend in Tucson who might have contacts in Mexico. But you'll have to have the money."

"How much?"

"I have no idea, but you can count on it being several hundred dollars."

I swallowed hard. "Between Patty and me, we can probably get the money," I lied. In fact, I had no idea where to find that kind of money.

"Okay. I'll call my friend. Maybe she can help."

I breathed a sigh of relief. "Thank you. Thank you very much. Really. You're the only person in Rosales that I can talk to about this."

"And I'm the only person in Rosales who's not going to tell all the gossips in town that Patty Burleson got knocked up. Josh, dear, I've been where she is. I know what she's going through, and I know how some of those good Rosales Mormons wouldn't think twice about ruining her life and yours. Call me tomorrow. Now get your sweet little ass out of here before someone arrests me for corrupting the youth of Zion."

Riding my bike back into town, I felt relieved knowing that Lucy was going to help. It also felt strangely good to know that she suspected me of being gay without making anything of it. As promised, Lucy contacted her friend in Tucson, but the news was not good. Her friend knew of a reliable doctor in Nogales, but he wanted $400, with half of the money up front. Patty and I had a long conversation on how to raise money and hide a trip to Nogales, but nothing seemed remotely doable. Patty considered pawning some of her mother's jewelry, but she knew that she would get caught. I had access to the till at my father's garage, but no way could I steal from my dad. Another problem was getting to Mexico. Maybe Bercilak could make a 500-mile roundtrip, but how would we explain being out of town?

In the meantime, the clock was ticking. Patty missed her third period, and her cheerleader's costume was starting to feel tight. The Home Economics teacher, a very nice lady named Mrs. Waltz, started asking Patty if she was ill, or if things were okay at home. Subtext: Mrs. Waltz suspected that Patty might be pregnant. Never a good student, Patty's grades started to slide for which her mother grounded her indefinitely, or at least until her grades improved.

Then I remembered Sheldon, a.k.a. Mike. When he first proposed introducing me to a "generous" man, the thought of selling sex seemed so remote that I hardly took it seriously. I now needed money and could see no other way of getting it. Using a pay phone so my parents wouldn't know of the call, I dialed the number Mike had given me. Fortunately, he answered the phone after the first ring.

"Hi, this is Josh."

"Josh? I don't know any Josh."

"I mean Nick. You know me as Nick. We met a couple of times at the truck stop."

"Nick," he exclaimed with false enthusiasm, clearly intended for someone else. "Good to hear from you! What's up?"

"You said I might need money sometime. That time has come. Can you help me?"

"Give me the number you're calling from, and I'll see what I can set up."

Five minutes later, Mike called the pay phone to confirm that the following evening, a Friday, he would meet me at the truck stop and introduce me to a generous man.

Chapter Twenty: Blair

Friday happened to be a few days after my seventeenth birthday. To prepare for entering the world of prostitution, I took a second shower for the day to be properly groomed and perfumed. Before dressing, I examined myself in the full-length mirror on the bathroom door—an inventory of the merchandise, one might say. Although I never considered myself particularly good-looking, what I saw did not displease me. Approaching six feet tall and weighing around 150 pounds, I was a bit on the skinny side but not bad for a seventeen-year-old. I now had to shave every day—a pain—but I liked the look of my beard shadow.

Thanks to pushups, pull-ups, and weightlifting, I could see the outlines of chest and arm muscles. A thin line of hair connected my navel to my now abundant crotch hair. Several guys had told me they liked my penis, as did I. Straight and symmetrical when erect, it was on the large size of normal but without being gross. Remembering Father Tovar, I wondered what it would be like to have a foreskin, but alas, what's gone is gone.

As agreed, Mike was waiting for me at 7 PM at the truck stop, his large pickup parked next to a late-model Cadillac DeVille coupe. The drivers of both cars stepped out to greet me. "Nick," Mike said, "Meet Blair. Blair, meet Nick."

With an extended hand and a deep voice, Blair said, "Hello, Nick. I'm Blair. Blair Huxley. I'm pleased to make your acquaintance. Mike tells me that you are a bright young man and that you and I might become friends." Like Mr. Barnes, the high school principal, Blair was big without being fat. He had a handsome face for an old guy and a full head of dark hair mixed with gray. He spoke with no trace of a hick accent and knew enough grammar to say "you and I" instead of "you and me." Taking his large hand in mine, I mumbled something profound like, "Pleased to meet you," although, truth be told, I was nervous as hell. Mike bid us a quick farewell, and I soon found myself in the passenger seat of a new Cadillac headed east on I-40.

"Nick," Blair said, "Don't feel nervous. Tonight, we're just going to get acquainted."

"Mike says that you'll pay me."

Frown. "Now Nick, let's not ruin things by talking about money. I know how to be generous, so let's just leave it at that. For the time being, let's just see if we can become friends."

Reverting to BS-Speak, I explained, "I didn't mean to offend you. You'll have to forgive me, but I'm new to this."

The Boy Scout charm worked. "No offense taken," he said with a smile, "and there's nothing to forgive. We're going to take a short drive to my guest house and get acquainted. If at any time you feel uncomfortable, just say the word, and I'll take you back to your pickup."

I already felt uncomfortable, but thinking of Patty, I said nothing. Blair asked all the obvious stuff about how old I was, if I was a student, if I had any hobbies, etc. I lied about my age, saying that I was nineteen while in fact I had just turned seventeen. It occurred to me that if I ever did this again, I would need to invent a consistent story to avoid contradicting myself.

After a couple of miles, he exited onto the frontage road and then onto a dirt road going north. Soon, we arrived at a small, well-maintained one-story stucco house with a tiled roof and a large front porch surrounded by pine trees, a windmill, a water trough for cattle, and several utility sheds. Blair had done nothing to scare me, but I was scared. What was I doing in the middle of nowhere with an old guy I knew nothing about? What if he was a serial killer who liked to gut and quarter teenage boys?

The living room had a flagstone fireplace and some nice leather upholstered furniture. Wall decorations included an expensive-looking Navajo rug, a couple of western landscape paintings, and a large oval mirror above the mantelpiece. After starting a fire in the fireplace, Blair asked, "Would you like a drink? Maybe some nuts and a Coke?"

"Sure. That would be nice.

Setting two soda pops and a bowl of almonds on a coffee table, Blair sat next to me on the sofa, placed his right arm over my shoulders, and gently pulled me towards him. Feeling me stiffen, he said, "Now Nick, you need to understand what's going on here. For right now, this is a world of make-believe. Your job is to make believe that you enjoy being close to me. If you act like I'm a repulsive piece of shit, it won't work. Besides, you might actually like me if you give me a chance."

So, I tried to relax, placing my left hand on his thigh. This was the first time a man my father's age had embraced me. Despite my father's undeniable devotion to his children, I never had any physical contact with him beyond a handshake. I was surprised to find myself enjoying the warmth of Blair's body and the size and firmness of his arms and chest. Whatever his age, he stayed in shape. As a young man, he must have been a real knockout. With his arm across my shoulders, he began caressing my right shoulder. But he seemed oddly pensive. Suddenly, he pulled away and looked carefully at me as though for the first time.

"Are you okay?" I asked. "Why are you looking at me like that? Am I growing a second head, or is there a foot sticking out of my ear?"

He chuckled. "No, I see no sign of extra appendages. It's just that you remind me of someone I used to know. In fact, you remind me of him a lot."

"I hope he was good looking."

"He was," he answered with a grin. Then, after a long silence, he said, "Nick, I'm going to make what might strike you as a really strange request."

"Like what? That I stand on my head and recite Shakespeare sonnets?"

He smiled at my feeble joke. "No, nothing that onerous." Then, all serious again, he said, "I'd like to give you a massage. Nothing sexual. Just a massage. Are you okay with that?"

I consented, partly because I had never had a massage before, but also because I wondered where such a bizarre request might end up. He led me to a bedroom that, like the front room, had wall decorations in western motifs but was dominated by a large bed with a leather headboard.

"Now Nick, I won't try any funny business, but I'd like you to take off all your clothes."

"You're not going to try to fuck me, are you?"

"Right now, sex is the farthest thing from my mind. Just lie down on your stomach and relax." I removed my clothes and lay face down on the bed. He rubbed lotion on his hands and with slow, firm strokes began massaging my upper back, shoulders, and arms. His hands were large, strong, and warm. He then started kneading my feet, slowly working up to my calves and

124

thighs. Not since Father Tovar had anyone paid so much attention to my body.

Contrary to all expectations, I started enjoying it. Even more surprising, images of my father flashed through my mind as I fantasized what a massage from him would be like. While caressing my upper legs, Blair brushed my balls several times and I felt myself getting hard. By the time he rolled me over on my back, I was fully erect. "Oh my," he said. "Your body isn't the only beautiful thing about you. I promised you no funny business, but do you mind if I have taste?"

"Go ahead."

He then gave witness to a profound truth: experienced older guys give great head. After climaxing, I asked, "Is it my turn now? Do you want me to return the favor?"

"No. Right now, I just want to cuddle a bit. Would you mind?"

Since up to this point, he had asked permission for everything, I consented. He stripped to his boxers, lay down next to me, and gently pulled my head onto his chest. Lying on my side, I started running my hand through his profuse chest hair and was surprised to find it soft and spongy. After several minutes, he said, "You know, Nick, this is as good as it gets. Just feeling the warmth of another human being. If it weren't for these moments, I could probably do without the sex."

"It does feel nice," I said. "Thanks."

"And thanks to you. You're a beautiful and very polite young man. May I ask you a question?"

"Do I have to tell the truth?"

"No, but I suspect that you will. You don't look like a poor kid, and you don't talk like a punk or a hayseed. So, why are you so anxious to get money? Are you feeding a drug habit? Is someone extorting money out of you? Are you in debt to a loan shark?"

After considerable hesitation, I told him that I needed money to help a girl who was in trouble.

"Is she your girlfriend? From what Mike told me, I didn't think you had a girlfriend."

I assured him that Patty was not my girlfriend, that her baby was not mine, and that her life would turn to shit if her parents found out that she was pregnant.

"If you're telling me the truth, you're being a good friend."

"I'm telling the truth. Now it's my turn. May I pose a nosy question?"

"Pose? You've got a fancy vocabulary," he said grinning. "Go ahead. *Pose* whatever you want."

Continuing to rub the hair on his chest, I asked, "How old are you?"

With a smile in his voice, he replied, "I don't use the word *old*: I prefer the word *mature*."

"Okay. How *mature* are you?"

"I'll give you a hint. I'm probably about three times your age."

Which—God forbid—meant that he was what? Fifty? Fifty-plus? Even more surprising, I was increasingly finding his warm, furry body very pleasant to be with. "Can I ask another question? What's it like being your age and liking guys?"

"I can ask you the same question. What's it like being your age and liking guys?"

"I asked first."

"Fair enough." After a long pause, he answered, "It's not easy, especially in a place where most people know each other. I stopped picking up guys anonymously a long time ago. But I have friends like Sheldon, the guy you call Mike, who occasionally introduce me to someone like you. And I know a few rodeo people who like to fool around. We meet largely by word of mouth."

"When did you figure out that you were gay?"

Frowning he said, "*Gay* is a new word to me. In fact, none of us call ourselves gay, although I guess that's what we are." Then with a smile, "We usually just call ourselves *special*."

"Okay, when did you start feeling *special*?"

"A long time ago. Are you in the mood for a story?"

"Sure. I love stories."

"Okay, but let's get dressed and eat something first. I can't tell stories on an empty stomach."

Chapter Twenty-one:
Blair's Story

He made a great sandwich—homemade bread, sliced tomatoes, cold cuts, lettuce, mayo, and mustard. Beckoning for me to sit down, he placed the sandwiches on the coffee table in front of the sofa and asked, "How much do you want to know about me?"

"Whatever you want to tell."

"You know, Nick, it's hard to talk to most kids your age. They're too flighty and obsessed with themselves. But you're different. You ask real questions. Do you have older friends?"

I thought of Father Tovar and Lucy. "Yeah, a few. And I find most kids my age kind of dull."

"Why?"

"Because they talk about dumb stuff."

"Like?"

"Oh, you know. Sports and girls."

"Well, I enjoy talking about sports, but I never talked much about girls."

After we finished our sandwiches, he placed another log on the fire. We sat facing each other, semi-reclined on opposite ends of the sofa, shoes off and legs touching. After a short hesitation to gather his thoughts, he folded his arms and began his story.

"I suppose I was always special, or gay as you would say. But I didn't figure it out until college. My parents wanted me to get a top education, so when I was barely eighteen, they put me on a train and sent me to Columbia University in New York City. This was back in the early days of the Great Depression. My dad owned a lot of land, but they were strapped for cash. Sending me to Columbia was a big sacrifice for them, although Columbia gave me a tuition break because I played football.

"One night, after the last game of my freshman season, a bunch of us got drunk. I ended up spending the night with a senior named Andrew, a teammate who had his own apartment off campus. That was the first time I had sex with another man. Or with anyone for that matter, since I had never been with a woman either. Of course, the next morning we went through that old routine of 'My God, I was so drunk that I don't remember a thing about last night.' But Andy continued inviting me over, and we always ended up in bed. By then, it was clear that I liked guys.

"Andy and I never socialized since I was a lowly freshman from the sticks, and he was a mighty senior from a rich family in Greenwich, Connecticut. The following year, he went to law school at Yale, which was just up the road in New Haven. I went up to see him once, but he told me to get lost and stay lost. He wanted to appear normal and knew that being a fairy or a pansy—those were the words that we used back then—could sabotage the law career he wanted.

"Later in my sophomore year, I met other students who shared my interests. We started exploring pick-up spots in New York. In the 1930s, men were so available in New York that sometimes we felt entirely normal. Even a few city cops were in on it. Of course, I was young, and I was athletic. A lot of men found me attractive."

"You still look pretty good."

"That's sweet of you to say, but I wasn't fishing for compliments."

"Do you think you're abnormal? Do you think I'm abnormal?"

"Nick, normal is a statistical term. People like us are a minority. A small minority. That makes us statistically abnormal. But what's normal for some people is not normal for others. For me, I'm normal. I'm the normal me. And I can't be someone else. I tried that when I got married, but it was wrong for me, and it was wrong for my wife. We shouldn't try to be who we aren't."

"You were married?"

"Don't look shocked. Yes, I was married. After graduating from college, I returned to Arizona to start working with my dad. I married a local girl from a good family because that was what I was supposed to do, particularly since I was an only child. The Huxley name had to go on. We produced two great boys, but sex never became part of our lives. Occasionally, I'd do something with a guy, usually a rodeo rider or a race jockey. Nothing permanent and nothing visible. I had to be careful.

"Then, in 1941, when I was in my mid-twenties, the war broke out. My dad owned a small crop duster, so I had some flying experience. I joined the Army Air Corps—this was before they created the Air Force—and ended up in England. I flew reconnaissance missions over France and Germany. Fortunately, I was never shot down. I was really lucky because a lot of my friends never returned."

"That must have been really sad."

"You have no idea," he said, looking toward the floor and blinking back some tears. "We're conditioned for the death of older people, but nothing prepares us for the death of a young person. Anyway, I became good friends—much more than good friends—with another pilot, a young Jewish kid from Detroit named Jacob Berkowitz. He was tall like you, with curly hair and green eyes like yours. You remind me of him." With a catch in his voice, he added, "In fact, you remind me of him a lot."

Clearing his throat, he continued. "Jacob was the first person I ever fell in love with. Between missions, we were inseparable. After making love, he and I used to give each other massages just like the one I gave you. Then one morning, he didn't return from a night bombing mission. His plane was shot down somewhere over Germany. That was when I realized how much I loved him. Please don't think I'm ghoulish, but as I was giving you a massage tonight, I kept thinking of him."

After a long silence, he continued in a hoarse voice laden with emotion, "You asked if I'm okay about being gay. The answer is that there was absolutely nothing wrong with the love Jacob and I had for each other. It was the purest, most wonderful love imaginable. No one can tell me otherwise. I have never grieved anyone's death so much. But of course, I couldn't let on. One of the biggest problems about being *special* is that you can't tell people about your love for another man, much less your grief when that man dies. No one at the time knew about Jacob and me."

After an uncomfortable silence, I asked, "So you came back to Arizona after the war?"

"Yeah. My parents were getting old, and my dad needed someone to take over the family business. But I never got back into my marriage. Isabel and I continued living together, but basically like brother and sister. We raised the boys and saw that they got a good education. I fooled around with guys occasionally, but strictly on the sly. Isabel may have had a fling or two. I hope she did because God knows she wasn't getting any sex from me. By the time the boys were grown, she was spending most of her time in our apartment in Scottsdale to be near the boys and the grandkids. Then she got cancer and came back to the ranch where I took care of her until she died. It was very sad. She was a good person and a great mother to our kids. She deserved a better husband. It's not fair to marry a woman unless you're really attracted to her."

"Do your boys know about you?"

"They probably suspect. I have a special friend, a guy named Barkley, who was in my class at Columbia and is now a big-time lawyer in San Francisco. I ran into him at a class reunion about fifteen years ago, and much to our surprise we developed a romantic relationship. We meet several times a year and take trips together. Some people might call him my lover, which is a term that I like since I love him, and he loves me. My boys have probably put two and two together. But they don't intrude in my private life. They have families and are busy building their careers. I visit them often, and sometimes they come up here. I'm a good grandfather. But I stay out of their lives, and they stay out of mine."

"Your friend in San Francisco doesn't mind you being with other people?"

"You mean for sex?"

"Yeah, for sex."

"Why would he mind? That monogamy nonsense is for married people. And believe me when I tell you that it doesn't work for most of them either. I'm Barkley's lover, not his property. I feel the same way about him. Besides, sex is nice. Why should I limit myself to one person? And if Barkley meets a handsome guy, someone like you for example, why shouldn't he enjoy it?"

"What about Sheldon?"

"We're just friends. His family has a small spread north of here. I knew him when he was a teenager and always suspected he might be one of us."

"Why did you suspect him?"

"It's hard to say. Maybe because there was a certain sweetness about him, and he was a little chattier and funnier than other kids his age. You develop a sense for finding people. When I learned that we had rodeo friends in common, we confessed to each other and became friends. He's basically living the life I lived thirty years ago, what with a wife and a couple of kids. And when he meets someone nice like you, he introduces them to me. So how about you? By the way, I didn't believe much of what you told me in the car. Would you like to start over again?"

Embarrassed that he knew I had been lying, I began by telling him that my real name was Joshua Chastain and that I lived in Rosales. Since virtually all Anglos in Rosales were Mormon, he asked if I was LDS. I told

him that I was but that I didn't go to church much—
which wasn't true.

"Nick—I mean Joshua—that must be really hard,
being a Mormon and a homosexual."

"It's not easy."

"I've known a few Mormon guys. Some of them had
a hard time of it. Disowned by their families. Kicked
out of the church. Do you know how you're going to
handle it?"

"No idea. Maybe there'll be a miracle and God will
make me straight."

"Don't count on it. If there is a God, he made you
what you are, and you had best enjoy it." Then, looking
at his watch, he added, "And I need to get you back to
your car. What do you tell your parents when you're
up here carousing around?"

I told him about tutoring and playing the piano for
rehearsals. At that, his eyes lit up. "Next time, you'll
have to come to my main house and play my piano. It
belonged to Isabel. It would be nice to hear it again. I'll
make sure that it's tuned."

As we stood up, he suddenly hugged me. I was
totally transfixed by the powerful embrace of this older
man and imagined myself being Jacob Berkowitz,
Blair's first love. After a long embrace, he gently pushed
me away. "You need to get home." Back at the truck
stop, he handed me an envelope. "Josh, you're a nice

kid. Here's my phone number and something for your friend Patty. Give me a call. I'd like to see you again."

I got into Bercilak and opened the envelope. Along with Blair's business card were two hundred-dollar bills. I could hardly wait to tell Patty about the money but of course without revealing how I got it. Driving back to Rosales, I kept thinking about Blair, his love for Jacob, his marriage, and his friend Barkley. What a strange evening! After an uncomfortable beginning, things had moved in a surprisingly pleasant direction. His kindness, his courtly manner and educated speech, the massage, the feel and touch of his body, and the story about the "purest, most wonderful love imaginable" between Jacob and him. Do straight boys have experiences like that? Or do such things happen only to gay men? Whatever the answers to these questions, my eighteenth year got off to a warm and memorable start.

Chapter Twenty-two:
Mother Nature Intervenes

The following morning, Patty called the garage where my dad and I were both working. Frightened and crying, she said that she was in terrible pain and starting to bleed. I told my father that Patty needed to go to the doctor as soon as possible.

"What's wrong with her?"

"Some kind of female problem. She's by herself, and she's bleeding a lot."

Recognizing the danger, my father told me to get her to the doctor's office as fast as possible. I raced to Patty's house, helped her into Bercilak, and hurried to the hospital. After years of depending on part-time doctors who served several small Arizona towns at once, Rosales had managed to hire its first full-time doctor, a childless widower named Dr. Berman who ostensibly accepted the job because he wanted a small, country practice. The truth, according to Craig's father, was that Dr. Berman had run into disciplinary problems in Michigan and needed a job elsewhere, even if it meant relocating to a small Arizona town. As a recent arrival, he didn't know the town well, which turned out to be a very good thing for Patty and me.

Seeing Patty's condition, the receptionist ordered me to take a seat and quickly hustled Patty down the hall. She returned a few minutes later and asked how to reach Patty's parents. Wanting to talk to the doctor before he talked to Patty's parents, I gave her my home number since I knew that no one was there to take a call. About an hour later, Dr. Berman poked his head into the reception area and asked me to join him in his office.

"Are you the young lady's boyfriend?" he asked.

"Yes," I lied. "How is she?"

"She didn't get here a minute too soon. She was starting to hemorrhage badly and is still quite weak. But she's going to be okay. The emergency has passed. We stopped the bleeding, and I've given her something to help her relax. She had a miscarriage. Did you know she was pregnant?"

"No," I lied.

"Do you know how to reach her parents? I'll have to tell them."

A million alarm bells went off in my head. After a tense pause, I said in my steeliest voice, "You can't tell her parents anything."

Taken aback by my aggressive response, he said, "But I have to tell them. She's a minor, and they have a right to know. I could get in trouble if I don't tell them."

"And she'll get in trouble if you do tell them."

"She will have to work that out with her parents. I have no choice in the matter."

My mind was racing. How could I keep this doctor from telling Patty's parents that she had been pregnant? Her mother would have a fit, and once the word spread, Patty would be tarnished for life. Suddenly I had an idea that ironically was inspired by AMPS. "If you tell her parents, I will tell everyone that when I came in for a physical, you fiddled with my dick until I got hard, and then tried to stick your dick up my ass."

"What?!? What?!? What in the hell are you talking about?!? That is a total and outrageous lie! Something like that could ruin my life."

"And if you tell Patty's parents that she was pregnant, you will ruin her life. So, let's make a deal. You don't tell anyone that she was pregnant, and I don't tell anyone that you tried to rape me."

"But that's such a despicable lie! No one will believe you."

"They'll believe me long enough to ask why you had to leave Michigan." This last bit was a shot in the dark, but it evidently hit a target. For once, Craig's father's gossip proved useful.

Behind his rimless glasses, Dr. Berman's watery blue eyes showed a mixture of fear and anger. He looked old, beaten, and sad. For a second, I felt sorry for him and considered backing down. But I couldn't let anyone find out about Patty. After staring at me for what seemed an eternity, he asked, "Do you have her parents' phone number? I promise not to tell them what really happened." He then sent me back to the waiting room. About twenty minutes later, Mrs. Burleson tore through the front door, demanding to see her daughter. The receptionist led her back into the hospital area where I suppose she saw Patty and talked to Dr. Berman.

Sometime later, Mrs. Burleson returned to the waiting room. All teary eyed, she hugged me and thanked me for saving Patty's life. With considerable temerity, I asked her what had happened. She replied that her daughter had developed a severe infection that had produced some sort of toxic shock. Nothing about a miscarriage. Dr. Berman had come through as promised, and I was very grateful. Mrs. Burleson took me back to the hospital room where Patty was lying in bed. She looked pale, but was able to squeeze my hand, thank me, and tell me that everything would be okay.

She went home two days later and was soon back in school. No one knew what had happened, and things quickly returned to normal. Patty continued on the cheerleading team, and I continued writing her English papers and helping her cheat on exams. She and I remained best friends and dance partners, and no one was the wiser.

My first stop after Patty's ordeal was Lucy's Outpost. After hearing the story, Lucy gave me a big hug. "Josh," she said, "You've been very brave through all this. You'll make some woman a great husband." And then with a wink, "Or maybe you'll just be some guy's best friend." I blushed but again felt a strange comfort knowing that Lucy suspected that I was gay and didn't seem to mind.

My second task was to write a short note to Dr. Berman thanking him for giving such superb care to Patty and for agreeing to be Rosales's doctor. Of course, he never replied, but on the few occasions our paths crossed, he acknowledged me with a cool solemnity that made me feel like an adult if not a co-conspirator.

Chapter Twenty-three: Things Turn to Shit

In mid-April everything turned to shit. One late Saturday afternoon, I went to the high school weight room to work out. The only other person there was Burt Larson, one of the duh-duh's who also happened to be quite attractive. With bowling-ball biceps and incredible pecs, he had the most developed body in the high school. In the shower room after we finished working out, he started to beat off and got an admirable hardon which he was flopping around entirely for my entertainment. He then said, "Follow me and I'll let you suck it."

An alarm bell went off in my mind. Burt was sexy, but he most certainly was not a friend. But my mind numbed into truck-stop mode as I followed him into a bathroom stall. As soon as I knelt in front of him, he grabbed the back of my head and started thrusting into my mouth, making me gag. Fortunately, he came almost immediately. After he pulled his dick out, I immediately spat his cum into the toilet. "Next time," he said, "You gotta swallow it." Then without a goodbye much less a thank you, he walked away. Feeling used and angry, I vowed to never do anything with Burt again, great pecs and bowling-ball biceps notwithstanding.

The following Monday evening while walking home from a rehearsal, I noticed that Barry Cummings, another duh-duh, was following me. No one else was in sight. Barry was the love child of a dotty older woman, Noni Cummings, who ran off with a truck driver when she was still in high school. She returned a few months later, very pregnant and very unmarried. She never identified Barry's father, but whoever he was, their son was a brute and a slob—the kind who always appear on the verge of deodorant failure. With a pimply face and greasy hair, he wore low-slung jeans buckled under a protruding belly. It was hard to tell how much of his bulk was muscle and how much was fat, but he was clearly bigger than I was. He caught up with me, grabbed my shoulder, and roughly turned me to face him. With no preliminaries, he said, "Hey, Q-B. I hear you're a cocksucker. I want you to suck my cock."

I replied, "I am not a cocksucker, and I have no interest in sucking your cock."

"Why? What's the matter? You think you're too good for me? You weren't too good for Burt."

I started to say, "Actually, I am too good for you …" but he suddenly sucker punched me hard in the gut. I bent over in pain. He then knocked me to the ground and began kicking and hitting me. After fisting my face a couple of times, he snarled, "Pay attention, Q-B. When I want a blowjob, you give it to me. Next time will be worse."

He then lumbered off, leaving me lying in the street. One of my eyes was starting to swell shut, I could taste blood in my mouth, and I felt an intense pain in my side where he had kicked me. I managed to stand up and slowly limp home. Mother let out a shriek when she saw the blood on my face. "What happened? Who did this to you?"

My father immediately came into the room and said, "We need to see the doctor. We can discuss the details later." They got Dr. Berman out of bed to attend to me. With no indication that we had ever met, he cleaned my wounds and applied a tight bandage to the cut over my eye. He palpated my entire body, found no sign of broken bones, and recommended icepacks for my swollen lip and black eye. After a silent drive home, my father asked, "Who did this to you?"

"I can't say."

"Sonny, roughhousing is one thing. But somebody wanted to hurt you. Bad. Who was it?"

Against my better judgment, I confessed that it had been Barry Cummings.

Chapter Twenty-four: Suspended

I stayed out of school for the next two days and was glad to see that the ice packs Dr. Berman had recommended were bringing down the swelling and discoloring around my eye. On Thursday morning, my father took me to Principal Barnes' office to demand that Barry be held accountable. Barnes called Barry into his office. In front of my father and me, Barnes asked, "Barry, are you responsible for what happened to Josh?"

"Yeah," he said with a smirk.

"Why did you do it?"

"Because he tried to grab my dick. He's always tryin' to grab guys' dicks. I don't want no queer touchin' my dick. That's why I hit him. Any normal guy would do the same. And if you don't believe me, ask Burt Cummings. He'll tell you the same story."

Barnes then asked my father and me to wait in the front office. Minutes later, Burt swaggered in. With something between a smile and a sneer on his face, he entered Barnes' office. While we waited, my father asked, "Josh, is any of this true?"

"None of it is true. I never did any of that. They're lying."

"Why would they make up a story like that? Is there something you're not telling me?"

"No."

"Sonny, I'm on your side. I want to do what's best for you. Tell me what's going on."

I responded with a stoical silence, doing everything possible to avoid looking at him. After a few minutes, Mr. Barnes called us back into his office just as Burt was leaving. Seeing that no one was looking at him but me, Burt placed his third finger alongside his nose, subtly flipping me the bird and mouthing the words, "You're fucked."

Mr. Barnes looked at me for a few seconds, and then ducked his head as though talking to me made him nervous. "Josh," he finally said, "do you find boys attractive?"

I thought a long time and finally replied, "I don't want to talk about it."

"You know that Burt and Barry have made a serious accusation against you."

What was I supposed to say? Tell him that Burt got a hardon in the shower, wanted a blowjob, and almost choked me with his huge dick? Or that Barry had beat the shit out of me when I refused to give him a blowjob? Choking back tears, I said in a soft voice, "I really don't want to talk about it. I do not want to be here. I hate this school, I hate everyone in it, and I never want to come back."

Barnes asked me to sit in the front office so he could talk to my father. They talked for a long time, and I heard Barnes make a couple of phone calls. He then called me back in the office. "Josh, I cannot ignore what Burt and Barry are saying about you. I want to do some more investigating, but in the meantime, I think you should take tomorrow off. Your father will explain why."

My father and I walked quietly back to the garage. "We'll need to talk to your mother tonight," he said. I was glad to focus on fixing tires and servicing cars for the rest of the day as though nothing had happened— anything to avoid thinking about my situation. I was also still sore, but thankfully my black eye had started to clear up. I was also glad that the following day was Saturday, so I wouldn't have to go to school.

That night, my parents sat me down at the kitchen table. My father had told Mother everything. She started out, all tears, doing the Loretta thing. "You can't be that way. We've given you everything. And the church! You know what the church teaches. This is worse than sin. It's not normal." Grave but calm, my father said quietly to my mother, "Lily, that's enough. He feels bad enough as it is." His words were probably too gentle to be a reprimand, but at least they shut her up.

Then turning to me, he said, "Sonny, we want to help you through this. This afternoon, Mr. Barnes called LDS Social Services in Salt Lake City. They recommended a Mormon psychologist in Phoenix who runs a place called Croft House that specializes in helping adolescent boys like you. On Sunday afternoon, I'll drive you to Phoenix so you can work with him for a couple of weeks. I'm sure it will be a good place for you."

That night, as I was trying to go to sleep, I heard some boys shout something from a passing car. I couldn't make out all the words, but I distinctly heard "Q-B" and "cocksucker." And I wondered if some of my "friends" were in that car.

Chapter Twenty-five:
Lucy and Gabe

By Saturday, I still ached a lot, although my black eye and cut lip were almost healed. Even so, I worked a full day at the garage. Sunday morning, I asked to stay home from church. Surprisingly, my parents didn't object, perhaps because they feared what other kids might say to me. The minute they left the house, I called the only person in town who might offer sympathy: Lucy Ramírez. I told her that I'd got beat up and that I needed to talk to her. Without hesitation, she told me to meet her at the Outpost. It didn't open on Sundays, so no one would be there.

Although most of the swelling had gone down, she took one look at my face and exclaimed, "God Almighty! What happened to you?" She beckoned me into her office, closed the door, and took a closer look. "Okay, Josh. Who did this to you, and why are they still alive?"

I tried to talk, but I choked up and couldn't. Lucy pulled me onto the small sofa she kept in her office and put her arms around me. "It's okay, Josh," she said. "No one is going to hurt you here. Just tell me what happened."

After collecting myself, I told her how Barry had beat me up because I had refused to have sex with him.

I didn't tell the whole story, but enough to explain my bruises and my black eye.

After a long silence, she said, "Josh, I'm not going to pry, and you don't need to tell me anything you don't want to. But I want to tell you a story. How much do you know about me and why I went to Alaska?"

"Just what I've heard," I replied.

"Well, since the Rosales gossip mongers have probably mucked things up, let me tell you the real story. First, you probably know that I'm not really a Perkins."

"I've heard rumors."

"Not surprised. This town does well with rumors. My mother was an only child who grew up on a ranch. She married Clay Perkins just after graduating from high school. He was a widower and had a couple of grown boys from his first wife. He was a lot older than Mom, but he needed someone to take care of him, and she wanted a reason to get off the ranch. Clay owned a farm and several rental properties, so he was well fixed for Rosales. He was also a diabetic and a heavy drinker. Since Rosales didn't have a regular doctor back then, a Dr. Rosen used to spend a couple of days per week in Rosales. My mother and him had an affair, and that's where I came from. Clay died shortly after I was born so, as far as the town knew, he could have been my father. It was a shock when my mother told me who my real father was, but I was relieved not to be a Perkins.

"Fortunately for my mother, Clay was on bad terms with the two boys from his first marriage, so he wrote an ironclad will leaving everything to my mother. His sons challenged it in court, but Mom fought them to a standstill. She ended up with a decent income, managing the rental properties and paying someone to run the farm. She was a smart lady, she read a lot, and she made sure that I went to school and participated in things. I was not raised Mormon for which I am grateful, but I did a lot of school stuff, cheerleading, honors society, and that sort of thing. But I never felt accepted because I was the only non-Mormon Anglo in the school.

"Anyway, in my senior year, a young Mexican guy named Gabriel Ramírez started flirting with me. Gabe was one of the most beautiful men God ever created. He had dark eyes, wavy black hair, a handsome face, and a great smile. He was three years older than me and had a good job with the county. His parents died in a car wreck when he was just a little guy, so his grandmother had raised him. She died just after his high school graduation, so he was on his own when we met.

"In my senior year, we started dating. He was pushy about sex. Just before graduating from high school, I realized that I was pregnant. I told my mother. She surprised me by saying that I should marry Gabe and move someplace else as soon as possible. So, Gabe and I got married at the courthouse and left for Alaska the following day. Gabe got a job in construction, and we settled into a tiny two-bedroom apartment in Anchorage. I started preparing one of the rooms for a nursery. We got really excited when the doctor told me that I was going to have twins.

"During my pregnancy, Gabe could not have been nicer. He worried constantly about my comfort, brought groceries home, cooked for me, and worked hard to decorate the nursery. We didn't have sex since he claimed that sex during pregnancy wasn't safe for the babies. This of course was bullshit, but what did I know? After the twins were born, Gabe spent lots of time with me and seemed overjoyed with the girls. I became a full-time mother, and Gabe was a great father. When the girls cried at night, he was the first to get up and bring them to me so I could feed them. And he was a lot better at changing diapers than I was. But still no sex. He said he wanted to save some money before having another kid. And of course, I believed him.

"A few months after the girls were born, Gabe started to change. He'd get in dark moods and not want to talk. He started drinking, sometimes to the point of blacking out before he could get to bed. Then he stopped coming home some nights. When asked where he had been, he'd mumble some lame excuse about late-night poker or whatever. The shit hit the fan when I developed a bad itch in my private area. Thinking it was an infection, I went to the doctor who told me that I had crab lice. Josh, do you know about crab lice?"

"Not a thing."

"Well, they're called crab lice because they look like little crabs. They live in your pubic hair, and they're usually communicated through sexual contact. But you can also get them from a towel that was used by someone who has them. That's how I found out that Gabe was fooling around. I confronted him. After a long argument, he confessed. I asked if he liked whores more than he liked me, and that's when he admitted that he was having sex with men. Gabe was a homosexual."

"Did you suspect?"

"Josh, I never suspected a goddamned thing. I sometimes wondered why he avoided sex, but it never crossed my mind that he might be homosexual. God Almighty, I hardly knew what a homosexual was."

"Did you hate him after he told you?"

"Did I hate him? I can't tell you what I felt. Of course, I was mad as hell because he'd brought filth into our home. He had infected me and could have infected our daughters. But I hated him mostly because he'd been lying to me from the beginning. The first lie was when he pretended to find me attractive. Gabe

154

somehow had the idea that if he could get it on with a woman, he would lose his attraction to men. He used me like a guinea pig to prove that he wasn't homosexual, and that's how I got pregnant.

"Of course, he didn't change. He couldn't change. He still wanted to be with men. Anchorage was full of single men back then. I imagine that quite a few of them were open to sex of any kind, including other guys. He may have been fooling around from day one for all I know. He also made me into a liar because every week I'd send my mother a letter telling her how wonderful everything was. I never did tell her the truth about Gabe."

After a short silence, she continued. "So yes, I hated him. Sometimes, I wanted to kill him. Sometimes I'd yell at him and call him horrible names, which really upset the girls. I wanted to hurt him just like he had hurt me. But he never fought back. I soon realized that I wasn't saying anything to him that he wasn't saying to himself. You see, Gabe hated himself for being homosexual. I think his love for the girls and even for me was sincere. But he couldn't love himself. Gabe's tragedy was that at some point he decided that his life wasn't worth living, and that he might as well throw it away through drinking and screwing around."

She suddenly stopped talking. Her jaw quivered slightly, and her eyes filled with tears. As gently as I could, I said, "You don't have to go on if you don't want to."

She held up her hand, gesturing for me to wait. "You're very sweet, but I've never told this whole story to anyone, and I probably won't ever tell it again. So, I need to go on. Where were we? Oh yes, you asked if I hated him. And the answer is yes. I cannot tell you how much I hated him. But I also loved and felt sorry for him. It's terrible to watch a beautiful, gentle man like Gabe come to hate himself so much that he wanted to die. Another reason I couldn't hate him was that every time I looked at my beautiful daughters, I saw something of him. They have his eyes, his hair, and some of his sweetness. Those girls are the best thing that ever happened to me, so at some level I have to be grateful to Gabe."

"What happened to him?"

"He eventually moved out. I stayed in Anchorage because I had no place else to go, but also because he continued to take care of us. Every few days he'd show up with groceries and enough money for me and the girls to get by. But he was in bad shape. Each time I saw him, he looked more tired and more worn down. He was probably drinking himself into an early grave, and God only knows what else he was doing. It was like watching a slow suicide. Then one day, just before the girls' second birthday, a man came to the apartment to tell me that Gabe had been killed in a construction accident.

"The company paid me a small death benefit which I used to arrange a nice funeral at the local Catholic church. Several of Gabe's friends and co-workers showed up at the funeral. I wondered if some of them had been his lovers. We buried him in Anchorage. Every year, I send a check to the church, so they'll maintain the grave. I then called my mother and told her that I needed to come home. As it turned out, she needed me as much as I needed her because she was getting too old to take care of herself and her properties. She wired me enough money to buy plane tickets to Phoenix, and we came back to Rosales.

"Of course, the decent folks in Rosales thought it served me right for getting pregnant and running off with a Mexican. I resolved to never give them the satisfaction of seeing me fail. I took over my mother's properties and eventually bought some new ones. I made sure that my girls were the best students they could be, I got involved in the PTA and other civic projects like the public library where I met you, and I just smiled at everyone, especially the ones I didn't like. I also really enjoyed taking over The Outpost. It was a dive when I bought it, but I've turned it into a nice place and a good business. What you see now."

"Do you have a boyfriend? Did you ever want to marry again? I think you're really pretty."

"That's very sweet of you but words aren't enough. Every woman deserves to feel that she's so beautiful that some man is just dying to touch her. She'll never get that from a homosexual no matter how nice and gentle he is. That's probably the worst thing Gabe did to me. He made me feel unattractive. Undesirable. So yes, I've had some boyfriends over the years. They made me feel attractive, and I needed that a lot. But I couldn't see myself marrying again. I didn't need some man to help raise my daughters or run my business. I'm happy with my life. My girls have graduated from college and are doing well. They visit often, and sometimes I run down to Phoenix to see them. Carmen is starting to get serious with some guy, so maybe I'll soon be a grandma!"

"Do you ever think of moving?"

"Why would I move? I've got a good income and a business that I enjoy. I have friends, including a few drunks and Jack Mormons. I volunteer in the community, and occasionally, I meet someone like you who reminds me that there are decent people in the world. So that's my story. I wanted to tell it to you. But I particularly wanted you to know about Gabe."

I remained silent, trying to digest all that she had said. I wasn't drinking myself into an early grave, and I wasn't using some poor girl as an experiment. But I knew how it felt to wonder if a gay life was worth living. Finally, with great difficulty I confessed what I had never confessed to a straight person: "Lucy, I think I'm like Gabe."

She put her arms around me and pulled me close. In a soft voice she whispered, "If you can be as nice as Gabe, that's a great start. Just make sure you don't throw your life away like he did." After a long hug, she asked, "Josh, what's next for you? What are your parents going to do?"

I told her about the Mormon clinic my parents were taking me to later that afternoon. Her response: "Josh, be careful. Be really careful. That clinic could be a dangerous place. They're going to throw everything they can at you to make you change. Don't let them make you hate yourself. And if you ever need anything, you have my number."

We hugged again. She then gave me a little shove towards the door and said, "You need to go. Take care of yourself. You're a really great kid."

As I rode home, I wondered if I had already begun thinking that a gay life wasn't worth living. That's what drove Gabe to throw his life away, and that was probably why Billy Schaeffer smashed his car into a concrete column. But I was relieved that Lucy knew about me and still thought that I was a great kid.

Part II

Chapter One:
Croft House and Dr. Chandler

My father and I left for Phoenix shortly after my conversation with Lucy. Some church event kept Mother in Rosales which spared me a four-hour rant about filling the measure of my creation. The date was April 26, 1970. I remember it well since even then I intuited that it marked an important pivot point in my life. After a long silence, my father began speaking haltingly, in a soft and gentle voice. "Sonny," he said, "Your mother and I have always wanted the best for our kids. Jeff, Terri, and Clarissa have graduated from college, Jeff and Keith have completed their missions for the church, and Keith will start law school in the fall. We want you to go on a mission too when the time comes. Finding money for all this hasn't always been easy. Mother's income as a teacher helps, and I do okay at the service station. But what I most want you to know is that I am on your side. With Heavenly Father's help, we'll get you through this."

His words moved me because they were heartfelt and hard for him to say. But what did he know about my side? Until Barry beat me up, the thought of homosexuality probably never crossed his mind. How could my parents understand much less accept a gay son when the LDS church had such horrible ideas about gay people and gay sex? Mother Harold once told me that, of all minorities, gay kids may be the only ones raised by the enemy or at least by parents unlike them. Little Jews learn from Jewish parents. Little Black kids learn from Black parents. But almost by definition, little gay kids do not learn from gay parents. Sometimes gay kids' worst enemies are their own parents—a terrible fact that neither the parents nor the child may be aware of.

We drove into a small parking lot marked by a sign saying *Croft House*, written in curvy letters meant to look inviting. The building was a one-story, flat-roofed affair made of cinderblock painted light yellow with glass double front doors, evenly spaced rectangular windows, and a few plantings feebly trying to approximate landscaping. The receptionist, a portly, white-haired woman with a big smile, stood to greet us.

"You must be Josh and you must be Brother Chastain" she said in a warm voice. "Welcome to Croft House. I'm Sister Farr. We've been waiting for you. Let me call Dr. Chandler. He's anxious to meet you, and you'll just love him. He's very smart. He has a doctorate from Harvard, you know."

She pressed a button on the intercom. "The Chastains are here." Almost immediately, a tall, lanky man with a full head of slightly mussed salt-and-pepper hair came into the reception area. Dressed in a rumpled tweed jacket, chino pants, and a button-down white shirt with no tie, he took my hand in both of his and said, "You must be Josh. Welcome. We're so very glad you're here." Then, giving my father the same double-handed handshake, he said, "And you must be Brother Chastain. We talked Friday afternoon on the phone. I'm looking forward to getting to know you both, especially Josh. I know that he is a very special boy."

All smiles and affability, Dr. Chandler invited us into his office which was just a few doors from the reception area. Chandler evidently shared the building with other therapists since several doors had nameplates for people with PhDs or MSWs after their names. The interior of Chandler's office looked totally out of place in the cinderblock building. It had real wood paneling, flowery drapes, a couple of overstuffed armchairs with a matching sofa and a large wooden desk. Centered on the wall behind his desk was a framed Harvard diploma surrounded by stylized reproductions of winter landscapes. A little piece of New England right in the middle of cinderblock Phoenix. A working man with no high school degree, my father seemed ill at ease in Chandler's office. Anxious to make conversation of some sort, he said "I hear you studied at Harvard."

With a self-satisfied smile, Dr. Chandler responded, "I can see that Sister Farr has been talking too much. Yes, I got my doctorate at Harvard, but I really don't put much stock in the Harvard name. I went to Harvard only because Harvard gave me a full-ride scholarship." Smile again.

For someone who didn't put much stock in the Harvard name, he had just managed to drop the Harvard name four times in three seconds, he was wearing a five-pound Harvard ring on his right hand, and a framed Harvard diploma adorned the wall opposite the entry door, making it the first thing people noticed. And just in passing, he let us know that he had not only gone to Harvard, but that he was so damned smart that Harvard had paid him to study there. I was tempted to ask, "Were those *Harvard* courses taught on the *Harvard* campus by *Harvard* professors in a *Harvard* building in the company of other *Harvard* students?" But I kept my mouth shut. This was a time for BS-Speak.

Chandler motioned for my father and me to sit in the cushiony armchairs as he plopped down on the sofa opposite us, spreading his legs in a manly manner. Resting his elbows on his knees, he leaned towards us as though to create a circle of confidence. "So, let's get acquainted. I know your name is Joshua Chastain, but I don't know much about you." He then asked some obvious questions about my age, my hometown, my hobbies, my favorite and least favorite courses in school, my friends, my family. All easy stuff. Then he asked, "Are you LDS?"

I answered in the affirmative although in the back of mind I recalled how the buck-naked Father Tovar had almost converted me to Catholicism.

"Josh and Brother Chastain, I have two anchors in my practice. First, my training as a psychotherapist at Harvard (that word again) and second my testimony of the Church of Jesus Christ of Latter-day Saints. I've never found these to be in conflict. The gospel teaches us the commandments and tells us that righteous living will bring us joy. Psychotherapy gives us the tools to take control of our lives and live according to God's plan. Josh, at Croft House we want you to get to know your true self and grow closer to God. After two or three weeks, we'll do an evaluation and decide what steps to take next. Do those sound like good goals to you?"

I could tell that my father was awed by the guy, so of course I said, "Yes."

"Yes what?"

"Those sound like good goals."

"Good boy, Josh. I see that you and I are going to make real progress. Now, before your father leaves, would you please join me in prayer?" It was more a command than a request, so following his example, we knelt in a circle. Closing his eyes tightly, he began to pray.

164

"Dear Heavenly Father. Hallowed be thy name. On this night, we a few of thy children kneel humbly before thee to render thanks for thy many blessings and for bringing us to this place where the broken can be made whole and the lost can be brought back into thy presence. Lead us to a true understanding of who we really are. Help us discern the plan that thou hast made for us. Teach us to guard against Satan and his minions. We know they walk among us, telling us that unnatural things are natural, and that evil actions are good. Give us the wisdom to not be deceived by the lies of the father of lies. Help us to understand thy divine plan so that we may be stalwart in the faith and bring forth righteous sons and daughters to build thy kingdom. Be with us now and at all times. In Jesus' name. Amen."

In seventeen years of attending Mormon services, I had never heard a prayer quite like Chandler's. The message was crystal clear. Being gay is not our true identity. If we believe that gay is okay, it's because we've been deceived by the father of lies, yea even Satan himself whose minions walk among us. And God's plan for Mormon men is to impregnate women, have lots of kids, and build the kingdom. Leaving me in the reception area, Chandler followed my father out to the car where they conversed for what seemed a long time. Finally, my father looked at me through the glass doors, waved, and got in his car.

I couldn't get Chandler's prayer out of mind. But I also remembered Mother Harold's advice: "Joshua, never take shit for being gay, especially from dickwad shrinks and douche-bag religious fanatics. They are the worst. The VERY worst." If anyone filled the definition of a dickwad shrink and a douche-bag religious fanatic, it might be the esteemed Dr. Chandler.

Chandler returned to the reception area and in a hearty voice said, "Sister Farr, please show Josh to his room. Josh, tonight we just want you to settle in. Tomorrow evening you will meet with a discussion group of fine young men like yourself who are here to work through a few personal issues and grow closer to Heavenly Father. I'm sure you'll enjoy hearing their stories as they progress towards a more fulfilling life. Then you and I will have our first personal meeting on Tuesday after dinner. Don't worry about anything. You are where you need to be."

Located at the end of one of the halls, my small room contained a bed, a built-in desk with a bookshelf, a chair, a nightstand, a closet with drawers, and a small bathroom. On the bookshelf were the Mormon scriptures—the Bible (*King James* Version of course), the *Book of Mormon, Doctrine and Covenants* (these being mostly revelations given to Joseph Smith), and *The Pearl of Great Price* (consisting mostly of translations Joseph Smith allegedly made from Egyptian papyrus scrolls). At first, I felt lucky to have

166

my own bathroom, but then I realized that Croft House would not want communal showers lest guys be tempted to pecker-check.

Chapter Two:
Sunday Evening at Croft House

A half-hour later, Sister Farr led me to her small office to explain the schedule. The day would begin at 6:30 AM followed by showers, breakfast, and tutoring from 8:30 to noon. Croft House used a home-schooling curriculum which, according to Sister Farr, was recognized by the State of Arizona so no one would lose time towards graduation. After lunch and more study, at 3:45 PM we would have a ninety-minute gym period followed by showers and dinner at Croft House. On Monday and Wednesday evenings I would meet with a discussion group. On Tuesday and Thursday evenings, Dr. Chandler would meet me for one-on-one sessions. After evening prayer, we would return to our rooms at 10 PM with lights out by 10:30. On Friday afternoons my parents could pick me up for the weekend, but I would need to be back by Sunday evening. I could leave the building only with permission. Although Sister Farr explained all this in a sweet voice, the subtext was clear: I was basically a prisoner.

The cafeteria was a medium-sized multipurpose room that also served as a classroom, a study hall, and a meeting room for group sessions. Dinner was a meager affair—breaded patties of some sort, instant mashed potatoes, waterlogged string beans, and a salad consisting entirely of chopped iceberg lettuce and bottled dressing. Some ten boys were in the dining hall, most of them about my age. Only one seemed interesting, a guy named Ronnie Richards. Actually, he was more than interesting. With red-tinged brown hair, dark brown eyes, thick eyebrows, and light brown freckles, he was strikingly handsome. We couldn't help but notice each other.

After bussing our tables, we began reading hour. Since I had nothing to read, I asked Sister Farr for permission to get a book from my room. I returned with the only book I had brought, Dostoevsky's *The Brothers Karamazov,* which I was reading partly because I was going through a Russian phase, but also (might as well confess) because I wanted people to know that I read serious stuff. Ronnie smiled ever so slightly when he saw the title.

Evening prayer was led by the senior resident who introduced himself as Brother LeGrand Stewart. More pretty than handsome, he was a small-framed, nervous man with delicate features, intense blue eyes, and meticulously parted, slicked-down brown hair. He spoke in an artificially low voice and had a strange way of keeping his arms folded or his hands in his pockets as though needing to contain his own body. At a distance, he seemed no older than the boys in the group, but up close one could see stress lines in his forehead and tiny wrinkles around his eyes. Despite the large wedding ring on his left hand, he immediately tripped my gaydar. As we left the room, Ronnie handed me my copy of *The Brothers Karamazov.* "You left your book in the study hall." Back in my room, I saw a note in the book. I quickly closed the door and read it.

Welcome to the funny farm. Follow my lead tomorrow and Coach Charlie might let us run back from PE on our own. Ronnie

Chapter Three:
Running with Ronnie

The next day, a Monday, unfolded exactly as Sister Farr had said. Up at 6:30, showers, scripture reading and prayers, breakfast, and tutors beginning at 8:30. The tutors were a married couple, Brother and Sister Sonderegger, both retired high school teachers who seemed very nice. She taught English and social studies while he oversaw math and science. They gave me diagnostic tests in math, verbal reasoning, and reading—easy stuff.

At 3:45, we dressed for PE and took the Croft House van to a large LDS meeting house about two miles away. Like most Mormon churches, it was as much a community center as a religious structure what with a chapel, classrooms, and a large multipurpose room that served as both a gymnasium and an auditorium. Our PE teacher, Coach Charlie, was an aging jock with a nice smile. We started with the usual stuff—running in place, jumping jacks, pushups, sit-ups, and the like.

During a short break, Ronnie engaged Coach Charlie in a private conversation and beckoned for me to join in. He argued that Ronnie and I had been high school athletes (a total lie in my case) and that, to stay in shape, we would like to jog back to Croft House.

After some hemming and hawing, Coach Charlie said, "If you can give me twenty-five good pushups, I'll let you do it."

So, we both dropped to the floor and gave him twenty-five stunning pushups.

"Okay, go ahead, but leave now so you'll get there at the same time that the van does."

As we began running, I fixated on Ronnie's good looks. With reddish hair, dark eyes, full lips, a square chin, and the faint shadow of a beard, he had the face of a catalogue model. He was on the short side (five foot seven maybe?), but like lots of short guys, he had well-defined muscles. And I loved the way his gym shorts revealed muscular hairy legs and a gorgeously sculpted bubble butt.

"Hey, pervert" he said with fake annoyance. "Stop staring at my ass. We have serious things to talk about. We're running together because we need to talk. Do you know why you're here?"

Forcing my eyes away from his lovely posterior, I replied, "I'm here so Dr. Chandler can teach me not to be a homosexual and help me become acquainted with my true self."

"That's the bullshit he peddles. Are you a homosexual? Do you find guys sexy?"

"Yeah, but…"

"Tell me something. When a boy and girl walk towards you, which one do you look at first?"

After a moment's thought, I answered, "Always the boy. How about you?"

"Damn rights, the boy. It's been that way my entire life and I'm sick and tired of people telling me there's something wrong with it. If you always look at the boy before you look at the girl, that should tell you who you are. You don't need Chandler to say that your real self is somebody else."

"If you've already made up your mind, why are you here?"

"Because I'm still seventeen, my dad is married to a religious fanatic, and they won't let me out until Chandler says I'm cured."

"Are you a senior or a junior?"

"Still a junior. My dad made me start grade school late so I wouldn't be the littlest kid in my class. How about you?"

"Also a junior. Do you ever think of running away?"

"All the time, but there's a small detail. When my mom died, she left me a trust fund, but I can't access it until I'm eighteen and enrolled in a university. My birthday isn't until October. So, for the time being I'm dependent on my dad, and I have to convince that quack Chandler that I am a red-blooded, pussy-obsessed heterosexual so I can get out of here."

"If Chandler's such a quack, why does he have Croft House?"

"Because the Mormon church is filled with guilt-ridden gay boys and their parents who think that Chandler can make them straight. Lots of shrinks think that homosexuality is totally normal for some people. But Chandler tells them that homosexuality is a sin and that he can cure them and bring them back to God. In the meantime, he's raking in the cash."

I suddenly felt guilt pangs. How much was Croft House costing my parents? I didn't like the idea of Chandler gouging them for money. Interrupting these thoughts, Ronnie asked, "So, what's your story?"

I told him about Burt and Barry and how my dad brought me to Croft House to make me straight. I also told him that I had come willingly to get out of Rosales where the Burts and Barrys of the world would make my life hell.

"Do you think Chandler can change you?"

"I have no idea. This is all new to me. I know some nice gay people, so I'm not sure I want to change. But I know what the Church teaches, and I'm worried about my parents and family. They've been good to me, and I don't want to hurt them."

"Josh, if you're gay, you're gay, and the sooner you accept that fact, the sooner you can start making a life for yourself. Your parents just need to get used to it. You can't live your life for them."

This sounded harsh, but I feared he was right. When we reached Croft House, he said, "We need to talk some more. Tonight, just after lights-out, around 10:35, I'll knock on your door. Be ready to sneak out."

"Won't the guard see us?"

"There's only one guard at night, a big guy named Sanders. I'll arrange for him to let us out."

"How?"

"Money, my dear, money. Remember, my dad's rich, and he gives me lots of money, so he won't feel guilty about sending me to be raised by my grandparents. Besides, I think Sanders might be one of us."

Chapter Four:
The First Group Therapy Meeting

After dinner I went to my first group meeting. It consisted of about twelve guys in their late teens and early twenties. Except for Ronnie and a couple of guys I had seen in the cafeteria, the group members were locals. Brother Stewart, the pretty senior resident with the huge wedding ring, led the discussion. Speaking in a pious, artificially low voice, he explained, "The purpose of the group is to help us compare experiences, learn from each other, pray together, and grow together. We are all blessed to be members of God's only true church, the restored church of Jesus Christ. Through our efforts in this group and our work with the individual counselors, we can learn to live righteous lives and channel our desires in ways that are consistent with gospel teaching."

Two of the outsiders and I were new to the group, so we had to introduce ourselves. One of them, a sweet-looking guy named Glenn, was up front about his "homosexual tendencies" and his need to be free of them in order to live "according to Heavenly Father's commandments." The second guy, a nelly queen named Billy, lisped his way through a testimony of how Mormonism was the only true church and how much

176

he loved Heavenly Father and how he knew that Joseph Smith was a true prophet of God, and… If Brother Stewart hadn't cut him off, he could have lisped the night away. I said as little as possible about myself, something about wanting to get to know myself better—which in fact was true.

"Okay," Brother Stewart began. "Do any of you have anything to share with the group?"

After an uncomfortable silence, a skinny guy named Spencer who seemed all knees and elbows said, "I'd like to tell you about my new girlfriend."

Several boys oohed, and others applauded. I couldn't tell if they really approved or if they were making fun of him.

"Great!" exclaimed Brother Stewart with theatrical enthusiasm. "Where did you meet her?"

"At church. Since she doesn't date much, I knew she was available. So, I asked her to go to the movies with me."

Doesn't date very much? Available? Sounded like a desperate Mormon girl looking for a man to take her to the Celestial Kingdom.

"That's really wonderful," Brother Stewart said encouragingly. "How did it go?"

"We had a good time. I kept thinking about how Dr. Chandler wants us to become physically comfortable with a girl, so about halfway through the movie, I put my arm across her shoulders."

"And how did she react?"

"She snuggled in close to me. It felt good, so last Saturday night we went to a church dance together. I don't dance very good, but she didn't seem to mind. Afterwards, when we got to her house, she let me kiss her. Maybe Dr. Chandler is right. All I have to do is experiment a bit to get in touch with my heterosexual feelings."

Everyone seemed okay with this until Ronnie asked, "Does she know that you're experimenting? Do you plan to tell her that you're a homosexual using her as an experiment?"

"I'm not just using her as an experiment," he protested. "Maybe I really like her."

"Would you be with her if Dr. Chandler hadn't recommended it?"

"Well, no but…"

Brother Stewart immediately interrupted. While clearly annoyed that Ronnie had deviated from the unwritten list of acceptable questions, he seemed to relish the possibility of putting Ronnie in his place. Speaking rapidly with his voice rising to what was probably its natural pitch, he asked, "Ronnie, isn't dating always an experiment? Two people trying to find out if they're compatible and maybe, if things work out, they can join their lives together in eternal marriage, in a marriage accepted by God? In some sense, every date is an experiment."

"It's not the same thing. If a heterosexual guy asks a heterosexual girl out on a date, and she accepts, we can assume that they are already attracted to each other. They just need to find out if they like each other in other ways."

With even more stridency in his voice, Brother Stewart responded, "Ronnie, you seem to think that there is such a thing as a homosexual. No one is a homosexual because God would not make a homosexual. Now some people experience homosexual attractions, but these are temptations to be resisted, just like we resist smoking or drinking alcohol."

"Smoking and drinking are different. No one would want to smoke or drink without first being exposed to tobacco or alcohol. But how many of us have 'homosexual tendencies' (he placed air quotation marks around the term) without ever having been exposed to a homosexual? I was attracted to guys long before I knew anyone else was like me. You can't say the same thing about tobacco and alcohol."

While Ronnie was talking, one of the boys, a heavy kid with a red face, was getting increasingly agitated. He suddenly stood up and almost shouted, "Ronnie, stop arguing. When we prayed at the beginning of the meeting, we asked the Spirit of the Lord to be with us.

179

But because of your negative attitude, you chased God right out of the room, and I can't feel the Spirit anymore."

Silence fell on the room, although several guys seemed to nod in agreement. Brother Stewart lifted his eyes toward the ceiling as though seeking divine guidance. Then, looking directly at Ronnie, he intoned in his low manly voice, "Ralph is right. The Spirit of the Lord cannot abide where there is a spirit of discord. Ronnie, I think you owe an apology to the group."

Clearly embarrassed, Ronnie squirmed a bit but finally muttered, "Okay, I'm sorry people got upset. I'll keep my mouth shut next time."

"No one is asking you to keep your mouth shut, Ronnie. It's just that you need to learn to help and not hurt." Fixated mostly on Ronnie, he assured us that he knew of many happy marriages in which a devout Mormon girl had helped a boy with "sexual identity issues" to become a happy heterosexual in a marriage blessed by God. I wondered if Brother Stewart might be in one of those happy marriages. I also remembered what Lucy suffered because Gabe used her as an experiment. Evening prayer followed the group meeting. Of course, all I could think about was Ronnie's promise to sneak us out of the building later that night.

Chapter Five: Ronnie's Story

I returned to my room, turned out the lights at 10:30, but did not undress. A few minutes later, I heard a light knock on the door. Ronnie was waiting for me in the hall. Sanders beckoned us to one of the emergency exit doors and let us out into the night. Ronnie explained that Sanders had disarmed the alarm so that we could get back in the same way.

"Where are we going?" I asked.

"I know a place. My dad belongs to a country club near here, and I know how to sneak into the golf course. Don't worry. Nobody's there this time of night."

We walked a few blocks through a fancy neighborhood and eventually came to a fence surrounding a golf course. Ronnie showed me where to crawl under the fence, and we soon found ourselves on one of the fairways. The night was warm, and a full moon illuminated the grassy stretch ahead of us. Finally, yielding to the electricity between us, Ronnie took my hand, and we interlaced our fingers in a tight grip. He led me to a grassy patch in the middle of a small clump of trees. After staring at each other for a moment without speaking, he pulled me towards him in a full embrace. I loved the feel of his hard, compact body and the way his erection was pressing against mine. "Wow!" I thought. "If this is only my second night at Croft House, I might come to like this place."

I placed my hand on his erection, but he gently pushed it away, saying, "Don't be in such a hurry. There's more to me than my cock. Let's pretend that we're blind and that we can get to know each other only through touching."

With closed eyes, I concentrated on the faint musk and feel of his body, the gentle curve of his shoulder muscles as they connected to his well-defined biceps, the soft hair on his forearms, the indentation where his back muscles joined at his spine, the gentle swell of his ass at the base of his back. I ran my hands through his hair, and touched his ears, his eyebrows, his lips, and the stubble on his chin. I pushed my hand up under his t-shirt and felt the beginnings of a nice patch of chest hair. And I loved feeling his hands explore my own body with the same tender intensity. I kissed him lightly on the mouth. He responded with a sensual deep kiss that I gladly prolonged. We began undressing each other and slowly sank to the grass. Ronnie's body was more compact than I was used to, but it was perfectly shaped, from his impeccable chest to his beautiful symmetrical cock. For a fleeting moment, I realized that this was the first time I had ever had real sex with a guy my own age. With utter abandon, we kissed, we went down on each other, and we licked each other's ears, nipples and armpits, relishing the feel and the aroma of each other's body. When the tension became too great, we brought each other off in a powerful climax that left us both breathless. We then lay on the grass, legs and arms intertwined, and began to talk. "Okay," I said. "I told you about my life this afternoon when we ran back to Croft House. Tell me about yours. When did you figure out that you were gay?"

"I'm not sure. It was sort of gradual. In the eighth or ninth grade, I started noticing guys sexually and having wet dreams about them. It soon became clear that I was gay, especially since I had zero sexual interest in girls."

"When did you first have sex?"

"It was with the Filipino guy who gardened for my grandparents. I was like fourteen. I'm not sure how old he was. He was very handsome, and we got it on several times."

"Did you ever get caught?"

"Yeah, my grandfather caught us with our pants down in the pool house and told my dad. So, my dad sent me to a shrink, a Dr. Adler. But he chose the wrong shrink since Adler thought that gay was okay and that I should learn to like who I am. Totally different from Chandler."

"So how did you end up at Croft House?"

"Okay, there's a pre-history here. My parents were career lawyers and didn't get married until their late

183

thirties. Mother was nearly forty when I was born. She died when I was five of some weird kind of cancer. I don't remember her very well. I just remember her being really nice." Then with a note of sadness, "I envy kids who have real mothers."

I could have noted that real mothers can be histrionic, drug-addled, and crazy-religious, but I preferred to hear the rest of his story. "What happened after she died?"

"About a year later, my father married this devil-bitch from Hell, someone he met at church. My dad has made millions of dollars in commercial real estate development, so a lot of women were after him, especially Mormon women frantic to find a man to take them to the Celestial Kingdom. He's also good-looking for an old guy. He dresses well and stays in shape. The devil-bitch was sticky-sweet nice while they were courting, but once they got married, she turned into the meanest thing that ever drew a breath. She hated my guts and took every opportunity to show it. When my dad came home earlier than usual one afternoon and found me locked in a closet being punished for God knows what, he sent me to live with his parents, Daddy Jake and Mama Claire. That's what I called them since they didn't like being grandpa and grandma.

"In the meantime, the devil-bitch popped out three kids, all boys, and did her best to keep me away from them. For some stupid reason, she saw me as competition, maybe because my mother had been a successful lawyer, and she was only good at having babies and being a world-class asshole. My father visited me regularly and sometimes brought me to this very club to swim and play tennis. He feels guilty about pawning me off on his parents and tries to make up for it by giving me nice presents and plenty of money. But I don't know my half-brothers, which is fine with me if they take after their mother."

"That still doesn't tell me how you got to Croft House."

"Daddy Jake died very unexpectedly of a heart attack when I was fifteen years old. About the same time, Mama Claire started having memory problems, like she'd get lost in her own house. Before she got really bad, she taught me how to pay the bills and supervise the house cleaners and the gardener. I got good at forging her signature. I hid her condition because I did not want to live with my dad and the devil-bitch. Taking care of an old woman who is slowly losing her mind wasn't a picnic, but I kept up the charade until the summer before my junior year. Then, one day she wandered naked down to a shopping mall, making it obvious that she had gone bonkers. She's in a home now and doesn't recognize anyone. It's really depressing to visit her."

"So, did you go live with your father and the devil-bitch?"

"Well, that story also got more interesting. Just after Daddy Jacob died, my dad started shagging his secretary. The devil-bitch found out, divorced him, and got him excommunicated for adultery. She's probably soaking him for lots of alimony and child support. She also got the house and the Mercedes, but he's still far from poor. By the way, the devil-bitch lives in this neighborhood."

"Goodie, goodie," I enthused. "Let's go visit her!"

"Only if you have a silver stake to drive through her heart. Anyway, my dad met another woman at church, a total bimbo who coaxed him back into the church. He probably went through some sort of repentance routine to be reinstated. Since the LDS church likes rich guys and repentant sinners, they made it easy for him to return. He bought a house in Scottsdale, so I went to live with them after Mama Claire went crazy. By then, they already had a baby. Dad made the mistake of telling his wife about me and the gardener, which totally freaked her out. She started nagging him to send me to a Mormon shrink. My dad wasn't big on the idea. But when the bimbo caught me trading blowjobs with a neighbor boy, she threw a fit. That's when my dad took me to Croft House, which was only last week. So, now you know the story of my life."

"Did you always go to church?"

"Yeah. I did the whole thing—Boy Scouts, Aaronic priesthood, MIA, you name it."

"Did they lecture you about being morally clean?"

"Of course. Thanks to them my body is unsullied by the touch of woman." He looked at his watch. "We need to get back."

"Why? It's not that late."

"No, but 6:30 is that early."

As we walked back to the fence, I grabbed his hand, and we laced our fingers tightly together. I was suddenly overcome with that same intense sense of gratitude that I had felt in the hotel room after meeting Mother Harold. No guilt. No shame. Just a profound thankfulness for having found a friend like me. As we approached the emergency exit that Sanders had left unarmed, Ronnie pulled me behind a tree, gave me a big wet kiss and whispered in my ear, "Let's do this again."

Chapter Six:
Tuesday at Croft House

He was right. 6:30 came awfully early, and I felt mildly sleep-deprived. But I regretted nothing about the night before and fantasized that some of Ronnie's smell was still on my body. As I expected (forgive the lack of modesty), I had aced the diagnostic tests, so much of the morning was spent planning a course of study. A retired English teacher, Sister Sonderreger said that she wasn't going to waste time following the state curriculum for high school juniors. She asked what I was reading and was delighted to learn that I was just finishing *The Brothers Karamazov*. With a slight smile that was both kind and mischievous, she said, "Now that I know you can take tests, let's see if you can write an essay. Could you write a short paper on whether Dostoyevsky believed in God, based on evidence in the novel?" After seeing my test scores, Brother Sonderreger suggested that I take the high school graduate equivalency exam and consider skipping my senior year altogether.

At noon, my father called to say that he would pick me up the following Friday evening to take me back to Rosales for the weekend. I dreaded going back, but I needed to empty my high school locker and get some clean clothes. I also missed my piano. Towards the end of the PE hour, Coach Charlie again gave Ronnie and me permission to run back to Croft House. Our conversation began awkwardly. Finally, I ventured, "Last night was quite something."

"That it was."

"Something quite nice, I meant to say."

"And I would agree. By the way, I told you stuff last night that I've never told anyone else."

"Like what?"

"Like my father's adulterous life and his attraction to horrible women, my mother excepted. I also told you about having sex with the gardener and then getting caught blowing my neighbor only three weeks ago. You mentioned the two guys who got you in trouble, but I know that wasn't the first time you had sex."

"How do you know that?" I asked coyly.

"Because you're a good kisser and you give great head. That comes with practice."

"You're not bad yourself."

"Okay. Cut the crap. Tell me about all the guys you've had sex with."

"Actually, I've sort of lost count."

"Smart ass. Stop bragging and start talking."

I told him about the Boy Scout circle jerks, which thoroughly amazed him since nothing like that happened in his high school much less in his Mormon Boy Scout troop. I then gave a brief account of Harold and Father Tovar. He was terribly impressed that I had had a thing with a Catholic priest. I wanted to tell him that my relationship with Father Tovar included much more than sex, but somehow, I couldn't find the words. How could I explain that we had managed to combine great sex with moving discussions about religion? I also told him about visits to the truck stop and was not surprised that he had had similar experiences in bathrooms at shopping malls and public parks. We reached Croft House, just as the van drove up.

"Can we see each other again tonight?" I asked.

"Of course. Same arrangement. I already paid Sanders to let us out."

After dinner, I had my first individual session with Dr. Chandler. Greeting me with that same two-handed handshake, he said "Hello, Josh. Please have a seat." This time we sat in the overstuffed chairs facing each other. "How are things going? Is the food okay? How do you like your tutors? Isn't Coach Charlie the greatest? Can you believe he's over seventy years old?"

I mumbled something that sounded affirmative to which he responded, "Josh, it's time to get down to business. Now, why do you think you're here?"

"Because my father brought me."

Toothy smile. "He can do that because you are underage. But the real question is why does your father want you to be here?"

"Because he doesn't want me to be a homosexual."

"Do you think you're a homosexual?"

"I find men attractive and suspect that I might be a homosexual."

After a long silence, a pained frown, and a bit of staring at the ceiling, he said, "Josh, you know, there is really no such thing as a homosexual. Some people feel same-sex attractions and sometimes commit homosexual acts, but that doesn't mean that they are homosexuals. Homosexual is an adjective, not a noun. So, we speak of homosexual behavior or homosexual acts, but there is really no such thing as a homosexual."

Thinking about Ronnie's comments in the previous evening's group meetings, I asked, "Does that mean there's no such thing as a heterosexual? Just heterosexual acts?"

Smiling, he leaned forward, and gave me a friendly slap on the knee as though we were great buddies. "That is a very intelligent question. You just confirmed what I already suspected. You are a very bright young man. Josh, the word homosexual is a relatively new term. In fact, the word heterosexual was invented a little later to give us a way of contrasting one with the other. But that is the language of science. We also have the language of scripture. In his Epistle to the Romans, St. Paul clearly condemns men who leave, as he puts it, "the natural use of the woman, burning in their lust one toward another." Leviticus also offers clear condemnations of homosexual behavior. Then, there is the story of Sodom and Gomorrah. Do you know the story of Sodom and Gomorrah?"

"The one where Lot's wife gets turned into a pillar of salt?"

Smile. "That very one. You have no idea how many people can't answer that question. You can be proud of yourself for knowing the answer. Do you know what happened just before then?"

"Sort of. A couple of angels came to Lot's house and told him that he'd better leave because God was going to destroy the city."

"Two cities, actually. Sodom and Gomorrah. Do you recall what the men of Sodom wanted?"

"No."

"They wanted him to bring the angels out so they could 'know' them. This passage of scripture has many interpretations, but one interpretation holds that the men of Sodom wanted to know them in the Biblical sense."

"Like they wanted to have sex with them? Can you have sex with an angel?"

"That's not the point. The point is that Sodom and Gomorrah were very wicked cities, and it is generally agreed that one of their sins was homosexual behavior. This gave us two of our first terms for men who have sex with other men: sodomy and sodomite."

"Does that mean I'm a sodomite?"

Smile. Shaking of head. "No, but it does mean that the sin of homosexual behavior is a lot older than the word homosexual. And whatever its name, scripture teaches us that it has always been a sin. Our modern-day prophets have reaffirmed this, that homosexual behavior is a grievous offense to God because it perverts the gift that God gave us for creating life. My goal here is to give you the tools of modern psychology to help you control thoughts that might lead you to sin and to the unhappiness that sin causes. I would remind you of the verse in the *Book of Mormon* where the prophet Alma says to his son, 'Wickedness never was happiness.'"

I had no response to any of this. I briefly thought of my wonderful sex with Ronnie the night before. Was that sodomy? Were we sodomites? If wickedness never was happiness, how come I felt so wonderful with Harold, Father Tovar, and Ronnie? Had we really offended God? Did God really give a shit about such things? Doesn't he have worlds without end to worry about?

Observing my silence, Chandler asked in a soft voice. "Josh, tell me about your sexual experiences. Have you ever had sex with another boy or maybe even a grown man?"

No way was I was going to tell him about Harold or Father Tovar, much less the truck-stop guys, so I simply answered that I had masturbated with some of my classmates.

Knowing smile and understanding nod. "That's quite common. Adolescent boys often compare themselves to each other, but then they grow out of it. Have you masturbated since arriving here?"

"No," I lied, not wanting to hint at the marvelous experience of the previous night with Ronnie.

"Good. You realize, of course, that sin of any sort, including masturbation, alienates the spirit. We cannot expect God to help us if we do things that drive Him away from us. How about the boy who beat you up? Did you masturbate with him?"

"He wanted me to do something that I didn't want to do. When I refused, he attacked me."

"What did he want you to do?"

When I didn't answer, he said, "Josh you can use whatever language you want here. I study sexual behavior and I know all the words. So, if you want to say fuck, blowjob, jerk off, or whatever, go right ahead. Our goal is to get to the truth no matter what it takes."

"Okay. He wanted me to give him a blowjob."

"Why did he think you might give him a blowjob?"

"One of his friends once forced me to suck his dick."

"Forced you? You didn't want to?"

"Okay, I sort of wanted to, but it turned out to be a horrible experience."

"Where did this happen?"

"In the bathroom at the school gym. We were alone."

"Why was it a horrible experience?"

"Because he crammed his dick in my mouth and was really rough with me."

After a long pause, Chandler asked, "Do you want to tell me any more about it?"

"There's nothing else to tell."

He stared at the ceiling, frowned, and then looked at me very intently. "Josh," he said, "as someone trying to live the Lord's commandments, I am not only concerned about your mental health but also about your spiritual welfare. I therefore have to ask you if you've committed any sins that might require Church involvement."

"What does church involvement mean?"

"When you talk to me, you're talking to a therapist. But some of your activities may require confession to the appropriate church authority."

"Like what sorts of activities?"

"Have you ever penetrated another man? Or been penetrated by another man?"

"Penetrated?"

"Fucked. Stuck your dick up another guy's ass or had a guy stick his dick up your ass. Anal intercourse."

Chandler had warned me that he could use terms like these, but I was stunned by the vehemence with which he said them.

"No," I said. "I've never done any of those things." Of course, I was lying. I had fucked Harold numerous times, and Father Tovar and I had taken turns topping and bottoming for each other. I had also "penetrated" guys at the truck stop and at Mike's party. But I chose not to tell Chandler about those experiences because I didn't want him siccing church authorities on me. So, I asked, "Why does fucking make a difference?"

"Because anal intercourse between men is so heinous that forgiveness is possible only through confessing to church authorities and submitting to a program of repentance and rehabilitation."

"What does rehabilitation include?"

"It depends on the case. Usually for a first offender, it means being disfellowshipped for a short period of time during which the sinner receives spiritual guidance from his priesthood leaders but cannot participate in Church activities. For more serious cases, especially for people who return to their sin after supposedly repenting, it might mean excommunication. The Church's goal, of course, is not to punish sinners but to assist them in their journey towards forgiveness through sincere repentance. Church disciplinary councils truly are courts of love. It is because God loves you that his church marks out a path to obtain forgiveness." Pause. "Now are you sure you have never done any of those things?"

"No," I lied for the second time.

"No what?" he probed.

"No. I've never done those things".

Long pause with a frown because he probably knew that I was lying. Change of tactic.

"Josh, do you believe that the Church of Jesus Christ of Latter-day Saints is the only true church, Christ's own church restored through the prophet Joseph Smith?"

Choosing honesty, I replied, "Sometimes I have doubts."

"Those doubts may be a consequence of sin. The apostle Paul in First Corinthians tells us that the spirit of God cannot dwell in an unclean temple. So, if you have sinned, the spirit may withdraw from you, and that could be the source of your doubts."

He again peered into my eyes for what seemed a very long time. He clearly didn't believe me and was hoping I would say more. After a long, uncomfortable silence, he moved in a new direction. "Josh, how much contact have you had with girls?"

"My best friend is a girl."

"Do you find her sexually attractive?"

"No. She's just a friend."

"Have you had much physical contact with girls?

"I've made out with some girls."

"Did you enjoy it?"

"It was okay."

"Did you get an erection?"

"Sometimes." Which was true. But I got erections all the time, so they didn't mean anything. In fact, I always carried a book around to hide that involuntary bulge in my pants whenever it occurred.

"Josh, do you want to lead a normal life, a good Mormon life with a loving wife and children?"

"Is that what you want?"

"What I want doesn't matter. What you want and what God wants are all that count. Now I can help you overcome your homosexual attractions and teach you to enjoy sex with your wife. Homosexual feelings are sort of like diabetes. They may never go away entirely, but you can learn to channel your sexual feelings in healthy directions. But I need to count on you to work with me and to be honest with me. Are you willing to give it a try?"

I said "yes" because "no" was clearly not an option.

"Good boy. Our time is up, but you and I will meet again on Thursday. Next week, we will start you on some exercises to help channel your desires in healthy ways. Does that sound okay?"

I nodded yes and stood to leave his office. On my way out, he gave me a manly one-armed hug. I did not like being touched by this man.

Chapter Seven:
Tuesday Night with Ronnie

During evening prayer, all I could think about was sneaking out again with Ronnie, Chandler's admonitions notwithstanding. Promptly at 10:35, I heard Ronnie's light knock. Sanders let us out and we walked back to the golf course. When we got to the trees, we immediately embraced—a full body hug that lasted several minutes. No way can I describe how good he felt. His solid, compact body, his deep kisses, and the sheer joy of his touch. I started to unbutton his shirt but, placing his hand on mine, he said, "Could we hold off on the sex? I just want to talk for a while."

We lay down, his head resting on my chest. "Okay," I said. "What do you want to talk about?"

After a few silent moments, he asked, "Do you really think the Mormon church is the only true church and that God wants what Dr. Chandler wants?"

"I'm not sure," I replied. Before I could tell him how the beautiful, naked Father Tovar had almost made me a Catholic, he said, "I'm pretty sure that Mormonism is not what it claims to be. You've got to admit that all that stuff about the Angel Moroni and the gold plates sounds farfetched. Have you ever read the *Book of Mormon?* "

"I never made it past the first fifty pages," I answered. "I got tired of all the 'beholds' and 'it came to passes.' Then I got to the bit about how the small plates of Nephi just happened to show up to replace the pages of the translation that Martin Harris managed to lose, and it was just too convenient."

Ronnie responded, "My big problem with the *Book of Mormon* are the characters. They don't seem real. The good people are really, really good, and the bad people are really, really bad. And if they're good, they are white and delightsome. And if they're bad, they're loathsome and cursed with a dark skin. But if the dark-skinned people repent, they become white and delightsome, and if the white and delightsome people become sinful, they turn dark and loathsome. So, it's easy to keep track of who's good and who's bad because they're color-coded. Nephi, Alma, and Mormon— they just don't seem real. Compare them with some of the people in the Bible.

"Take David for example. He all but seduces a king with his singing and harp playing, then the king gets mad at him, so he runs to the arms of his friend Jonathan. They hug and kiss until David comes in his pants. It's too bad that David didn't shack up with Jonathan for the rest of his life because later he gets the hots for Bathsheba, gets her pregnant, and then does everything he can to get her husband to come home and fuck her so that no one will suspect that David is the father of her baby. But the dullard of her husband refuses to sleep with her since he wants to rejoin the troops, so David sends him to the front lines where he is sure to be killed. Then, David's son Absalom rebels against his father and gets killed, and David ends up being a broken and sad man. Now that's someone I can believe is real."

"Where does it say that David came in his pants?" I asked.

"Pervert! I knew you'd like that part," he said with a grin. "It's there. I'll give you chapter and verse tomorrow. But getting back to the subject at hand, the *Book of Mormon* is filled with unbelievable characters, and that's why I think it's a fraud. It's not about real people."

"Do you think that Joseph Smith made the whole thing up?"

"He must have. Which is not to say that he wasn't a clever guy with a great imagination. It just means that it's not a history of real people translated from gold plates that he got from an angel. And it's kind of suspicious that he gave the plates back to the angel, leaving no physical evidence."

"You've thought a lot about this, haven't you?"

"Of course I have, and so should you. Chandler is trying to tell us that homosexuals don't exist because God wouldn't create a homosexual. But that's Mormon bullshit."

"How about the Harvard degree?"

"Harvard didn't teach Chandler that homosexuality is sinful. He gets that from Mormonism. Besides, my previous shrink came from a fancy school, and he said that there's nothing wrong with being gay. If you're gay, you're gay, and you'd better learn to like yourself and live with it.'"

I was impressed. I had never shared my growing doubts about Mormonism with anyone before, nor had I ever met anyone like Ronnie. He was smart, and he certainly knew how to make an argument. "All that stuff about the *Book of Mormon* and King David was really impressive" I said. "Did you think it all up by yourself?"

He grinned and whispered in my ear, "Okay. I'm a fraud. A lot of it came from Mama Claire."

"Your grandmother!? But I thought she was a good Mormon."

"Actually, she didn't believe any of it. She went through the motions to keep Daddy Jacob happy, but she picked and chose what she would do for the church. She was always the first to take food to people with a death in the family or to visit sick people. But she kept instant coffee hidden in the cupboard and had her cup of java every afternoon—her symbolic rebellion."

"Why did she tell you all this?"

"Probably because she needed to tell someone. After Daddy Jacob caught me with the gardener, she said, 'Ronnie, don't be like me and spend your life pretending to be someone you're not.' I sometimes wonder if she didn't go crazy on purpose. She was tired of living a lie."

"But we can't be honest with people. Look how I got beat up for giving a blowjob to one guy and refusing to give one to his shithead friend. People hate us. I can't march around saying, 'Hi, I'm Josh and I'm a homosexual.' I wouldn't last two days, least of all in Rosales.

"Being honest doesn't mean telling everyone that you're gay. But we can be honest with ourselves and with each other." With a naughty grin on his face, he pulled me towards him and added, "Like maybe right now."

We started to make out. Two seventeen-year-old Mormon boys in the middle of a Phoenix golf course, lying on the grass and getting lost in the feel and smell of each other's bodies. Just like David and Jonathan several millennia before. Or maybe like Jacob Berkowitz and Blair Huxley who had loved each other so intensely during World War II. As I went down on Ronnie, I imagined myself being David's Jonathan, or Blair's Jacob. And I felt a peculiar oneness with gay people everywhere who like Ronnie and me had discovered the beauty of men loving men.

Chapter Eight: Wednesday

The next morning, I began scouring *The Brothers Karamazov* to figure out what Dostoyevsky thought about God. I quickly realized that Sister Sonderegger, clever old girl that she was, had given me an impossible assignment because so much of the novel consists of conversations about God, about moral behavior, and about whether there can be moral standards without God or the possibility of divine judgment. Figuring out Dostoyevsky's position was all but impossible because he hid behind his characters. So, that's what I wrote about—how novelists create fictional characters to hide their real feelings. I gave it to her just before lunch.

"Are you done already?" she asked with genuine surprise.

"Well, sort of. I'll be glad to revise it if you want."

"Let's talk tomorrow. I need time to read it."

After lunch, Ronnie slipped me a note with a scriptural reference on it: 1 Samuel 20:41. Immediately after getting back to my room to dress for PE, I looked it up:

"*And* as soon as the lad was gone, David arose out of a *place* toward the south, and fell on his face to the ground, and bowed himself three times: and they kissed one another, and wept one with another, until David exceeded."

Ronnie evidently thought that "exceeded" meant that David came in his pants, or his robe, or whatever Israelite boys of his time wore. While running back to Croft House from PE, I asked Ronnie, "Do you really think that David's 'exceeding' means that he came in his pants?"

He grinned. "No, but it's the interpretation that I like. I asked the Hebrew teacher at my high school what it meant. He said that in Hebrew it was something like he grew large with emotion, or that he was overcome. Sounds like an orgasm to me, wouldn't you say?"

"Of course. What else could it be?" I replied in mock agreement.

"Well, now that we've gotten that out of the way, tell me about what you did in high school and in Rosales, that is, when you weren't beating off with the Boy Scouts."

"You're just jealous."

"Yeah, I'm jealous, but I'm also sure that circle jerking wasn't the only thing you did."

I told him about playing the piano, studying the organ, and singing in all-state choir.

"What kind of music do you play?"

"Just classical. Bach is my favorite, but I know pieces by other composers. And I've done a lot of accompanying. I accompanied our community *Messiah* last Christmas."

"Really? That shit's hard. My high school choir sang some choruses from the *Messiah*. We had to bring in an accompanist from the community, so you must be pretty good."

"I'm okay when I practice."

"Will you play for me sometime?"

"Sure, but you'll have to find a piano."

Enigmatically, "Let me think about it. By the way, do you know why I don't mind being gay?"

"Because guys are gorgeous?"

"That's part of it of course. If God had wanted me to be straight, he wouldn't have made men beautiful. But another reason is that I don't like most straight guys. I don't want to be like them."

"What do you mean?"

"Think of the straight guys you know. Most of them are slobs. They are always the loudest, they want to have the last word on everything, and they think that the highest form of humor is hearing someone fart. It only gets worse when they're older. You should meet the pathetic guys who hang out with my dad. Everything is about who has the biggest car, who has the prettiest wife, who makes the most money, who has the last word, and probably who has the biggest dick."

"Now you're not saying that they get together and compare dicks, are you?"

"They sure do! Watch straight guys in the shower rooms. They're always checking out each other's equipment. Dr. Chandler rattles on and on about how heterosexuals are so happy but think about it. How many happy heterosexuals do you know?"

It was a good question. I thought of Ronnie's father now in his third marriage as the result of an adulterous affair and a divorce from Wife Number Two. I thought about the devil-bitch who had forced Ronnie to live with his grandparents. I thought about my father's two younger half-brothers, both in their second marriages with messed-up kids from both marriages. I thought about my mother's parents, divorced partly because of my grandfather's alcoholism. I thought about one of my mother's brothers, now married to his second wife, with whom he fought constantly. I thought about my piano teacher, the magnificent Mrs. Jespersen, who was widowed when her husband died in a car wreck while returning from a tryst with his mistress. I thought about Mrs. Bumstead and her three sons by three different men who were not her husband. I thought about Mrs. Perkins, mother of the wonderful Lucy, who had been seduced by a horny, itinerant doctor. I thought about AMPS, his fat wife and his two ugly children, not to mention the time he tried to rape me. I thought about my own parents. Looking from the outside in, most people would think they had a good marriage. But the inside story was more complicated. While my parents clearly loved each other, my father worried a lot about my mother's pill addiction. Other people? Maybe Principal Barnes and his wife Alma, my favorite Sunday-School teacher? Maybe the Sondereggers?

I compared these heterosexual couples to the few gay men I had met. Sweet, funny, effeminate Harold; beautiful Father Tovar and his faith in God; Blair with his gentle caresses as he remembered his wartime lover; and now my intense new friendship with Ronnie. So, Ronnie had asked a good question. Just where was all the heterosexual bliss that Dr. Chandler kept yapping about? As we ran into the Croft House parking lot, I said, "You know, I can think of only a few happy heterosexuals."

"And you can't be sure about them. That's one more reason to not believe Chandler's bullshit."

Chapter Nine:
Second Group Meeting

At the group meeting after dinner, Brother Stewart seemed more uptight than usual. I wondered if he was still mad at Ronnie. Like the night before, he began with a prayer, but this time he added, "And let there be no more spirit of discord among us, lest we offend thy Spirit. Let thy light of truth shine on us so that we may no more be deceived by the Evil One." Clearly, the prayer was directed more towards Ronnie than towards God. The prayer was not, however, a great way to start a discussion. A couple of guys bravely stepped forward, talking about their conversations with girls and their intentions to ask them out on a date, but after a few minutes a general silence fell on the group. Finally, Brother Stewart started to talk.

"In our last meeting, a spirit of contention entered our discussion, and I feel that we lost some ground. So, let's get back to basics. Why are we here?"

Knowing that he was the cause of the contention, Ronnie kept his eyes glued to the floor. After a long silence, Spencer, the guy with the experimental girlfriend, responded almost robot-like, "So we can learn to control our tendencies towards sin and live a righteous life."

"And why does God want us to live a righteous life? Is it just a matter of what God wants?"

Silence.

"What does the *Book of Mormon* teach us?" Pause as he looked around the room. "I know that you all know the verse I have in mind, so let me start you out. 'Adam fell that man might be; man is…'"

Philip, a pimply little guy who up to that point hadn't said anything, completed the verse: "Adam fell that man might be; man is that he might have joy."

"Joy!" exclaimed Brother Stewart. "Not happiness, not pleasure, not good times, but joy. Joy! We were created to have joy. Now let's go back to my first question. Why are we here? And when I say 'here' I'm not just talking about Croft House. I'm talking about 'Why are we here on earth?'"

"To find joy?" ventured Phillip.

"Right, Phillip. Exactly right. And what is the path to joy?"

Silence.

"Okay," continued Brother Stewart, "Let's start off with another verse of scripture that I'm sure some of you memorized in Sunday School. 'There is a law, irrevocably decreed in heaven…'"

Phillip again completed the verse: "There is a law, irrevocably decreed in heaven before the foundations of this world, upon which all blessings are predicated—And when we obtain any blessing from God, it is by obedience to that law upon which it is predicated."

Switching on his smile, Brother Stewart said, "Phillip, I can see that you have received a good religious education. Can you tell me where these scriptural citations come from?"

"The one about joy is in the *Book of Mormon*. I think the second one comes from one of Joseph Smith's revelations in the *Doctrine and Covenants*. I can't give you chapter and verse."

"Chapter and verse don't matter. What does matter is that we understand three basic principles. First, that wickedness never was happiness, as Alma tells us in the *Book of Mormon*. Second, that man is that he might have joy. And third, that to receive the blessings of God we need to obey the laws on which those blessings are predicated. There is no other way."

Then raising the pitch of his voice and speaking with increasing intensity, he continued, "So if someone tells you that God made homosexuals, that person is a liar and an agent of Satan. And if someone tells you that homosexual behavior is normal and can lead to joy, that person is a liar and an agent of Satan. And if someone tells you that you can receive God's blessings without obeying God's commandments, that person is also a liar and an agent of Satan. They've lied to me, and they've lied to you." Then, looking directly at

Ronnie, he added, "And in our last session, some of those lies crept into our discussion."

This attack on Ronnie stunned us into silence. Ronnie, however, did not remain silent for long. "Brother Stewart," he asked. "Are you married? To a woman, I mean?"

Touching his large wedding ring with his right hand, Stewart retorted, "Of course I'm married to a woman. What a stupid question. Men don't marry men."

"Did you have homosexual tendencies, learn to control them through Dr. Chandler's program, start experimenting with a woman, and then finally get married?"

Brother Stewart turned bright red. Swallowing hard, he managed to stammer out, "We're not here to talk about me. We're here to talk about you."

"Yeah, but it would help if you could be our role model, someone who once had homosexual tendencies, overcame them, and is now living a heterosexual Mormon life filled with joy. Is your life joyful? Or are you still experimenting, like, you know, is your marriage just another experiment?"

Turning bright red, Stewart snapped, "Do you have any idea how insulting your question is? How dare you suggest that my marriage is an experiment? My wife and I are very happy. We're even expecting a child. You have no right to question our marriage."

"Yet it was alright for you to suggest that I brought lies into this discussion and am somehow an agent of Satan. Why was that okay?"

Through clenched teeth, Brother Stewart replied, "Ronnie, I think you should go to your room. But before you leave, you should know that I am very happy with my wife and very thankful that God has saved me from a fate worse than death. Now leave."

Ronnie noisily pushed his chair aside, and slowly stood up. But before leaving, he said, "Okay, I'll leave. But if you are a homosexual pretending to be something else, we have right to know. And so does your wife."

Ronnie slowly exited the room with Stewart's eyes following him all the way, eyes filled with a mixture of hatred and (dared I think it?) desire. Once Ronnie closed the door, Brother Stewart uttered in his low sanctimonious voice, "Brothers in the priesthood, we have just seen an example of why homosexuality is so evil. Its goal is to attack and destroy. To make a nice person an instrument of evil. I think it's time to end this meeting with a prayer. And in our hearts, let us all pray for Ronnie." In a low and somewhat tearful voice, he prayed:

"Dear Heavenly Father. We bow our heads to thank thee that this night some of us have glimpsed a great truth—the truth that through obedience to thy commandments we can be heirs to the joy that thou hast promised us. Empower us with thy spirit so we can pursue a path of righteousness. And grant us a spirit of discernment to recognize the snares of the Evil One and resist his agents who tell us that evil is good, that abnormal is normal, and that we are unable to escape the bondage of sin and evil desires. Stay particularly with thy son and our brother Ronnie. Bless him with a spirit of love and openness to truth so that he may humble himself and appreciate those who want to help him. In Jesus' name. Amen."

At the end of the prayer, Brother Stewart's eyes were wet with tears. We left the room silently, the lucky ones to go home, and those of us residing at Croft House to face another scripture reading and prayer. I could hardly wait to tell Ronnie how proud of him I was.

Chapter Ten:
Wednesday Evening

Just after 10:30, Ronnie tapped on my door. As we left the building, I eagerly (joyfully?) squeezed Ronnie's hand. "How are you doing? That was quite an argument you had with Brother Stewart. And you were FABULOUS! I think half the guys there wanted to stand up and applaud."

"Yeah, and the other half wanted to kill me. It wasn't a real argument. It was him telling us a bunch of shit that he probably doesn't believe himself. Talk about a gay boy trying to be what he's not."

"You think he's gay?"

"Does the pope wear a beanie? Everything about him screams gay. And have you noticed how he is constantly checking you and me out. Tonight, I was sitting right across from him. Whenever I spread my legs, his eyes went straight to my crotch. So yes, he's a total gay boy and a total hypocrite. If he's what you become after Dr. Chandler finishes with you, I don't want any part of it."

"And think of his poor wife."

"Actually, I would prefer not to think about either of them. By the way, we're going to a different place tonight. I hope you don't mind." We walked down the hill away from the golf course. After several blocks we came to a Mormon meeting house.

"Why are we here? Haven't you had enough church for one evening?" I asked.

"Just wait."

A large A-frame structure, the building was outlined by concrete beams that peaked at the top. Ronnie slipped his hand under the base of one of the beams and gleefully extracted a key. "It was here ten years ago, and it's still here. I just found a piano for you to play."

Within minutes we were in the chapel where there was a small Knabe grand piano in the choir loft behind the pulpit. Ronnie ceremoniously raised the top of the piano to full-stick and with theatrical imperiousness said, "Play."

"What do you want to hear?"

"Something beautiful."

So, I played, starting with Brahms' Intermezzo in A-major from Opus 118. Ronnie sat very quietly in a pew beside the piano. When I finished, he said in a hushed voice, "That was really beautiful. Please play something else."

So, I continued to play and ended with the gigue from Bach's first partita. I glanced at Ronnie several times to make sure he wasn't bored. He appeared entirely absorbed in the music. After the last note of the partita, I pivoted on the piano bench to face him.

"You had enough?" I asked.

"Enough for now, maybe. But never enough. You play beautifully."

Feeling myself blush, I mumbled something about how the real geniuses were the composers.

"Of course," he said. "But they're not here to play for me, and you are." He then placed his hands under my arms, raised me to my feet, and pulled me towards him. We held each other in a tight embrace, right in an LDS chapel and behind a pulpit where countless good Mormons might condemn us as sodomites. But we did not feel condemned. We felt pure, warm, intimate, spiritually joined. We walked to the exit with our arms around each other's waist, after which Ronnie returned the key to its hiding place under the beam.

As we walked slowly back towards Croft House, I could tell that this wasn't a night for sex. So, I asked, "Do you believe in God? You didn't sound like much of a believer last night."

He drew a deep breath. "I'm pretty sure that if there's a God, he's not the Mormon god."

"Why?"

"Because of what we talked about last night. If Joseph Smith made up the *Book of Mormon*, the whole thing falls apart. So, I guess that the answer's no. I don't believe in the Mormon god. Besides, the

Mormon god doesn't like gay people, and he actually sounds sort of simple-minded."

"Simple-minded?"

"What's all this stuff about every blessing being predicated on obedience to some commandment? That can't be true. Look at all the bad people in the world who live comfortable lives and all the good people who suffer all the time. Besides, it makes God sound like an accountant, checking off a list of commandments and then passing out the blessings people have earned. Look at all the beauty in the world that we never earned and don't deserve. Sunsets. Friends. Music. Consider the music you just played. What did we do to deserve Brahms or Bach?"

"Is this you or Mama Claire speaking?"

"It's probably more her than me," he replied with a grin. "So, no. I do not believe in God, or at least not in the Mormon version of God. I just can't buy it. How about you?"

I thought about the paper I had just written for Sister Sonderegger about how some of the characters in *The Brothers Karamazov* argue that if God doesn't exist, nothing is forbidden. But not wanting to give up on the idea of God, I answered, "I want there to be a god because, without God, there's no reason to be good. There's no reason to be kind or generous."

"Why can't you be kind and generous just because you're kind and generous? Why does there have to be a god who punishes bad behavior and rewards good behavior? Can't you be good just for the sake of being good? Why does everything have to have a reward or a punishment attached?"

"How do you know that some behavior is good, and some behavior is bad?

"Most of the time, I just know. And when I don't know, I think about it and try to do the right thing. Do you do everything because you want a reward? A star on your forehead?"

"No. Actually I haven't thought about it very much."

But I tried to think about it. Why had I tried to help Patty? It certainly wasn't because of God. Everything about her pregnancy—her having sex with Rod when she was supposedly studying with me, our trying to arrange an abortion, my having sex with Blair for pay (although I ended up liking him), my threatening to make up a despicable lie about Dr. Berman if he told Patty's mother about her miscarriage—everything I did for Patty violated one commandment or another. Yet, it felt like the right thing to do because I was helping a friend who was in trouble. And then there was Lucy, the most godless woman in town. What did she get out of being kind to me? Why did she contact her friend in Tucson to ask about getting an abortion for Patty?

Why did she tell me the story about Gabe? Maybe Ronnie was right. Some people are kind, some people are mean, and God doesn't have anything to do with it. But I wasn't ready to give up on the idea of God. After a long silence, I asked, "Can I tell you about my reaction after first having sex with Harold?"

"Sure."

"You promise not to laugh and make fun?"

"Promise."

"When I got back to the hotel after my first time with Harold, I felt overwhelmed by a sense of thankfulness. Thankful that I had met a guy who was like me. A gay guy. And thankful for the sex because without the sexual attraction, we would never have become friends. But to be thankful for something, you need to be thankful to someone. So, I prayed and thanked God for letting me meet Harold. Does that sound too weird—that I thanked God because being gay led me to a friend? I felt the same way when I was with Father Tovar. And I sort of feel that way about you. I'm grateful that I met you, and to be grateful, I need someone or something to be thankful to. Maybe because of gratitude I can't give up on the idea of God."

He didn't laugh and he didn't make fun. Rather, he put his arm around my waist and said, "And I'm very thankful that I met you. I'll just have to figure out if you can be thankful without being thankful to someone."

As we approached Croft House, I asked, "Can we sneak out again tomorrow night?"

"Absolutely. I wouldn't miss it for the world."

Chapter Eleven:
My Second One-on-One with Chandler

The following day I had a long conversation with Sister Sonderegger. She liked my paper on *The Brothers Karamazov,* although she thought that I was too harsh on Dostoyevsky. We talked about empathy and how fictional characters help us see the world through other people's eyes, including the imagined conversations between Dostoyevsky's quirky characters. She gave me a copy of another Dostoyevsky novel, *Crime and Punishment.* For the following week, she assigned me an essay on why Rodion Raskolnikov felt guilty for committing a crime that he considered justified. I had no idea what she was talking about, but I was anxious to start the book.

During lunch, Ronnie told me he would miss PE because Dr. Chandler had scheduled some sort of special session with him. Of course, I was disappointed since that meant that we couldn't run back to Croft House together. "Can we still meet tonight?" I asked.

"Of course. Same time, same station."

At dinner, Ronnie looked pale and uncharacteristically tired. I wanted to ask if he was okay, but Sister Farr sat with us and spent the entire time rattling on about her beautiful, brilliant grandchildren. After dinner, I had to rush to my one-on-one with Dr. Chandler but not before whispering to Ronnie, "Catch you later."

I knocked on Chandler's door for my next appointment. Standing to greet me, he gave me the familiar two-handed handshake. After some small talk, he asked me how things were going.

"Can I ask you a question?" I asked.

"Of course." Toothy smile. "That's one of the reasons I'm here. To answer questions if I can."

"Do you believe in the devil?"

Pensive frown. Measured delivery. "Josh, people can laugh all they want, but evil is real, whether we call it Satan or something else. He's smart enough to never show himself, but I see the hand of Satan in evildoing and the unhappiness it brings. We have extreme examples of evil like the Nazis, but they don't worry me personally because I'll probably never meet a Nazi. But I do know people, some in my own profession I'm sorry to say, who claim that homosexual behavior is okay, that it is normal. That is a lie. It's a big lie. But it's a very good lie because it convinces lots of smart people. It's the kind of lie we should expect from the Prince of Lies."

Smart people like Ronnie's first shrink? Like Ronnie himself? Did Chandler really want me to think that Ronnie was one of Satan's minions?

"I know it's a lie," he continued," because every day I see how homosexual behavior makes people unhappy, how it alienates them from God, from the church, from family, and from life-long friends, condemning them to lonely, sterile lives. Take you for example. What do you think people back in Rosales are saying after what happened between you and those two boys?"

"I don't really care because I never plan to go back there."

"Are you sure that you don't care? If that's true, why have you hidden your homosexual feelings from your parents? The fact that you hide these feelings suggests that you are ashamed of them."

"That's not quite true. I don't hide my feelings from everyone. Just from people I don't trust."

"Don't you trust your parents? If you're not ashamed, why haven't you told them? What about the heartbreak you've caused them? I'm certain that you have friends who are worried about you and are praying for you. In fact, God himself is crying right now as He thinks about you. That's why I know that homosexuality is wrong. It's a cancer that spreads misery. And the most miserable person of all is likely to be you if you don't break the pattern."

Okay. He had touched a nerve. My father had always been kind to me, and my mother—however drug-addled and fanatical—was not a mean person, so of course I was concerned about their feelings. But God? Is the God of all creation from somewhere beyond the Andromeda Galaxy weeping copious tears because I sucked Ronnie's dick? Knowing that nothing would be gained by arguing with him, I changed the subject. "So why do I find guys attractive?" I asked. "That's something that has always been there. I didn't choose it."

"Your real self does not find guys attractive because your real self is God's creation, and God does not make people homosexual. We learn desire. And what we learn, we can unlearn. I can teach you how to develop wholesome desires and find the strength to choose righteous thoughts instead of evil thoughts. Free agency is God's greatest gift to us. You have the God-given ability to choose."

"Are you saying that I chose to have homosexual feelings? When did I do that? Do people choose to have heterosexual feelings?"

Supercilious smile. "Josh, those are very clever questions—the kind of questions some of my psychotherapist colleagues might ask when they argue that homosexuality is not a matter of choice. But it's the wrong question because we will probably never know where homosexual interests come from, and obsessing about the causes of homosexual behavior distracts us from the right question, which is: What do you choose to do now? Will you use your free agency to make right choices now? From a practical standpoint, I see homosexual behavior as a temptation like any other temptation. And as with any temptation, we can learn to resist it."

"But you're doing more than asking me to resist temptation. You're asking me to enter a sexual relationship with a woman. I feel no inclination in that direction. I've made out with girls, and I've even done a bit of groping. I've tried to see in girls what some of my classmates see in them, but it just isn't there. I feel no sexual attraction for girls."

"Josh, desire is learned. It might be learned at such an early age that you are unaware of it, but believe me: desire is learned. This means two things. First, you can unlearn unhealthy desires. And second, you can learn new desires, desires that lead to a happy life that conforms to the will of God. At Croft House, we understand that choosing is difficult, especially for people indoctrinated into thinking that they have no choice. Now, I'm convinced that, somewhere in you, there are heterosexual desires that can be cultivated and developed—if you choose to do so. Our basic goals at Croft House are to help you discover those natural tendencies and to give you the tools to choose them, to trust in the power of your free agency and in God's willingness to help you."

"Like what kinds of tools?"

"We start by teaching you better habits, by helping you to control your responses. Next week, we'll start you on some exercises that can move you in that direction. You'll be surprised at how quickly you can learn to control your sexual feelings and re-channel them in more positive directions. Eventually we will encourage you to seek greater intimacy with a woman. I know there is a very special woman out there waiting to meet you. We also urge you to pray for success. I promise you—I testify to you—that God will hear your prayers and bless you in this process."

I wondered if that "special woman" might be someone like Lucy, and if I would end up doing to my "special woman" what Gabe had done to her. As for invoking the help of God, I remembered how I was moved to thank God for letting me meet Harold and Father Tovar. Of course, I had asked God to make me heterosexual, but only because I thought I was supposed to—never because of the spontaneous gratitude I felt after meeting Harold and Father Tovar.

Observing my silence, Chandler leaned over, squeezed my knee, and said, "But right now, I just want to get to know you better." He then started asking questions about my family and my childhood. I made the mistake of telling him about the guy at the county fair who had pushed his hardon between my naked legs when I was five years old. He was much taken with the story although I told him that I didn't assign much importance to it.

"That's what you tell yourself. But experiences like that leave an imprint on our subconscious. We'll have a chance to talk about it again, but in the meantime don't dismiss its importance." He then asked about my first orgasm. I lied and said that I couldn't remember.

"You know, Josh, there's good research with regards to sexual preference and the importance of one's first orgasm. Try to remember. Sometimes that first orgasm is the beginning of habits we need to unlearn."

This from the guy who only minutes earlier was telling me that the causes of homosexual desire did not interest him! I had been ogling men since I was five years old, considerably before that first wonderful orgasm after seeing the naked Mike Grieber in the swimming pool shower room. My first orgasm had nothing to do with it. Fortunately, we were out of time. He ended the session with the same one-arm hug.

Chapter Twelve:
Third Night with Ronnie

At evening prayer, Ronnie looked distracted and a little sad. Dr. Chandler usually didn't attend evening prayer but that night he not only attended but chose as the reading an excerpt from the *Book of Mormon* affirming that the only two sins greater than sexual transgression are denying the Holy Ghost and shedding innocent blood. He closed the meeting with a prayer in which he said in a tearful, pleading voice, "And dear Father, if any here have fallen into serious transgression, empower them to repent and to confess their sins to one of thy chosen representatives." Subtext: he did not believe that I had never fucked anyone or allowed myself to be fucked. After prayer, he walked over to Ronnie, gave him an arm over the shoulder hug, and whispered something in his ear.

The most beautiful thing I heard that day was Ronnie's knock on my door after lights-out. We were soon on our way to the golf course. After a couple of minutes in silence, Ronnie said "I've been suspended from Brother Stewart's discussion group because I'm too disruptive. Chandler wants me to have some extra individual sessions with him before letting me return to a group, not Stewart's but someone else's. By the way, how far along are you with Dr. Chandler?"

"So far, I've met with him only three times, once with my father and twice this week."

"And what do you think?"

"I'm not sure he's a nice person. He put a real guilt trip on me tonight about all the people I hurt by being gay. He even said that God was crying because of me. He also harps on and on about there being no such thing as a homosexual because God would never create a homosexual."

In an angry and emotional voice, Ronnie exclaimed, "You know that's total crap, don't you? I am a person who also happens to be a homosexual. I am a homosexual person. I am not just a behavior. And I'm sick to death of all these assholes telling me that my real self is someone else."

The fierce independence of these words lifted my spirit. They also brought to memory Mother Harold's advice to never let dickwad shrinks and douche-bag religious fanatics tell me who I am. We crawled under the fence into the golf course and were soon lying together in our special little grove of trees. Ronnie pulled me next to him and asked, "Has Chandler hooked you up to his dirty-picture machine yet?"

"No. What is it?"

"Have you seen the door with the sign that says 'Laboratory'?"

"Yes, but I don't know what's there."

"I hope you never find out. It's where Chandler makes you put on a special pair of shorts that has little buzzy things that sit right next to your balls. He then has you watch pictures of naked people as they are projected on the wall. The pictures change automatically, but you can press a remote control and make them move faster. If you look at the pictures of men too long, your balls get zapped with an electric current. If you change to the female pictures, the current goes away. But the machine keeps flashing more pictures at you, so when you see a naked man, you need to push the remote right away to avoid getting a shock."

"What is that supposed to accomplish? Are these the tools he keeps talking about?"

"Yes. These are the tools. It's called aversion therapy. He wants you to associate looking at guys with unpleasant experiences."

"Does it work?"

"You learn very quickly that staring at the men's photographs will lead to a shock. He tells you not to think. You're just supposed to react so that it becomes habitual not to look at men. He calls it reflex conditioning. I think it's total crap, but, hey, maybe that's what they teach at Harvard."

"Are the guys handsome?"

"There are all kinds—mostly younger guys like us and lots of athletic types, some of them with really ripped bodies and big hardons. There are also some naked little kids with their asses pointed at the camera, which is awfully gross. There's a timer attached to the remote to keep track of how long you look at each picture. He measures 'progress' (air quotation marks) by how quickly you look away from the pictures of men."

"Sounds primitive."

"It is primitive. I can't believe that anyone with half a brain thinks that it works. But it gets worse. In fact, it got a lot worse this afternoon when I was supposed to be at PE."

"What happened? Is that why you looked so sad at dinner?"

"You would look sad too. This afternoon, some other guy was with Chandler, maybe a medical doctor or a nurse. He gave me a shot of something. Then they started the dirty picture machine, but this time there were only pictures of naked men, and they didn't give me the remote. The drug made me feel awful, like nauseous but without being able to vomit. I was forced to look at pictures of naked men, but I couldn't turn them off because I didn't have the remote. I finally closed my eyes and begged them to stop but they kept at it until I almost passed out. I was crying when they finally stopped. Then the medical guy gave me another shot that slowly made the nausea go away. Afterwards, that asshole Chandler gave me a big hug and said, 'We've made a lot of progress today.' The guy is insane. I will not go through that again."

"What do you plan to do?"

"Run away."

"Run away? Where to?" I asked, hoping that the panic I felt didn't show in my voice.

"Los Angeles. I've been there a couple of times with my dad, and I loved it."

"Won't your dad come looking for you?"

"I don't know what he'll do. His bimbo wife doesn't want me around so he may just want me to leave. I intend to tell him about Chandler and his dirty pictures. I'm also thinking of contacting my journalism teacher. He knows people at *The Arizona Republic*. I'd love to get some reporters on Chandler's tail. There has to be a law against showing pornographic photos to guys our age."

Terrified that I was about to lose another friend, I asked, "When do you plan to run away?"

"Next Monday night. But there's more. I want you to come with me. You're the best friend I've ever had. Maybe the only real friend I've ever had. You're gay, you grew up Mormon, and I can talk with you about things that no one else understands. In fact, I may be falling in love with you."

234

This was a lot to process. Had I ever been able to talk with anyone the way I talked with Ronnie? No. Did I want to stay at Croft House and continue with Chandler's "treatment"? No. Could I go back to Rosales without lying to my parents that I had been cured? No. Could I face people in Rosales who now know that I'm queer? No. Did I want to see the triumphant smirk on AMPS' face? Absolutely not." Was I falling in love with Ronnie? Probably.

"I'm pretty sure that I love you too."

"It took you a long time to say that you're only pretty sure," he chided.

"I had to think. I've really been in love only once before, and that was with Father Tovar. But we had no future together. With you it's different because we're almost the same age, and we might have a future together. When do we leave?"

"Could you be ready by Monday night? I'll talk to Sanders tomorrow, so he'll let you out."

Without hesitation, I responded, "I'll be ready. I'm not sure how to handle my parents, but I'll figure something out."

"How will they react?"

"They'll be sad and worried. But it's high time that I simply tell them that they have a gay son, and that they need to get used to it. I might also tell them about you. My father will try to understand although I'm not

235

sure he can. My mother is such a religious fanatic that she'll probably never accept it. She'll just cry a lot and rattle on about how much God loves a repentant sinner. Besides, I really want to be with you."

"Does this mean we are boyfriends?"

"Like going steady?" I asked with a grin.

"More than that. We're going to live together."

"Does that mean that you'll never, ever have sex with another guy?"

After a short silence, I saw a smile playing at the corners of his mouth. "I guess it depends on how cute he is."

"So, I could be replaced as soon as you find someone who's cuter?"

He frowned and suddenly was not teasing anymore. "I didn't say that. It's just that we shouldn't make promises we might not be able to keep. We're together now, but who knows where we'll be a year from now? This is a complicated subject. I think of my dad. He's rich and good-looking, and women are always after him. If he could just dip his wick occasionally with no strings attached, maybe his marriages would work. So, let's not make promises we may not be able to keep."

We embraced each other and remained silent for several minutes, sobered perhaps by his plan to run away. We started to kiss. I reciprocated and soon we were both naked, lying on the grass, with the bright moonlight overhead. After prolonged lovemaking, we talked well into the wee hours about what our life together might be like. Ronnie wanted to attend a prestigious school, possibly Princeton, supported by his mother's trust fund. My future was less certain. Up until my fatal encounters with Burt and Barry, I had planned to study music at BYU where I would receive some financial help from my parents. Without their support, things would be less certain. We returned to Croft House shortly before sunrise, dead tired and anxious, but also excited and very happy.

Chapter Thirteen:
Friday and Saturday

The following day dragged on, partly because I had hardly slept the night before, but mostly because I was worried about the future. PE was suspended on Fridays because parents started picking up their kids in the midafternoon. A late-model Mercedes showed up for Ronnie. Before walking to the car, Ronnie gave me a big hug—a real no-no at Croft House—and then whispered in my ear, "See you on Monday night just after lights-out. Don't be late. I'll be waiting by the emergency exit."

I watched him load his backpack into the Mercedes, his copper-red hair glistening in the sunlight and the movement of his well chiseled muscles perceptible underneath his t-shirt. I marveled at how fond I had become of him in four short, intense days.

My father arrived a couple of hours later in our 1965 Ford Galaxie, fortunately without Mother. As we entered the Rosales valley, my father dropped a bombshell. "Sonny," he said, "your mother and I think that Rosales High School may not be the best place for you after all that's happened. So, we called your Uncle Hyrum in Panguitch. He's agreed that you can live with him and Aunt Leeanne next year and finish your senior year at Panguitch High School. You've always liked Hyrum and you'd be far away from Rosales. Panguitch will be a good place for you."

Actually, I thought it would be a horrible place for me. My mother's youngest brother, Uncle Hyrum was employed by the church education department. Like Master Bateman, he taught high school seminary. Worse, he was a hopeless jock who wore his maleness like a badge of honor. A year with him, Aunt Leeanne (whom I did like), and their seven kids (whom I tried to ignore) in a small-town in southern Utah sounded like Siberia. I murmured an affirmative-sounding response to my father's proposal, but only because I knew that the following Monday I would flee to Los Angeles with Ronnie.

We arrived home late. Mother was still awake, but she had taken one (or several) sleeping pills and was too dopey to talk. I spent the next day, a Saturday, working at my father's garage. Fortunately, it was a busy day that allowed no time for me to dwell on my problems. That afternoon, Mr. Barnes came by the garage to take me to the high school to empty my locker. He asked me how things were going, but as with my father he didn't want details.

Someone had written CS on my locker door with a felt pen. Cocksucker no doubt. I found three notes that kids had pushed through the locker vents. The first said simply, "Cocksuker [sic]. Your [sic] going to die." No doubt a love letter from Burt or Barry.

The second was from Patty. Written in her girly handwriting with little valentines over the i's instead of dots, it read, "I really miss you and hope you come back soon. I know that those awful stories about you aren't true because I know that you are not that way." Patty was a close friend. I had written homework assignments for her, helped her cheat on exams, facilitated her affair with Rod, and helped her through the nightmare of her pregnancy and miscarriage. I knew she loved me as a friend, but for the time being she couldn't accept me as homosexual.

The third note was from Craig Bowen. Short and concise, it read, "Next time, bite the bastard's dick off so he can't reproduce." This unexpected gesture of sympathy warmed my heart, but it also made me sad. Why had I never trusted Craig's friendship enough to share my secret with him?

Chapter Fourteen:
Blair and Barkley

Before returning to the garage, I ducked into a public phone booth and placed a call to Blair Huxley. Why Blair? I had met him only once, but I desperately needed the company of a gay person. Blair answered on the second ring and recognized my voice immediately. "Josh! It's so good to hear from you. I have been hoping you would call. It's been over two weeks. How's your girlfriend?"

"There's a lot to tell. Patty's okay. She had a miscarriage which was truly scary but ultimately a good thing. I've also been out of touch because I was suspended from school, and for the last week I've been stuck in a Mormon clinic in Phoenix where my parents sent me to make me straight."

"They what!?" he exclaimed.

"They put me in a Mormon clinic to cure me of being homosexual."

After a long pause, he asked, "Josh, are you free this evening? Could you come up for dinner? I'm at my main house, so I can offer you something more elegant than sandwiches. I had my piano tuned hoping to hear you play. Also, there's someone I want you to meet." I accepted with relief because I did not want to stay

241

home. I needed to be around gay people. I finished the workday, cleaned up, and told my parents that I was meeting Patty for a drive. A total lie, of course, but I had to tell them something.

Blair's main house lay a few miles north of I-40. The entry to his property was bracketed by two stone pillars. The road curved around a wooded hill, ending in a parking area near a large ranch house hidden from the highway and surrounded by a wrought iron fence, large pine trees, and a well-tended yard. Blair greeted me with an affectionate hug, saying, "Welcome! It's so good to see you. Come in and make yourself at home."

The living room was a much larger version of the front room of his guest house, with a comfortable seating area, a large flagstone fireplace, and tasteful paintings of nearby Arizona landscapes—the red rocks of Sedona, the cliffs of Canyon de Chelly, and of course the Grand Canyon. Dominating the far end of the room was a midsized grand piano with an ornately carved mahogany case—a stunning piece of furniture. Noticing my fixation on the piano, Blair laughed, "Well, I can see what caught your eye! Show you a piano and everything else disappears!"

"I'm sorry. I didn't mean to be rude, but it's hard to ignore a piano that beautiful."

"I had it tuned in hopes of hearing you play. But first I want you to meet someone."

Standing behind us next to the fireplace was a tall, handsome man with a well-coiffed head of gray hair, a trim body, and a craggy but attractive face. "Josh, this is Barkley. Barkley Gibson. He's the friend from San Francisco I told you about."

Barkley and I shook hands. Speaking in a smooth baritone voice with the slightly elongated vowels and leisurely cadence of the American South, he said, "I'm delighted to meet you, Nick. Blair has told me so much about you. All of it good. But right now it appears that what most interests you is the piano, so why don't you play something for us."

The piano was a Steinway and certainly one of the most beautiful pianos I had ever played. The action was sluggish from lack of use, but it had a gorgeous round tone. Since Blair and Barkley were not interested in a recital, I performed a couple of short Chopin etudes and the last movement of Bach's first partita, which, with all its hand crossings, is quite a showpiece. They complimented my playing, and I praised the piano. Blair explained that it was wedding present from his wife's family, "Perhaps," he joked, "because she was getting such a lousy husband."

We moved to the dining room where Blair introduced me to two Mexican men. "Josh, please meet Manuel and Javier. They're my right-hand men around here and are truly essential to keeping things running." They smiled broadly as they shook my hand but then indicated that they needed to get back to the kitchen.

After they left the room, Blair explained that they lived on the ranch, helped with the livestock, and kept the house presentable. "They came to work for me about fifteen years ago on the bracero program. Seeing how the other workers teased them, I realized that they were a couple. I also noticed that they worked hard and were good with cattle, so I put them on salary and asked them to stay on permanently. They've been here ever since. I couldn't get along without them."

Dinner consisted of a green salad, a grilled T-bone steak, buttered asparagus, and garlic mashed potatoes. The food was tastefully served on china plates, with real silver, real crystal stemware, an ironed tablecloth and cloth napkins—items virtually unknown in my parents' home. If being gay required that level of elegance, I would need to up my game. As we ate, Blair asked about my previous two weeks. I briefly described my fateful encounters with Burt and Barry, my suspension from school, and my week at Croft House.

"Croft House sounds perfectly dreadful," Blair exclaimed. "How are you dealing with it all?"

"Well, there's actually a silver lining," I replied, and I told them about Ronnie.

After oohing and awing a bit, they indulged in some gentle teasing. "You'll have to forgive us," Barkley said, "but deep down inside Blair and I are just a couple of sentimental old queens. We are in love with love, and we particularly love young love." Then, much to my surprise, he added, "You know, I've actually heard of Dr. Chandler. He sounds like a real piece of work."

"How do you know about Chandler? Don't you live in San Francisco, and aren't you a lawyer of some kind?"

"Yes, to both questions, but right now I want more dirt on Dr. Chandler. As a lawyer, I do pro-bono work for an interfaith ministry called The Bay City Recovery Center. The Center helps kids who have either run away from home or been tossed out on the street by their parents. Most are gay with a history of using and selling drugs. Many have also worked as prostitutes—survival sex they call it. The Center provides counseling to help these kids get their lives together. It's not easy. They come with lots of problems, mostly addiction and depression as well as a history of abuse."

"So, you heard of Chandler through these kids?"

"Only through one of them, a sweet kid named Kevin. When he was a missionary for the Mormon church, he had an affair with another missionary and got sent home in disgrace. He went through Chandler's program and some sort of church disciplinary program, after which he was pronounced cured. He started school at BYU, but of course, nothing had changed. He was still gay. He fell off the wagon and started seeing a guy who unfortunately confessed everything to his bishop and also ratted out Kevin. Kevin was simultaneously kicked out of BYU, excommunicated from the church, and disowned by his parents. Without a red cent to his name, he came to San Francisco and eventually got arrested for prostitution. He contacted the Center, and I became his legal counsel."

"How is he now?" I asked.

"He's doing well. Since he's a bright kid with marketable skills, we got him a job as an office temp. He's going back to school in the fall. He'll be okay, but he needs to get Chandler out of his system. Now, everything I know about Chandler is through hearsay. But from what I gather, he subjects kids to something called aversion therapy. Do you know anything about it?"

I described Ronnie's experience with the dirty-picture machine, the ball-buzzing shorts, and the nausea drugs.

"That sounds genuinely horrible," Barkley said with a frown. "No wonder Kevin is so messed up. I'd like to see the photographs. If they include minors, they are patently illegal."

"Ronnie says that there are even photos of naked little kids."

"Then Chandler ought to be busted. And the sooner the better."

After a few moments of silence, Blair said, "Barkley, why don't you tell Josh something about yourself? You didn't grow up Mormon but growing up Southern Baptist wasn't a lot better."

"Do I have to?" Barkley asked with a pained expression on his face.

"No, you don't have to. But hearing your story might do Josh some good."

"Okay, but let's go in the living room for coffee and dessert. I tell better stories with caffeine in my system and a soft chair for my derriere."

Chapter Fifteen: Barkley's Story

We gathered around a coffee table where Manuel and Javier served three ample dishes of apple cobbler with ice cream. Turning to Barkley, I said, "So you were going to tell me about your church. Was your family super religious?"

"You have no idea," he replied. "My father's father and grandfather were Baptist preachers. My name is Barkley Gibson IV. Why the fourth? Because I'm named after my great granddaddy, my granddaddy, and my daddy's oldest brother, all of whom were Baptist preachers named Barkley. My daddy tried his hand at preaching, but he was no good at it. He was also not good at producing heirs, since I am an only child. So, he spent his time hounding me to carry on the preaching tradition. He was not, by the way, a nice man, may he rest in peace. He was mean by nature and religion gave him an excuse to be even meaner. He regularly threatened me with damnation and a beating if I didn't go to church three times a week and memorize the right number of scriptures every day. At first, it seemed that he would get his wish because I was a child wonder. By the age of twelve, I was witnessing and calling people to Jesus right and left. I could recite hundreds of Bible verses from memory, and I was especially good with the clobber verses."

"Clobber verses?"

"The ones they use to clobber homosexuals. But when the juices of life started flowing, I became aware of the irresistible beauty of the male members of our species and realized that those clobber verses were talking about me. I started fooling around with guys in my early teens. Once I started, I couldn't stop, no matter how much I begged God to free me of such sinful proclivities.

"So, I stopped preaching and attending church, which led to horrible arguments with my daddy. In our last argument, he asked if I was a sodomite. I told him to mind his own business, so he gave me a whipping. A real whipping—with his belt. Left big welts on my back and butt. When my mother saw what he'd done, we moved in with her aunt Lydia, a spinster lady who was a retired schoolteacher."

"Did your mother share your daddy's religious beliefs?"

"Hard to say. We were country folk. That was the only religion we knew. After my parents separated, we stopped going to church, but Mama never stopped reading the Bible. Mama got a job clerking in a J.C. Penney's, and I started working part-time jobs. We lived pretty much hand to mouth, but we managed. My daddy died a couple of years later of some mysterious ailment. Probably choked on his own meanness. But since my parents never got divorced, his estate went to my mother. She stashed the entire amount in an education fund. She had set her heart on getting me out of the South and seeing me attend an Ivy League university, so she pushed me in school.

"Her dream came true when I was accepted at Columbia. Columbia gave me a scholarship, so with Mama's help, money from my daddy's estate, and my income from part-time jobs, we financed a Columbia education. I felt out of place at Columbia. I had a southern accent and none of the polish the other kids had learned at home. But I got both my BA and JD there, so I'm grateful to the place. After law school I took a job in San Francisco, and I've lived there ever since."

"Did your mother know you were gay?"

"Of course she knew. But she never asked any questions. In Southern culture, certain things are never discussed. She passed several years ago. I will always be grateful to her. Without her help, I'd probably be in South Carolina working as a store clerk."

Barkley's description of his mother helped me understand him. Although I wouldn't call him effeminate, there was an unhurried gentility in his language, accent, gestures, and facial expressions. I suspected that I was seeing a male version of his mother. "Were you and Blair friends at Columbia?" I asked.

"We hardly knew each other. I was aware of him, of course, because he was so handsome. But he was a rich kid, and I was a poor Southern brat. We moved in different circles."

Perhaps with a note of sarcasm in my voice, I asked Blair, "Is that true? Were you a rich kid?"

"By Arizona standards, my family was well fixed. But contrary to what Barkley says, I didn't move in fancy circles at Columbia. Old money—old WASP money—counted for a lot back then, and I wasn't in that social class. Barkley and I didn't get acquainted until a class reunion about fifteen years ago."

With a smile and wink, Barkley added, "Well, to tell the truth, we got a bit more than acquainted, but my Southern discretion prevents me from going into detail. Anyway, we've been seeing each other ever since."

"Do you ever miss your church?"

"Yes and no. I may have left it, but Lord knows it never left me. I can still sing the songs and quote thousands of Bible verses from memory. But there's no church I want to attend. I may rethink that decision someday. Church people help run the Recovery Center, and they're truly fine people. According to our counselors, some of our kids need to work out their problems through religion and not against religion. Maybe that's what I should have done. But it's too late now."

After a short silence, Blair asked, "What's next for you Josh? Are you going back to Croft House and Dr. Chandler?"

"I'm going back for one night, but then on Monday Ronnie and I are going to run away. We're going to live in Los Angeles."

Worried expressions. After a long pause, Barkley said, "Josh, what you're saying worries me. Every day I see young guys lost in a big city with no way of making money and no direction to their lives. What will you do for money?"

"I'll get a job and maybe take some night classes. I know about cars and tires, and I can learn to do other things. I might even get a job as a church musician."

After a long silence, Blair said, "Josh, I admire your courage, but there are so many ways this could go wrong. If you ever need anything, give me a call. I don't want you ending up like one of those kids in San Francisco."

It was past time for me to go. As I was preparing to leave, Blair went out of the room. He returned with an envelope that he stuffed into my back pocket. ""Josh, you're a bright boy. It would be a shame if you didn't go to college. Here's a bit of pin money for you, and there's more where that came from. Stay in touch and let me know how I can help. You already have my phone number, and there's a card with my mailing address in the envelope."

They walked me out to the front porch, gave me a big hug, and watched me leave. As I waved goodbye from Bercilak, my eyes grew moist as I thought about how generous and sweet these two men were. Could God really hate them because they were gay? It was also good to meet older gay men who seemed to be getting along just fine. At the stop sign before getting on the frontage road, I opened the envelope Blair had given me. It contained two new $100 bills.

Chapter Sixteen:
My Last Day in Rosales

The next day, a Sunday, I begged off attending church with my parents. Mother started a Loretta episode about how our family had always gone to church together, but my father put a gentle stop to it. "Lily, I'm sure that it's okay for him to miss today." Actually, I think my father was afraid of what some kids might say to me.

So, I stayed home. To prepare for running away with Ronnie, I filled my backpack with clean clothes and a couple of books along with the $200 Blair had given me after our first encounter and the $200 he had given me the previous evening. $400 in 1970 could go a long way. I also packed a street map of Phoenix in case my plans with Ronnie fell through. After church, my parents took me to lunch at one of Rosales' two restaurants. Several townspeople came over to our table to say hello, but no one asked about me, perhaps because I made them uncomfortable. After lunch, Mother told me that Mrs. Jespersen would like me to stop by her house before I returned to Phoenix.

Knocking on Mrs. J's door on a Sunday afternoon seemed strange since I had only been in her home for music lessons. Still wearing her church dress, she invited me in, quietly closing the door behind us.

"Josh," she began, "Thanks for coming. I fear that we may not see each other for a while. That's why I wanted you to drop by. I want to discuss a couple of things with you. I hope it's not an inconvenience."

"It's no inconvenience at all. I appreciate the invitation."

Looking uncharacteristically nervous, she said, "Please have a seat. I've prepared some hot chocolate and cookies for us. I'll be right back." As she stepped into the kitchen, I looked around her front room and remembered how much that space meant to me. The two grand pianos, the bookshelves filled with musical scores and books about music. But I also noticed the photo of Mrs. J's husband on the mantelpiece. Could there be any truth in what Craig had said about him? And about Mrs. Jespersen and Madame Arnaud?

She returned with a tray carrying two mugs, a small teapot, and a plateful of cookies. "Josh," she said as she sat down, "This conversation makes me a little nervous, so I'll get straight to the point. I am not unaware of the problems you've had at school. Nor am I unaware of how awful people like Burt Larson and Barry Cummings can treat a boy like you."

A boy like me? Did she mean musical? Smart? Or maybe queer?

"I also know that Mr. Barnes and your parents think that they are doing what's best for you by sending you to that special school in Phoenix. And maybe they are.

I'm in no position to judge. After all, your parents are your parents, and Mr. Barnes is an honorable and well-intentioned man. That's not what I want to talk about."

After an uncomfortable silence, she continued. "Josh, you must know that you are exceptionally talented. I've been teaching piano for over thirty years, and I have had very few students as good as you. Add to that, your voice. Jackie feels as strongly about your singing potential as I do about your promise on the piano. In fact, your biggest problem might be that you are too talented, that you'll be tempted to not work as hard as you should because things come easily to you."

"Don't I work hard enough?"

With a sigh of exasperation, she replied, "No, that is not what I mean. What I want to say is that you need to get out of Rosales. You need to be around people like you." Then with a slight blush, she quickly added, "I mean as talented as you. Look for scholarship opportunities. Listen to good musicians and learn what beautiful music sounds like. Look for the best teachers and places to perform. And try to be around students who will challenge you to be your best."

"My parents want me to go to BYU."

Stiffening a bit, she replied somewhat hesitantly, "BYU is a fine school in many ways." She then added somewhat cryptically, "But you will find people at

BYU who think like Burt and Barry. You would have to be very careful there."

She didn't know about my growing disillusionment with Mormonism and the church's founding stories, so yes, she was talking about me being queer, albeit in a roundabout way.

"But that's a few months away," she continued. "What you most need now is to finish high school and apply to good universities. Plenty of fine schools find ways to support someone as promising as you." Subtext: don't apply to BYU. Then, with some discomfort, she continued, "There's something else I want you to know, but you must promise not to tell anyone. Do you promise?"

"I promise."

"I plan to retire at the end of this term and will be moving away from Rosales. I've given my entire life to ASC, this town, and to my family. It has been a good life, and I've found much joy in my students. But it is time to move on."

"Where will you go?"

"I'm moving to Tucson where I'll be living with Jackie. She has no family, and my family increasingly sees me as a doddering old woman, more an annoyance than an asset. I was never so happy as when Jackie and I roomed together in Cincinnati. We've stayed in touch ever since. We plan to set up a music studio, and we might do some teaching at the U."

Then looking at the clock on the mantelpiece next to her husband's photo, she said, "I promised your mother that you'd be home by two. But before you leave, I want to give you something. Please wait here."

She went into a back room and returned with a small, blue felt bag tied with yellow drawstrings. She opened it and pulled out a gold lapel pin in the shape of a four-leaf clover. "Have you ever heard of my brother Lars?" she asked.

"No," I replied. "I know your other brothers and sisters because they're grandparents of some of my classmates. Should I know Lars?"

"Lars never got old enough to be a grandparent or even a parent for that matter. He was the youngest of my parents' children. My little brother. He was killed in the Normandy invasion in the Second World War. He had barely turned twenty-one. Such a tragic waste! Lars was a gifted violinist. I gave him this pin when he graduated from high school. He wore it whenever he performed because he said it brought him good luck. I would like you to have it. When you perform, you might wear it and think of him and remember me."

As we stood up, I thanked her profusely, not just for the pin but for all she had given me. Then, quite to my surprise, she gave me a big hug. As she held me, she said in a soft voice, "Let's not say goodbye because neither of us knows what the future will bring. I know that you're going through a bad patch right now, but things will get better. Best of luck."

I was not pleased to learn that Mother was driving with us back to Phoenix. I expected the worst, and she delivered in spades. For four hours she harangued on how the LDS church was the only true church, how the only ordinances God recognized were those performed by LDS priesthood holders, and how I had clearly been a choice spirit in the pre-existence in order to be born into a good Mormon family and not in darkest Africa. She went on and on about how this earthly existence was a probationary period to see if we could prove worthy of the Celestial Kingdom and fill the measure of our creation. And of course, she mentioned several times that sexual transgressions were second in gravity only to shedding innocent blood and denying the Holy Ghost. My father tried to change the subject several times, but to no effect. Ever the actress, she was on a holy rant, and no one was going to push her offstage.

Chapter Seventeen:
Beginning to Say Goodbye

As I watched the taillights of my parents' car disappear, I felt a great sadness coming on. Despite my mother's hysterical religiosity and drug use, they were conscientious parents who had given me a great deal— books, material well-being, piano lessons with Mrs. Jespersen, and the best of everything Rosales offered. But they had also sown seeds of guilt and shame, not just about what I had done, but about who I was. If Chandler had accomplished anything, it was bringing that shame to the surface. I wondered when I might see them again.

In my room after dinner, I recalled the conversation with Ronnie in which he did such a fabulous job of describing the characters in the *Book of Mormon* as stick figures. Okay, he did confess that most of his ideas came from Mama Claire, but still, by any standard, it was a virtuoso performance. I also recalled what Chandler had said the first time we met, that his authority rested on two pillars: the truth of Mormonism and his training at Harvard. Ronnie's experiences with aversion therapy and my own interactions with Chandler convinced me that he was a quack. But the LDS Church?

I decided to try reading the *Book of Mormon* again. I'm a fast reader and I know how to skip boring sections of a book. After finishing I Nephi, I could see exactly what Ronnie meant. The plot was engaging— so yes, Joseph Smith had a good imagination—but, just as Ronnie (or Mama Claire) had said, the characters were paper-thin, what with the good ones being so very good and the bad ones being so very bad. And yes, they were color-coded since the good ones were "white and delightsome" and the bad ones were "loathsome and cursed with a dark skin."

I thought of Father Tovar's beautiful brown body. He proudly claimed ancestry from the Tarahumara Indians of northern Mexico, which according to the *Book of Mormon* would make him one of the cursed Lamanites. Was he loathsome? Absolutely not. Was his dark skin a curse? Hardly. He was gorgeous from head to toe. I know because I had explored, kissed, caressed, smelled, and loved his entire brown body on numerous occasions.

But what really got me about the *Book of Mormon* was how much Joseph Smith had lifted verbatim from the *King James* Bible, including entire chapters from Isaiah which this small group of Israelites had allegedly brought from Jerusalem in 600 BC. But if their scriptures preceded the *King James* Bible by nearly two millennia, how could they be virtually identical to the *King James* Bible?

Only one way: Joseph Smith copied them verbatim. His penchant for copying stuff is particularly outrageous in III Nephi where Jesus supposedly visited the New World and repeated nearly word for word the Sermon on the Mount as recorded in Matthew's gospel. How could Jesus do this? Note cards? A teleprompter? Or just a weakness for recycling his own material? Again, there is only one explanation: Joseph Smith filched it straight out of the *King James* Bible. Perhaps I was reading in bad faith, but by the end of the evening, I no longer believed.

That night I had a most peculiar dream. Retelling this dream may be the most difficult part of my story since words can only trivialize it. I was surrounded by darkness, walking on a rough, narrow trail that hugged the side of a steep mountain. I was completely alone and greatly feared falling to someplace where no one could find me. In my confusion, I glimpsed a pinpoint of light far away in the distance. I knew that I had to reach the light but that reaching it would be very difficult and perhaps impossible.

Struggling toward the light, I was overcome with fatigue and overwhelmed by darkness. I stumbled several times and came close to sliding into the black abyss below. Just as I was about to give up, the light suddenly reached out and engulfed me. I became aware of a man whose naked torso, chest and arms were clearly visible to me, but not his face. There was nothing overtly sexual about the dream, but I was overwhelmed by his male beauty—by his exquisitely sculpted body, glowing translucent skin, and large strong hands. I felt an incredible warmth emanating from his body. For the briefest of moments, I felt united with him, in him, through him. Caressed by him. I was totally at peace—accepted, protected, loved, and overwhelmed by gratitude. I awoke with a start, devastated that the beautiful dream had ended.

I have never ceased puzzling over the dream and its meaning. Who was the man? Was he really a man? Why was he naked? Why couldn't I see his face? Why was I fixated on his maleness in a way that was intensely homoerotic without being sexual? Would I ever again feel such peace and acceptance? Maybe the dream was prompted by the anxiety I felt about leaving the LDS Church. But maybe—and this is what I choose to believe—maybe for a moment I was united with a god who accepted, embraced, and caressed me with his love. So, while I had come to doubt the god of Mormonism, I was not ready to give up on the idea of God altogether.

Chapter Eighteen: Monday

On Monday morning, I tried to lose myself in *Crime and Punishment.* But never far from my mind was the thought of running away with Ronnie that very night. Just before lunch, a man dressed in chinos and a tight golf shirt barged through the front door and stomped toward Dr. Chandler's office, totally ignoring Sister Farr's attempts to stop him. With reddish hair, moderate height, and a compact muscular build, he was clearly Ronnie's father. He pushed open Chandler's office door without knocking. We then heard him shout, "What the hell did you do to my son? What's this about shock treatments and drugs? Who gave you permission to torture my boy like that?"

Chandler quickly shut the door. The shouting continued but we couldn't make out the words. A few minutes later, Ronnie's father strode out, but before slamming the door, he said in a loud voice, "You'd better get a good lawyer because you're going to need one. The police are going to hear about this." We heard his tires squeal as he tore away from Croft House. Without a word, Chandler left the building, also in a great hurry. Remembering how Barkley had said that Chandler's methods might be illegal, I fantasized that Chandler might have to stand trial and maybe even go to prison.

At dinner, Brother Stewart announced that the group session had been canceled, but that everything would return to normal the following day. Evening prayer was mercifully short. Back in my room, I began the most difficult task of the day: writing a letter to my parents. After several revisions, this is what came out:

Dear Mother and Dad,

This is a hard letter for me to write because I don't want to worry you or cause you any more pain than I may have already caused you. You have been wonderful and generous parents. I love you both very much, and I will always be grateful to you. But recent events and accusations have made it impossible for me to return to Rosales. Nor can I remain at Croft House since I do not agree with Dr. Chandler's ideas on therapy or religion.

What I'm going to write now may be hard for you to accept, but your knowing and accepting it are conditions for any future contact between us. I am a homosexual. I have known that I was different since I was very young and that I was a homosexual ever since I first heard the word. Asking me to change is like asking me to be a different person. Being homosexual is not something I chose, nor is it something I can unchoose. It is my nature. It is how God made me. I understand that what I'm saying contradicts LDS teachings. But I cannot be anyone other than who I am. Moreover, I will no longer allow other people to tell me who I am or try to make me change.

The good news is that here at Croft House I have made a wonderful new friend. Like me, he grew up Mormon, and like me he knows that he is homosexual. His name is Ronnie, and we plan to make a life for ourselves together in California.

I'll send you another letter as soon as we are settled to let you know that I am okay. But for the time being, I need to be on my own. Please do not try to find me, and please, oh please do not send the police looking for me. If you send the police after me, I promise to disappear forever.

I love you very much. I'm deeply grateful for all that you have done for me and for the sacrifices you have made. Forgive me for any pain I have unintentionally caused you. When we see each other again, I hope you can find it in your hearts to still love me and even be proud of me. I will always love and be proud of you.

Love,

Josh

PS Please sell my pickup and use the money to recover whatever you spent on Croft House. I do not want to ever be a financial burden on you again.

Planning to mail it the following day, I placed the letter in an envelope addressed to my parents but with no return address. At 10:35, I sneaked out of my room with my backpack to wait for Ronnie. I waited by the door for what seemed an eternity. No sign of Ronnie.

Thinking that I might have misunderstood the plans made the previous Friday, I walked out to the street, past the tree behind which Ronnie and I had shared goodnight kisses. I looked up and down the street. No sign of Ronnie. I walked back and forth several times between the emergency exit and the street, increasingly worried because Ronnie was nowhere to be seen. With growing anxiety, I waited over an hour, hoping against hope that he would show up. By midnight, I knew that something was wrong and reluctantly returned to my room.

I lay down on my bed, too anxious to cry and too worried to sleep. Where was Ronnie? Why had he not shown up? Had he been in an accident? Had his father found out about our plans and locked him up somewhere? I couldn't believe that he had ditched me altogether, although that dreadful thought did cross my mind. Worse yet, I had no way of contacting him since we never considered a Plan B. After much tossing and turning, I fell into a fitful sleep.

Chapter Nineteen: Tuesday

Still wearing my regular clothes, I awoke as the sun was coming up. It took me a moment to remember that I was still at Croft House and that Ronnie had not met me the night before. As casually as possible, I asked Sister Farr at breakfast if Ronnie had come back. She replied tersely, "After the fuss his father raised yesterday, I am certain that he won't return. And good riddance. I don't know why people refuse to recognize all the good that Dr. Chandler does."

During study period, I tried to read more of *Crime and Punishment,* but somehow Raskolnikov's problems—murder, guilt, need for punishment— seemed less immediate than mine. I was worried sick about Ronnie and couldn't imagine that he had just blown me off. Ronnie was not only someone I loved; he was the only option I had considered for starting a new life elsewhere.

Just before noon, Sister Farr called me out of class, saying that my father was on the phone. Imagine my elation when I heard Ronnie's voice! "Josh. It's Ronnie. We've got a big problem. I'll have to talk fast. Don't let on that it's me. I told Sister Farr that I was your father."

Following his lead, I said with false enthusiasm, "Hi Dad. What's up?"

After a short silence, Ronnie answered, "You're talking on the phone at the reception desk, and Sister Farr can hear everything you say. Right?"

"Yeah, that's pretty much it."

"Okay. Listen carefully. I told my father that you and I were going to LA. I thought that he'd be glad to get rid of me, but then he turned into a super asshole, took away my car keys, and basically locked me in the house. This morning he announced that he's sending me to some wilderness survival program to make a man of me. Sounds more like a prison."

"That sounds awful," I said, noting that Sister Farr was playing close attention to the conversation while pretending to concentrate on something else. "So, what happens now?"

"I have no choice. Until my eighteenth birthday, I'm his prisoner. I turn eighteen on October 8. After that, my father will have no legal hold on me, and I will also have my own money." He paused and then asked, "Do you know where you'll be?"

"No idea."

"So, here's what I propose. On the third Sunday of this coming October, look for me at noon in the waiting room of the Los Angeles train station. Have you ever been there?"

"No."

"Well, you have several months to find it. I've got to run. My jailers just drove up. See you in October. Don't forget that I love you."

"And I love you too."

He hung up abruptly. With more than normal curiosity, Sister Farr asked, "Is everything alright? Your father didn't sound quite like himself."

Time for a BS-Speak lie. "That's because he's so worried about my mother. She had an attack of some sort and had to be taken to a hospital in Winslow. He'll be there for several days and might not be able to take me home this weekend."

"That won't be a problem. I'm sorry to hear about your mother. Is it really serious?"

Time for more BS-Speak. "They're not sure what it is, but it could be bad. She has a history of heart trouble. My dad's going to call tomorrow with an update." I then fled back to study hall before she could ask more questions.

A huge burden had been lifted from my shoulders. Ronnie was alive, he loved me, and we had a plan to meet again. In the meantime, how was I supposed to get to LA and stay alive once there? Of course, the most pressing matter at the moment was escaping from Croft House before someone discovered my lie about Mother being sick.

While dressing for PE, I stuffed what I could into my backpack and checked the Phoenix street map that I had brought from home. Croft House was near North 67th Avenue, a major artery that led almost directly to a truck stop on Interstate 10 where I might hitch a ride to Los Angeles. After PE, Coach Charlie let me run back to Croft House on my own. Without anyone noticing, I grabbed my backpack out of the van and headed for 67th Avenue. As I had hoped, a city bus ran the length of the Avenue. I boarded, paid the fifty-cent fare, and prepared for the next episode of my life—but not before dropping the letter to my parents in a mailbox. I was excited to be going somewhere even though I had no idea of what lay ahead. It was May 5th, and the bus was festooned with small Mexican flags in observance of Cinco de Mayo, one of Mexico's national holidays. Perhaps my imagination got away from me, but I wondered if there wasn't some parallel between Mexico's victory over the French and my escape from Croft House.

PART III

Chapter One: Ape Arms

After a ninety-minute bus ride and a sweaty half-mile walk, I arrived just before sundown at a large truck stop just off I-10. My mind kept recycling my brief phone conversation with Ronnie earlier in the day. Was it stupid to be in love with someone I had known for less than a week? Would this wilderness experience that his father was forcing on him mess up his head? Would he meet me in October? That was nearly six months away. How much would we both have changed by then? How would my parents react to my letter? I certainly did not want to hurt them, but there was no going back. Freeing myself from them, their society, and their church struck me as the only path forward. But forward to what? I had no idea.

I approached several truck drivers who were fueling their rigs. Some said they weren't headed for LA, others that they were finished for the day, and still others that they didn't give rides. Finally, a large man with ape-hairy arms covered with tattoos, a protruding paunch, and massive muscles said that he could take me as far as Ehrenberg. "I'll have to leave you at the truck stop," he said, "but you won't have no trouble getting a ride from there to LA."

His huge size made me nervous, but I couldn't be picky. I climbed into the passenger seat and placed my backpack on the floor between my feet. He squeezed his huge body into the driver's seat and steered the eighteen-wheeler onto the freeway. He gave me several sideways glances that made me uncomfortable. I kept my eyes glued to the road to avoid looking at him. Finally, he asked, "How old are you kid?"

"Nineteen," I lied.

"Hmm," he said. "You look younger than that." After a few more miles of silence, he said, "There's a weigh station down the road that I'll have to stop at. Can't ignore regulations."

Sure enough, at the bottom of a long hill, a weigh station came into view. But as we got closer, a sign also came into view saying that it was closed. "It's not open," I said, perhaps with too much relief in my voice.

"It's open for what we need," he replied with a nasty smile. He pulled off the road and drove behind the weigh station into an empty parking area out of sight of the highway. Fearing that something awful was about to happen, I opened the passenger door as he was stopping the truck and threw my backpack onto the ground. But before I could jump out, he slammed on the brakes and smashed his massive right forearm into my chest and throat, pinning me to the seat and making it almost impossible for me to breathe.

"Don't get any ideas about running off, sissy boy. You've got a real cute ass, and it's time you learned what it's good for." Turning off the engine, he twisted himself towards me while keeping his arm pressed tight against my chest. I tried pushing him away, but he was too strong for me. Suddenly without warning he smashed his left fist hard into my chest. "Hey bitch," he growled. "You keep fightin' back, and you're gonna' really get hurt. If I hit you again, it'll be your face. And I'd hate to mess up that pretty little face." He then pushed me downward until my butt was half off the seat. With his left hand he ripped open the buttons of my fly. After mauling my genitals a bit, he slid his hand under my butt. After several tries, he managed to jam a finger into my asshole. I let out a scream because it hurt like hell.

In a girlish voice, he said, "Oh my. I'm so sorry. Did that hurt? I didn't feel anything. In fact, what I'm feeling feels real good. I love a tight young butt hole. Besides, sissy boy, you know you really want it. Ever had a big dick up your little boy twat? No? Then you're in for a real treat."

The pain was excruciating, but all I could think about was getting air into my lungs. Finally, I managed to force out the words, "Okay, I'll be good. Just let me breathe and don't hit me again."

"That's more like it. I like my bitches to be good little girls." He then slipped his right arm behind my back, seized my right wrist, and twisted it hard up towards my shoulders, forcing me to turn towards the door.

"Easy does it," he said as he forced me out of the truck with his massive body right behind me. I almost gagged at the stench of his unwashed body, made worse because he was now sweating profusely. Once we were both standing outside the truck, he said, "Okay sweetie. Time for the real fun. Just turn around, bend over, and kiss the floor of the truck. I'll take care of everything else." He slowly twisted me around and pushed my head towards the floor of the cab. Fully aware of what was about to happen, I heard from a distant recess of my mind the voice of Father Tovar saying, "Fucking is special. When you're inside of me, you become a part of me." No way did I want this monster inside of me.

He jerked my pants and shorts down to my knees. Keeping my right arm twisted high behind my back, he managed to lower his pants with his other hand. I then heard him spit on his hand and felt him pushing his finger into my asshole again. Worse than the pain was the thought that he would soon shove his dick into me and fill me with monster cum. He pulled his finger out and then tried to enter me with his dick, but it was too soft. Breathing hard, he started to masturbate. Realizing that he was having trouble getting hard, I had an idea. In my best BS-Speak, I said, "Maybe it would help if I sucked it."

"Huh?"

"You know. A blowjob. Then when you get hard you can finish what you started."

"You want it now, don't you?" he asked with a nasty chuckle.

Continuing in BS-Speak, I answered, "Yeah. I want it a lot. You've got a great body, and it was starting to feel good. So why don't you let me help you?"

Thank God, my wannabe rapist was dumbass stupid. He slowly pushed me into a squatting position and twisted me around to face him, but without letting go of my right arm. He quickly realized that for me to take his dick into my mouth, we would both need to straighten up, which meant that he would have to release my arm.

"Okay," he said. "I'm going to let go of your arm, but if you try any funny stuff, I'll knock your brains out."

Kneeling in front of him with his hands resting on my shoulders, I took his stinky dick into my mouth and began giving him a real blowjob. It took all the control I could muster to keep from gagging at the sour taste. God only knew when he last took a shower.

"You've got a great cock," I said in BS-Speak. "It tastes really good." As I spoke, I slowly brought my hands to his crotch and began fondling his sweaty balls. Sighing with pleasure, he let go of my shoulders, slowly pulled up his t-shirt, and started pinching his nipples with both hands.

Which was colossally stupid on his part because as soon his hands reached his nipples, I bit his dick as hard as could, squeezing and twisting his slimy balls at the same time. He roared with pain and pulled away from me, clutching his crotch and bellowing like a wounded bull. I leapt sideways, barely escaping a blow to the head that could have killed me. But I couldn't move fast enough because I was hobbled by my pants which were down around my knees.

He lunged toward me and grabbed my left ankle, causing me to fall forward as he pulled himself toward me. I kicked back at him with my right foot and felt a very satisfying crunch as my shoe connected with his face, causing him to gasp in pain. I then managed to pull free, pull up my pants, and run towards the desert away from the highway. Almost immediately, I realized that my backpack containing everything I owned, including my savings, was lying a few yards behind the truck. Following my gaze, he lunged towards it but not soon enough to keep me from grabbing the backpack and scooting into the desert behind the weigh station.

"You fucking son of a bitch!" he bellowed. "You are dead meat." He started to chase me but quickly realized that I was too fast for him. I continued running into the desert until I was a safe distance from the weigh station. I could see him clearly because of the single streetlight over the parking area. But he couldn't see me because night had fallen, and I was standing in total darkness.

"Hey, lard ass," I yelled. "How does your dick feel? Do you like those teeth marks? Your dick tastes like shit, by the way. I'm sorry I didn't bite it off."

"Shut up, you fucking asshole."

"Come and make me. Come on. Let's see how well you run with sore balls and half a dick."

He remained in the parking area for what seemed an eternity, peering stupidly into the night. After what seemed like forever, he gave up and limped toward his truck. With great satisfaction, I noted that he was holding his legs wide apart and moving slowly. I watched his taillights fade into the distance and then cautiously returned to the parking lot, avoiding the lighted area for fear that he was watching from a distance. It soon became clear that he was gone.

It was then that the panic set it. My heart started racing and I began gasping for air. I sank to my knees and started vomiting, more dry retching than vomiting because I hadn't eaten since lunch. Once the nausea passed, I stretched out, face up on the desert ground. Images of AMPS attacking me when I was thirteen flooded my mind along with the recent memory of Ape Arms pushing my face toward the truck floor as he jerked my pants down and rammed his finger into my asshole. I lay on the ground for several minutes waiting for my body to return to normal. Well, sort of normal because my asshole and chest still hurt, and I couldn't spit enough to get the foul taste of Ape Arms' dick out of my mouth.

As my mind cleared, I became more aware of my predicament. The desert is filled with vermin, including rattlesnakes, scorpions, and tarantulas. It isn't a place to spend the night. I slowly got to my feet, picked up my backpack, and started walking towards the highway.

Chapter Two:
The Bonneville Samaritan

What to do? I had no idea how far it was to the next town going west, nor did I want to risk running into Ape Arms again. I decided to hitch a ride back to the Phoenix truck stop and try again to find a ride to LA. I briefly considered returning to Croft House where at least I had food and a warm bed. But only for a moment. Going back was not an option.

Dodging traffic and struggling through the sticker-infested median to reach the other side of the divided highway wasn't easy, but I finally made it. To look as presentable as possible, I picked the stickers out of my clothes, dusted myself off, and did a quick spit-wash of my face with my handkerchief. I then stood beside the road, stuck out my thumb, and hoped for the best.

Lots of cars passed without reducing their speed. Several drivers slowed down, looked at me, and then sped away. After what seemed an eternity, a white 1969 Pontiac Bonneville slowed down. The driver looked me over and then stopped about fifty yards away. I ran towards the car as he backed up towards me. Before unlocking the passenger door, he scrutinized me see how scary I looked. I evidently passed muster because he leaned over and opened the passenger door.

"Where are you headed?" he asked.

"To the truck stop just this side of Phoenix. It's an easy bus ride from there to my home," I lied, "and the bus runs all night."

"Where's home?" he asked.

"South Phoenix."

"Okay. Get in. The truck stop is sort of on my way."

He eased the Pontiac back onto the Interstate. Middle-aged, potbellied, tired-looking, and dressed in a rumpled, baggy suit, he wore his hair in a comb over held tightly in place with lots of Vitalis. Nothing about him looked dangerous, which was a relief after Ape Arms.

"What brings you out here?" he asked. "This is an odd place to be hitching a ride."

Time to lie. "I was headed to a friend's ranch when my fuel pump stopped working. I crawled under my pickup to see what was wrong. That's why I'm all dirty. I'll have to come back tomorrow and replace the belt."

"You a mechanic?"

"Sort of. My dad runs a garage, and I've worked on a lot of cars. I guess that kind of makes me a mechanic. Replacing the belt shouldn't be hard. I just hope the fuel pump didn't freeze up. Finding and installing a pump replacement will be a lot more work than replacing a broken fan belt."

"You sound like a mechanic to me. I wouldn't know a fuel pump from a hole in the wall."

Glad to have a civilized conversation after my experience with Ape Arms, I asked "How about you? What do you do?"

"I'm a sales rep for a company that provides school rings, sportswear, and yearbooks to high schools. I cover most of Arizona and parts of Nevada and California. Where do you go to school? Maybe your high school is one of my customers."

Time to lie again since I knew nothing about Phoenix schools. Fortunately, I remembered that Father Tovar had attended a boarding school in Phoenix, so I said, "I attend the Jesuit High School in Phoenix."

"Jesuit? Isn't the Jesuit high school called the Brophy School?"

Oops. Caught in a lie. "Yeah, it is Brophy," I said as casually as possible, "but most of us call it Jesuit because the word Brophy doesn't tell outsiders very much."

"I didn't know that. Maybe if I started using their right name, they'd become one of my customers. So, are you Catholic?"

"Uh, yeah. All my life," I lied.

"Do you go to church?"

"It's required."

"Do you like church?"

Needing a readymade lie, I continued ventriloquizing Father Tovar. I had already adopted his school, so why not his life? "Yeah. I really love the church," I answered. "The Catholic Church is a major part of my life. In fact, I plan to become a priest."

He frowned and with a pensive tone in his voice, he said, "There's a lot of confusion about religion these days. People want religion but they don't know where to look. What do you know about the Mormon Church?"

God help me! I was trapped in a car with a Mormon who wanted to reconvert me to Mormonism! Since Mr. Vitalis had rescued me from the Sonoran Desert, I didn't want to be rude, so I mumbled, "I don't know much about Mormonism at all." A big lie of course since I knew a lot about Mormonism and was trying to get away from it.

His next question followed a script formulated by the LDS Church to interest potential converts: "Would you like to know more about the Mormon Church?"

"Not particularly. I love the Catholic Church, and I cannot imagine being anything else. I love our liturgies (I didn't know what liturgies were, but it was a nice word that Father Tovar had used) and I love the fact that our priests can forgive sins." I then asked disingenuously, "Can your priests forgive sins?"

Startled by the question, he responded, "Well, actually we don't have priests as such."

"Then how do you know if your sins are forgiven?" I needled.

"We believe that only God can forgive sins."

"But that's not what Jesus said. Right there in John's gospel, Jesus tells his apostles that they can forgive sins. Check it out for yourself. It's in the twentieth chapter of John."

The poor man was absolutely dumbfounded by this detailed response. As was I! In what corner of my mind had I retained what Father Tovar had taught me, including the Bible citation? Then, just to tease Mr. Vitalis a bit more, I added, "You know, if the Mormon church can't forgive sins, maybe you should find a church that can. Why belong to a church whose priests can't forgive sins?"

Teasing this poor Mormon guy was so much fun that I had almost forgotten my horrific experience with Ape Arms and how much my body hurt. Finally, he responded with a lame "Boy, they have really indoctrinated you, haven't they."

With feigned firmness, I responded, "It's not indoctrination when it's true."

Frowning, he said, "Well you have your truth and I have mine. Let's just leave it at that."

Which was exactly where I wanted to leave it. But then the guilt pangs started. Mr. Vitalis had risked picking up a stranger late at night, not knowing if I was an axe murderer or worse. By wanting to tell me about Mormonism, maybe he wasn't a trophy hunter. Maybe he just wanted to share something that meant a lot to him. To make amends, I said in BS-Speak, "By the way, I really want to thank you for picking me up. You never know when you'll meet a Good Samaritan."

A sad smile played at the corners of his mouth. "Thank you for thanking me." Then, with a plaintive note in his voice he added, "I don't hear a lot of thank-yous these days."

I looked at him carefully. Who was this lumpy, middle-aged man? What was his life like if he didn't get a lot of thank-yous? Did he have a wife and a family? Did he enjoy trying to support a family by selling class rings and yearbooks to high school students in three states? Did he believe that being a Mormon and having a family were steps towards becoming a god? Or was he another one of those not so blissful heterosexuals trapped in an unhappy marriage? Looking at his rumpled suit, his out-of-shape body, and his Vitalis hairdo, I regretted not being kinder. As we neared the truck stop, he asked, "Where do you want me to leave you?"

"In the parking lot near the restaurant will be fine." While putting on my backpack, I said, "It was nice talking to you. And I really want to thank you for picking me up. Only a good person would do that."

"I also enjoyed talking to you. You will make an excellent priest."

Chapter Three:
Angelo

I bought a Coke and a bag of peanuts in the minimart. It wasn't much of a dinner, but I needed to save money. Seeing a sign saying "Showers" I asked the cashier if I could rent a shower. "Sure" she said. "Twenty-five cents if you have your own towel and soap, and fifty cents if you need a towel and soap from us."

I gladly paid the fifty cents. The shower stall had a small anteroom with a bench, a mirror, a sink, and a couple of hooks for hanging clothes. I slowly removed my shirt and was shocked by the huge purplish bruise on my chest where Ape Arms had hit me. Worse was the memory of how he crammed his ogre finger into me and almost raped me. The shower felt great. I rinsed out my mouth repeatedly and scrubbed myself hard, partly to clean my body but mostly to purge the memory of that horrendous experience. After toweling off and changing into my only extra set of clean clothes, I walked out to the parking lot. Purged, cleansed, and reenergized, I still faced the problem of getting to Los Angeles.

Vowing to be more discriminating this time, I walked to the pump area to try again to hitch a ride. After several refusals, I approached a guy who was facing away from me. A little shorter than me, he had broad shoulders and longish dark hair. "Sir," I said, "Could I catch a ride going towards Los Angeles?"

He turned around and gave me a quick once-over. "It's a bit late to be looking for a ride, but I'll take you as far as Ehrenberg. That's where I plan to spend the night."

As he spoke, I almost forgot to breathe. His loose t-shirt revealed the contours of an athlete's body. With dark hair and eyebrows, olive-colored skin, and intense sapphire-blue eyes that seemed out of sync with his complexion, he was gorgeous. He needed a shave and a haircut, but the rest of him looked, oh so fine. I gratefully accepted his invitation and wondered how I could nearly get raped and then that very night feel drawn to this beautiful man.

As we drove onto the interstate, he offered me his hand. "Hi. I'm Angelo. Angelo Moretti. What's your name?"

"Josh. Josh Chastain."

"So, Josh, what takes you to Los Angeles? Shouldn't you be in school?"

Time to start lying—again. "I'm going to Los Angeles to live with my grandmother. I'll finish high school there."

"Why are you hitching rides? A bus fare can't be that expensive."

Time for more fibbing. "I had to leave home in a hurry because my mom's boyfriend threatened to kill me."

"Whoa! That's heavy stuff. Why did he want to kill you?"

Inventing a new identity was getting fun. "Because" I answered, "I was tired of his bullshit and starting to stand up to him. He has a good job, and we live in an okay house, but at night he gets drunk and sometimes beats up on my mother and me. She cries and begs him to stop, and then he goes all maudlin and tells us how much he loves us. After that, he drinks until he passes out. I left because I couldn't take it anymore. Besides, without me in the house, maybe he'll be nicer to my mom. He never liked me since I was some other guy's kid."

"What happened to your real father?"

Warming to my improvisation, I answered, "He's an even bigger loser. He's a hopeless drunk who can't keep a job. He basically mooched off my mom although she didn't have much money because she worked at a Circle K. He disappeared when I was about twelve. I never want to see him again. My mom is a nice lady, but she has a penchant for finding atrocious boyfriends."

After what seemed an eternity, Angelo asked quietly, "Josh, can I tell you something?"

"Sure. What?"

"I don't believe you. You just used the words *maudlin, penchant,* and *atrocious.* Those aren't words that I would expect from the child of a no-good drunk and a Circle K mother. Do you want to tell me your real story?"

Well damn! No way could I tell him my real story. Who would believe all that stuff about my drug-addled apocalyptic mother, Father Tovar who almost made me a Catholic, and Dr. Chandler and his dirty-pictures machine, not to mention angels and gold plates? So, I asked, "Do I have to tell my real story? Do you need to know all that Oliver Twist stuff?"

"Oliver Twist stuff?" he asked with a chuckle. "You're a pretty smart kid for a kid. No, you don't have to tell me your whole story. A lot of us have stories we're trying to get away from. But you do have to tell the truth about one thing. You're not running from the law, are you?"

"Absolutely not. I've never been arrested. I just can't go back home."

"Why?"

"I'd rather not say."

After a long pause, he said, "Okay. I can accept that. Maybe later."

After a few minutes of silence, I said, "Tell me something about you. Who is Angelo?"

"Who is Angelo? Well, that's something I'm trying to figure out," he said with a nervous laugh.

"Okay. Where does Angelo call home when he's not driving a truck?"

"Another good question. My family has a printing business in Houston, but Houston is not big enough for both me and my ex-wife Betty."

"Why? What's wrong with her?"

An angry shadow fell over his face. Through clenched teeth he answered, "You mean aside from being a lying, money-sucking, conniving, castrating cunt?" This sudden show of anger frightened me because it was so unexpected. After several deep breaths, he continued in a more controlled voice, "We have a kid, a sweet little guy named Mario who just turned three. But the marriage was a nightmare. She would love to stick me for more child support. That's one of the reasons I drive truck. It makes me hard to find, and since I'm paid by the job, she never knows how much I earn. Can you believe it? I hide my income, so she won't grab more of it. I keep up with the child support payments because I love my kid, but I refuse to give that lying cunt a penny more. How about you? Do you have a girlfriend?"

I hate that question. Why do people assume that anyone with a penis has a wife or a girlfriend? I could lie, but Angelo had already proven good at detecting lies. I could tell him about Ronnie, although I wasn't ready to tell this beautiful stranger that I was gay. Thinking of Patty, I answered, "I have a friend girl, a girl who is a really good friend, but no, I don't have a girlfriend."

"That surprises me. A handsome kid like you, I'd expect girls to be standing in line for you."

Noting that he had just called me handsome, I asked, "Do you have a girlfriend?"

"No. Never did until Betty."

"You don't ever want a girlfriend again?"

"Not right away. Of course, it would depend." Then carefully weighing his words, he added "Maybe with the right person."

Ah-ha! That telltale word, *person*. Not a girl or a woman but that noncommittal, non-gendered word, *person*. So, I decided to tip my cards. "Well, actually there is a *person* I'm kind of in love with."

"Does this person have a name?"

"Yeah."

"Do you care to tell me this person's name?"

Since he was playing along with the person stuff, I decided to open up. "Yes, *he* has a name. *His* name is Ronnie." Angelo hunched his shoulders over the steering wheel, took a deep breath, and asked in a gentle voice, "Is that why you're running away from home? Because you're gay?"

"That's the main reason. Will you hate me for being gay, throw me out of your truck, beat me to a bloody pulp, and abandon my limp, battered body to the vultures?"

He let out a hearty laugh. "Josh, you have a way with words and a gift for drama. No, I won't do any of those things. In fact, since you're gay, maybe I'll like you even more." Before I could follow up on this enigmatic response, we reached the exit to the Ehrenberg truck stop, which gave him an excuse to change the subject and concentrate on his driving.

Chapter Four:
Ehrenberg

The truck stop consisted of a minimart, a fast-food joint, restrooms, shower facilities, and about a million gas pumps. "Are you hungry?" Angelo asked.

"A little." In truth, I was famished. Except for a bag of peanuts and a Coke, I hadn't eaten since noon at Croft House.

"Tell you what. Let's take a shower. Then, I'll treat you to a hamburger."

My second shower of the evening felt just as good as the first one. Maybe I was finally getting rid of Ape Arms' germs. Angelo took a long time, but when he stepped out of the individual shower stall, I almost fainted. He had shaved and was wearing clean levis and a t-shirt. There was nothing—absolutely nothing—wrong with his looks. Thick black hair parted in the middle, intense blue eyes, chiseled facial features, full sensuous lips, and a compact, well-muscled build—he had it all. Put a beard on him and he could be Titian's John the Baptist. After buying me a hamburger and fries, he asked if I planned to look for a ride.

"What are my chances of finding a ride this time of night?" I asked.

"Pretty lousy. Tell you what. There's a bed in my truck behind the passenger seats. That's where I sleep. Maybe you can improvise a bed using the front seats. Then we can go on to LA tomorrow. Sound like a deal?"

It sounded like the only deal I had. He crawled into the "bedroom" behind the cab where I was aware of him undressing. In the meantime, I removed my Levi's and T-shirt, hoping to use them as a pillow, and tried to get comfortable. After watching me squirm from one awkward position to another, Angelo said with an odd tension in his voice, "Okay, Josh. That's not going to work. You'll have to sleep in here with me. This is supposedly a double bed, so we should fit."

Wearing only my jockey shorts, I clambered between the two passenger seats into the space behind the cab where indeed there was a double bed but not much else. "Hey man, how did you get that bruise on your chest? That looks painful. Did someone hit you?"

"Uh… I had an unfortunate experience this afternoon."

"What happened?"

I gave him a very abbreviated version of my encounter with Ape Arms. With a mix of concern and curiosity in his voice, he asked softly, "Josh, tell me the truth. Did the guy rape you?"

"He tried, but I got away. I'd prefer not to talk about it."

Frowning and shaking his head, Angelo said, "Well, whatever happened, I'm glad you escaped. If I ever meet the bastard, I'll put him in a body cast. Let me put something on that bruise." He pulled a small medical kit out of a little cabinet above the bed and tenderly rubbed salve on the bruise. Under normal circumstances, I would have found his touch a sexual turn-on. But at that moment, I only felt gratitude. I suddenly teared up. With an alarmed look on his face, Angelo gently placed his hands on my shoulders, saying, "That's okay, buddy. Cry if you need to. You've had a terrible day." Then, somewhat nervously, he added, "Maybe you'll feel better if we lie down."

After considerable maneuvering, both on his part and mine, we found ourselves in a spooning position, my head on his left bicep, his chest against my back, and his right arm draped lightly over my body. We were clearly in a lovers' embrace—something neither of us was ready to acknowledge. Incongruously, I recalled an old hymn, something about "Leaning on the Everlasting Arms." Why is it that every time I feel embraced by a kind man, I think of God? Feeling brave, I took hold of his right wrist with my left hand and pulled his arm more tightly around me. He didn't resist. After several minutes, he asked, "Do you feel better? Are you comfortable now?"

"Very comfortable. Thank you for being so kind. Are you okay?"

"More than okay," he replied. "This feels good. Let's just be quiet and go to sleep."

Eventually, we disengaged, and he turned over on his right side with his back to me. He quickly fell into a deep sleep. His soft, regular breathing seemed almost musical. After a few moments, I too drifted off, but not without marveling that on that very day I had escaped from Croft House, I had almost been raped by a monster, I had been rescued by a Good Samaritan who wanted to convert me to Mormonism, and I was now sharing a truck-cab bed with a kind man who reminded me of Titian's John the Baptist.

Chapter Five:
Angelo's Story

At the crack of dawn, Angelo nudged me awake. "You up for a run?" he asked.

"A what?" I asked through a big yawn.

"A run. I go for a run every morning. It makes me feel good for the rest of the day. Come on. You'll like it. Let's go before it gets hot."

Barely awake, I pulled my sneakers out of my backpack, slipped into my PE clothes, and followed him outside. "Where are we going?" I asked.

"Just a couple of miles up the road," he answered, "but first we need to do some stretching."

Miles? I hoped I was up to it. After a quick pee break, he did some elaborate stretches that I tried to imitate, painfully aware of how clumsy I looked in comparison. I barely managed to keep up with him, perhaps because he wanted me to know that he could outrun me. As we walked out of the shower building, Angelo suddenly turned toward the cinderblock wall and slugged it with both fists. Seeing the shock on my face, he smiled and raised his fists to my eye level. They looked hard and meaty. "That's how I keep these babies in shape," he said. "I never know when I'll need them."

After a quick breakfast, we settled in for what was going to be a drive of several hours, "Can I ask you a nosy question?" I asked.

"Sure," he answered with a grin, "just as long as I don't have to answer."

"Why did you get married if your wife is so awful?"

"Because she set me up. I had just got back from Vietnam and wasn't in the best mental state."

"You fought in Vietnam?"

"Yeah, but don't make me talk about it. Vietnam is fucked up and it really fucked me up."

Noting the anger in his voice, I sought safer ground. "So, how did your wife set you up?"

"We met at a mixer for single Catholic adults that my parents talked me into joining. They wanted me to marry and settle down. Betty was quite aggressive, so we had a couple of dates. She swore she was on the pill, so we started having sex. But she lied about the pill and got pregnant. That was the trap because she knew that, as an honorable Catholic boy, I would feel obligated to marry her. So, we got married although I knew it was a terrible mistake."

"How did you know that?"

"Because I didn't like her. I felt trapped in a marriage I never wanted."

"Did you keep having sex?"

"She wanted to, but I couldn't get into it. After Mario was born, I refused since the last thing I wanted was another kid, least of all with her."

"Couldn't you just get a divorce?"

"Not when you're Catholic. Of course, as a good Catholic boy I shouldn't have had sex before getting married, but I was curious, and you know how that turned out. I come from a devout Catholic family. My parents saw that I got an intense Catholic education, first at an all-boy Catholic grade school and then at an all-male Jesuit high school. After that, I did four years at St. Thomas University in Houston, a very conservative place run by the Basilian fathers."

"Bazillion as in millions and millions?"

"No, dummy. Basilian as in the Order of St. Basil. It's a French-Canadian order of monks."

"So, if you were such a serious Catholic, what finally made you get a divorce?"

After a long pause, he said, "I'm going to tell you something that few people know. You promise to keep it a secret?"

"Who am I going to tell?"

"Whom."

"Okay 'whom' Mr. Persnickety Grammar Geek. Just finish your story."

"I became friends with a guy at the dojo, a guy named Jason. After workouts, we'd go out for beers and joke around a bit. One night after some beers, he walked me to my car. It was dark and we thought we were alone in this big parking lot. When I turned to say goodbye, he grabbed me and started to kiss me. At first, I was shocked, but I didn't stop him. Maybe—and I have a hard time admitting this—because I wanted it to happen. After a couple of minutes, he pushed me away, and said 'We'd better go. I'll look for you at the gym.' And that was the last time I saw him."

"Is that the end of the story?"

"God, I wish it were the end of the story. Unbeknownst to me, bitch Betty had hired a private eye to follow me. Since I was avoiding sex with her, she assumed that I was seeing other women. Her private eye took night photographs of the thing between Jason and me. The next afternoon, her lawyer showed up with the photographs and told me that Betty was suing for a divorce, but that if I met her demands, she'd keep the photographs secret. He also told me to find someplace else to sleep. She basically kicked me out of my own house. Sure enough, two days later, a county marshal cornered me with a divorce summons. Betty wanted everything, but what she most wanted was full custody of Mario."

"Couldn't you fight her?"

"I hired a good lawyer and told him everything. His advice was, 'Angelo, she's got you by the balls. If she brings up the Jason stuff, Texas courts may never let you see your kid again.' I had to sell the house and my part of the business since she demanded half of all I owned plus child support. My father and brother bought my third of the business, which was a real hardship for them. So, you see, the bitch hurt both me and my family. The judge, of course, didn't know that she was blackmailing me and probably wondered why I didn't fight harder. But with those photos, she held a powerful trump card, especially in Texas. The best I can do is pay child support and stay out of sight. That's why I'm driving truck in the middle of the Mojave Desert and telling my sad story to a teenage hitchhiker I hardly know."

He looked so sad. I wanted to reach over and take his hand, but I didn't dare. Finally, I said, "You must really hate her."

"Why wouldn't I?" he answered, raising his voice. Then, with no warning, he was suddenly very angry, just like the previous day. In a hard voice that was almost a shout, he continued, "Of course I hate her. Look how she fucked up my life! The cunt tricked me into getting her pregnant and shamed me into marrying her. Then she blackmailed me with those photos, took away my kid, and took away my life. That's why I'm living like a migrant worker. Why wouldn't I hate her? I'd kill her if I could. Maybe I should have killed her when I had the chance."

Red-faced with anger, he seemed an entirely different person. After a few deep breaths, he calmed down and started talking in a more subdued voice. "The divorce was really hard on my parents. I was always their golden boy—a good kid, a good student, and a nice Catholic boy who confessed every week and never missed mass. My dad died of a heart attack a year after our divorce. I feel guilty about his death and wonder if maybe I had something to do with it. But then I force myself to remember that he was overweight, never exercised, and smoked two packs of unfiltered cigarettes every day."

"Does your family know why you got divorced?"

"I told everything to my brother Enzo but nothing to my parents. They couldn't understand. There was no reason to tell them."

"Enzo's okay with it?"

"Yea. Enzo supports me no matter what. He's always been on my side." After a long pause, he continued in a soft voice, "Josh, I can't go on like this. Hating Betty and being angry all the time doesn't get me anywhere. At some point, I'll need to calm down, go back to Texas, and fight for more time with Mario."

Remembering what he said about Jason, I asked, "Do you think you might be gay?"

The question hung in the air for what seemed a very long time. Then, in a testy voice, he answered, "Why do you think I might be gay? Do I look gay? Do I act gay?"

Fearing another outburst, I carefully weighed my reply. "I don't know what gay looks and acts like. I'm sorry I brought it up."

"It's okay. No offense taken." Then, looking at me, he asked, "Let's talk about you. You seem pretty sure of yourself. How did you figure out that you were gay?"

"There wasn't much to figure out. I was attracted to guys even when I was a little kid." I told him some of my story—about growing up Mormon, the circle jerks with classmates, my friendship with Harold, the Burt and Barry story, Ronnie, and how I ran away from Croft House. I left out Father Tovar since I was unsure of how Angelo would react to my being with a priest.

After a long silence, he said, "You know, Josh, you're the first person I've discussed any of this with. It feels good to talk about it. Or at least to hear you talk about it. I'm so pathetic that I don't have much to tell."

Although knowing that I was treading on sensitive ground, I dared ask, "Did you find Jason attractive?"

"I never let myself find anybody attractive. I suppressed all thoughts about sex by studying hard and working out a lot. I was in total denial about my sexual feelings."

"Why?"

"Josh, do you have any idea what it's like to grow up Catholic, like really strict Catholic?"

"It can't be much worse than growing up Mormon."

"Don't be so sure. For me, it was mostly awful. The nuns in grade school scared the shit out of me about sin and hell. I remember a large painting of the last judgment over the main staircase in my grade school, where God is sending the good people to heaven and the bad people to hell to burn for eternity but never be consumed. I even remember washing dishes a second time on Thursday nights to make sure that not a single molecule of meat remained on them for fish-only Fridays. Maybe it wasn't the same for other kids, but I grew up scared shitless. The Jesuits who taught me in high school were better than the nuns, but even some of them harped constantly on avoiding the near occasion of sin."

"What's that? The near occasion of sin?"

"Anything that might lead to sin. Like thinking about sex. I entered puberty later than most, like around fourteen. I was the runt of the class, which was one reason I got into martial arts. As soon as puberty hit, I started having wet dreams. They were always about guys, although I didn't want to admit that to myself. And that's how I grew up. Lots of guilt, lots of worrying about going to hell, lots of sports, very little information about sex, and lots of trying not to think about my dreams. Oh, and I was also an A-student. I do have to thank the nuns and priests for that. Except for their bullshit about sex, sin, and hell, they gave me a good education."

After several moments of silence, he said, "Josh, I'm going to propose something that makes me nervous as hell. I need to unload the truck at a warehouse in Compton. If you want to help, I'll ask them to pay you for your work. Then we can spend another night together in a motel. Does that sound okay?"

"It sounds more than okay. By the way, I don't have a grandmother in LA."

"I figured as much."

Chapter Six:
First Night in LA

The warehouse was in a scuzzy part of town. The foreman guided the truck into a large bay. As we climbed out of the truck, Angelo greeted the foreman, whom he apparently knew. "Hi, Henry. How's it going? This is my nephew Josh. If he helps us unload, can you pay him anything?"

"It's against the rules since he isn't a regular employee, but I tell you what. I'm shorthanded and really want your truck out of here before five o'clock because a couple of others are due later this evening. If you, your nephew, and what's left of my crew get the truck unloaded by 5 PM, I'll say you worked overtime and give you some extra money for your nephew. Deal?"

"Deal." I joined in tackling the cargo with Angelo. It consisted of lots of large crates that had to be unloaded with a forklift. The crates contained hundreds of smaller boxes that had to be delivered to different sections of the warehouse. A couple of Mexican guys worked with us to make sure that everything got in the right place. I worked hard, partly because I wanted to finish on time but also because I wanted Angelo to admire my manly prowess. Thanks to my dad, I knew how to work, and I wasn't a weakling. I kept up with the other guys, and sure enough by 5 PM the truck was empty.

"What's next?" I asked Angelo.

"A rental car, a motel room, and a nice dinner. You may have noticed that we skipped lunch."

"When do you start driving again?"

"I'm not sure. I've asked Henry for a couple of days off. Let's see how things go."

One of the Mexican guys drove us to a discount car rental place where Angelo picked up a used 1965 Oldsmobile. We then got a motel room on Western Avenue just south of Sunset. By evening we were settled in a room with two double beds, ratty curtains, and some faded prints on the wall. Despite pretending otherwise, we both felt an awkward sexual tension in the air. After showers, he asked, "You up for dinner?"

"Yeah, but I want to buy. After all that lucrative work at the warehouse, I'm rich now."

He smiled and asked, "Will this make me your date?"

"Sure. After all you've gone through, it's about time you had a date."

We were back in the motel by nine-o-clock. He seemed nervous. The night before, he had held me because I needed comforting. But now there was no excuse, so I made the first move, placing my hands on his shoulders and then lacing my hands behind his neck. He responded by pulling me into a full-body embrace. We held each other for what seemed a very long time. Then, pulling his head towards me, I kissed him, first on his cheeks and then on the lips. He was a clumsy kisser, which suggested a lack of experience. The bulge in his pants, however, said that he didn't want to stop.

We continued making out and started to undress each other. His well-muscled chest was lightly covered with hair that narrowed into a straight line down to his navel that then expanded into an inverted V towards a very hairy crotch. I slowly pulled down his pants and shorts and slipped my mouth over his dick, which was on the small side of average but still, as Mother Harold would say, a nice mouthful. He placed his hands lightly on my head, running his hands through my hair, as I sensed his growing excitement. Suddenly, he pulled me to my feet and said, "Josh, would you mind if I gave it a try just to see what it's like?"

Clearly, I didn't mind. Again, his lack of experience showed, but he was a fast learner and showed great potential for becoming a proficient cocksucker. Fully naked, we lay down on one of the beds, hugging, kissing, and blowing each other. Eventually, the tension became too great. Looking deep into each other's eyes, we jacked off to climax, coming on each other's body. With a towel from the bathroom, I cleaned us both off. Temporarily sated, we embraced each other and interlaced our legs, gently rubbing each other's body.

After a few minutes, I remembered the massage that Blair had given me. Repeating that ritual, I turned Angelo over on his stomach and began massaging his body, starting with his feet. Dark short hair covered his legs, but not so much that I couldn't appreciate the well-defined muscles of his calves and thighs, and the delicate blue veins visible through his translucent olive-colored skin. Every inch of him was beautiful. And then I had a God moment. Sensing the warmth of his body, his heartbeat, the air moving in and out of his lungs, and the magical feel of his skin, I thought, "This gorgeous man was made in the image of God. I am touching a sacred object."

Intruding in my God-thoughts, Angelo whispered, "Now it's my turn." Led partly by curiosity, he massaged every part of my seventeen-year-old body. I luxuriated under his touch, marveling at how those hands capable of punching cinderblock walls could also be so tender. After this mutual massage, we relaxed in a loose embrace, but before long we started making love again. After another amazing climax, we nestled in each other's arms. Before drifting off to sleep, Angelo whispered, "Josh, I never knew it could be this wonderful. Maybe I'll finally figure out who I am." I sensed that he already knew who he was. But knowing it and liking it would turn out to be two different things.

Chapter Seven:
A New Life

The next morning, I woke up before he did. We had slept the entire night in each other's arms. As I gazed at this beautiful man at my side, my mind kept going back to that fleeting intuition that Angelo's body—anybody's body maybe? —was a sacred object not to be trifled with. Just then, Angelo yawned, pulled me towards him, and kissed me on my forehead. "What are you thinking about?" he asked.

"About how handsome you are."

"You're not bad yourself," he answered as he gave me another kiss. "I have the day off, so let me show you a bit of LA."

We started with a big breakfast at a Norm's, an LA version of Denny's but with larger portions and a quirkier clientele. Next was Venice Beach—my first time to see the ocean. Although new to me, the sound of the waves seemed familiar, as though remembered from a previous life. As we wandered toward Santa Monica, Angelo told me more about his family, his older brother Enzo, whom he called his best friend, and his mother who had worn black ever since his father's death. I told him about music and state choir. He was much impressed that I played the piano.

Walking back to the car, we passed a small building with a sign in Chinese letters followed by "Venice Beach Martial Arts." Angelo had to check it out. A well-muscled, compact Asian man greeted us and allowed us to look over the facility which consisted of a smallish dressing area and two large rooms covered with large floor pads. A few guys were working out in what looked like shadow boxing to me—lots of posing, kicking, and mock hitting. Angelo was utterly entranced. Noting my curiosity, he explained some of the moves, whispering at times why some guys were better than others. He then asked, "How would you like to study martial arts with me? I'm a helluva good teacher and you could use the training."

I agreed, not realizing that we would soon be frequent visitors to the dojo. After lunch at a taco stand, we drove out the Pacific Coast Highway and took Topanga Canyon Road over into the San Fernando Valley. We eventually made it to Hollywood and parked on Selma Avenue, just a block from Hollywood Boulevard. We spent an hour looking at the names of movie stars embedded in the sidewalks. Angelo not only recognized a lot of them but also gave detailed descriptions of their careers. Obviously, when not being a good Catholic boy, an A-student, and a martial arts expert, he watched old movies and musicals—like every gay boy should.

That night over dinner, Angelo seemed nervous as though he wanted to say something but couldn't quite get it out. But he finally started talking. "Josh," he said. "I've really loved these last two days. I feel like I'm doing things I should have done years ago. I've told you stuff that I've never told anyone else. And I really like being with you. As you know, I drive truck largely to keep out of Betty's sight. But I'm tired of being alone all the time, so I'd like to make you a proposition. Why don't we rent a small apartment for just the two of us? I could drive truck locally for Henry, and maybe you could take classes at a community college and finish high school. We could also train together at that dojo we visited. It could be a lot of fun. Maybe we both just need to slow down."

I accepted without hesitation. Back at the hotel, he said "And now you have to do me a favor."

"Like what?"

"Come and see."

He took me into a darkened meeting room behind the motel lobby where there was a Yamaha baby grand. "You have to play for me."

He pulled up a chair just to the left of the piano bench, and I began to play, mostly romantic stuff— Brahms, Schubert, and Chopin. After I finished, he said, "That was so beautiful. Do you know any Bach?"

Bach!! This guy was too good to be true. I played the opening movement of Bach's first partita. He begged me not to stop, so I played the entire piece.

After finishing, I turned towards him and was shocked to see tears in his gorgeous blue eyes. "Josh, that was beautiful. You play like a god."

Never knowing how to respond to compliments, I mumbled a thank you. When we got to the room, he said, "Josh, you need to thank your parents for making it possible for you to play like that. You're a smart, accomplished kid. You didn't get that way by accident."

He was right of course, so that night I wrote a short letter to my parents, letting them know that I was alright, thanking them for all they had done for me, and telling them not to worry. Angelo arranged for a fellow truck driver to mail the letter from somewhere other than Los Angeles so my parents wouldn't know where I was.

Chapter Eight:
Almost Married

Within a week, we were practically a married couple. I occasionally wondered if I was being unfaithful to Ronnie, but then I remembered Blair's assertion that Barkley and he could be lovers and still enjoy sex with other people. I saw no reason that the same couldn't be true for Ronnie and me. Yet, I marveled at how I could have such warm memories of Ronnie while moving so quickly into an intimate relationship with another man. I had told Angelo about Ronnie in our very first conversation, but it was apparently a subject neither of us wanted to pursue.

We found a furnished two-bedroom apartment on Ocean Park Boulevard in Santa Monica that rented by the month. Angelo helped me get a California driver's license with our Ocean Park address—no mention of Rosales. He continued driving truck, but only for local deliveries, which meant that he came home every evening. Henry loaned us an old Volkswagen bus, and I bought a used bicycle.

To contribute to household expenses, I took a part-time job at a Lucky's supermarket, a short bike ride from our apartment, that required me to work four hours every morning, mostly checking inventory and stocking shelves. It was mind-numbing work, but it gave me a little spending money and a discount on groceries. Neither of us could cook, so we learned together and prepared remarkably good meals for a couple of amateurs. Thank God for Betty Crocker and Good Housekeeping.

We joined the dojo on Venice beach, which fortunately was only a few blocks from our apartment, and started working out most afternoons. Watching Angelo was like watching ballet. His movements were beautiful, fluid, perfect. He gave me a couple of lessons, but I soon decided to work with another instructor. Angelo knew his stuff, but teaching brought out an authoritarian strain in him that made me uncomfortable. Somehow, he always managed to communicate that he could really hurt me if he wanted to. Still, I found martial arts fun and was surprised to see myself succeeding at something so manly and athletic.

We had sex almost every night. He wanted to try everything and surprised us both by preferring the passive role in anal intercourse. But lest I mistake passive for passivity, after sex he often initiated supposedly playful martial arts moves that always resulted in me being pinned. Perhaps, as the passive member in intercourse, he needed to show domination in other ways.

As our friendship deepened, I came to know Angelo as a profoundly complicated person—highly intelligent and well-read, but also seething with subliminal anger, flashes of which could be quite frightening. At first, he seemed to have no trouble accepting his sexuality. Recognizing himself as a gay man helped him understand why he had never wanted to date women, how he had used Catholic teachings to avoid recognizing his sexual orientation, and why he often felt uncomfortable in the company of straight men. But he had trouble saying, "I'm gay" and often made snide remarks about effeminate men.

Angelo may have been the first real intellectual I ever met. By intellectual, I mean someone who loves ideas, reads serious stuff, and seeks thoughtful conversation. I quickly learned that he expected me to talk like an adult rather than a snarky adolescent (which I was good at). Through him, I became acquainted with high-toned magazines like *Harper's, The New Republic, The Atlantic,* and *The New York Review of Books.* His favorite nighttime reading ranged from Shakespeare plays to histories of the Roman Empire.

We received *The Los Angeles Times* daily, which was my first contact with a decent newspaper. One day, the *Times* published an article on aversion therapy as a cure for homosexuality. Dr. Chandler of Arizona State University was quoted prominently as an authority on the efficacy of such treatment. The article quoted psychotherapists who agreed with Chandler's methods along with others who claimed that aversion therapy had no scientific justification and could be dangerous.

This was in 1970, several years before the American Psychiatric Association determined that homosexuality was not a mental disorder.

We also talked a great deal about religion. Angelo's experience of the Roman Catholic Church was the exact opposite of Father Tovar's. Whereas Father Tovar had found in Catholicism a source of comfort, Angelo remembered only mindless legalism, sexual and intellectual repression, and a system of control based on fear of punishment. In a discussion on St. Thomas, he described how Catholicism condemned homosexuality as a violation of natural law, explaining that sex should be used solely for procreation. On similar grounds, he explained that the Catholic Church opposes birth control because it thwarts the natural use of sex, prompting me to ask, "So, essentially natural law says that you can use your dick only for pissing and for making babies?"

He laughed. "I doubt that St. Thomas used those exact words, but yeah, that's the basic idea.

"Does natural law mean that it's a sin to stand on your head or walk on your hands? Obviously, your head and hands were not designed for those purposes."

"Good questions. If I ever meet St. Thomas, I'll be sure to ask him."

"What if what's natural for one person is not natural for another one? Being gay is the natural me. Does natural law allow for such differences?"

"No, because exceptions smack of relativism, which is something Roman Catholicism hates. They want certainty—dogma—with only the church itself authorized to say what is true."

While interesting, these conversations sometimes made me uncomfortable because Angelo could not talk dispassionately about certain subjects, specifically his ex-wife, the war in Vietnam, and the Catholic church. Worse, he would often turn conversations away from the subject at hand and attack me personally when I disagreed with him or ventured a differing opinion. Once or twice, he said something like, "And here we have the opinion of a seventeen-year-old queer boy from Arizona who still hasn't graduated from high school."

I once retorted, "Would you mind disagreeing with my opinion instead of insulting me?"

"Where's the insult? Did I say anything that was untrue? Aren't you a queer boy from Arizona who hasn't graduated from high school? Where's the insult? I'm just stating the facts."

"I've been around a lot of college graduates—some of my numbskull high school teachers, for example—and I've seen no evidence that a college degree guarantees intelligence."

"So, now you're insulting me!"

319

I never prolonged these conversations because he refused to let me have the last word. Lest our disagreements escalate into a full-fledged argument, I chose either to agree with him or simply to stop talking. My silences annoyed him and took an emotional toll on me since I was never good at holding my tongue. I especially resented being called "queer boy". After all, what was he? Still, I kept my mouth shut, largely because I feared his temper.

Chapter Nine:
Vietnam

Soon after moving into the apartment, I awoke in the middle of the night to hear Angelo mumbling incoherently. His eyes were tightly closed as though not wanting to see something. Recognizing it as a nightmare, I tried to wake him up, but he pushed me away, almost violently. He finally opened his eyes, sat up, and looked around as though not knowing where he was. Slowly he started to breathe normally, and then started to cry, almost like a little kid. "Oh Josh. Josh. I'm so sorry you had to see me like this."

"It was just a bad dream," I said. "Everything is okay now." He curled up next to me and thanked me for being so good to him.

"How could I not be good to you?" I asked. "You're a wonderful person."

"I'm not a good person. You just don't know me that well."

"What were you dreaming about?"

"Fucking Vietnam. Always fucking Vietnam. I'll never get it out of my head."

We eventually fell asleep in a loose embrace. Over the next few days, he started talking about his Vietnam experiences. He hated the war and could get frighteningly furious in denouncing the policies that led to it. Kennedy, Johnson, McNamara, Nixon, Kissinger, Westmoreland—for him, all were war criminals. He described seeing friends die and feeling guilty for the suffering inflicted on the Vietnamese people. One of his tasks had been euphemistically called "education" which meant distributing flyers to inform villagers that their homes were about to be napalmed. I was never sure if telling these stories did him any good since the anger never seemed to dissipate.

In mid-May, I heard an announcement on Pacifica Radio that UCLA students had organized a rally to protest the Vietnam war and commemorate the students killed at Kent State. Given Angelo's feelings about the war, he was easily persuaded to attend. It was my first time on the UCLA campus, and I immediately fell in love with the place. Hundreds of people attended the rally, mostly students but also famous people like Joan Baez and my childhood heartthrob, Harry Belafonte, who spoke eloquently of how devastating the draft was to young Black men. After the rally, Angelo pulled me onto the sofa and said, "It's time you and I had a heart-to-heart chat."

"What about?" I asked nervously. "Have I done something wrong?"

"No, you've done nothing wrong but you're not doing enough right. Seeing those students tonight, I kept thinking 'Josh should be one of them. It's not right that he's not in school.' So, tomorrow I want you to go over to Santa Monica College to see about enrolling in summer school. That way I won't feel like you're totally wasting time with a broken-down vet like me. Besides, neither of us should count on our relationship lasting forever. At some point, I'll have to return to Texas, and you need to be thinking about a career. You're too smart to be a stockboy at Lucky's for the rest of your life."

Although these hints about ending our relationship made me nervous, they also made sense. I was seventeen years old, he was twelve years my senior, and he had a life back in Texas. I also remembered Mrs. Jespersen's advice about planning for a career.

Chapter Ten:
Mr. Hazen Takes Care of his Own

The following afternoon I met with an academic counselor at Santa Monica College, a Mr. Hazen. Slightly overweight but immaculately dressed in a tweed jacket, a cuff-linked starched blue shirt, and a paisley bow tie, he reminded me of Mother Harold, complete with the lisp, the pursed lips, and the floppy wrists. After introducing ourselves, he asked, "Josh, how old are you?"

"I turned seventeen last April."

"Have you graduated from high school?"

"No."

"Are you attending high school now?"

"No."

Frown and long pause. Pudgy index finger pressed against pursed lips. Finally, he said, "Well, to enroll at SMC, you need to have a high school diploma or be enrolled in a high school that allows students to take college courses. So why don't you go back to high school?"

"I can't. I dropped out because I had to leave home. My parents live in Arizona."

"Why did you leave home?"

"Because I wasn't safe in my hometown."

"Were the police after you?"

"No, it was something else. Some of the guys in school don't like people like me, and they were making my life miserable. My parents don't approve of me either because they're really religious." In sum, I did everything short of jumping on the table and shouting that I was queer.

"I understand" he said. "In fact, I understand only too well. But I still need information about your academic potential. Have you taken any national tests?"

"Yeah. I took the junior national merit exam last February."

"How did you do?"

"I scored in the 99th percentile."

"The 99th percentile? You wouldn't lie to me, would you? You know I can check these things."

"Go ahead and check. I'm telling the truth."

After a moment's pause, he said, "Checking will take time. It's easier to just believe you. So, here's what you can do. In California, you can take what's called a High School Proficiency Examination. The HSPE. If you pass, it's as good as a high school diploma and will allow you to apply to any college or university in the state. You should register for the exam immediately since the registration deadline is next week. You will have the results by July."

"July is a long time from now. Can I take courses at SMC before getting the results?"

"If you're not enrolled in a high school, you'll need a special waiver."

"How do I get one?"

With a slightly conspiratorial smile, he replied, "You get it from your new friend, Mr. Hazen." He then filled out a form for the registrar. I thanked him profusely for his help to which he answered, "No need to thank me. I'm just doing my job." The following day, I registered for the HSPE. With Mr. Hazen's waiver in hand, I also enrolled in two summer courses: introductory French and music theory—all free since at that time California colleges did not charge tuition.

Classes started on June 1, and I loved them from the first day. My French teacher was a Mr. Byrd who wanted us to call him Monsieur Loiseau. My music theory teacher was a Ms. Vogel. I was delighted to learn that Vogel in German also meant bird. I told Angelo that I had gone to the birds, which I thought was quite clever. He failed to see the humor even after I explained it to him. Puns don't translate. One of my French classmates immediately set off my gaydar. His name was John, but he insisted on being called Jean-Pierre. Surfer-blond, blue-eyed, and nicely built, he invited me to lunch the second day of class. Midway through a sandwich, he abruptly asked, "Are you gay?"

I answered hesitatingly. "Is it that obvious?"

"No, it's just that I think all cute guys are gay until proven otherwise. Would you like to have dinner with me on Saturday? I know this cool French place in Beverly Hills that you'll just love."

I told him that I was living with my boyfriend and not interested in dating.

"*Quel dommage*," he replied. "I had hopes that we might become more than friends. Does your boyfriend mind if you fool around with other guys?"

"Like sex?"

"Well, yeah. That's what fooling around means."

"We've never talked about it, and I don't want to ask. We've got a good thing going, and I don't want to mess it up."

We continued having lunch together almost every class day. I couldn't understand Jean-Pierre's living situation. His parents were divorced, his father lived in Westwood with his former secretary, and his mother lived in Pacific Palisades, but Jean-Pierre had an apartment in West Los Angeles. When asked why he didn't live with his mother, he responded vaguely about needing to be on his own. He showed great interest in my sexual history and was intrigued by stories about Boy Scout circle-jerks and truck-stop sex.

Yet, when asked about his own sexual experiences, he replied evasively with something like "Let's just say that I've been around the block a few times."

In the meantime, Monsieur Loiseau turned out to be a superb French teacher. A World War II veteran, he had perfected his French in the post-war occupation of Europe and could have been a Maurice Chevalier impersonator. He told us that a good way to learn a language was through talking to oneself, posing questions and then answering them out loud—creating prose in one's head as he put it. So, I started holding profound conversations with myself, much to Angelo's amusement. *Joshua, comment reconnaissez-vous qu'un autre homme est gai? C'est une question très intéressante. Merci à vous pour me la posez.* And I would then generate some sort of answer, but only after complimenting myself for asking such a brilliant question in the first place.

Music theory was just as exciting. Learning to hear intervals, spell chords, and take harmonic dictation seemed like second nature to me. At first, the students with perfect pitch intimidated me, but I soon learned that I could sight-read and identify intervals just as well as they. I have always resented people with perfect pitch. It's like they're going through life with a cheat sheet. Ms. Vogel shared my distrust of perfect-pitchers and often transposed sight-reading exercises so that they would have to either transpose or calculate intervals like the rest of us instead of just identifying the notes. She also arranged time for me on a practice piano. It was a beat-to-death upright Hamilton, but at least it allowed me to keep my fingers in shape.

Chapter Eleven:
Another Side of Angelo

A couple of weeks after classes began, I heard on Pacifica Radio that Evelyn Hooker was scheduled to give a lecture at UCLA. Prof. Hooker had done groundbreaking research on gay men that concluded that sexual orientation had nothing to do with happiness, mental health, or success in life. At first, Angelo refused to go because he didn't want to be seen at a gay event. But he finally accepted, bending to my argument that it was merely a university lecture.

Angelo paid close attention to Prof. Hooker's lecture, but he seemed more interested in the audience. Noticing that several same-sex couples were holding hands, I reached for Angelo's hand at one point, but he brusquely pushed me away. As we drove back to the apartment, he was uncharacteristically silent. Finally, I asked, "So, what did you think? Did you enjoy the lecture?"

Upset about something, he answered, "I don't want to talk about it. Maybe when we get home." Once we were settled in our small living room, me in our single armchair facing him as he sat on our small sofa, I asked again what he thought of the lecture. Grudgingly, he replied, "She was okay, but did you notice the people there?"

"Yeah, sort of. But not really."

"You didn't see those really effeminate guys? The ones with red and green streaks in their hair and painted fingernails who minced and pranced around like girls?"

"Not everyone was like that. In fact, most of them looked normal to me, and some of the guys were really built."

"Don't think for a minute that those guys with gym-bunny muscles aren't gay."

"Why wouldn't I think they are gay? Since it was a lecture on a gay subject, I assumed that many in the audience would be gay. Besides, what's wrong with being gay? Why can't people just be themselves? You know, like you and me?"

An angry shadow came over his face, one that I had seen before and learned to fear. "What do you mean like you and me? I'm not that gay."

"Really? The guy I fucked last night seemed pretty gay to me."

No sooner were the words out of my mouth than I wished I could take them back. Angelo's face hardened in rage. He stood up, kicked the coffee table aside, and hit me with a closed fist in the chest, as hard as he could. "You want to brag about fucking me?" he muttered. "Try this on for size." Then he hit me again.

Stunned by the outburst and the pain radiating from the blows to my chest, I tried to explain. "I wasn't bragging. I was just pointing out …" but before I could finish the sentence, he hit me again. I tried to stand up and pull away from him, but he tackled me, smashing my face into the floor with his left hand and pummeling my back and sides with his right fist—a fist hardened through years of martial arts and a stint in Vietnam.

I pulled into a fetal position to protect my face and hands, but he continued hitting me. After several more blows, he finally stood up, breathing hard. Hoping that it was over, I crawled into a sitting position, but not before he kicked me, sending me sprawling toward the front door. He then fell back on the sofa, staring at me with a puzzled facial expression as though he couldn't understand why I was on the floor.

I stood up slowly, keeping my eyes on him lest he attack me again. Turning quickly, I opened the front door. He sprang toward me, but this time I had the sense to close the door halfway so the edge of it caught him squarely in the face. By the time he recovered, I was on my bicycle, pedaling as fast as I could towards the beach. I heard him running after me, shouting for me to come back. He could run fast, but he was no match for me on a bike.

Hurting, crying, raging, I biked to the park overlooking Santa Monica Beach. Sitting on a deserted park bench, I tried to process what had just happened.

The only person to ever hit me like that was Burt Cummings. But that was different because Cummings was a moron and a bully. Angelo was as smart as anyone I had ever met and someone I had come to love. But I now recognized that he was also a trained fighter with an unpredictable temper who could kill me with his bare hands if he wanted to.

I stepped into one of the park restrooms to see how much damage he had done. Although my body hurt like hell, there were no bruises on my face. Angelo had hit and kicked me only on my back, butt, and upper legs. With my clothes on, no one could see the bruises. Was this by design? Had he done this before—beat someone in a such a way that no bruises were visible afterwards? Betty came to mind. According to Angelo, she sought a divorce because her PI had photographed him with Jason. But was there more to the story? How many times had Angelo said that he would like to kill her? Had he ever come close? Was Betty a battered spouse? Just how far had his temper outbursts taken him? How could this beautiful, intelligent, and often sensitive man do such horrible things? His perfect body that I had caressed and loved was also a brutal weapon. No doubt he could hurt me much worse. What if I hadn't escaped?

On returning to the park bench, my mind turned to practical matters. Wearing only levis, a T-shirt, and sneakers, I was keenly aware of how cold the Santa Monica night was becoming. I had no place to sleep, and everything I owned, including my savings, was back in the apartment. I had heard how battered spouses continued living in unsafe situations. At that moment, I understood why.

Such concerns, however, eventually turned to pure grief. I started to cry, the kind of crying I had experienced only once before, when Father Tovar and I said goodbye. Father Tovar had loved me, taught me a great deal, and was unfailingly kind. With Angelo, I had enjoyed similar moments of great tenderness and wonderful conversations about religion and politics. But his anger lay just under the surface, and I had just experienced an extreme version of where it could lead. Just who was he, and what sort of relationship did we have? How could I share so much with him, have great sex, and then suffer a brutal beating? Heartbroken and exhausted from crying, I suddenly noticed that someone was sitting on the other end of the bench. With a start, I saw that it was Angelo. In a soft voice, he said, "Josh, I've been looking for you."

I stood up and backed away. "Why are you looking for me? Do you want to beat me up again? Didn't you get enough last time?"

"Please sit down. I only want to talk."

Stepping further away from him, I grabbed my bike, poised to take flight. "Well, maybe I don't want to talk to you."

Suddenly he started to cry, real tears and real sobs. "Josh, you have no idea how awful I feel. I am so, so, so very sorry. You must believe me. I've never loved anyone as much as I love you. I can't believe what I just did. Now, will you please sit down? I can't talk to you like this."

I slowly sat down, but on the opposite end of the bench, as far from him as possible. We remained silent for several minutes. Finally, he said, "You'll have to come back to the apartment tonight. All your stuff is there, and you have no place to sleep."

"Like I'm trapped? Like I'm your property now? A queer boy for a good fuck whenever you're in the mood? Or your punching bag when I might remind you that you're gay? How do I know you won't attack me again?"

"I'm not going to attack you again. Ever. I don't know what came over me. I cannot tell you how sorry I am. I would never hit you."

"But you did, didn't you? You hit me and kicked me. Several times. And if I hadn't managed to run off on my bike, you could have killed me. How do I know that something like that won't happen again?"

After a long silence, he said, "It's just that I don't always feel comfortable being gay, and I don't like having it smeared in my face."

"What changed? A couple of weeks ago you were saying how lots of things made sense now that you recognized yourself as gay. Why you never dated women, for example, and why you feel uncomfortable around straight men. What changed?"

"Nothing changed. I just don't want to be like some of the guys we saw at the lecture, and I don't want people to think that I'm like them."

"What do you want to be like?"

After a long silence, he said, "Josh, it's hard to accept something you've spent years trying to deny. In my head, I know that I'm attracted to men and basically indifferent to women. But so far, my heart has not caught up with my head. Maybe I know who I am now, but I don't know what to do with it. I don't know how to be gay. I don't know how to cope with what other people think. I don't know how to live a gay life."

"What's to know? You do what we've been doing for the last month. You eat, you drink, you work out at the dojo, you read, you play, you talk, you make love, and if you're lucky you have friends. People like me, for example, if you can keep from beating them to a bloody pulp. You just live your life, and if other people don't like it, they can go fuck themselves."

"That's easier said than done." After a long pause, he begged, "Now, would you please come home with me before we both freeze to death?" I eventually consented and helped him load my bike into the

Volkswagen bus. Back in the apartment, he nudged me onto the sofa, placed his arms around my shoulders, and held me as though his life depended on it. Against all my intentions, we ended up going to bed together. My feelings were all over the place. I could not forget that earlier that day he had assaulted me, causing me great pain, and that my body bore the bruises of his attack. But neither could I forget that I loved this man. Nor could I doubt the sincerity of the tears in his eyes as he gently and affectionately applied salve to the bruises he had inflicted on me.

Chapter Twelve:
Nearly Normal

We eventually fell back into our usual schedule, but things never returned to what they had been. Lurking in the back of my mind was the fear that some minor provocation might lead to another attack. It was like living with a beautiful but unpredictable wild animal. His blue moods and nightmares continued. One afternoon after our workout at the dojo, he announced that he was planning that night to attend a discussion group for Vietnam veterans up at the VA just off Wilshire. "I need to talk to people who might understand why I'm so screwed up," he said. "They might also help me get my temper under control. I'm so tired of being angry all the time."

The group meetings started as twice-a-week affairs, but Angelo was soon attending almost every weeknight. He often returned from the meetings depressed and agitated—exactly the opposite of what I had hoped for. Once when I asked how it went, he told me to mind my own business. He later apologized for being distant and rude. One evening, a Friday, I took pains to prepare a nice dinner only to be greeted by a curt "I'm not hungry" when he came home. Seeing the hurt in my eyes, he said, "Josh, right now I'm not fit for human company, so just leave me alone." Turning his back on me, he walked into the second bedroom, slamming the door behind him. Or maybe he didn't slam the door, but that was what I heard. It almost felt like he hit me.

I put my carefully prepared dinner in the refrigerator, grabbed my bike, and took off towards the beach. I was hurt and angry, but I was also worried because the Angelo I had just seen reminded me of the guy who had attacked me a few days earlier. I found a secluded bench in the park overlooking Santa Monica beach. The sun had just slipped behind the western horizon, revealing at a distance the profile of the Santa Catalina Island. The sky was a frenzied mosaic of blues, pinks, and dark reds—totally out of sync with the darkness of my mood. Angelo had warned me several times that our relationship couldn't last—warnings I had always pushed out of mind. Maybe our time together was now coming to an end.

After about a half-hour by myself, an older guy sat down on the opposite end of the bench. He glanced sideways at me and started to rub his crotch. Refusing to acknowledge him, I rode off on my bike, annoyed that he had interrupted my thoughts. But then I remembered the guys at the truck stop who, however briefly, wanted to feel attractive to other men. Back at the apartment, Angelo was sitting quietly on the sofa. "Can I say hello without getting yelled at?" I asked.

In a quiet voice, he answered, "Yes, you can say hello. And no, I won't yell at you. It's just that sometimes I can't help being an asshole. Josh, we need to talk, but first let's have dinner." With admirable effort, he had reheated the dinner I had prepared, set the table with candles and cloth napkins, and served "my" dinner in a more beautiful presentation than the one I had conceived.

After eating, he pulled me over to the sofa, put his arms around me, kissed me, and began speaking. "Josh, I've come to love you as much as I've ever loved another human being, and I owe you so much. The last few weeks have been incredible. Because of you, I've come to know myself a lot better, and we've had wonderful times together. But I need to face my responsibilities as a father and a brother. I need to return to Texas. Soon."

"What happened? Have things changed with Betty?"

"Lots. I have had several phone conversations with Enzo and my lawyer, including a long conference call this morning. Several weeks ago, Betty started dating someone who didn't like having Mario around, so the hypocritical bitch started buttering up my mother because she needed a free babysitter. Her parents aren't available because they retired to Florida. She broke up with the first guy and now leaves Mario with my mother several nights a week. Sometimes, she doesn't pick him up until the next day. Enzo hired a private investigator to start following her. She's really falling apart. Lots of drinking, lots of pick-up bars, and lots of one-night stands. On the nights she leaves Mario with my mother, it's usually because she's drunk and fucking her brains out with some pick-up. Sometimes she even brings guys home when Mario is there. My lawyer thinks that he has enough evidence to charge her with child neglect."

"Won't she bring up the photos of you and Jason?"

"If she does, my lawyer has plenty of evidence to charge her with being an unfit mother, in which case we could both lose custody. Neither of us wants Mario to end up in foster care, so if I'm lucky I might get shared custody. I might even become his sole caretaker."

"I'm very happy for you and for Mario, but this seems awfully sudden."

"I know it's sudden. I apologize for not talking to you sooner, but in my defense, I wasn't aware of how bad the situation had gotten until just a couple of days ago."

"When do you leave?"

"This weekend. My lawyer has scheduled a court date for next week, and I have to be there. I talked to Henry earlier today. He's loading a truck for me to drive back to Houston. I expect him to call me tonight."

Seeing tears in my eyes, he pulled me close to him. We embraced for what seemed an eternity. I felt moisture on my cheek and realized that he too was crying. Eventually, we disengaged, and he said, "I've paid the rent through the end of August, so you'll be able to stay in this apartment for the next few weeks. Henry needs the bus for one of his kids, but you seem to manage okay on your bike. I have also rented a mailbox for you at the post office on Seventh Street in Santa Monica. Here's the number and the key. I'll drop you a note from time to time to let you know how things are going. And I expect you to do the same. I don't want to lose touch."

Just then the phone rang. Although I heard only half of the conversation, I knew that it was Henry and that he had scheduled a truck for Angelo to drive to Houston. After hanging up, he confirmed what I suspected. "I leave tomorrow. Henry wants me on the road by noon."

It was bedtime. We slowly undressed each other. Despite my familiarity with Angelo's body, I never tired of his beauty. We lay down on the bed and quickly fell into our familiar spoon-position, with both of us lying on our sides, my head resting on his right bicep and his chest pressing against my back. Sort of like that first night in the truck. Neither of us felt like sleeping. After several minutes of silence, he asked, "Isn't there a better way to say goodbye than this?"

"Like what?" I asked disingenuously. "Like this," he said as he reached around me, placing his hand on my crotch. Making love that night was slow, tender, and prolonged. It was a warm and beautiful experience, but it was also very sad because we both sensed that it was the last time.

The following morning, I phoned my supervisor claiming to be ill. I prepared Angelo's favorite breakfast—three poached eggs on heavily buttered multigrain toast with coffee, grapefruit, and grits. (To cook for a Texas man, one makes grits.) After breakfast, he finished packing and by eleven o'clock was ready to leave.

Before opening the front door, he pulled me toward him. We held each other for a long time. He then kissed me on the forehead and gently pushed me away, saying, "We need to get on with our lives. I have your mailbox number. I'll send you a note as soon as I get settled, and I expect you to write me. Stay in school, and don't stop writing your parents. They need to know that you're okay."

Watching him get into the Volkswagen bus, I felt a great sadness coming on. But I was also somewhat relieved. Although Angelo had beat me only once, I feared his temper and never ceased wondering if he might attack me again. We met on May 5, 1970, and he left LA to return to Texas on June 13. In the nearly five weeks that we lived together, I had basked in his beauty and come to love him a great deal. But I had also become afraid of his temper and his physical strength. No adjective was big enough to describe this very complicated man. Although worried about my future, for the time being I had a place to live, a boring job, and courses at SMC that I loved. A small consolation prize: the day Angelo left, the postman brought a letter saying that I had passed the HSPE exam and could now apply to any college or university in the State of California.

Chapter Thirteen:
Eviction

The following week, after work and classes, I ran, went to the dojo, and exercised at the beach—activities that allowed me to imagine that Angelo was still around. I lingered well into the evening to avoid the empty apartment and to numb the ache in my heart. I longed for the comfort of Angelo's company, the warmth of his body, and the intense blue of his eyes. Now that he was gone, I easily put the bad times out of mind. Perhaps it would have been easier if we had separated in anger after a big argument, the way some lovers do. But for me, there was no anger. Only a hollow sadness and fears about the future.

In the meantime, I spent extra time on my classes and sneaked often into the practice room to pour out my sorrows on the piano. Following Angelo's insistence, I dropped a note to my parents telling them that I was okay and that I had enrolled in a junior college. I also wrote Lucy and Blair, gave them a few details about my life, and included my mailbox number. I assured them that things were going well, although they clearly weren't.

The following Saturday, exactly a week after Angelo left, I returned to the apartment after work and found that my key wouldn't work. I told the manager that there was something wrong with my key. He gave me a nasty little smile. "There's nothing wrong with your key. You don't have a key anymore because I'm kicking you out of the apartment. I changed the lock and want you out by this afternoon."

"But you can't do that. Angelo paid you two months' rent in advance and said that I can stay here through the end of August."

"Is that what your faggot boyfriend told you? He didn't pay me shit."

"He told me he did, and he wouldn't lie."

"Do you have a receipt? Do you have proof that he paid?"

"No but…"

"So that's the end of it. I've been watching you boys. I know what you are, I know what you do, and it's really disgusting. I don't want people like you in my building. I'll let you back in the apartment so you can pack your stuff. But at three o'clock this afternoon, a cop will be here to make sure that you leave, so don't get any funny ideas about trashing the place. As far as the cop is concerned, you are an illegal squatter. You leave or you go to jail. You hear?"

"But where am I supposed to live?"

"Where am I supposed to live?" he echoed in a derisive falsetto. "That's your problem. Maybe you can find another faggot to sponge off of. There's plenty of them around."

PART IV

Chapter One: On the Streets

Having no desire to see the manager again much less tangle with his rent-a-cop, I left the apartment well before 3 PM with just my bike and whatever I could cram into my backpack. This meant leaving behind linens and kitchen items that Angelo and I had bought together—reminders of a possible future that never happened. Where to go? Where to sleep? Remembering that the practice rooms were open on Saturday, I biked to the SMC campus and poured out my sadness on a practice-room piano. Just before five, the janitor informed me that the building was closing.

I rode down to Venice beach and worked out a bit on the outdoor exercise bars. Just before nightfall, I biked up to the Santa Monica Mall, dined on a Big Mac combo, and people watched. I recognized several gay guys, laughing it up and having a good time, and wondered what it would be like to have friends like them. Around nine o'clock, the stores began closing, and by midnight the last movie goers exited the theaters. Eventually, a cop told me that I couldn't spend the night in the mall and would have to move on.

I rode down to the park overlooking Santa Monica beach and found the same bench I had commiserated with the night that Angelo attacked me. I locked my bike to the park bench, placed my backpack under my head, stretched out, and eventually fell into a fitful sleep. Just as the sun was coming up, I awoke with a start realizing that someone was tugging on my backpack. I jumped up, grabbed one of the straps, and got into a tug-o-war with a skinny, stringy-haired kid no older than I. After a few pulls, I connected a good karate kick with his upper thigh. He let out a howl and limped off into the dark, shouting, "Fucking asshole! You broke my leg!" "Fucking thief!" I yelled back. "Next time I'll break your neck!"

Fully awake, I noticed other people sleeping in the park, some on park benches like me and others in improvised cardboard tents. Was that my future? Realizing how much trouble I would be in if the wannabe thief had succeeded in stealing my backpack, I rode over to the post office, placed most of my cash savings in an envelope, and left it in the mailbox that Angelo had rented. Not much of a safe deposit box, but at that moment it was my best option.

What to do for the rest of the day? I bought an egg-McMuffin for breakfast and then biked slowly up Santa Monica Boulevard. Sunday morning traffic was light, leaving me ample time to appreciate the expanse and variety of my new hometown. Shortly after crossing under the 405 freeway, I caught sight of the huge Mormon temple with the Angel Moroni atop its spire, blowing a trumpet to proclaim the restoration of God's only true church. I rode to the intersection where Overland dead ends at Santa Monica Boulevard.

Leaning on my bike, I stared up at the massive white building. Imposing, daunting, and imperiously perched on top of a hill, it reminded me of the Great Sphinx, with the central tower being the head and the two side wings, the Sphinx's huge feet. Although church photographs had conditioned me to consider this building a holy place, it seemed more threatening than beautiful. Mormons have two types of worship buildings: ward houses that anyone can attend and temples open only to church members holding a certificate attesting to their righteousness. Such certificates, or temple recommends as they are called, must be renewed annually, subject to a satisfactory interview with the local bishop. Paying a full tithe is one of the requirements—ten percent of one's gross income. Sort of a pay-to-play arrangement. Although marriages "for time and all eternity" are solemnized in the temples, the buildings' primary purpose is to perform ordinances by proxy for dead people.

Before turning twelve, I made several trips with other Rosales kids to the LDS temple in Mesa, Arizona where we were baptized for dead people whose names were collected through the Church's far-reaching genealogical research. Mormon doctrine holds that through giving dead people a valid baptism by proxy

(Mormons consider other churches' baptisms invalid), they open the door for dead folk to continue their path of eternal progression. Hence, the urgency of genealogical research to identify all those souls stranded in spirit prison awaiting a valid baptism.

Dressed in white, we lined up to enter the baptismal font, a large round pool resting on the backs of twelve sculpted oxen—a design based on the description of a purification pool in Solomon's temple (1 Kings 7:23-26). As each of us entered the font, the baptizer gripped us firmly, leaving one hand free for us to pinch our nose and avoid inhaling water during the immersion. He then said, "Having been commissioned of Jesus Christ, I baptize you for and on behalf of (name of the dead person), who is dead. In the name of the Father, and of the Son and of the Holy Ghost." We were then pushed backward until fully immersed under the watchful eye of two witnesses whose job was to ensure that water covered our entire body. If any part of the body failed to immerse, the ritual was repeated.

Viewing the Los Angeles Temple, I was engulfed by these memories, making me aware of how deeply I bore Mormonism's imprint. But I also remembered the church's odious teachings on homosexuality, my conversations with Ronnie, and my personal disillusionment with the *Book of Mormon*. Could I ever consider this massive building and the church that it represented to be true, or for that matter welcoming? Were such things even possible for a gay person? On multiple occasions, I had committed sins that according to Dr. Chandler and my mother were second only to murder. The temple seemed to glower down on me in condemnation. Thinking of how much Mormonism had formed and deformed me, I wanted to glower back but felt powerless to do so.

To get a better view of the temple, I rode my bike up Manning and then turned left onto Ohio where I soon came to the Westwood Ward chapel, which is through the block behind the temple. On approaching the building, I heard people singing what was probably the opening hymn of the nine-o-clock Sunday school. The hymn was one of the most elegant to come out of Mormondom, "Sweet is the Work, My God, My King" composed by Joseph Daynes, the first Tabernacle Organist.

A wave of nostalgia engulfed me. It was in the Mormon church that I first played the organ, first led the congregational singing, first learned Bible stories, and first gained a taste for doctrinal disputation. The Rosales Mormon community also introduced me to good people like Mrs. Jespersen and my church-choir friend, Leona Barnes, who were striving to live good lives and make the world a better place. I remembered particularly the kindly church women who taught my first Sunday school classes and organized activities for little kids.

For a moment, I wondered if I could go back. It would be easy to walk into the Westwood meeting house and introduce myself as a newly arrived Mormon fallen on hard times who needed a place to stay. I would immediately be embraced by a community of people anxious to get me back on my feet and accept me back into the fold. But then I remembered: I'm gay, I have committed grievous sins, and I am on the verge of becoming a nonbeliever. I also remembered the high cost of belonging to a Mormon community— particularly the demands for conformity, time, and money. Overcome by conflicting emotions, I felt betrayed yet needful of the very thing that had betrayed me. I also felt angry—angry that Mormonism had marked me so deeply that I could not just walk away from it. What a blessing indifference would be! To feel no anger, no sense of betrayal, no nostalgia, and no guilt. Just blessed indifference. I also wondered if there was not a hole in my soul—a hole exactly the shape of the Mormon church.

Chapter Two:
A Very Strange Sermon

Casting these thoughts aside, I continued up Santa Monica Boulevard, eventually entering a lush area with huge homes and carefully landscaped yards—my first glimpse of Beverly Hills. I passed two churches and noticed that one of them had a choral service scheduled for 11 AM. I continued up Santa Monica, but by the time I reached West Hollywood, the road had narrowed and become less friendly to bicycles. On a whim, I returned to the church with the choral service. Perhaps hearing a good choir would lift my spirits.

As I approached the front door, an usher started to hand me a bulletin, but then pulled it back, saying, "We don't do soup kitchens on Sundays." Not realizing the implication of her words, I naively answered, "I'm here for the eleven o'clock choral service. I'm not looking for the soup kitchen. Is that okay?" Still looking suspicious, she handed me a bulletin while adding, "You know, you can hear the choir better from the balcony. Perhaps you'd be more comfortable up there."

More likely, she thought I was a bum who had to be kept out of sight. And why wouldn't she? I had spent the night on a park bench, I carried a backpack, my hair was a mess, and I had not showered, shaved or changed clothes for two days.

After a lovely organ prelude, someone from the back of the church said in a loud voice, "This is the day that the Lord has made; let us rejoice and be glad in it." As the choir and the clergy processed to the front of the church, we sang a triumphant Easter hymn that I had never heard before, "The Strife is O'er, The Battle Done." I loved the processional cross carried by a beautiful young woman wearing a long robe and flanked by two male acolytes, also in robes and carrying tall candles; I loved the choir in robes; and I loved the priest carrying a bible aloft as they processed towards the altar—all supported by a robust pipe organ and enthusiastic congregational singing.

I sang at the top of my lungs, particularly the "Alleluias" that close each verse. It felt wonderful to sing and to think that this body of mine, though ill-clad, unwashed, and homeless could still sing. Several people turned to look at me, but I was not deterred. Singing felt too good. The third scripture reading was the parable of the prodigal son, after which a priest so old that he had to be helped to the pulpit, prepared to give the sermon. He gripped the top of the lectern as though fearing that he might fall, closed his eyes, and began to speak. Or better said, to mumble. Paradoxically, his mumbling had the odd effect of making me listen more closely.

He began by saying that it was good to be back, explaining to newcomers that he had previously been the congregation's rector but was now retired. With a sly grin, he added, "No doubt some of the folks up here are nervous about what this old geezer might say. One of the few pleasures of old age is being able to speak your mind and damn the consequences."

After recounting the parable, his sermon took an odd turn. He contended that people might identify with the prodigal's father when they see themselves in a position to forgive and show mercy. Or they might identify with the older son who kept the commandments and resented his brother's getting something for nothing. But then he added words to this effect:

"In my fifty-plus years as a Christian pastor, I have met many more prodigal sons than fathers and elder brothers because sometimes we all find ourselves in a far country, alienated from others, suffering from broken relationships, and estranged from God's love, not because God rejects us but because we don't feel worthy of God. We don't feel acceptable."

Was he talking directly to me? In a far country? Estranged from others? Feeling unworthy and unacceptable? Nothing could have described my feelings better.

He continued: "Note please that the prodigal's father accepts him but asks for nothing in return. Had the prodigal earned the elegant robe and the expensive ring? No. Did the prodigal deserve the sumptuous feast? Of course not. Did the father put conditions on his gift, demanding some kind of payback? Again, no. So why did the father accept him so generously? Because the father loved him.

"In the father's act of love and acceptance, we see the scandal of the gospel. It is scandalous because of God's lavish, promiscuous, undeserved, unearned, and un-earnable love. God's love makes no sense because we live in a world where we are supposed to earn things. Where we are supposed to deserve things. Where getting something for nothing seems wrong. Yet in Christ Jesus, we get everything just for believing. Consider, for example, those very familiar words in John's gospel: 'For God so loved the world that he sent his only begotten son that whosoever believeth in him should not perish but have everlasting life.' You all know that Bible verse. You probably had to memorize it sometime in your life. I see it occasionally on billboards and bumper stickers.

"But I wonder how many people consider the sequence of what John is saying. First of all, God loved the world. Not because we deserved it, not because we earned it, and not because God owed us anything, but because it is God's nature to love. And that is the scandal. We cannot earn God's love, we cannot buy it, we cannot negotiate for it, and we cannot do anything to deserve it or make ourselves acceptable. God's love is freely offered because otherwise it becomes a commodity, something to purchase or bargain for—like a used car or a piñata down on Olvera Street. The biggest challenge to our faith is to know that we are accepted and to accept that acceptance."

Utterly transfixed, I realized that I was hearing a radically non-Mormon sermon. I remembered the checklist of the bishop's interviews where if we answered a few questions correctly we were considered righteous and deserving—worthy for example to enter the temple on Santa Monica Boulevard just a few blocks away. Yet, this elderly priest maintained that there was no checklist. I remembered Joseph Smith's teaching that to earn a blessing we must obey the commandment on which it is predicated; yet, according to this old priest, we cannot earn blessings because God's blessings are not commodities to be bargained for. As a gay person in the Mormon church, I was constantly aware of my unworthiness; yet this old guy maintained that worthiness had nothing to do with being loved of God, that God's love was a given. Did that include me? Did it include the homeless people with whom I shared a park?

Lost in these thoughts, I have little memory of the rest of the service. The closing hymn was the very familiar "All Creatures of Our God and King" which I sang with all the gusto I could manage. After the service, remembering my exchange with the usher, I tried to sneak out a side door. But a tall, handsome woman with perfect hair and immaculate nails cornered me on the way out, introducing herself as "Flo—you know Flo as in Florence Whitmore." She seemed to expect me to know who she was. I had barely told her my name when she said, "Josh, you've got a spectacular voice. Why don't you join the choir?"

Caught by surprise, I answered, "I'll have to think about it. I don't actually live here."

"Where do you live?"

"I'm staying with a friend," I lied.

"Well, if you stay in town, give it some thought. I want Dr. Riedel, our minister of music, to hear you sing. You might even qualify for a staff position."

"What's a staff position?"

"You know, a section leader and sometimes a soloist. The paid singers. Here's my card. Call me if you'd like to talk more." She handed me a card and grabbed my hand. "Please come back," she said. "And be sure to call me. This is a good place, and you have a spectacular voice. We'd love for you to join us." As she blended into the crowd, I slinked toward my bicycle. I didn't want to talk to anyone else because I felt dirty, unkempt, and malodorous. Surely, Flo had noticed although she apparently didn't mind.

Despite the old priest's sermon, I did not feel acceptable much less accepted. Maybe he was wrong. Mormonism's exchange of obedience for blessings seemed to make sense. But isn't that what the old priest said—that God's love is a scandal because it doesn't make sense? This was my first encounter with the doctrine of grace, a shocking realization for someone who grew up in a nominally Christian tradition that hardly speaks of grace. I was also intrigued by Flo's mention of a staff position. Maybe by working at Lucky's and getting a church job, I could earn enough to stay alive and remain in school.

Chapter Three:
The Proposal

I spent the next couple of hours biking around Beverly Hills, trying to ignore people's suspicious looks. Young, unkempt biker with a backpack—I could hardly imagine what they were thinking. I eventually found myself on Sunset Boulevard and followed the signs to the UCLA campus, a spectacularly beautiful enclave in the middle of the sprawling city. I found a shady incline on the lawn across from Royce Hall where I stretched out, my backpack under my head and my bike at my side.

I must have fallen asleep because the next thing I knew the sun was low in the western sky. After a cold-water shower at Venice Beach and a Big Mac combo, I found my way back to my park bench. Several benches were already taken by homeless people planning to spend the night in the park, just like me. Remembering the morning sermon, I wondered if my homeless park mates were lavishly and promiscuously loved by God, and if so, why were they (we) living on the street and sleeping in a park?

I woke at the crack of dawn, just in time to get to my job. After my shift at Lucky's, I pedaled to SMC for my French class, painfully aware that I had been wearing the same clothes for three days and needed a shave. When I walked into the French classroom, Jean-Pierre did a double-take and asked "Are you okay? You look like shit. Rough weekend?"

"I've had better."

"You can tell me all about it at lunch. I want details," he added with a salacious grin.

"It wasn't rough for that reason, potty-brain."

After class, we bought sandwiches at the campus deli and sat at a table under some trees.

"So, what happened this weekend?" Jean-Pierre asked. "Why do you look so awful?"

"Where do I start? Last week, my boyfriend left me. On Saturday I got kicked out of my apartment. I spent Saturday night and last night sleeping on a park bench. And I have no idea where I'm going to sleep tonight. Does that sound like a great weekend?"

"Sounds pretty shitty. Are you looking for a place to live?"

"Yeah. You got any ideas?"

"In fact, I do. My roommate moved out a couple of weeks ago. You interested?"

"I probably can't afford it."

"I pay $80 a month for a furnished two-bedroom apartment. Can you afford $40 per month?"

"That's expensive for what I earn. I wouldn't have any money for food after paying the rent."

"Where do you get your money now?"

"I work twenty hours a week at a supermarket for a dollar fifty an hour. It was okay when Angelo was here because he covered the rent. But now. . . You do the math. No way can I come up with $40 a month for rent."

He scrutinized me as though seeing me for the first time. With a slight frown, he said, "I have a business proposal for you. But you have to promise not to be shocked."

"I don't shock easily, so shoot."

"You're gay, right?"

"Yeah. We already discussed that."

"I just wanted to make sure. Now. . . have you ever been paid for sex?"

Two things bothered me about this question: first, it was a total blindside. And second, I didn't want to confess that both Mike and Blair had paid me for sex. Hesitantly, I confessed. "Yeah, a couple of times."

"Good. Then you've had some experience. So, here's the deal. There's a guy named Arnie who sets me up a few times a week with guys who like having sex with outrageously sexy teenagers like me and you. Arnie arranges everything. Then his partner, a total thug named Oscar, picks me up and takes me to a motel where I meet a guy. We have sex. An hour later Oscar picks me up and gives me twenty-five dollars a pop. It's the easiest money in the world."

I did the arithmetic. I made around $30 per week for twenty hours of work. Three tricks a week would more than double my salary.

"How does Arnie find the guys?"

"The johns? Or the clients as he likes to say? I have no idea. I leave that to him. But on a good week, I can turn up to five or six tricks—which means an income of over $400 dollars per month. What do you think? Do you want to give it try?"

"What are the guys like?"

"All types. They're generally older. Some are deep in the closet and terrified that someone will find out that they're queer. Others just want a quickie and are tired of trying their luck in bars. Quite a few are married to women."

"Are they gross?"

Somewhat impatiently, he answered, "You're not looking for a boyfriend or great sex. You're merely providing a service. It's what Arnie calls transactional sex. Pay for services. Nothing more. He claims that it's the most honest sex in the world because each guy knows exactly why he's there."

"Sounds pretty cynical."

"No more cynical than any other business arrangement. You mow someone's lawn? They pay you. You fuck someone? They pay you. What's the difference?"

"What if you don't like them? What if they're disgusting?"

"Then you just close your eyes and think of England."

Seeing me frown, he explained that the line referred to English women who hated sex with their husbands but needed to procreate for the good of the empire. "By the way," he asked. "Do you have any trouble getting it up?"

"Like getting a hardon? No, I get hardons all the time, even when I don't want them."

"Good. That's all you need. Just think of the money, and you'll be fine." Then after a long pause, "So what do you think? You up for it?"

I thought of Mike who paid me for sex, took me to an orgy, and introduced me to Blair. I thought of Blair who paid me once for sex and then became a friend and gave me $200 just because he thought I needed it. I wondered how long I could sleep on a park bench and carry everything I own in my backpack. I thought of my weekly income of $30 per week. I thought of having to work fulltime to stay alive, which would mean dropping out of SMC. It didn't take me long to decide.

"Okay. I'm interested, but I'd like to know more."

"Good. Arnie's going to want to meet you. He'll also want to check you out. Physically. So be prepared. The one you want to be careful with is Oscar, the big guy who drives you to and from your tricks. He enforces the rules and pays you the money. You want to obey the rules."

"Which are …"

"It works like this. First, Arnie finds the contacts. You don't go looking on your own, and you never give your phone number to a client. When it comes to turning tricks for pay, Arnie owns you. Second, you don't discuss price with the clients, and you do not accept tips. Take the twenty-five dollars Oscar gives you, say thank you, and don't ask any questions. Third, Arnie sets up the visits. He leaves a message on my answering machine twice a day, once at noon and once at four o'clock. You call the answering machine for the message and then call him back immediately at whatever number he gives you, always from a pay phone. He will then explain the arrangements for that evening. Fourth, you don't befriend the clients. If someone wants a repeat with you, they go through Arnie. And fifth, his shtick is that we are innocent and unsullied preppies, which means that you need to buy new clothes, get a haircut, and spiff up a bit. That ragged jeans and dirty t-shirt look won't work. Other than that, you look pretty good. I'm sure that Arnie will like you."

"I can't afford new clothes," I said, which was a bit of a lie since I still had over $300 remaining from the money Blair had given me.

"Don't sweat the money," Jean-Pierre said. "I'll spot you for the clothes and rent until you can pay me back. I'm not worried because you're going to make lots of money. What do you think?"

This went way beyond anything I had done with Mike and Blair. But I needed the money. "Okay," I said. "I'll give it a try."

"Great! Let's get you settled in the apartment and then buy you some clothes. I can't introduce you to Arnie the way you look now."

Chapter Four:
Arnie

A half hour later, we met in his apartment, a first floor, furnished two-bedroom on Mayfield Avenue in West LA. True to his word, I had my own bedroom and a double bed. After a shower and a shave, I felt somewhat human again. While emptying my backpack, I found the card from Florence Whitmore, the church lady. I set it aside, thinking that a paid job as a church singer would be nice and smiling at the irony of hoping to become a church musician while starting to work as a hustler. Around sundown, Jean-Pierre and I hit the stores.

Or better said, the store. He took me to the Bullock's in Westwood Village. By the end of the evening, I had a small but decent preppie wardrobe complete with button-down shirts, penny-loafers, new sneakers, and several pairs of chinos. Before going to bed, he gave me an affectionate hug, after which he said, "You're cute, but I don't do sex with business partners. I need to save myself for the johns."

"Was your previous roommate also selling sex?" I asked.

"Yeah, but he started seeing guys on his own, including people he had met through Arnie. A very big no-no because Arnie wasn't getting his cut. Oscar found out, roughed him up a bit, and told him to leave town. Let that be a lesson to you. You can earn good money if you play by Arnie's rules. Really, this is a Cadillac operation. Compare what I do with what those street hustlers on Selma Avenue go through. Besides, the rules are easy to keep. Oh, and by the way, some of Arnie's clients like threesomes. So, my dear Josh, *toi* and *moi* might end up being sex partners one of these days. But it will be strictly business."

"Okay," I replied. "I'll keep that in mind and try not to enjoy it."

"Wise ass. I think you and me are going to get along just fine."

The following afternoon, Jean-Pierre took me to a barber shop. "You need to look your best because Arnie will want to check you out. No need to be nervous. Just do what feels natural, and he'll be satisfied."

Promptly at seven o' clock, the doorbell rang. Jean-Pierre opened the door and introduced me to a short, muscly but slightly overweight guy with bug eyes, a bushy mustache, and dark hair parted in the middle. He was wearing baggy black trousers, a frilly white shirt, and a linen sports coat at least one size too small. At his side was a massive man in western clothes with a braided ponytail and a mean-looking face. After a cursory hello to Jean-Pierre, the short guy took my hand and didn't let it go. "Hi. I'm Arnie and this is

Oscar. You must be Josh. You'll need a new name for work. What do you want me to call you?"

"Nick," I said, since that was my name with Mike and Blair.

"Nick will do fine, since I don't have another Nick in my boy collection." He continued holding my hand as he looked me over. Frowning, he said, "I need a better look. Come with me."

Jean-Pierre gave me a quick wink as Arnie led me to my bedroom, shutting the door behind us.

"Okay," he said as he hoisted himself onto the bed. "Undress. All the way, including the shoes and socks. Some of our clients like feet."

I did as he said, intensely aware of his eyes following my every move. Once I was buck naked, he said, "Okay. Turn around. Slowly."

I did as he said, feeling like a pig at a 4-H show. He then hopped off the bed, ran his hands all over my body, ending with a good grope of my genitals.

Standing up, he asked, "Do you do sports?"

"I run, do some martial arts, and lift weights. Nothing major."

"Well, whatever you're doing, it seems to be working. Okay, put your clothes on and meet me in the living room."

His explanation of the job was only slightly more detailed than Jean-Pierre's. All dates would be made in advance. Calling from a pay phone, I was to check the apartment answering machine at noon and four every day. If Arnie had a job for me, he would leave a phone number with some fake business name that I was to call, again from a payphone and never from the apartment.

"Be sure to write each number down because it won't always be the same. I'll then expect you to call me immediately. Be prompt. I don't have all day, and the clients are waiting. You got it?"

"Got it. What else?"

"I will tell you when and where to meet Oscar, and he will take you to meet the clients. No client gets more than an hour unless he's paid for more. Then, when you're done, Oscar will pick you up and bring you home or take you to your next client. He'll also pay you. You can't accept money from the client. Not even tips. My price covers all services, and I handle the finances."

"Am I expected to do whatever the client wants? Like, what if I don't want to get fucked?"

"Just say so. I'll tell the client that you're a straight boy who doesn't take it up the ass. That'll turn some guys on because they fantasize having sex with a straight boy. One last thing. These men are clients. A lot are repeaters because I furnish a good product. But they're not friends and you shouldn't try to befriend them. They are paying for sex and anonymity. If they want to see you again, they go through me. Don't tell anyone how to contact you directly. Also, you work with me and nobody else. No moonlighting. I tell you this for your own good. Most of the managers out there (he didn't say pimps) don't treat their people nearly as good as I do. I'll supply you with plenty of business. But that means you can't go out looking on your own. I'll be your best friend unless you break the rules. You understand?"

Seeing Oscar's hulking body sitting on the sofa and remembering what happened to Jean-Pierre's previous roommate, I understood only too well. Then, a bit nervously, I asked, "When do I meet my first customer?"

"Probably tomorrow. Just check your answering machine every day at noon and at four. Sometimes you'll have a date for that very night. Sometimes two. Sometimes we can set up appointments several days in advance. It all depends. With that, Arnie squeezed into his undersized sports coat and hugged both of us. "Boys," he said, "I'll be in touch. Stay clean and healthy." Then with a wink, he added, "And Nick, keep working out. Those muscles look good on you." During this entire conversation, Oscar had not said a word.

Chapter Five:
Myron

The following day, promptly at noon, Jean-Pierre showed me how to get messages from his answering machine using a payphone. Sure enough, Arnie had left a message asking me to call a number identified as Milo's Cleaners that ostensibly had clothes for me to pick up. His instructions were quick and succinct. Oscar would pick me up on the southeast corner of Barrington and Santa Monica at 6:30 PM. All I had to do was show up.

"Why all the secrecy?" I asked Jean-Pierre. "Why all this stuff about calling a different number with some fake business name and never calling him from the apartment?"

"Because Arnie's operation is totally illegal. If the vice squad catches him, he'd be in big trouble for both pimping and corrupting minors. By making us call from payphones and using different numbers, he makes it hard for the police to track him down. Just do as he says and enjoy it while it lasts."

"Are you and I in danger?"

"I doubt it. We're minors. The worst they can do is send us to a shrink. Besides, the vice squad is so stupid that they think only women do this kind of work. Also,

Arnie is careful. He uses guys like us, you know, middle-class students and stuff. He's not one of those trolls who pick up runaways and druggies at the bus station. Oscar is also careful. They use only a few motels where I'm sure they're paying off the managers."

That evening, promptly at 6:30, I was standing at the appointed place. Oscar appeared out of nowhere. "Let's go," he said. "My car is just around the corner."

I tried to start a conversation with him, but he would have none of it. "Nick," he said, "my job is to get you to and from your jobs, keep you safe, and get you paid. I'm not into conversation."

I made an apology of some sort to which he didn't respond. He entered the 405 Freeway using the Santa Monica onramp going south. After a short drive, he exited on Sepulveda Boulevard and headed towards the LA airport. We came to an area filled with dozens of nondescript two-story motels, most with rooms opening to a parking lot, thus allowing easy access from the outside.

"That's the motel," he said, pointing at an unexceptional two-story building with a flashing neon sign that read "Ocean Breezes Motel." He stopped the car and said, "Walk back to the motel. Your client is waiting in room eighteen. It's on the first floor in the back. Meet me on this street corner in an hour and fifteen minutes. That gives you an hour with the client and fifteen minutes to get back to the car. Don't be late. I don't like to wait."

Dressed in chinos and a preppie button-down checked shirt, I was the perfect image of a university-bound high school student. Nervous but curious, I found room eighteen and knocked lightly on the door. The door opened immediately, and a man invited me into a dimly lit room. Singularly unattractive, he was short, bald, and pear-shaped. Staring at me through small, squinty eyes, he brought the term *porcine* to mind. Remembering Jean-Pierre's advice to just close my eyes and think of England, I smothered a chuckle.

"Are you laughing at me? Do you think I'm funny-looking?" he asked with considerable annoyance in his voice.

"Not at all," I lied. "It's just that I'm new to this and kind of nervous."

"Your name is Nick, right?"

"Yeah, and your name is …?"

"Myron. Just call me Myron"

"Got it," I said. Myron seemed a perfect name for this blobby guy.

He started rubbing my arm and shoulder muscles, closed his eyes, and sighed, "So nice. So very nice." He then began unbuttoning my shirt, but after getting halfway down, he said, "This is too slow. Let's just undress."

I removed my clothes, trying to ignore his flabby muscles, paunchy belly, and irregular clumps of body hair. But I also noticed that his hair was damp from a recent shower and that he smelled of cologne and toothpaste. He had done his best to look good for me. I started feeling sorry for him, so I decided to be nice. After all, isn't that what he was paying for?

Myron acted like I was the most gorgeous creature to ever draw a breath. He had me lie down, and began running his hands all over my body, muttering things like, "So nice. So very nice. So beautiful. Should be in an anthology." He turned out to be an enthusiastic and very needy bottom who was easily pleased. We both climaxed after about twenty minutes. Now what? I didn't want to stand around waiting for Oscar, so I said, "We've got some time left. Would you like a massage?"

"Really? Would you do that for me?" he asked in a voice that sounded like a little kid who never got Christmas presents.

I turned him over on his stomach and started giving him a backrub. "Nick," he mumbled. "No one has ever been this nice to me before. Are you sure you're just doing this for the money?"

"I want you to feel good," I answered, which in fact was true. Somehow, making this unattractive guy happy gave me a good feeling. While massaging Myron's flabby body, I couldn't help but remember

Angelo's gorgeous hard body—everything that Myron's was not. I remembered wondering if Angelo's perfect body was a holy object made in the very image and likeness of God.

Was that true of Myron's unshapely body as well? Was Myron made in the very image and likeness of God, just a little lower than the angels? Did God know or care that he was unattractive? Did God love him, lavishly and promiscuously, just like the old priest said? After finishing, I said, "Myron, I need to leave pretty soon. Is there anything else you want?"

He suddenly leapt from the bed, threw his arms around me in a tight embrace that felt like being accosted by shag rug. I hugged him in return and sensed that he could have prolonged that moment forever. "You've been so nice to me" he said. "None of the other boys have treated me this nice. Can I see you again?"

"You'll have to arrange that through Arnie."

"My apartment is near here. Visit me there, and I'll cook a nice dinner for you."

"Can't. If you want to see me again, you need to go through Arnie."

He watched me dress with hungry-puppy eyes. Just as I was ready to leave, he hugged me again, and said, "Thanks so much. You've made me very happy."

I let myself out and walked toward the corner where Oscar was to meet me. What to think? Myron was unattractive. Myron was starved for human and sexual contact. Myron said that I had made him happy. In a weird way, I felt satisfied because of a job well done. Wondering if my Mormon work ethic made me a better hustler brought a smile to my lips. The squeal of Oscar's tires ended these thoughts. "Get in," he ordered. "You're right on time. I like that. Here's your money." Twenty-five big ones for doing very little. After Oscar dropped me off, I biked down to the Santa Monica post office to collect money from my savings and start paying off my debt to Jean-Pierre. I was pleasantly surprised to find a letter from Angelo waiting for me.

Dear Josh,

I'm back in Houston. I can't tell you how much I miss you. I know we had a couple of difficult moments, but we also had some great times together. I'm doing a lot better now. I owe you a lot.

Things are happening here. The private investigator hired by Enzo and my lawyer has evidence that could hurt Betty in court. My lawyer says that this is a good time to threaten her with a charge of child neglect and maybe negotiate a joint custody arrangement that would allow Mario to live with me part time. The lawyer also thinks we might negotiate something about the photographs with Jason and put all that behind us.

I've moved in with my mother, which feels strange, but she's all alone in a big house and likes having me around. This allows me to spend time with Mario. I wasn't much of a husband, but I'm a good father. I'd do anything for Mario. I'm even teaching him some elementary karate moves!

It's good to be working with Enzo again. The business is doing well. No more hiding on long truck runs. But I miss you, and I miss running on the beach and working out at the dojo. I miss cooking with you and talking about the stuff we read together. But I'm where I need to be. There's no going back. By the way, I told Enzo all about you and me. He's totally okay with it. I couldn't ask for a better brother.

How about you? Are you taking good care of our apartment? Do you still work out at the dojo and exercise on the beach? Are you still the smartest student at SMC? Are you still playing the piano? It would be good to hear from you. You can use the return address on the envelope.

Miss ya ...

Angelo

PS Are you sending your parents a note every week like you promised?

I reread the letter several times. I missed him tremendously and was amazed by how easily I put his anger attacks out of mind. But I didn't know how to reply. Should I tell him how the landlord stiffed him for two months' rent and threw me out on the street? Should I tell him about my new source of income? Angelo and I had shared a lot in the almost two months that we were together. But I didn't want him to know that I was hustling to stay alive.

Chapter Six:
Transactional Sex

Over the next two months, I averaged six to eight tricks a week, occasionally two on the same night. I had several repeat customers, including Myron who never ceased extolling my beauty, somewhat to my embarrassment. I quit my job at Lucky's, leaving my entire day free for classes, study, exercise, and my new line of work. Jean-Pierre turned out to be a good roommate—clean, orderly, and almost never there. I met several of his Pacific Palisade friends, all of them gay and all of them boring. How many Judy Garland stories can gay boys tell before brain death sets in? I missed talking about serious things—the kinds of conversations I had with Ronnie and Angelo. I continued to buy the magazines that Angelo had hooked me on, namely *Harper's, The New Republic,* and *The Atlantic. The Los Angeles Times* continued to be a daily friend.

My day soon settled into a well-organized routine, for which I had to thank that "maven of time management" Mother Harold. Every morning I jogged on San Vicente Boulevard, a lovely street with lots of trees and a wide, landscaped median running down the middle. I then showered, had breakfast, biked to SMC, studied a bit, and attended my two classes. I faithfully called our answering machine at the appointed times, and Arnie almost always had one or two tricks lined up for the evening. I continued spending time at the dojo and took great satisfaction in my growing martial arts prowess. With earnings from hustling, I settled my debt with Jean-Pierre, opened a real savings account, and bought a used Vespa, which greatly facilitated getting around town.

I soon discovered that sex work was real work. Some of the johns were attractive, and occasionally the sex was enjoyable—the old truck-stop thing of wanting men to find me attractive. But most of the time, especially with the less appealing guys, I had to close my eyes and think of England. I set limits. I avoided deep tongue kissing and never bottomed. Following the pattern set with Myron, I often gave clients a short massage after sex. This surprised and pleased them, giving me an inkling of how much people need to be touched and feel touchable.

Luckily, I never had an abusive client. In fact, most tried to make a good impression as though my opinion of them mattered. Several wanted to adopt me, promising that they would support me through school and get me out of the life that they were paying me to be in. I had a couple of trysts with a Mormon guy, recognizable from his temple garments, these being underwear Mormons use after making special vows in a temple ceremony. Why ever did he visit a hustler wearing temple garments? I tried to imagine him with his wife and kids, having family prayer, blessing his children when they were ill, attending church, and performing temple ordinances for the dead—the whole shebang—while having gay sex on the side.

How did I feel about hustling and how do I feel about it now? I never thought that I was selling my body since my body remained intact. I sold a service. Transactional sex, as Arnie said. Nothing else. During hustler sex, I learned to fake enjoyment and developed a kind of mind/body separation in which I watched myself perform while maintaining the illusion of not really being a participant. Later in life, I discussed my hustling days with a couple of therapists. They probably didn't believe me when I insisted, and continue to insist, that my short career as a hustler left little impression.

Chapter Seven:
The Parade

What did leave a deep impression, however, was the first Los Angeles gay pride parade. In mid-June of 1970, shortly after Angelo left, *The Los Angeles Times* carried several articles about attempts to organize a gay pride parade to commemorate the Stonewall riots that had occurred a year earlier in Manhattan. Much to my amazement, the main organizers were Christian clergymen. The LA Chief of Police at the time, the odious Edward Davis, initially refused to issue a permit. Frustrated in this attempt by a court order, he demanded a $1.5 million security deposit. Again, thanks to a court order, the amount was reduced to $1500 and eventually waived altogether. The parade organizers got permission only two days before the parade was scheduled, but miraculously, it came off anyway on June 28.

Nervous about the possibility of appearing on TV or in a news photo, I was initially reluctant to attend, but Jean-Pierre insisted. He drove us up to Hollywood and found parking several blocks from the parade route. Approaching the Boulevard, we were amazed to see hundreds of gay people gathering under signs proclaiming gay liberation and demanding a halt to gay oppression. The enthusiasm of the crowd soon drew us into the march.

My initial nervousness gave way to a giddy excitement I had never felt before—the joy of belonging to a gay and lesbian community forged by shared experiences and a common struggle for the freedom to be ourselves. In my fantasies about being David's Jonathan or Blair's Jacob, I had glimpsed a historical community. That day on Hollywood Boulevard, I realized that the community exists in the here and now. It was an exhilarating moment and the beginning of a long involvement with gay political activism, a passion I would carry for the rest of my life.

Following a sound truck blasting out disco music, Jean-Pierre and I danced, marched, and shouted chants of various sorts in unison with our fellow marchers. Eventually, we fell in with an exuberant group of shirtless men who at one point formed a circle around us and started chanting, "Take it off, take it off." So, we removed our shirts and waved them around like flags of liberation. After nightfall, we tried to enter a couple of bars on Santa Monica Boulevard, but we were too young to get in. We ended up at a House of Pies that, given the very raucous, very gay, and very happy crowd, could just as well have been a gay bar. We got back to the apartment well after midnight— tired, sweaty, and very happy.

Chapter Eight:
The Inimitable Dr. Martin Riedel

Grades came out for the first summer session. I received an A in both French and music theory and a personal note from Ms. Vogel congratulating me on a perfect final. With fake annoyance, she wrote, "Since students never make perfect scores on my finals, I corrected yours twice and still didn't find any mistakes. Congratulations! But beware: my next exam will be harder. See you next session!" Jean-Pierre barely passed French. I wasn't surprised. He claimed that, rather than bothering with grammar, he just said what sounded good. The problem: he didn't sound good.

I needed no encouragement to enroll in the second session of both French and Music Theory. Monsieur Loiselle had been replaced by a UCLA graduate student from France named Pierre Laflamme—a very appropriate name because the guy moved and talked like a flaming queen. He was also cute. Jean-Pierre warned me, however, not to jump to conclusions about his sexuality because "with the French, you just never know."

That night, I accidently found Florence Whitmore's card in my nightstand drawer, she being the lady who invited me to audition for her church choir.

Remembering how much I missed singing, I gave her a call. She immediately recognized my name. "Josh!" she exclaimed. "I've been so hoping you would call. A position for a bass staff singer just opened, and Dr. Riedel is looking for a replacement. Can we set up an audition for you this coming Sunday after the 11 AM service?"

After the service, Flo—as always with impeccable clothes, impeccable hair, and impeccable nails—seized my arm as though we were old friends. "Josh dear (dear?), it's so good to see you," she enthused. "Dr. Riedel cannot wait to meet you." She marched me to the choir rehearsal room where Dr. Riedel and the organist, a nervous skinny guy named Alexander, were waiting for me.

Dr. Riedel was a man of exceptional height and girth, well over six feet tall and weighing at least three hundred pounds. He wore his pants up to his belly button, so that in profile he looked like an obtuse triangle standing on one of its points. Despite his gargantuan size, his gestures were dainty and precise, complete with a mincing walk, floppy wrists, and pursed lips.

Offering his hand and speaking with a slight lisp, he said, "It gives me extraordinary pleasure to make your acquaintance. Please take a seat so we can begin assessing your musical capabilities and evaluating your possible contributions to the music ministry at St. Mark's." Folding his huge arms on his ample belly, he asked about my musical training and appeared surprised and skeptical when informed that I had studied piano, organ, and voice. "Well, Mr. Chastain. Let's see if that training did you any good."

Put off by the pretentious way he talked, I asked, "Why don't you call me Josh? When you say Mr. Chastain, it sounds like you're talking to my father."

"What a charming request!" he responded with a wintry smile that quickly turned to a scowl. "Actually, I disapprove of that deplorable American penchant for reducing every name to a monosyllable. So, for the time being, I prefer Mr. Chastain, and you should address me as Dr. Riedel. Now then, if you will be so kind, stand in the curve of the piano so I can assess your musical capabilities."

Clearly, BS-Speak and my country charm had no effect on this persnickety man. The audition was amazingly thorough, almost to the point of making me wonder if he wanted me to fail. Fortunately, I had a good ear, a good foundation in music theory, and solid vocal training from Mme. Arnaud. Towards the end of the audition, he said with something of a sly smile, "Well, that was nice (nice?). Now let's see if you can read music. Have you ever sung Johann Sebastian Bach's motet *Singet dem Herrn ein neues Lied?*"

Suddenly Flo spoke up. "Martin (which I guess was Dr. Riedel's first name), we performed that piece in our spring concert last year. It took the choir forever to learn it. Isn't it a little difficult for a sight-reading test?"

"Dear Flo," Dr. Riedel answered with affected patience. "No one knows better than I that it is a difficult piece. As you may recall, *it was I* who struggled so *heroically* to teach it to the choir. Besides, I'm going to request that Mr. Chastain sing only the opening of the Alleluia section in which the entire text consists of repeating the word 'Alleluia.' No German for the time being."

He handed me an open score, pointed out the section I was to sing, and marked a tempo with one of his huge hands. Turning to the organist, he said, "Alexander, would you be so kind as to help us on the piano?"

"I think I can sing it without the piano if you give me a minute to study it."

Feigning shock, Dr. Riedel answered, "My. Oh my, oh my! You do not lack for self-confidence, do you, young man? Of course. Take some time, but then we will expect utter perfection. Agreed?"

I ran through the notes in my head and realized that the passage was easier than it looked. Lots of sixteenth notes, but no tricky intervals or rhythms.

"Mr. Chastain, your preparation time is up. Alexander, please give him a pitch, and be prepared to jump in when he falters."

But I didn't falter. When I finished, Dr. Riedel almost looked disappointed. Pressing a fat index finger against pursed lips, he stared at me for a moment before asking, "Are you certain that you have never sung this before?"

"Absolutely certain. In fact, I've never heard of it before."

"Really? Well, goodness me. That is extraordinary. Utterly extraordinary. So, let's get down to business. I have an opening for a bass staff singer. I would like to employ you for a three-month probation beginning with this coming Wednesday's rehearsal. The rehearsal starts at 7 PM and lasts for two and half hours. Warm-up on Sundays starts at 8:20 with a service at 9 and another at 11. We often rehearse in the interval between services, so you need to set aside approximately four hours every Sunday morning. You will receive ten dollars per rehearsal and ten dollars for each of the Sunday services. This will amount to $30 per week, which, I must inform you, is a very good wage for a beginning singer. Do you agree?"

I quickly ran the numbers in my mind, comparing his offer with how much I made hustling. Giving up Wednesday nights for only $10 would put a dent in my income. For two tricks in the same three hours, I could earn $50. Seeing me frown, Flo immediately intervened.

"Martin, since Josh is a college student, we can supplement his salary with money from the Spicer Fund."

"Ah, yes," Dr. Riedel sighed. "The famous Spicer Fund."

"Josh," she explained, "the Spicer Fund is a special endowment for supplementing the salaries of student employees of the parish. People like you." Then turning back towards Dr. Riedel, "So, you take $30 per week from the music budget, the church puts in $30 from the Spicer Fund, and Josh's salary will be $60 per week instead of $30—which I might add is what you already pay some of your singers who are no better than Josh." Then, turning to me, she asked, "Josh, does that sound acceptable?"

How could I say no? I would later learn from other staff singers that Flo was "richer than God" and a major force in both the parish and Los Angeles cultural life. Dr. Riedel didn't like being outmaneuvered, but he had no choice. "Very well, then," he grumped. "We will give Mr. Chastain three months' probation and see how he does." Then, looking intently at me, he added, "Mr. Chastain, I will see you this coming Wednesday evening promptly at 7 PM. You've been given a notable talent, and you are remarkably accomplished for your age. Since St. Mark's will pay you such a *generous* salary, I urge you to remember the words of Jesus: 'Where much is given, much is expected.' Can you find your way out?"

"He can come with me," Flo said. After closing the door behind us, she gave me an unexpected hug. "Josh dear, you absolutely floored Dr. Riedel! You were so good. I've never seen a harder audition. It was almost as though he wanted you to fail. But you came through like a champ." Then with a girlish giggle, she added, "I even think he was little jealous! By the way, are you by any chance Episcopalian?"

"No. I'm not anything," I answered—which was more an aspiration than a fact.

"That's not a problem. People who aren't anything often end up becoming Episcopalians. Now go home and be happy." Hugging me again, she added, "You really did knock him dead. I've never seen him speechless before. Such fun! See you on Wednesday!"

I had heard the term Episcopalian but had no idea of what it meant. Still, when Flo said the word, it appeared in my mind in Gothic print. Arnie was not pleased that I would no longer work on Wednesday nights, but on learning that I'd be singing in a church, he lightened up, probably because he could now market me as a choirboy.

In rehearsal the following Wednesday, Dr. Riedel proved to be an excellent conductor. Prissy mannerisms and affected speech aside, he knew the music well and had great ears—so unlike my high school music teacher who read only the soprano line. It was a level of choral singing I had experienced only once before: at Arizona all-state choir with Lara Hoggard. And I loved it. So, even if the fussy Dr. Riedel wasn't the warm and fuzzy type, he was certainly someone I could learn from.

In August, Dr. Riedel and the choir took a month's break, leaving the eight staff singers to provide the service music, coordinated by Alexander. We mostly sang anthems for mixed quartet, but I sang a couple of solos. One night after rehearsal Alexander asked if I would like to try out the organ. It was a big Aeolian-Skinner with four keyboards and oodles of stops. Alexander complimented my playing. Several times he gently squeezed one of my biceps or let his hand rest on my shoulder a little too long, tacitly suggesting that he'd like to do more. Remembering Mother Harold's eleventh commandment—Thou Shalt Not Fuck the Flock—I did not encourage him.

Chapter Nine:
Mr. Hazen Again Takes Care of his Own

Second-session classes were going well. I continued jogging every morning and working out at the dojo most afternoons while still turning one or two tricks for Arnie on my free nights. I stayed busy and was happy to see my bank account growing. Yet no matter how welcome the money, I worried about the future, remembering Mrs. Jespersen's advice on the importance of attending a good university. I also wondered about my future with Ronnie. Would he be at the train station on the third Sunday in October? Would we connect again? Should I tell him about hustling? Would he consider me used goods?

Throughout my life, I've often felt that someone or something was looking after me, particularly in view of some of the risks I took. Stealing exams in high school, truck-stop sex, Dr. Chandler, Ape Arms, hitch-hiking, Angelo's temper, homelessness, and prostitution—all could have ended badly, but they didn't. To mix metaphors, things could easily have gone south, but I always landed on my feet, usually with help from other people—my saints as it were. In August of 1970, another miracle occurred. The last day of the second summer session, Mr. Hazen sent a note asking me to come to his office. Both Mr. Hazen and Ms. Vogel were waiting for me. After the usual greetings, I asked, "What's up? Am I in trouble?"

"Anything but," Mr. Hazen replied. "Josh, Ms. Vogel and I have discussed your achievements and promise at length. I've also discussed your case with the admissions office at UCLA. UCLA has a small program that allows exceptional students to enroll off-calendar without going through a regular admission process. We believe you to be such a student and want to nominate you for that program. We like having you at SMC, but at UCLA you will have a greater variety of courses and the opportunity to interact with better students. UCLA also offers individual keyboard and vocal instruction as well as financial assistance and housing. Ms. Vogel tells me that you are entirely on your own (true) and supporting yourself by working part time at a grocery store (not true, but for obvious reasons I didn't correct him). I can't imagine how you make ends meet. (I avoided making a rotten pun about making ends meet.) You will be better off at UCLA which is why we are having this conversation. To get to the point: would you like to enroll as a freshman at UCLA? Classes begin in about a month, the last week of September. What do you think?"

Almost too flabbergasted to reply, I managed to blubber out something like, "That sounds truly amazing. Is this really possible? What do I need to do?"

"I'll help with the paperwork, and Professor Vogel will arrange the auditions. You might qualify for both a music and an academic scholarship. You will need to take the ACT exam post haste. You shouldn't find it difficult, and I'll help you prepare. What do you say? Are you okay with this plan?"

Almost in tears, I said, "I am more than okay. I'm overwhelmed. Thanks to both of you. Thank you very much. Uh, what's next?"

Next was registering for the ACT exam and working with Mr. Hazen to prepare. He explained that being familiar with the format and structure of the questions was half the battle. He also helped me complete the application forms for admission. Ms. Vogel arranged two auditions for me, one in voice and another in organ. Both went well.

Second-session classes ended, I received an A in both my courses, and a near perfect score on the ACT, thanks in part to Mr. Hazen's coaching. A few days after sending my ACT score to the admissions office, a fat envelope arrived from UCLA announcing that I had been accepted as an incoming freshman into the UCLA honors program with a scholarship that covered room, board, and academic fees while also paying me a small stipend for working ten hours per week in the music library. This plus church income would allow me to give up hustling and still live well.

I made an appointment with Mr. Hazen to thank him for all he had done for me. Somewhat embarrassed by my gratitude, he brushed me off with "I'm just doing my job. Besides, if we don't help people when we can, what are we good for?" I remembered Ronnie's argument that some people are good just because they're good. But I also wondered if Mr. Hazen thought that homeless gay boys needed special attention.

The Wednesday after Labor Day, church choir rehearsals began anew, one for the 9 AM service, which sang easy stuff, and another for the 11 AM service with a more difficult but more interesting repertoire. One Sunday, Flo had me and the other staff singers over to her house (mansion) in Hancock Park for a lovely brunch. She was undoubtedly one of the nicest people on the planet. She knew everyone in the choir and seemed to keep track of everyone's problems. "How is Ginny doing in school? How does your husband like his new job? I am so sorry to hear that Phoebe is in the hospital again. Can I do anything to help?"

I began paying more attention to the sermons and was impressed that punishment and rewards—so essential to Mormon doctrine—seemed totally absent in what I heard from the pulpit. But I also sensed underlying tensions in the parish regarding women's ordination, the peace movement, and racial justice. In mid-September, the old priest who so impressed me three months earlier was back in the pulpit. In his mumbling style, he delivered another shocker.

The gospel reading was the parable of the good Samaritan. He explained how the Jews of Jesus's time saw the Samaritans as ethnically impure—i.e., not true descendants of the original twelve tribes of Israel—and heretical in their beliefs. "Tainted blood and tainted religion" as he put it. But the clincher came when he asked, "If Jesus were to retell this parable from this pulpit, who would play the role of the Samaritan? A communist? An atheist? A drug-addled hippie? Or maybe a homosexual? Which of these would shock us the way Jesus shocked the people of his time?" I had never heard the term homosexual from the pulpit before and certainly not in such positive terms.

Chapter Ten:
Busted

With church income and anticipated financial support from UCLA, I resolved to stop hustling. Pity I didn't quit sooner. On Thursday afternoon in the third week of September, I phoned our answering machine, called Arnie at the number he supplied (supposedly a pet supply store), got my instructions, and met Oscar at the appointed time. He took me to a motel we had used before near the airport. I knocked on the door and heard someone say, "Come on in; the door is open."

In the dim light, I made out a man sitting on the bed and another man standing at the foot of the bed near the door. I immediately sensed that something was wrong because I had never done a threesome with two clients.

"Hello, Nick," the man on the bed said. "I've been wanting to meet you. How are things going? Ready to suck some cock?"

No client had ever talked that way. I stepped back towards the door, but the second man had moved to block my way out. Both men were fully dressed, and they most certainly did not look gay.

"Don't try to run away Nick. Just tell me if you're ready to give me a blowjob. My partner here might enjoy a pair of hot lips on his dick as well. How much do you charge?"

I felt blood run to my head as my vision focused on the man's face. Stammering, I replied, "I don't want to do any of those things with you."

"Why? Is there something wrong with us? You've done things like that and worse with lots of other men, haven't you? Come on. Tell us how much we have to pay you."

"I don't charge."

"Nick, don't waste our time. We know you don't do this for free, so stop playing games. My name, by the way, is Officer Gonzalez, and the man behind you is Officer Malone. We're from the LAPD vice squad, and we're arresting you for prostitution. We've been monitoring your friend Arnie for several weeks. He has quite an operation. Such a pity that we have to blow it up. By the way, both him and your driver along with your cocksucking roommate and the night manager of this flea-trap motel have also been arrested, so don't expect any help from them. Could you show me some ID?"

Fumbling badly, I fished out my wallet and handed him my driver's license. He turned on the table lamp next to the bed and squinted at the small print. "I see that your real name is Joshua. Joshua Chastain. Do you still live on Ocean Boulevard?"

"No. I moved."

"Where to?"

"An apartment on Mayfield."

"Any other lies on your license?"

"Everything else on the license is true."

"That means that you were born in 1953, had a birthday last April, and are now seventeen years old. That's good news for you, Josh, because it means we can't arrest you as an adult. Do you have a criminal record? Have you ever been arrested before?"

"No."

"If you're lying, we'll find out."

"I'm not lying."

"Have a seat, Josh. We need to talk."

My mind was starting to clear. I had seen enough movies to ask, "Isn't there something about me not having to answer questions if I don't want to?"

"Clever boy. Where did you hear that?"

"I read newspapers. I'm not illiterate."

"Not illiterate, huh? That's a big word for a cocksucker. Well, as it turns out, you have the right to remain silent, and yes, just like you heard in the movies, anything you say can be used against you in a court of law. So, we have two options. You can answer our questions now, or we can put you in jail with a bunch of butt-fuckers who will pound your ass to a bloody pulp, after which you might decide that cooperating with us is not such a bad idea. What will it be?"

"Don't I have a right to make a phone call?"

"Too many movies, Josh. Too many movies."

"You didn't answer my question. Don't I have a right to make a phone call?"

He groaned. "Yes, Josh, you can make a phone call. Do you have a lawyer?"

"Yes," I lied, although the only person I could think of was Flo Whitmore who I did not think was a lawyer.

They cuffed my hands behind my back, shoved me into the back of a caca-brown Crown Victoria, and drove me to a police station on Culver Boulevard. After they fingerprinted me and took my photo, I asked, "Can I make my phone call now?"

"If you must. Use the telephone behind the reception desk. Keep it short."

I dialed Flo's number. Much to my relief she answered after the second ring. "Flo, this is Josh." My voice broke as I tried to choke back tears. I hated telling her about my situation.

"What's wrong Josh? You sound upset."

"Flo, I'm in trouble, and you're the only friend I have."

"What kind of trouble?"

"I'm at the police station on Culver Boulevard. I've been arrested."

"For what?"

"I'd rather not say over the phone. Can you help me?"

"Of course I can help you. I'm not a lawyer, but I can find one. This time of night, it might take a while. Don't answer any questions until a lawyer representing you gets there. Can you let me talk to one of the policemen?"

I handed the receiver to Officer Gonzalez. I couldn't hear what Flo said to him, but I saw his facial expression grow increasingly grim. He responded once with the word "prostitution" and a couple of times with "Yes ma'am." He then handed the phone back to me.

"Josh, I'll have a lawyer there shortly," Flo said. "Try to be brave. And remember: no matter how nice the police seem, don't answer any questions until your lawyer gets there."

As I placed the receiver back in its cradle, Gonzalez was scowling at me. "Josh," he said, "How does a cocksucking little piece of shit like you know Florence Whitmore? Does she know that you're a butt-fucking whore?"

I didn't reply. They led me to a small room with a table and several chairs. Maybe because Gonzalez had already shown himself to be a consummate asshole, Malone took over, trying to sound nice. "Josh," he said, "why don't you tell us about Arnie's operation. He's the one we're after. Not you. If you help us, we'll help you. What do you think?"

"If I answer your questions, does that mean I'm no longer a cocksucking little piece of shit?"

Gonzalez intervened. "Ooh! Touchy aren't we. Sorry if I offended you. But, as they say, the truth hurts."

"Well, the truth is that I'm not answering any questions until Flo's lawyer gets here."

"'Flo, is it? Like you and her are really good friends?"

"That's a question. I already said I wouldn't answer any questions."

"Have it your way. But just remember. If you don't help us, we won't help you, no matter how many rich friends you've got." He locked the deadbolt after leaving the room. A thousand thoughts swirled through my head. What had I gotten myself into? Would I have to stand trial, maybe spend time in jail, or be followed by a criminal record for the rest of my life? Could this keep me out of UCLA? I was Joshua Chastain, the Mormon boy from Rosales, Arizona who played the piano and organ, sang in a fancy church, and was headed to UCLA under a special admissions program. But I was also a gay boy, a runaway, and a prostitute under arrest who was facing… I had no idea what.

Chapter Eleven:
Joan Feldberg

About an hour later, Officer Gonzalez unlocked the door and said, "Your lawyer is here." A short, well-groomed, forty-something woman with bright brown eyes and short dark hair entered the room. Wearing a gray business suit, a white blouse, and a single strand of pearls with matching earrings, she projected an aura of authority despite her diminutive height. Shaking my hand, she said, "Hello. I'm Joan Feldberg. You can call me Joan. I'm the lawyer that Flo arranged for."

Without waiting for me to respond, she turned to Gonzalez and said politely but firmly, "Officer, I would like some time with my client, and I would like to see him in another room, one without a two-way mirror or microphones." Grudgingly, Gonzalez took us to a small, windowless room furnished with a small table and two chairs. As we faced each other, her expression softened as she laid her right hand on my forearm. Her touch was warm and reassuring. After thanking her for coming, I asked, "How do you know Flo?"

"I'm a defense attorney, but I also do pro-bono work for a shelter for abused women. Florence Whitmore is one of our major funders. She and I go way back, and believe me, you have no idea how lucky you are to know her. You couldn't have a better person in your corner."

"Are you expensive?"

"Don't worry about money. Let's worry about getting you out of here. Josh, I know the charges against you. They don't scare me, and they shouldn't scare you. You're still a minor, and I'm sure we can get you off on a lesser charge or maybe no charge at all. Also, because you are a minor, I can also ensure that there will be no record of your arrest. But you must tell me everything. Lawyer-client privilege means that our conversation will remain completely between us, so you can be totally honest with me. Do you mind if we start with some questions?"

"Can I ask you a question first?" I asked.

"Of course."

"Are you okay with defending a gay boy guilty of prostitution?"

"If you're gay, you're gay. Doesn't make a bit of difference to me. As for the prostitution charge, let's just say that there are better ways to earn a living. The charges against you don't make me think any less of you, nor do they make me less inclined to defend you to the best of my ability. So, tell me your story and how you got involved in this."

I started by telling her that I was a runaway trying to live on my own. To explain why I ran away, I touched on my Mormon background.

"Mormon, huh? They're a tough bunch. Got awful ideas about Black people. About gay people too, I'll bet. So go ahead. You ran away and then …?"

I told her how I got kicked out of my apartment, how a guy I'd met in my French class introduced me to Arnie, and how I started hustling to make money to stay in school. I also told her that I'd been hustling for the last two months but now wanted to give it up because I had a scholarship from UCLA and wouldn't need to hustle for money anymore.

"Flo told me about the scholarship and the special admission. Congratulations. UCLA doesn't give those to just anyone. So, tell me exactly how things worked with Arnie and how you met him."

I told her about Jean-Pierre and Arnie's operation. She listened carefully, took notes, and then asked, "So you never actually solicited anyone for sex?"

"No. Arnie always set things up in advance. The clients were always waiting when I got to the motel."

"Okay. Now this is important. Did Officer Gonzalez offer to pay you for sex?'"

"Sort of, but he didn't mean it."

"How do you know he didn't mean it?"

409

"Because of the way he said it."

"How did he say it?" Seeing my hesitation, she added, "Don't be afraid to use his exact words. I'm a big girl, and I've heard it all before."

"He asked how much I charged for a blowjob. That's when I knew that Arnie hadn't sent him. The clients paid Arnie, and Arnie paid us. We never took money from the clients."

"So, you turned him down?"

"Yes. Then they said that they were cops and that I was under arrest. That was when I remembered that I didn't have to answer their questions."

"Did you tell him that?"

"Yeah. Gonzalez said that I'd been watching too much TV and tried to ask me more questions. But when I refused to answer, he said that I would spend the night with some..."

"Some what?"

"Some butt-fuckers who would pound my ass to a bloody pulp."

"Charming turn of phrase. You know, these cops could get in trouble for entrapment and for threatening you with sexual violence, especially since you are a minor. I've dealt with entrapment cases where cops pretend to be interested in sex and then arrest some poor guy like you. It's a highly controversial tactic, and most judges don't like it. I think I'm going to enjoy my conversation with Officer Gonzalez. Did they inform you of your right to make a phone call?"

"I already knew about that and insisted on it."

"Good for you. Did they rough you up?"

"No. They just used a lot of insulting language."

"Like?"

"You know. Cocksucker. Faggot. Piece of shit. The usual stuff."

"Nice guys. Now are you sure they solicited sex and said they'd pay you?"

"I'm sure."

"And you're sure that you never asked for money?"

"Very sure. I only get paid by Oscar, Arnie's associate." Then, to add a bit of humor to a humorless situation, I added, "Besides, these cops really aren't very attractive."

Joan chuckled. "I'll be sure to let them know that they're too ugly for you. Anything else?"

"Not that I can think of."

"Good. I'm going to have a chat with Officer Gonzalez and his buddy. Do you mind waiting?"

"Of course not. I'm just very grateful that you're here."

"It's part of what I do. I shouldn't be long."

After a short wait, Joan returned. "Josh," she said. "I've talked to your arresting officers. They're not after you. They're after Arnie and Oscar and whoever else is involved in the prostitution ring. So, here's the deal. They will not bring charges against you if you dictate and sign an affidavit detailing your relationship with Arnie and Oscar. The affidavit will remain strictly confidential and not go on your record."

"There's not a lot to tell. I met Arnie only once. And I already told you how Arnie arranged for us to meet clients. Other than that, I know nothing about his operation."

"Then that's what you say. The police, by the way, already figured out most of Arnie's system. They had a tap on his phone lines. They also have your roommate's answering machine with a bunch of recordings. Your affidavit will merely reinforce what they already know."

"Do you think it's a good deal?"

"It's a great deal. You'll leave here with no charges filed, and, since you're a minor, nothing will go on your record. You may need to testify if the case goes to court, although I doubt that it will. After completing the affidavit, you should walk out as though nothing happened."

"That's really good news. I can't tell you how grateful I am."

"All in a day's work," she replied. Then with a rueful grin, she added, "All in a *good* day's work I might add. Things don't always go this well. Let me call the officers."

Gonzalez then took us to a larger room. He was carrying a tape recorder, some pencils, and a couple of writing pads. Joan said, "The police want to record your statement. I'll be taking notes for my own use. Just answer their questions. I'm here to make sure that your rights are protected."

Seemingly transformed by Joan's presence, Gonzalez asked straight-forward and professional questions, proving that he could tend to business when he wasn't being an asshole. When we finished, he explained that I would need to return to the police station the following afternoon to approve and sign a notarized transcription of my statement. By ten o'clock, I was ready to go home. Since Joan lived in Brentwood, only a short distance from my apartment, she offered to drop me off. I thanked her and asked again if I owed her anything.

"You can't afford what I charge, so let's call this one a freebie. When do you start at UCLA?"

"The dorms open on Sunday. Then, classes start the following Monday after orientation."

"You're going to love UCLA. That's where I got my law degree. It's a great university."

Chapter Twelve:
Jean-Pierre's Mother

I returned home well after midnight. Aside from the missing answering machine, nothing seemed out of place. Jean-Pierre was nowhere to be seen. Although exhausted by the day's events, I had trouble getting to sleep. What would have happened without Flo and Joan? And where was Jean-Pierre? Was he still at the police station, or maybe in jail being pounded by butt-fuckers?

Early the next morning, I awoke to the sound of loud voices and the smell of a cigarette. Wiping sleep from my eyes, I found Jean-Pierre in a heated argument with a leathery-skinned, peroxide blond, fiftyish woman wearing a flowery muumuu over a ridiculously skinny body. On seeing me, they stopped midsentence. After an uncomfortable silence, Jean-Pierre said, "Josh, meet my mother. Mother, this is my roommate Josh."

Blowing a cloud of smoke at me, she said in a raspy, near-baritone voice, "I hear you boys had quite an adventure last night."

Invoking BS-Speak, I answered, "Adventure is not the word I would choose, but yes, it was quite an evening."

Then, raising her voice and facing me, she said "Well, I cannot tell you how ashamed I am of John. And I can't imagine how upset your parents must be. John is coming home for the rest of the summer and will be grounded until classes start. Let's just hope he graduates from high school without getting expelled."

With an unfamiliar hardness in his voice, Jean-Pierre retorted, "Mother, we've already had this conversation. I'm staying right here. I may go back to high school, but I will not be living with you, so please don't start."

"Start? You're the one who started everything. I let you have an apartment for the summer so you can take some college courses, and you become a prostitute. How am I supposed to react?"

"Let's set the record straight. You did not let me have an apartment. I'm paying for this apartment with my allowance from Dad. I moved out of your house because I was tired of fighting with you, and I didn't want to catch you shagging Rodrigo again." Then turning to me, he explained, "Rodrigo is our gardener and handyman. Him and my mother have become very friendly in recent weeks. Of course, that was after I sucked his dick a few times. What can I say? My mother and I have a sexual timeshare on our handyman. Right Mother?"

In a subdued voice, "You have no right to say such things."

415

"Why not? If you badmouth me to Josh, shouldn't he know the truth about you?"

"I co-signed the lease on this apartment. I can pull it whenever I want."

"But you won't, will you. Because you need Dad's money as much as I do, and you probably don't want him to know about your fuck-fest with Rodrigo. Give me an excuse, and I promise to tell him everything."

Through clenched teeth, she muttered, "I'm sorry they didn't keep you in jail."

"Why? So, I could call Dad to get me out? Do you really want him to know what a great job you've done raising me?" Then looking at me, he added, "My father lives with his former secretary. My parents have a thing for fucking the hired help."

"Why do you keep using that word? And when… when did you do something with Rodrigo?"

"Why don't you ask him? I'm sure he remembers. It was probably the best sex he's ever had."

After a tense silence, she said, "You'll go to jail if the police catch you hustling again."

"Who said I was going to start hustling again? I'll work something out with Dad. He's pretty good about forking over guilt money to make up for leaving me in your tender care."

She suddenly started to sniffle. "This is so unfair. All I wanted was to be a good mother, and this is the way you repay me."

"Since when did getting drunk every afternoon and fucking Rodrigo make you a good mother? Or maybe you don't remember the times I had to pick you up off the floor and put you to bed because you were too shitfaced to make it on your own. Or maybe you're talking about the times you left me alone for days on end with just a credit card and the maid to look after me. So, tell me. When did you start being a good mother? Somehow, I missed that part."

By then, his mother was wailing. "Stop! Stop! How can you say such cruel things?"

"All of them true. So, turn off the crocodile tears before Josh thinks that they're real."

Amazingly, she stopped crying almost immediately—and there was no sign of real tears. Glaring at her son and biting her words, she declared, "Young man, you've not heard the end of this. But right now, I'm going home."

"That's a good idea. Maybe Rodrigo is waiting for you. And if he isn't, you can make yourself a nice triple martini. That usually puts you in a better mood."

Totally dry-eyed, she stomped out and slammed the door behind her. Jean-Pierre sat down heavily on the sofa and let out a long sigh. "I'm sorry you had to hear that. You see what a screwed-up family I have? God only knows why they wanted to adopt me."

"You're adopted?"

"Yeah, thank God. I'd hate to think I was actually related to those people."

Not knowing how to respond, I slowly sat down next to him. After a long silence, he pulled me next to him and laid his head on my shoulder. "So, what did you think of my mother? She's a real piece of work, isn't she?"

"I don't think I saw her at her best."

"She doesn't get any better. You should see her when she's drunk, which is most of the time. She starts drinking just after breakfast. By afternoon she is totally smashed. It's not pretty."

"Is she really having an affair with your gardener?"

"She was. I caught them going at it one afternoon when I ditched lacrosse practice. She tried to lie out of it, but with Rodrigo's pants down to his ankles, it was pretty obvious what was going on."

"Did you really have sex with him?"

"No. I just said that to drive her crazy."

"Where is your father?"

"He lives with his girlfriend in a condo up on Beverly Drive. He left my mother when I was in seventh grade. Can't say that I blame him for moving out. But I do blame him for leaving me with her. She is a hopeless alcoholic and impossible to live with. You saw her sober because it is still early morning." He fell into a long silence.

As gently as possible, I said, "But you were pretty hard on her."

"I was hard on her? You saw nothing. For the last several years, that's the way we talk to each other. And believe me, she can be one mean bitch when she wants to. She loved finding out that I was gay because it was one more thing to hold over me. She made the mistake of sending me to a couple of shrinks who convinced me that gay was okay and that I had shitty parents."

"But she did get you out of jail, didn't she?"

"As a matter of fact, she did not. I made a deal with the cops. I told them that I'd give them my answering machine if they wouldn't file charges against me. That saved them from getting a search warrant, so they agreed. Malone brought me back to the apartment. There are more than enough of Arnie's recordings on the answering machine to nail him. Then they took me back to the police station and recorded an interview with me. I have to go back this afternoon to sign a transcription of the interview."

"I do too. We can go together. So, how did you get home?"

"I took a taxi. The cops didn't mind bringing me here for the answering machine, but after that I was on my own. Of course, as a special surprise, one of the cops called my mother, which is why she showed up this morning. We started arguing, and then you walked in."

"Good thing. You might have come to blows."

"Nah. She really prefers not having me at home, but every so often she has a guilt attack and tries to act like a real mother, especially in front of an audience. None of that bullshit about me having to live at home and being grounded was true. She doesn't want me there, and God knows that I would never allow myself to be grounded."

"Where's your dad in all this?"

"He gives us money. He inherited a furniture chain from his father, so he's well-fixed. I spend weekends with him sometimes."

"He's okay with your being gay?"

"I think he was relieved. Just one more reason to ignore me." Then with a sad smile, he added, "So there you have it. I'm a poor little rich kid who also happens to be a faggot and a whore."

"Well, except for the rich part, I'm pretty much the same."

"No, Josh. Me and you are not the same. You're smart as hell and you're going to UCLA in a couple of weeks on a scholarship. I barely passed French."

"That's because you didn't work at it."

"That's where you're wrong. You know, smart kids like you don't understand that school is hard for some of us. I've been in good schools all my life, had tutors, even gone to special academic summer camps. But it takes me a long time to learn stuff. No matter how hard I try."

"What will you do now?"

"My father will keep giving me money, I'll graduate from high school, and then go to an easy college for rich dumb kids. Afterwards, my dad will probably take me into the furniture business, so I'll be okay. I've been taking care of myself for a long time and gotten pretty good at it." He pulled me closer. We reclined on the sofa for a long time, lying in each other's arms and sinking into the warmth of each other's body. Two faggots. Two busted hustlers. Two teenage boys with family problems. But my problems were nothing compared to Jean-Pierre's.

Chapter Thirteen:
Baked Howard

That afternoon, Officer Gonzalez was waiting for us at the police station with two typed affidavits ready for us to sign and notarize. Scowling as we left, he said "I'll keep an eye out for you boys. Don't think that you can get away a second time just because you've got fancy friends."

"Are you the one who called my mother?" Jean-Pierre asked.

With something between a gloat and a smirk, Gonzalez asked in a sing-song voice, "Did someone call your mommy? Why would anyone do that?"

Feeling Gonzalez's eyes on us as we walked out, Jean-Pierre said, "I'm sure he called my mother. He's mad because we got off with no charges. Don't be surprised if he finds a way to screw you too."

It was mid-afternoon when we got back to the apartment. I rode my Vespa down to the beach. After a workout with a couple of dojo guys, I took a run up to the Will Rogers beach and back. It was relief to have a Friday night to myself. Jean-Pierre was just waking from a nap when I returned to the apartment. "It seems strange to see each other this time of night," I commented.

"Even stranger having a Friday night with nothing to do. Or no one to do," he added with a salacious grin. "I have an idea. Why don't I take you to dinner? You're moving out on Sunday and leaving me all by myself. Let's celebrate our retirement as hustlers."

How could I refuse? He took me to a fancy French restaurant in Beverly Hills. Having recently acquired some expertise in French, I enjoyed pointing out the misspelling of baked lobster on the menu—*Howard au Four* instead of *Homard au Four*. This provided an excuse to flirt with the very cute French waiter by asking if Howard had consented to being baked.

The multicourse meal lasted several hours during which Jean-Pierre told me more about his mostly unhappy life. His parents had adopted him from a foster home when he was three years old. "Because I was the cutest kid in the litter, and my mother wanted a toy," as he put it. Until his twelfth year, when his parents separated, his primary caregiver was an Irish nanny whom he remembers fondly. He then spent three years at an all-boys boarding school in Virginia. At the end of his junior year, he was expelled for cheating and returned to Pacific Palisades to live with his mother who by then was an out-of-control drunk.

They quickly sank into a toxic relationship, impelled largely by her alcoholism. She often left him alone for weeks on end with just a credit card, a car, and a maid to look after his material needs. Tired of his complaining, his father increased his allowance at the end of his junior year so he could rent his own apartment. From early childhood, he had been in and out of psychotherapy. Unlike me with Dr. Chandler, he was grateful to his shrinks for teaching him how to cope. He reminded me a little of my friend Patty—a very good-looking, struggling student with a difficult homelife. Although we shared few interests, I ended up admiring his resilience. We were back in the apartment by 10 PM. "It's awfully early to go to bed," Jean-Pierre remarked. Then with a twinkle in his eye, "Unless you want to come to bed with me."

Already a bit horny from fantasizing about the French waiter, I accepted. Why not? I had not had sex just for the fun of it since Angelo left. So, Jean-Pierre and I enjoyed a lovely evening playing with each other's bodies and finally fell asleep in each other's arms. While fading into slumber, I realized how much I had missed real sex, the kind that celebrates mutual pleasure and friendship.

Chapter Fourteen:
A Love that Will Not Let Go

The following morning, I enjoyed a leisurely breakfast, read *The Los Angeles Times* from cover to cover, and took a long shower, fully anticipating a Saturday all to myself. As I was drying off, Jean-Pierre cracked open the door and told me that someone was waiting to see me.

"Who is it?"

"You need to see for yourself. I'll leave you two to yourselves."

Puzzled by the mystery, I slapped on some jeans and a t-shirt and walked into the living room. Much to my horror and astonishment, I found my father sitting on the sofa. He stood up and awkwardly shook my hand as though we were meeting for the first time. His hand was big and rough, the grease-stained hand of a country car mechanic.

"Sonny, how are you? I heard that you were in trouble."

"Did that cop call you?"

"Somebody called last night. He didn't give a name. He just told us what kind of trouble you were in and gave me this address. I jumped in the car early this morning and drove straight through."

425

"Who's watching the garage?"

"Your brother Keith is in town for the weekend. He just started law school at the U of A. But that's not what we need to talk about."

"So, what do we need to talk about?" I asked with maybe a trace of hostility in my voice. "Are you here to punish me? Drag me back to Rosales? Or make me return to that awful clinic?"

A painful expression crossed my father's face. "Sonny, when have I punished you? Have I ever hit you? And when did I drag you anywhere?"

"Well, you sort of dragged me to Croft House."

"We thought that was in your best interest. You may know, by the way, that Croft House is fighting a lawsuit of some sort. They tried to get us involved, but all we knew was that our son had disappeared. And you never gave us the opportunity to find out why."

Noting the veiled reproach, I responded, "I never tried to explain anything to you because I didn't think you would understand."

"Why didn't you give us a chance?"

"Because you're Mormon. I know what the church teaches, and I know that you never disagree with the church. If the church is on one side and I'm on the other, there's no way I can win. I would lose the argument before we ever started."

"Argue about what?"

"About who I am. You have to know. I am a homosexual, a gay person." Then with added emphasis, "A faggot."

He winced as though I had struck him, and I must admit, it was a brutal way to come out. Groping for words, he said, "Sonny, you will never hear me use that word. Besides, how can you be so sure that you're…" he was unable to finish the sentence.

"There, you see? You hate it so much that you can't even say the word."

He shook his head and looked at the floor. "It's just that I don't know how you can be so sure."

"Dad, I'm sure. Your youngest son is a homosexual. I am a homosexual. I've known for as long as I can remember. And thanks to Burt Larson and Barry Cummings, everyone in Rosales knows as well. What were my options? Stay in a torture clinic like Croft House? Go back to Rosales where everyone would ridicule me, if not worse? Or spend a horrible year with Uncle Hyrum? And how was I supposed to deal with the church? The LDS Church teaches that homosexuality is a sin second only to murder, and it excommunicates homosexuals all the time. Mother made church teachings on the subject very clear when you drove me to Croft House for the last time. Do you remember everything she said?"

He looked away from me. "Yes, I remember what she said. I wish I could take it back." After a long silence, he continued, "You know, over the last few years, your mother has not had an easy time of it. Women's problems, menopause, and all those damned pills she takes. She's a lot more rigid about religion than she used to be. You've not seen her at her best."

"Is she still taking pills after almost overdosing last year?"

"I can't keep track of her. She goes to doctors in different towns and never buys pills in the same place. I'm really worried about her. I keep my eye on her, but I can only do so much. I'm also worried about you. It's just that I cannot understand how a fella could …"

"Could what? Be attracted to another man? Why does everyone have to be the same?"

In almost a whisper, "Sonny, it's just not normal."

"Dad, maybe what's normal for some people isn't normal for others. Maybe being homosexual is the normal me. I don't expect you to understand it. But I do expect you to believe me. I'm the one who has lived it. Not you. Not Mother. Not the church. And not the Dr. Chandlers of the world who make money promising that they can cure us. Besides, things are going well for me here in Los Angeles. I've never been happier."

"How can you say that things are going well after you got arrested and all?"

"That is only part of the story. I needed money, and that was the easiest way to get it."

A sad expression came over his face. After an awkward silence, he asked, "Josh, do you remember your grandfather Chastain? My father?"

"Not well. He died when I was what—seven or eight years old? I remember his funeral. But I have only vague memories of him."

"There is a reason for that. For over twenty years, me and my father didn't hardly speak. We sort of reconnected after you were born, but we still had to overcome a lot of resentment. And then he got killed in a car wreck before we had things completely ironed out."

"Why did you go so long without speaking to each other?"

"My mother died when I was twelve years old, leaving my father with four small children to raise. I was the oldest. About a year later, he married another woman, Grandma Ursula as you know her. Ursula and I didn't get along, probably because I was starting to feel my oats and never gave her a chance. I wanted my real mother back. Ursula started having her own kids, and my dad got fed up with me and her squabbling all the time. So, he farmed me out to different relatives. I was passed from one family to another where I never felt wanted. When I got big enough to help on the farm, my dad took me back because he could use an extra hand. For a while, we kind of got along. To her credit, Ursula did her best to make me feel welcome, but I never felt like her home was my home.

"Then, when I was about your age, maybe a little younger, I went to a school dance with some friends. I was just a big kid and during the dance some of us snuck out behind the school and smoked a few cigarettes and took a few nips of whiskey that one of the guys had brought. More smart-alecky smoking and drinking than the real thing.

"When I got home, my dad was waiting up for me, which surprised me since he usually went to bed early. He asked me if I had been smoking and drinking. Maybe he could smell it on me. I might have been a little drunk and was feeling pretty full of myself. So, I sassed him and told him that it was none of his business. He said, 'Let's go talk this out in the barn where we won't wake anyone up.' As soon as we entered the barn, he sucker-punched me. Hard, in the stomach. Knocked the breath out of me with one blow. Then he started beating me. After a hard blow to my head, I blacked out, and he just left me there.

"After I came to, I walked to the highway and caught a ride to Phoenix where I lived for the next ten years. I was lucky to get a job with a good mechanic, Owen Lewis, who taught me almost everything I know about cars. But I never finished high school. Along the way, I picked up some bad habits, mostly smoking, drinking, and brawling. I got in fights for no good reason because, you see, I was angry all the time. Angry at the world, angry at my dad, angry at my relatives who hadn't treated me very good… just angry. And I'd take it out on anyone who got in my way. Owen sold his business, and the new owner wanted the property for something else, so I got a job driving a mail truck.

"One of my stops was the Tempe State Teachers College where your mother was a student and worked part-time in the mailroom. She was one of the prettiest girls I had ever seen. We got to talking and found out that both of us had grown up in small Mormon towns and had similar backgrounds. We started seeing each other. We soon fell in love and got married. Eloped. Neither of our families knew.

"She got a job teaching in Rosales, so I borrowed some money and opened a garage. That's when we started a family. She slowly persuaded me to give up my bad habits, and eventually got me back in the church. The church taught me to control my temper and the importance of being kind. In fact, I don't think any of you kids have ever seen me mad. When I feel my temper rising, I remember what my father did to me, and I just walk away. All I wanted was to be a good father.

"You see, I basically growed up without a father, and I don't want the same to happen to you. Your mother and me raised five kids. All of them but you have graduated from college, and both Jeff and Keith have completed church missions. Not a bad record for the kids of a high-school dropout like me. But most of the credit goes to your mother. She taught you good English, bought you books, and educated you in the finer things of life. She also supported you in music. Heaven only knows what would've happened to me without her. The Good Lord surely had his arms around me the day I met her on the Tempe campus."

He then fell silent as though trying to remember more.

"That's a nice story Dad. But why are you telling it to me now?"

"I'm not sure. Maybe I just want you to know what a good woman your mother is and what a good woman can do for you. I also want you to know how much I owe to the church. But I mostly wanted you to know about me and my dad. I don't want me and you to go twenty years without talking to each other. I want you to be part of the family."

Absorbing this much information left me without words. My father had never told me anything about his life, and I had no idea about him and my grandfather. Still, if the last few months had taught me anything, it was that I could not live the life of a good Mormon heterosexual. Finally, I answered, "Dad, your story can't be mine. There will not be a good woman in my

432

life to bring me back to the straight and narrow, and gay people cannot feel comfortable in the Mormon church."

"Are you sure? You're awfully young to make decisions like that."

"I may be young, but I know who I am, and I have to be me. I can't be someone else."

With fear in his eyes, my father asked, "Does that mean you're leaving the church?"

"How can I stay? I can't—won't—marry a woman. I know several cases (I knew about truck-stop Mike and Lucy's Gabe) where gay guys married women, and it ended up being unfair for all of them. Marriage and having kids are commandments for Mormons. And I can't do that. Besides, I'm not sure how much of it I believe."

"Sonny, the church helped me put my life back together. Without the church and your mother, I would still be a worthless carouser living in Phoenix."

"That's great for you, Dad, but I'm not you. I'm a different person. And I'm not living the life of a worthless carouser."

He folded his arms, looking so sad that I thought he might cry. After a long silence, he asked, "How about what that man on the phone told me? Is that how you want to live your life?"

"Dad, I needed money to stay alive and to stay in school. That was my best option."

"You could have asked me for money."

"Are you sure? Are you sure you wouldn't have demanded that I return to Croft House or go back to Rosales? Or maybe even called the police when you found out where I was and have them drag me home or put me in a juvenile detention center?"

He frowned. "I'm not sure what I would've done. I just wish you had talked to me."

"Dad, can I show you some of the rest of my life? I'm more than what that cop told you."

We drove to the dojo on Venice Beach where, at his request, I suited up and worked out a bit with one of the other guys. My dad, who had known me only as an unathletic musician, clearly enjoyed watching me. I then took him up to the SMC campus and told him about receiving A grades in courses of French and Music Theory, working as a staff singer at St. Mark's, and getting into UCLA. From there, we drove up to the UCLA campus where I showed him the dorm I would be living in and walked around campus. He was impressed. "When do you start at UCLA?" he asked.

"I move into the dorm tomorrow afternoon. Freshman orientation begins on Monday."

"Well, if you put me up tonight, I'll help you move in. Then, I need to drive back to Rosales so Keith can return to Tucson and not miss any classes. I need to be back at the garage on Monday."

"I can move myself. I don't have very much stuff. But I would like you to go to church with me tomorrow to hear me sing. You can leave after the first service and be back in Rosales by late afternoon."

With a glimmer of a smile, he asked, "Will they try to wash the Mormonism out of me?"

"Not a chance."

That evening, my dad and I enjoyed a long dinner at an all-you-can-eat steakhouse, his favorite kind of place. To my surprise, we found lots to talk about—family history, people in Rosales, the diphtheria epidemic that had killed half of his grade school class, and what life was like during the depression. He discussed his worries about mother and the changes in her personality since she got hooked on pills. He expressed concern about my sister Terri, who was living what he called a "worldly" life in San Francisco—his way of saying that she had left the church.

We talked politics—how loyal he felt to Franklin Roosevelt and the New Deal and how disturbed he was by the United States' involvement in Vietnam. "I remember several young guys who got killed in World War II, and as you may recall (I didn't) my uncle Lucian lost all three of his sons in World War I, the stupidest war in history. You know, sonny, there's always some damned fool out there wanting to start a war, and usually for no good reason. For example, what do they think they're going to accomplish in Vietnam? How many more kids need to die before they realize that there's no way for the United States to win? For every Vietcong we kill, there are three to take his place. It's not our country. We're the invaders." My father, the pacifist! I couldn't believe it.

Although we studiously avoided talking about sex and religion, this was the first time I had ever conversed with my father as equals. He didn't have my mother's verbal prowess (few do), and his grammar wasn't perfect, but he followed the news, enjoyed reading history, and had a strong sense of right and wrong. He had also slavishly devoted his entire adult life to his family. Still, I realized that he and I could share a past but, unless he could accept a gay son, we would not share a future. I also sensed that he was proud of my accomplishments—that I had stayed in school, passed the GED exam, and was going to UCLA. There was no more talk about me returning to Rosales.

Back at the apartment, he phoned my mother to let her know that I was okay. I reluctantly agreed to say hello, fearing a jeremiad against my sinful lifestyle. Fortunately, she was so high on Valium, Thorazine, or whatever that she could hardly sustain a conversation much less pronounce divine retribution on me. I felt embarrassed for her and sad for my father. Since he had had such a long day, I convinced him to let me sleep on the sofa so he could get a good night's rest in my bed. Before going to bed, he asked if we could pray together.

"Why Dad? What are you going to pray for? Are you going to ask God to make me straight? To guide me to the right woman? To make me stay in the Mormon church? How do I know you're not going to ask God to gang up on me?"

My answer stunned him. "Is that what we do? Ask God to gang up on you?"

"Think about it. Every time Mother or Dr. Chandler prayed, it was basically to ask God to make me someone I wasn't."

After a thoughtful silence, he said, "Maybe you're right. I'd never thought of it that way." Then, not wanting to force the issue, he said, "Sonny, I'm sorry we can't pray together, but I am going to insist on one thing."

"What's that?"

"I want your address at UCLA so I can send you some money every month. I helped the other kids through college, and I want to do the same for you."

"I don't need the money. With my job at St. Mark's and a scholarship, I'll make out just fine."

"Maybe you will, but I still want to contribute. It's the least I can do."

I suddenly wanted to embrace him. Everything about him was honest, generous, and kind. Even if he didn't understand me, he clearly loved me and wanted the best for me. But embracing wasn't something the men in my family did, so we separated with nothing more than a good night.

The following morning, he attended the early service at St. Mark's. The anthem was Haydn's "The Heavens are Telling" which has a short solo section for a bass, tenor, and soprano trio. I sang my best and could tell that my dad was proud of me. But I also sensed how out of place he felt—a country auto mechanic with chapped, grease-stained hands sitting among affluent, urban Episcopalians. I felt a twinge of class resentment wondering if some of those well-heeled people looked down on him. As I watched him leave for Rosales, I teared up thinking about how much he loved me even if he couldn't understand me.

In the warm-up for the 11 PM service, Flo went out of her way to say hello, but she didn't ask any questions about my encounter with the cops. I started to thank her, but she quickly shushed me. "Josh dear, that's water under the bridge. From now on, let's concentrate on the future."

Chapter Fifteen:
Hung Lo

That afternoon, I moved into the dorm. My half of the room included a built-in desk, a single bed, and a closet with a small space for clothes and toiletries. Already settled in, my roommate was a short Asian-American kid with a big smile, a mop of black hair, and a gymnast's build. He introduced himself as Henry Lo. Then with a totally straight face he informed me that his name in Chinese was Hung Lo. Continuing the deadpan, he explained "But you should just call me Henry. Guys get nervous when I tell them that I'm Hung Lo."

Seeing my consternation at this brazen dick joke, he broke into a broad smile and said "Gotta run and say a proper goodbye to my parents. Catch you later, Joshua Chastain. You'll eventually get used to my twisted sense of humor." I later learned that I had been placed on a special dorm floor for honors students, meaning that Henry (or Hung) was probably not just a smart mouth but also very smart.

Orientation week passed in a whirl. I was accepted into the Chamber Singers, the best choral group on campus, as well as into the organ studio I wanted. All my courses were honors courses, meaning that they were small and supposedly had the best teachers.

Thanks to the superb training given me by Mother Harold, that maven of time management, I found time for my classes, organ practice, and Chamber Singers in addition to ten hours a week working at the music library plus a weeknight rehearsal and two Sunday services at St. Mark's. I had never been busier, nor had I ever been happier.

I soon became aware of a large, gay subculture at UCLA and in Los Angeles. A hunky, hairy grad student named Gary, one of the other basses in the Chamber Choir, began flirting with me. We tricked a couple of times—sort of pro-forma sex since he liked sampling as many guys as possible, "like a hummingbird moving from flower to flower" as he put it. He introduced me to the two main tearooms on campus (tearoom: a public bathroom where gay guys meet and sometimes have sex), one in the Math Building and the other in the basement of the French department. The student gym was also cruisy—a new word I learned to identify places where gay men cruise for sex. Thinking of my upcoming encounter with Ronnie, I tried to keep my sexual urges under control, but it wasn't easy since sex was so widely available. This was also true for straight people, partly because inexpensive birth control pills had just come on the market. I was living what some remember as the sexual revolution and others as the glorious age of promiscuity.

My roommate Hung Lo turned out to be a raging heterosexual. After he tried several times to involve me in discussions about girls, I confessed that I was gay, to which he responded with wide-eyed amazement "Really! Like you do it with guys!? That is so cool! I've never met a gay guy before!" Henry was probably the happiest person I had ever met. He found almost everything totally awesome and greeted every development with a huge smile. He also worked his butt off in what appeared to be mostly science and math classes. Although irremediably straight, he was very curious about how gay guys meet and interact and pressed me for information about dick sizes. All men, I've decided, are closet size queens, as is obvious in public showers where guys—straight and gay—sneak glances at each other to compare equipment. But there was no question about Henry's sexual orientation. He loved women and seemed to fall in love with a different girl every week.

Chapter Sixteen:
The Court of Love

Remembering my promise to my father, I dutifully sent my parents a letter in which I gave them my address and telephone number. This turned out to be a mistake. Within days I started receiving missives from my mother—fifteen to twenty pages single spaced—lecturing me about not abandoning the faith of my childhood. Things got worse when two graduate students, Jack Huddleston and Greg Miller, came to my dorm room, introduced themselves as my home teachers, and welcomed me to the UCLA LDS student ward. My mother (who else?) had transferred my church records.

The LDS Church maintains a program by which two men known as home teachers visit individual members and member families at least once a month. Their task is to check up on the spiritual and material wellbeing of church members and to help out where they can. Although the home teachers often provide real help for the families they serve, some would argue that the program is also a veiled system of surveillance.

The two who showed up in my dorm room were nice enough guys, although I would have preferred to not have them around. Jack was a graduate student in nuclear engineering with a wife and two young kids.

Greg was a recent BYU graduate beginning doctoral studies in psychology. He wore no rings and was stunningly handsome. Gazing at the gorgeous Greg had its charms, but I did not want to talk about the LDS church. Indeed, I resented how much of my life-force had already been spent dealing with Mormonism.

Fortunately, my schedule as a staff singer at St. Mark's conflicted with LDS meeting times. Still, "my" home teachers promised to stay in touch, which I heard as a veiled threat. I wrote a curt note to Mother asking her not to send church representatives to visit me and to cease writing hortatory letters. Rather than stop, her next letter took on a particularly ominous tone, warning that I was subject to special divine retribution for not honoring my priesthood.

Only days later, Greg and Jack contacted me again, wanting to schedule a meeting in one of the dorm's group-study rooms. After putting them off several times, I reluctantly agreed, fully intending to make it our last meeting. I entered the group-study room at the appointed time and was not pleased to see that accompanying Jack and Greg were four other men, all of them older and clearly not students. Jack introduced them. "Josh, this is your bishop, Bishop Carson, and these are his two counselors, Brother Wiley and Brother Turley. The man sitting at the end of the table is Brother Taylor, the ward clerk."

It was an ambush. All stood, we shook hands, and then sat down in a tense silence. Beautiful Greg seemed particularly uncomfortable. Finally, Bishop Carson began speaking. An obese red-faced man with multiple chins and a tie too short to cover his belly, he asked, "How are things going, Josh? How's school?"

"School is fine. Is that why all of you are here, to ask me about school? Surely you've got better things to do with your time."

Not anticipating such an antagonistic response, Bishop Carson squirmed a bit before answering. "Well, actually we do have something else to talk about, something quite serious. But perhaps you would like to start."

"Start what?"

"Josh, is there anything that your bishop should know about you or about what you've done?"

"I can't think of a thing, so why don't we all go home."

"Josh, there's no need to be rude. We're here out of concern for you. You see, I received a letter from your mother and have since had several telephone conversations with her. We are very concerned about your salvation and the status of your soul."

"Maybe the status of my soul is none of your business."

"But it is, Josh. As your bishop, I need to know if you have fallen into serious transgression so we can call you to repentance and begin taking remedial steps towards helping you repent."

"It sounds like my mother should do the repenting for me."

"She's only concerned about your spiritual health. The Apostle Paul teaches us that where there is no law, there is no transgression. But you know the law. You also know that in LDS doctrine obedience is the first law of heaven. Moreover, you have been ordained a priest in the Aaronic priesthood, which authorizes you to act in God's name. God will not be mocked. It would be better for you to be out of the church altogether than to be a conscious sinner scorning the blessings that God has given you. Confession is the first step towards repentance."

"What am I supposed to confess? That I'm gay? Well, there you have it. I'm gay. I'm a homosexual. I have sex with men. Lots of men. Regularly. Is that confession enough?"

A stunned silence ensued. Finally, Bishop Carson asked, "Do you intend to repent of this sinful lifestyle?"

"It's not a lifestyle. It's who I am. It's my life. And no, I do not plan to stop being who I am."

I felt my temper rising, particularly since my mother, once again, had arranged for church leaders to gang up on me. I feared losing control of my emotions and showing weakness. But I didn't let that happen.

After all, I was seventeen years old and resolved to not let these men bully me. After a couple of deep breaths, I said, "So, let's get on with it. Kick me out of the church to relieve me of the burden of belonging to a church that I don't believe in."

"You question the truth of the church?"

"Have you guys ever really thought about what the church teaches? Gold plates? Reformed Egyptian? God's people as white and delightsome and dark skins as a curse? Black men excluded from the priesthood? Have you really considered how dumb all that sounds?"

In solemn tones, the bishop replied, "Josh, let me bear my testimony. I know that the Church of Jesus Christ of Latter-day Saints is true, that Joseph Smith was a prophet of God who restored the true Church of Christ, and that we are currently led by living prophets."

"And how do you know that? Maybe what you know is wrong. People know lots of stuff that's wrong."

"I know because the Spirit of God gave me a burning within and thereby confirmed to me the truth of the gospel as restored through Joseph Smith."

"Well, the next time that happens, take some Pepto-Bismol. It does wonders for heartburn."

Suddenly even more red in the face, Bishop Carson stood up and snarled, "I will not sit here and listen to you mock my testimony."

One of his counselors (Brother Turley?) touched him on the arm, gently trying to push him back into his seat, but not before I retorted, "Since when did recommending Pepto-Bismol become blasphemy? Is this the latest thing from Salt Lake City? Is Pepto-Bismol forbidden by the church?

After several deep breaths, the bishop squeezed his corpulent body back into his chair and seemed to get his temper under control. In a voice charged with emotion, as though he were having trouble breathing, he said "Josh, it truly grieves me to see that you have not only confessed to serious transgressions but that you are also in an advanced state of apostasy. God will not be mocked. We are here for your own good. We are here as God's representatives to call you to repentance and back to the life God marked out for you in the preexistence. Will you at least pray with us for God to soften your heart?"

"There's nothing wrong with my heart. So, I'm going to walk out of this room and hope to never see you again. And don't bother praying for me. I don't need your prayers." I stood up and began to leave.

The bishop stood with me. Biting each word, he declaimed in a loud voice, "Josh, I feel empowered by the Holy Spirit as your bishop and as a High Priest according to the order of Melchizedek to testify to you that if you walk out of this meeting, you are walking out of God's church. And it will be extremely difficult to come back."

"Good. That will make it easier not to return to a place I never wanted to be in the first place."

I stomped out of the room and would have slammed the door behind me if it hadn't had one of those hydraulic door closers—the kind that go whoosh and don't allow for dramatic door slamming. I went to my room and lay down on my bed. I was having a hard time breathing, sort of like after Ape Arms tried to rape me in the Arizona desert. Lying in the dark, I reviewed the details of my encounter with the bishop, his counselors, the ward clerk, and my home teachers.

I was angry for being ambushed but proud of how I had stood up to them. This explicit confrontation between me and LDS church authorities was long overdue. But I was saddened by the realization that whatever connection I had with the LDS church was now broken and that the breach between me and my family might never be bridged. I did not want to go twenty years without speaking to my father. As for Mother, I never wanted to see her again.

Three days later I received a notice from the student union post office saying that I needed to sign for a certified letter. Suspecting what it was, I went to my dorm room to read it. Alone.

October 8, 1970

Dear Brother Chastain:

My counselors and I express deep appreciation for your meeting with us on October 6 at 8:00 PM in Room 123 of Dykstra Hall on the UCLA campus. After careful consideration and much prayer, I, as your bishop, with the unanimous support of my two counselors, have decided that you are to be excommunicated from the Church of Jesus Christ of Latter-day Saints for conduct inappropriate for a member of the Church and a holder of God's holy priesthood. Specifically, we find you guilty, by your own confession, of violating the Law of Chastity and mocking church doctrine. We further deem our action appropriate since you show no sign of the "broken heart and contrite spirit" described in the Book of Mormon and identified by Church leaders as a necessary step towards true repentance.

As an excommunicated person, you cannot enjoy any of the privileges of Church membership. Your name will be removed from the Church records, you may not pay tithes and offerings, and you may no longer participate in any of the ordinances appropriate to a holder of the Aaronic priesthood. You may attend church meetings but will not be allowed to participate in class discussions, hold church callings, or sustain church officers and teachers.

In closing, I wish to emphasize that excommunication is an act of love and that our deepest desire is for you to recognize the error of your ways so that you might seek your way back into Heavenly

Father's kingdom by studying the scriptures, praying often, and heeding the counsel of our inspired leaders.

Please know that I am always available to guide you in the arduous path of regaining Church membership. In the meantime, be assured that my counselors and I will continue to pray for your spiritual regeneration.

Sincerely,

Bishop Willard Carson

So that was it. I didn't have to walk away. I had been pushed out. The patronizing tone of the letter angered me, but I felt relieved. A decision had been made. I wrote a curt letter to my parents informing them of my excommunication and asking that they suspend future contact with me.

October 8, 1970

Dear Mother and Dad,

Last Tuesday evening, I was ambushed by the bishop of the UCLA Ward, his two counselors, the ward clerk, and my two home teachers. I say "ambushed" because I knew nothing of the meeting's agenda and thought that only my home teachers would be present. Bishop Carson informed me that Mother had written him a letter and then had several phone conversations with him in which they discussed my "sinful" life. Based on this information, Bishop Carson asked me if I had anything to confess. I replied that I did not. He then asked if I was a homosexual and if I had sustained sexual relationships with other men. I answered yes to both questions while also holding that I did not consider such matters sinful.

Bishop Carson then bore testimony of the truth of the LDS Church and informed me that I would be excommunicated unless I showed remorse and a willingness to repent under the guidance of proper church authorities. I refused and left the meeting. This morning, I received a certified letter from Bishop Carson informing me that I had been excommunicated from the LDS Church.

I am pleased with the excommunication. It formally severs a relationship that I did not choose and that I no longer want to be in. I am not happy, however, with the fact that Mother went behind my back, betrayed me to Bishop Carson, and pushed him to confront me in what was basically an ambush. In short, she violated my agency and preempted a decision that should have been mine to make.

In view of these events, I wish to suspend all contact with you and the family. Moreover, as I am financially able, I will send you money from time to time to pay off my material debt to you. Perhaps in the future we can renew contact, but it will need to be on terms of mutual respect that, as revealed by Mother's actions, do not currently exist.

In closing, despite the events of this past week, I remain grateful for the good things you have done for me.

Sincerely,

Joshua

I sent the letter by certified mail to ensure its arrival. The cool distance I tried to project in the letter was totally out of sync with the turmoil I felt inside. Being excommunicated from the church and making a formal break with my family were not small matters. Further, this was probably the first time that I really stood up to my mother.

Late that evening, I rode my Vespa down to Santa Monica Boulevard and parked it across from the Mormon temple. As I stared up at the massive floodlit building, I realized that my separation from the LDS church had started many years earlier, perhaps when I was five years old and stood transfixed by the beauty of Mother's teenage helper, Manuel Guerrero. Still, the formal expulsion from my original church, family, and tribe left me emotionally drained.

Yet somehow, I did not feel separated from—dare I say it—God. Or something like God. I remembered the profound sense of gratitude that flooded my soul after my first sexual encounters with Harold, Father Tovar, and Ronnie. I remembered my dreams, the one in which Billy Schaeffer kept me from killing myself and the one in which I was lost on a dark mountainside and then suddenly engulfed by a light and embraced by a beautiful naked man with whom I experienced an intense spiritual connection.

These experiences were transcendent. Mystical might be a better word because they brought me into union with the numinous—a word I learned much later when I read Rudolph Otto's masterful *The Idea of the Holy*. Even more wondrous was the fact that each of these experiences began with homosexual desire. I therefore wondered if what made me hold on to the idea of God was a "perverse" sex drive that created conditions for these experiences to occur. Is that the real scandal? That God made sexual desire— in my case, homosexual desire—to keep bringing me back to him?

Monday evening my phone rang repeatedly for almost two hours, undoubtedly my mother, wanting to respond to my letter. I finally unplugged the phone, hoping that the calls were not for Henry. Two days later, I received a fat letter from my mother. I returned it unopened.

Chapter Seventeen:
Ronnie in Los Angeles

In the meantime, another *grand moment* was looming. The following Sunday would be the third Sunday in October, the day Ronnie promised to meet me at the Los Angeles train station. I told Henry (Hung) that for a few nights we might have a third person in our room. With some reluctance, I described my relationship with Ronnie to which Hung responded with his usual cheerful enthusiasm, exclaiming, "That is so great! Is he, like, your boyfriend? Are you going to, like, make love and stuff in our room?" And then with a wink, "Do I get to watch? Will it be gross?"

Fortunately, a student had dropped out early in the term, leaving an empty bed on our floor. It would soon be reassigned, but for the time being it was available to Hung. Our senior resident, a graduate student who tripped my gaydar, was okay with Ronnie staying in my dorm room while Hung used someone else's bed. Dr. Riedel grumped about my missing Sunday services, but even he managed a slight smile when informed that it was a matter of the heart.

Saturday night, I hardly slept. What should I expect from Ronnie after only four nights of intense conversation and incredible sex now five months past?

454

Did the trust-fund baby and the mechanic's son really have much in common? Was our friendship a hothouse plant that flourished only in the rarified environment of Croft House? And how much had we both changed? Two months with Angelo and two months of hustling had to have had some effect on me, not to mention recent sexual encounters at UCLA and the fact that I was now officially an ex-Mormon.

Not trusting my Vespa on the freeway, I took Sunset Boulevard all the way downtown. It was almost a straight shot from UCLA to Union Station, so I arrived well before noon. The breathtaking beauty of the train station along with its vast emptiness on a Sunday morning awed and inspired me. I tried to imagine what it was like in World War II when thousands of soldiers bade farewell from loved ones, perhaps for the last time. Maybe Blair or his pilot lover had passed through here. Just as the chimes started ringing the noon hour, I saw a longhaired guy with a full red beard approaching me. After a double take, I recognized him as Ronnie.

"Josh," he called. "Josh, is that you?"

"Better question: is this hairy man Ronnie?"

We looked at each other for several seconds and then fell into a spontaneous embrace. He seemed shorter than I remembered, but he was carrying more muscle, all of it rock hard. We held each other for a long time surrounded by the emptiness of the station.

Finally, he said, "I can't tell you how much I've been looking forward to this moment. Let's find someplace to talk. But can we grab a bite to eat first? I've been driving since six this morning, and I'm totally famished."

"La Luz del Día, one of the best Mexican places in town, is about a hundred yards from here over on Olvera Street."

After grabbing drinks and combination plates of tacos, enchiladas, and tamales, we crossed the street to the Plaza de Los Angeles and found a shady bench to share. "What's with the beard?" I asked.

"Evidently, I got my dad's genes for facial hair, which means that I'll probably have to shave twice a day just to look decent. Or maybe I'll just keep it like this. What do you think?"

"It's sort of sexy. Does it tickle?"

With a wink, "You'll have to find out."

"Okay, but not here. So, tell me! What was wilderness training like? Did they make you into a red-blooded heterosexual?"

"Before we start with the stories, let's talk about right now. I'm taking a week off from school and need to be back in Scottsdale a week from tonight. Can you put me up?"

"My roommate has generously offered to sleep in an empty bed in another room on my dorm floor, so you can stay with me. Just the two of us in one room."

"Roommate? Dorm? Where are you now?"

Realizing that my last conversation Ronnie was a rushed phone call about him going to a wilderness survival camp, I provided a thumbnail version of how I came to enroll at UCLA.

"Well shit! You're a mighty college student, and I'm still a senior in high school. Does that mean I have to kneel before you?"

"Depends on how badly you want blow me."

"Potty-brain."

"Are you living with your father and his bimbo wife?"

"I'm living with my father, but not the bimbo wife."

"Why? What happened to her?"

"My poor father. He just can't keep his dick in his pants. His wife found out that he was shagging some young thing at his office and kicked him out of the house. She doesn't want a divorce, but she won't have him back until he stops seeing his girlfriend and repents of his sins. So, he and I are sharing an apartment."

"Do you like living with him?"

"It's not so bad. When his brain isn't short-circuiting over some woman, he's a nice guy. We have a maid, of course (*of course!*), but we've started cooking a few meals together. It's been kind of fun. He's a better roommate than a dad."

"Is he okay now with your being gay?"

"He was always more or less okay with it. The problem people were his last two wives. Besides, given his sexual misadventures, he's in no position to criticize. By the way, he was all for my getting together with you. He even loaned me a car and a credit card for this trip. He wants a full report when I return to Scottsdale. So yeah, he has come around."

"And the church?"

"It's a big stumbling block. His wife won't take him back unless he accepts some sort of church disciplinary action. You know, the repentance thing. He was excommunicated once before and doesn't want to go through it again, so they're at a stalemate. If his marriage allowed him an occasional affair, he'd be fine. Men are just not made for monogamy."

Given my recent past, I had to agree with him. He followed me back to UCLA, me on my Vespa and he in his father's "spare" 1969 Mercedes 280SE. We found a twenty-four-hour parking lot in Westwood and by midafternoon were safely in my dorm room. No sooner had he put his backpack down than we began hugging and kissing. Within minutes we were having amazing sex. He had put on muscle and had more hair all over his body, including a beautiful furry chest. Afterwards, we lay naked in a loose embrace with our legs entwined. Sex with other guys had most certainly not diminished my attraction to Ronnie.

"You know," he said, "this is the first time that you and I have made love in a bed."

"Should we look for a golf course?"

"No, wise ass. I'm fine right here, although the open-air sex was pretty exciting."

"And so is this. Okay. Time for show and tell. Tell me about your life over the last five months."

"Why do I have to go first?"

"Because I asked first."

"That's a lousy reason but in the spirit of accommodation for which I am famous (not true), I'll pretend to find it convincing. First, my dad sent me to a sports camp in upstate New York."

"A sports camp? I thought you were going to a wilderness survival program."

"That came later. The sports camp turned out to be a good thing because I needed to train for the survival program. I did lots of running, climbing, swimming, and lifting. I got into good shape and put on some muscle, which (ahem) you may have noticed. I also started wrestling since I'm too short for tennis or swimming. And if you'll forgive the immodesty, I'm a good wrestler. After the first month, they asked me to join their staff as a junior fitness and wrestling assistant, so I stayed at the camp for another two months."

"What were the other guys like?"

"The staff guys were mostly older, but the camp participants ranged in age from twelve to eighteen. There were several programs, lasting from one to four weeks. A few dads came up wanting to bond with their teenage sons through sports. Watching them was sort of pathetic. There was also a bunch of Christian fundamentalists who repeatedly invited me to meetings to talk about Jesus."

"Did you argue with them?"

"No, I avoided them. I've decided that religion is a dead subject for dead people. I don't need it, and I'm tired of talking about it."

This was my first indication that Ronnie had changed in a fundamental way. Back at Croft House, he had no problem discussing religion.

"Any sex at the camp? All that wrestling must have done something to spark your hormones."

"Of course I had sex. That's what gay guys do. I first got it on with one of the wrestling instructors. Nothing serious. He was built like a brick shithouse, but dumber than dirt. He just wanted to get his rocks off. He'll probably end up marrying a woman and shagging guys on the side. I also got it on with a couple of the Christian youth counselors. They were seriously conflicted guys who will someday need to choose between sex and religion. Like lots of Mormons. Now it's your turn."

"Not so fast. So far, you've covered only the first two months. What happened after the sports camp?"

"You won't believe the next part. After three months at the sports camp, my dad sent me to an honest-to-goodness survival program—in Australia."

"In Australia!!?"

"Yeah, that island continent in the South Pacific. You may have heard of it."

"Yes, wise guy. I've heard of Australia. But why there?"

"One of my dad's business contacts is part owner of a survival program between Sydney and Canberra. It's a beautiful area."

"And …?"

Ronnie suddenly got very serious. "It gave me a different outlook on life. It was a genuine survival program. The goal was total self-reliance and independence. We read a lot of Ayn Rand and her ideas about the ethics of selfishness."

"Selfishness doesn't sound ethical to me."

"That's because you've been blinded by Christianity, which is basically a scam that allows mediocre, dependent people to sabotage the truly gifted. Have you read Ayn Rand?"

"Can't say that I have."

"Read her, and you'll understand what I'm talking about."

"So that's all you did? Wander around in the bush and talk about Ayn Rand?"

"Hardly. After several days of training, I spent a month in the woods with just my clothes, a poncho, and a knife. I had to live off the land. It was hard, but it wasn't awful. I'm glad I did it."

"Were you entirely by yourself? What if you got in trouble?"

"I had an emergency beeper but was not supposed to use it unless I was in real danger. The goal was to not depend on other people and to not let them depend on you. No sympathy for weakness, either in yourself or in others."

"No friends and no sex?"

"No friends and no sex. The head guide warned us that sex within the group would be a distraction that we couldn't afford. I was impressed that he openly addressed the fact that sex might occur in a group of men. But it didn't."

"So, a month in the wilds of Australia and then back to the US?"

"No. After the month in the bush, I spent a couple of weeks in Sydney to decompress."

"And that included sex?"

"God, you are so obsessed with sex!"

"It's just that I cannot imagine someone as cute as you being celibate."

"Okay. I confess. In Sydney, I met some great Australians. They are fun people, and the men are sexy. Are you happy now?

"Happy for you."

"Now it's your turn. How about you?"

I ended up telling a little bit of everything—Blair and Barkley, Ape Arms, Angelo, SMC, UCLA, and St. Mark's. I also told him that on several occasions I had accepted money for sex.

"Why would you do that?" he asked.

"Because I needed to pay the rent and feed myself."

"Oh," he replied as though one's needing money came as a surprise. Like most rich kids, he had never worried about money.

"Did you like it?"

"Not much. I don't plan to do it anymore now that I've got a job and a scholarship."

"Well, good. That means I won't have to pay you."

And that was it. The topic never came up again, perhaps because Ronnie found it repellent, uninteresting, or just something that a trust-fund baby would never think about.

That week with Ronnie started out as pure heaven. He attended classes with me, worked out with me, slept with me, and even attended a couple of my choir rehearsals. I took him to the beach and showed him the dojo. We had a great time comparing wrestling and karate techniques, during which the erotic touch of his body was never far from my mind.

As the week progressed, however, it became apparent that we would never recover the magic of those five intense days at Croft House. Our conversations were engaging, and the sex was great, but by the end of the week, we realized that we were headed in different directions. He had developed nothing but disdain for religion of any sort, not just for Mormonism. He pooh-poohed my growing fondness for Anglicanism as "exchanging one set of fairy tales for another." I winced just thinking of how he would scorn my mystical dreams or those transcendent moments when I sensed the reality of a nonmaterial world.

I also concluded that I could enjoy a very satisfactory life without hearing another word about Ayn Rand, the ethics of selfishness, or the right of the "truly gifted" to shit on everyone else. We came close to an argument only once—when I hinted that someone with a trust fund and daddy's credit card could hardly consider himself self-sufficient. Seeing how much this upset him, I never broached the subject again. I had once hoped that he might attend a university in the LA area, but he had his sights on an Ivy League school, someplace worthy of the truly gifted.

Anxious to get back to Scottsdale, he did not attend the morning service at St. Mark's, which hurt my feelings a bit since I wanted him to hear me sing. We vowed to stay in touch, although "in touch" at this point clearly did not mean "being together." I was both happy and sad to see him leave—happy about what had been and sad about what would never be.

Chapter Eighteen:
Greg

Several days after Ronnie's visit, just as I was leaving the music library, someone called to me. "Josh! Wait up." The speaker was none other than the gorgeous Greg, my erstwhile home teacher.

"Hi, Greg. I didn't think I'd ever see you again. According to my excommunication letter, I cannot enjoy any of the privileges of church membership which I suppose includes you."

Blushing, he replied, "I never considered myself much of a privilege, but can we forget for a moment that I used to be your home teacher and have a conversation like normal human beings?"

We strolled over to the outdoor deli next to Campbell Hall, ordered a couple of sodas, and sat down at a well-shaded table facing each other.

"First, I want to apologize for the way Bishop Carson treated you."

"Like for excommunicating me?"

"According to church policy, the bishop and his councilors have the right to excommunicate people, but he didn't need to be so nasty and trigger-happy."

"Trigger-happy or not, I am now officially an ex-Mormon. And even though I didn't appreciate being ambushed, I'm happy with the outcome. I shouldn't be a Mormon. I don't believe it, I'm gay, I have a sex life, and I do not plan to change. Of course, the gay part I can't change. It's who I am."

"That's what I want to talk about." Suddenly his eyes filled with tears. As he tried to blink them away, I noticed that the regulation temple garments showed through his shirt. After a long silence, he said, "Josh, can I tell you something about my situation?"

"Sure. I'm only a freshman, and you're a graduate student, but I'll be glad to hear you out."

"Josh, you grew up in the church, didn't you?"

"Born and bred. Fifth generation with pioneers and polygamists on all sides. So yeah. You might say I grew up in the church."

"When did you figure out that you were gay?"

"I kind of knew all my life. Why do you ask? Are you gay?"

"The church says there is no such thing as a homosexual, that there is only homosexual behavior."

"I know what they say. For a terrible week I was under the care of a sadistic Mormon therapist who never tired of saying that homosexual is only an adjective and never a noun."

"You don't agree?"

"Of course, I don't agree. I am a homosexual. I am a homosexual person. Homosexuality is not something I chose or something I do. It's something I discovered about myself, and it's something I am. The church's teachings on the subject are total bullshit—bullshit as in untrue and bullshit as in deliberately dismissive of the evidence."

Slightly stunned by my heated response, he said "You've thought a lot about this, haven't you?"

"I have thought about it, lived it, and I've heard stories from other gay people who say basically the same thing. We are homosexuals. Nouns. Real human beings who are fed up with other people telling us who we are. And that includes the LDS church."

"You're a little bit scary."

"Sorry, but I have no tolerance for the LDS Church's bullshit about homosexuality. Of course, they say that they love you and that they are only trying to help you become the person God wants you to be. Remember, according to Bishop what's-his-face, my excommunication was an act of love. But all they really do is make people miserable. Is that what you want to talk about?"

"Josh, I was a missionary in Argentina. While I was on my mission, I fell in love with another missionary. We got caught having sex. I was sent home

468

dishonorably and excommunicated. I then wanted to get back in the church."

"Why?"

"Because of my family, and basically because I believe it's true."

"That's your problem. You still believe it. That's something you need to get over."

"You make it sound like an illness."

"Maybe it is an illness. Or maybe just a destructive habit. It's not hard to become an unbeliever if you set your mind to it. Once I read the *Book of Mormon* carefully and studied some LDS history, choosing to become a non-believer wasn't that hard. So, what happened after you got home?"

"I went through a year's repentance routine in which I met with my bishop once a week. He spent a lot of time with me, and I really came to love him. We prayed together, we fasted together, we read scripture together, we did everything so that God would change me. Afterwards, I felt that I owed him something. So, a couple of years ago, I was re-baptized, and my temple covenants were restored. At the time, I thought that it was one of the happiest days of my life."

"First of all, did your bishop really love you or was he in love with the person he wanted you to be? My Mormon shrink said that he loved me, but it was all about control. I was his Eliza Doolittle. Not a person, but a project. Did all that fasting and praying work? Are you straight now?"

"I thought so. I started dating a nice LDS girl. We are engaged and planning to get married. By the way, she's okay with my story because she thinks it's all behind me."

"Then why were you crying?"

Choking up, he replied, "Because I haven't changed. I'm still attracted to men. I've just been play-acting to make other people happy. I'm really afraid."

"Afraid of what?"

"That people will find out and that I won't be able to control myself. But I'm mostly afraid of trying to sustain a sexual relationship with a woman."

"Greg, let me tell you what my friend Lucy told me. Every woman deserves to feel lovely, to feel beautiful, and to feel that there is some man out there who is dying to touch and hold her. Can you give that to your fiancée?"

He drew a deep breath. "I really do love her."

"That's not what I asked. Does she feel physically lovely and sexually desirable around you?"

Suddenly, he started crying again. "Josh, what am I going to do?"

Sensing how much he was hurting, I too was on the verge of tears. I laid a hand on his arm. "Greg, you've got to be honest with yourself. You cannot live your entire life as a lie. I've told you what I think, but right now I'm finding it unpleasant to be with you. I am just barely on the other side of what you're going through, and I am not ready to go through it again, even for a friend. Maybe we can talk some other time, but not right now."

I squeezed his arm, stood up, and began walking towards my dorm. I felt terribly guilty for not trying to help him, but at that moment, I wanted nothing more than to flee from his world of shame and guilt. I never saw him again.

Epilogue

"Are you just going to quit there?" asked Father Andy. "You were only a college freshman. Surely, a few important things have happened since then."

Of course, a lot has happened since then. Still, nothing in my later years matches the life-changing intensity of those teenage experiences, nor have I departed significantly from the path marked out after my first year in California. At both UCLA and St. Mark's, I determined that my professional homes would be the university and a non-LDS church. After graduating from UCLA, I completed a doctorate in music history and choral conducting at Indiana University. I currently teach at a well-known university in New England where I am also minister of music in a local Episcopal parish. As long as they don't require too much travel, I continue to sing solo roles for both professional and amateur choirs with *Messiah* being the perennial favorite.

This is not to say that everything since 1970 has been a smooth upward path. The decisions to accept my sexuality, find a religious alternative to Mormonism, and renegotiate relationships with my family have been processes of a lifetime. Like almost everyone, I have known blue moments. Helped by a couple of excellent therapists, I learned that depressive episodes are frequently triggered by a reemergence of the insecurities of my early years, not only about my sexual orientation, which I never doubted, but about how to deal with them.

Still, occasionally the notion haunts me that in some parallel universe another Joshua Chastain submitted to Dr. Chandler's therapy, recognized his homosexuality as something to be controlled like diabetes, married a woman, had children, lived the life of a faithful Mormon, and devoted himself to "building the Kingdom." But then I realize that such a person would be the product of other people's expectations and a betrayal of the authentic me. Worse, he most likely would have failed. Worst of all, I would never have met Benjamin—my partner, my spouse, the love of my life, and a marvelous human with whom I spent nearly forty wonderful years. I continue to grieve his death.

My father refused to accept as final the letter I wrote after being excommunicated. Proving himself the embodiment of the hymn "Oh Love That Will Not Let Me Go," he visited me several times in Los Angeles, never to preach or to scold, but merely to maintain contact. Since Rosales is a seven-hour drive from Los Angeles, he made these trips at considerable sacrifice. He took pride in my academic and musical achievements, and, although never comfortable with the subject of homosexuality, he made clumsy but well-intentioned inquiries about my social life. I enjoyed his company.

In my junior year at UCLA, my parents retired and moved to Utah where all my siblings except Terri had settled. My father eventually persuaded me to visit my parents' new home and renew contact with my mother and siblings. I developed a polite relationship with Jeff, Clarissa, Keith, their spouses, and their abundant progeny. But politeness is shared distance. We could share a past but not a present. Terri, the other fallen Mormon in the family, is the only sibling I'm close to. My father died of a heart attack in my second year of graduate work. I was deeply saddened by his death and remain profoundly moved by the memory of his tenacious love and generosity.

Of the vignettes painted in these pages, portraying my mother has been the greatest challenge. In championing my education, musical and otherwise, she gave me a great deal. But she also gave me tons of guilt. Many in Rosales idolized her as a mesmerizing, charismatic teacher—an enthusiasm I could not share. In these pages, I have exaggerated no item of her behavior. The enemas, her intrusive interest in my adolescent body, the drugs, the occasional violence, the interminable jeremiads on church teaching, and her outing me to my UCLA bishop which led to my excommunication—all are true. She never recovered from her addiction to prescription medicines, although she probably got more appropriate drugs.

After my father's death, I dutifully called her from time to time, but we never had a conversation in which her disapproval and disappointment in me were not evident. When I received tenure, partly for having written a prize-winning book, she responded with a tepid statement of congratulations followed by "Of course, it's very sad to climb a ladder only to realize that it was leaning against the wrong wall." The right wall, of course, was the heterosexual life of a devout Mormon. She died shortly after the tenure decision. It embarrasses me to confess that I do not miss her. Perhaps what I really miss is the relationship that we never had.

While I have had no official contact with the LDS Church for the last fifty years, I keep somewhat informed through news reports, family ties, a few Mormon acquaintances, and an occasional Mormon student. Still, just as Father Andy said, something of my Mormon background never left me, nor have I been able to leave it.

Although thousands of Mormons apparently derive great happiness from their religion and its unique ability to build community and sacralize the mundane, the LDS Church's mistreatment of gay people continues. Following the lead of "experts" like Dr. Chandler, for several decades the Church promoted various schemes for curing homosexuals. These included shock treatments, aversion therapy, excommunication, and intense regimens of fasting, study, and prayer. Once deemed free of sin, gay men were encouraged to marry women. These unions often ended in broken marriages, broken hearts, and broken lives. In her poignant memoir, *Goodbye, I Love You,* Carolyn Lynn Pearson tells the story of such a marriage.

In 2008, the LDS Church successfully spearheaded the campaign in favor of Proposition 8 in California which would deny marriage equality to gay people. But that "success" quickly backfired, provoking angry demonstrations in front of the Los Angeles Temple and the LDS visitors center and chapel that face Lincoln Center in New York City. Documents purloined from the church offices in Salt Lake City showed that the LDS Church had been the prime mover in financing and supporting the proposition. The whole mess was exposed in a superb HBO documentary titled *8: The Mormon Proposition.* Badly burned by the negative publicity, the church began softening its rhetoric against homosexuals with banalities about love and respect. But basic doctrines have not changed: non-celibate homosexuals are still subject to excommunication. Nor did the church officially abandon ex-gay strategies for changing sexual orientation until 2016.

Some gay Mormons hope that the church will change. In Mormon history, new revelations appeared just in time to deflect massive public condemnation on two occasions. The first occurred in 1890 when President Wilfred Woodruff yielded to public and legal pressure by ending plural marriages, thus removing one of the major impediments to Utah becoming a state. The church still accepts polygamy, however, since, if a widower takes a second wife in a temple marriage, he will, according to church doctrine, have both wives in the next life.

Just as dramatic was the reversal of the church's prohibition against ordaining African-descended Blacks to the Mormon priesthood. That issue came to a head in the early 1970s when civil rights demonstrations and lawsuits targeted the church, and universities began boycotting BYU athletic teams. Always sensitive to negative publicity, the church president announced a timely revelation in 1978 accepting Black men into the priesthood. Of course, women of all colors are still excluded.

Could something similar happen for gay people? It is unlikely that the kind of pressure that prompted the 1890 and 1978 revelations will develop on behalf of LGBTQ people. The LDS church's teachings on homosexuality match those of Roman Catholics and Christian fundamentalists, thus giving the LDS church plenty of allies. A bigger problem is the centrality of heterosexual marriage and childbearing in Mormon doctrine. Gay people have no place in the Mormon master narrative, nor has the church ceased viewing non-celibate gay people as sinners. Still, maybe one day we'll be surprised.

As with so many things, Mother Harold said it first and said it best: "If you're going to be an organist, you better make peace with the church because organs are in churches." After my position at St. Mark's in Los Angeles with the inimitable Dr. Riedel, I worked for several denominations as both organist and choirmaster. But I eventually felt the need to claim a religious tradition as my own. Remembering Father Tovar's lovely ruminations on Catholicism, I attended several RCIA classes (Rite of Christian Initiation of Adults) sponsored by a local Roman Catholic parish. Despite the kind and well-intentioned instructors, I quickly concluded that, having left one hierarchical, authoritarian, and patriarchal church, I was not about to join another.

Despite fond memories of Lutheran and Presbyterian parishes where I have worked, the Episcopal Church has long been my employer of choice. As an artist, I am drawn to the Anglican commitment to beautiful music, eloquent language, open-mindedness, and traditional liturgy. It was also in an Episcopal parish that I met Benjamin, my spouse, my partner, the love of my life. With Benjamin's encouragement, I began thinking about becoming officially Episcopalian.

My mentor in much of this process was a wonderful woman priest and formidable intellectual, Thelma Devries, who was raised in a strict Calvinist church that refused to ordain women, thus prompting her move towards Anglicanism. She held no stock with Biblical literalism and was given to pithy statements like "The opposite of faith is not doubt; the opposite of faith is certitude." Or "Faith doesn't mean belief; it means willingness to stay in a conversation." Or the one that most impacted me, "The opposite of love is not hate; the opposite of love is the desire to control another human being." Doctrinal certitude and control are essential elements of Mormonism and I suspect of most authoritarian religions. I thank Thelma Devries for steering me in a different direction.

In 2000, I was confirmed in the Episcopal Church. Afterwards, I wrote a note to Flo Whitmore, then in her nineties, recalling her statement that "people who aren't anything often become Episcopalians." In reply, she sent me a lovely handwritten letter of congratulations and a valuable copy of an early edition of the first prayer book of the American Episcopal Church. Do I think God is Anglican? Of course not. But in Anglicanism, I have found a place to practice my own peculiar religion, which may or may not be entirely Christian.

As I near my seventieth year and read over this manuscript, lurking in the background is the knowledge that I could suffer a cancer relapse at any moment or simply die from something else. Writing about my early years, however, has brought me a sense of closure and made more meaningful the plea in the *Book of Common Prayer* that "we might end our lives in faith and hope, without suffering and without reproach." This exercise in remembering has also convinced me that my gay life has been very worth living.

Reconstructing the life of a teenager more than fifty years after the fact has been an ongoing challenge and perhaps an ongoing failure. Still, I now understand better the connection between the young me and the old me. In addition, I have become intensely aware of my debt to people described in these pages who, in a very real sense, were my teachers, my protectors, and perhaps my saints. As I wrote down "my" ideas, I often heard other people speaking through me. At every point in my life when things seemed to be going south, a "saint" emerged—Dr. Jimmy, Father Andy, Mrs. Jespersen, Mother Harold, Father Tovar, Lucy Ramírez, Ronnie at Croft House, Blair and Barkley, Angelo (most of the time), Jean-Pierre, Flo Whitmore, Mr. Hazen, and Joan Feldberg—all offered me help when I needed it most.

Finally, I have become quite fond of the young Joshua Chastain. Of course, I am appalled (and amused) at how he helped friends cheat, stole answer keys to tests for his friends, placed nails under AMPS's tires, tampered with teachers' grade books, and lied with astonishing facility. If I met the young Josh today, I might find him arrogant and a little full of himself. But I think I would like him and hope that he would like me.

--Joshua Chastain